A CLOCKWORK OGRE

A CLOCKWORK OGRE

THE AMATHEREAN TALES
BOOK TWO

Bosloe

Podium

Published in 2025 by Podium Publishing
www.podiumentertainment.com

Podium

A CLOCKWORK OGRE

CHAPTER ONE

Training & Development

Faster," Lorna shouted at the trainees running laps of the training grounds. SJ felt her lungs would burst any second, as they had been doing laps for so long. One large orc trainee stopped, leaning forward on his knees, panting. Lorna whipped him on his rear with a wooden stick, making him move again. "No pain, no gain," Lorna shouted. Lorna was a weretiger, a member of the lycan race and the town guard's lieutenant. Her hair was a brilliant red which gave her an angry appearance. Her authority was only exceeded by the town guards' dwarven captain, Captain Broadaxe.

Eventually, after two more laps, Lorna called them to a stop as they reached the training rings again. "Okay. Take five minutes," she said.

SJ placed her hands on her head, trying to steady her breathing, and paced backwards and forwards. Slowly, she recovered and walked over to one of the water buckets. Her long silvery white hair was drenched with sweat from the exertion of the morning's training. She dunked her head in the barrel, revealing the green undertones of her hair, and as she pulled it back out, it trailed down her back, the cool water soaking into her dress and bringing relief from the heat of the day and exercise. The sun had been blazing hot, making running challenging.

It had been a week since the hobs' most recent raid, and this was the second three-day training session SJ had attended; each required at least one day's rest in between. Bordon and the hobs lived in the valley beneath the plateau where the town was situated. Since they'd arrived in the valley, they had raided several times. Each time, at least one town member had lost their life. During the last, largest defence of Killic, several town members had fallen, and SJ had sworn to uphold the quest for vengeance.

Quest: Vengeance
You have witnessed the heartache and torment caused by the evil that resides in Amathera. You may seek vengeance on those guilty of crimes against the town.
Kill Bordon the Brandisher: 1000xp
Kill Iratu the Mad: 700xp
Prevent any further hobgoblin raids on Killic.
Rewards: 1500xp, reputation with Killic. Usual level kill experience awards apply.

The training was helping. Her kata had improved to Level 5, and she hoped it would reach Level 6 soon. She had been practising the forms daily as part of the routine she had fallen into. She knew that at Level 6, it would unlock a second skill for her martial arts branch, she had held off selecting her next subterfuge choice until she knew what martial arts offered to see if anything would align with the other attributes and skills.

"Your running was much better today," Lorna said, walking over.

"Thanks," SJ said.

"I spoke to Jurgen. He has said he will teach you about fighting with claws."

"Really?" SJ said, grinning.

"Yes. He has agreed that he can train you on your off days. It won't be as arduous since it's more about precision and accuracy."

"That sounds amazing."

"We will see what you're saying after a session with Jurgen. He is a hard trainer and won't take mistakes lightly."

"I will do whatever it takes to improve," SJ said, happy at having another opportunity to grow her skills. The fluidity she had gained with reaching Level 5 in her kata was impressive, and she felt more agile, even considering the flexibility she started with because of her Dexterity. Her strike rate had increased, and she had regularly practised on one of the training dummies. Her ankles were also getting much stronger, and she could break the thinnest pieces of wood they used for training. They were only a couple of millimetres thick. She still had a long way to go to get anywhere near the level of Lorna, who could splinter two-inch-thick pieces of wood with a single strike.

After the rest period, Lorna called them all to the training ring. "Okay. We are going to do some sparring. I will pair you off, and we will use a two-strike rule. Once two strikes are received, you will be knocked out. The last person standing will win.

"First pairing is Greb and Pru."

Greb was a male kobold. Having trained under Lorna for a while, he served as a guard member. He was much better than SJ. Pru was a female gnoll who had taken up martial arts—from SJ's conversations with the other trainees—a year ago. She was not as proficient as Greb, but her size gave her a significant reach advantage.

Watching as the two sized each other up, standing on either side of the sand ring, SJ knew Greb would win. His smaller frame improved his agility, and his speed was insane.

"Fight!" Lorna called.

The two trainees moved towards each other, circling, before Greb, in a flurry of motion, moved in and kicked directly into Pru's stomach. The speed surprised her, and she staggered backwards from the blow.

"One point to Greb. Face off again."

Once Lorna called "Fight!" again, Pru didn't wait this time and came out on the offensive, making Greb dance backwards around the ring. Her punches kept him at bay and made him block continually. SJ thought Pru might get the point, but Greb ducked and swept his leg into her thigh. As he connected, there was a crunching sound, and Pru screamed, falling to the ground.

"Cleric!" Lorna called as she walked over to Pru, who now sat on the ground holding her leg, grimacing in pain.

The training ground cleric, who SJ had learned was named Kenzie, walked over and cast a healing light at Pru. Within moments, Pru could stand and move around again as normal. She returned to face Greb.

"Fight to Greb," Lorna concluded. The pair shook hands and walked out of the ring, chatting.

"Next fight. Quilti and SJ," Lorna announced.

The group had completed a couple of sparring bouts since SJ had trained, but as the newest member, she had always sat watching. With all eyes on her, she entered the ring. Quilti was an orc who towered over her diminutive frame. Slowly taking his position opposite her, he smirked. SJ's anger flared at the smirk, and listening intently for the call, SJ waited. As soon as she heard the first letter of Lorna calling "Fight," she reacted.

Launching forward before Quilti had even moved, she kicked straight out at him, catching him in the one place no male of any species ever wished to feel the weight of something forceful. His eyes flew open, and his hands automatically dropped to grab at his crotch, his knees giving way, and he fell to the ground holding his precious possessions, groaning loudly and rolling onto his side.

"That was a little evil," Dave said, his voice echoing in her mind.

SJ turned away from Quilti's sprawled body and whispered a reply to her AI administrator. "He shouldn't have smirked at me."

"One point to SJ. Quilti, are you good to go again?" Lorna asked.

The large orc was still lying on his side and waved his hand in response to Lorna's request. "Unfortunately, healing will only help so much with a blow there," she stated, trying to hold the amusement back from her voice. "Forfeit by Quilti. SJ wins."

The bouts continued until all the trainees had faced off. Only eight were left, and SJ wondered who she would face in the second bout. She quickly discovered.

"Greb versus SJ!"

SJ gulped, knowing she was facing off against the most proficient trainee. She entered the ring and stood calmly, waiting for Lorna to call the start. When it came, so did Greb. He was shorter than SJ, but his movements were fast. Fists and kicks flashed towards her; she dodged and blocked what she could until he found the opening he had been waiting for and brought his elbow inside her defences, crunching into her chest. The blow forced the air from her lungs. She staggered backwards, gasping for air.

"One to Greb. Face off."

SJ walked back to her side, rubbing her chest, and again faced her opponent.

She switched to her Shotokan stance rather than using the usual form Lorna had taught her. It was more defensive and didn't leave the same openings.

"Fight!" Lorna called.

Greb came at her again, a whirlwind of movement, with SJ using her original style. It confused Greb, initially throwing him off his usual approach, and where he had been expecting to find an opening, he found resistance. The form of her previous studies and her improved abilities from her kata practice lent her a boost of confidence. The bout continued for a few minutes, SJ on the defensive for 90 percent of the fight before she saw an opening and swept her leg around to strike at Greb's ankle. He saw it coming, leapt over her leg, and performed a jump kick, spinning his foot out as he did. SJ saw the kick coming too late to react—Greb's foot caught her squarely on the side of her face, making her see stars and stagger from the blow.

"Two to Greb. Winner Greb."

SJ shook out her limbs, looking at Greb, who walked over and offered her his hand; she took it.

"Good fight," Greb said. "What style did you use?"

"It's one I have known since I was a child."

"I was not sure how to get through to hit you. It looked more defensive."

"It is, but unfortunately, still not enough to stop you from winning," SJ said, smiling and rubbing the side of her face where his foot had connected.

"I think that is the longest round I have ever had to fight," he said, acknowledging her ability to last against him.

"Thanks, but next time, I will win," she said, still smiling.

Laughing, Greb walked to one of the water barrels to get a drink.

"That was some impressive movement," Dave said.

"It didn't feel like it," SJ whispered, sitting at the ring's side.

"He is a much higher level martial artist than yourself, and to last as long as you did was very well done. It obviously wouldn't help you in an actual fight because you would still have been killed, but for a training ground, it wasn't bad."

SJ let out a sigh. "Your confidence in me is astounding."

"I am just being honest. If he had activated his skills, he would have creamed you in an actual fight. I doubt your head would have stayed on your shoulders."

"Wow. Thanks," SJ said sarcastically.

The bouts continued, eventually reaching the final round. Greb would fight Mertylic in the last bout. Mertylic was an elf, a beautiful creature, all subtleness and grace—until he started fighting and it was as though a lion had been released. He fought with such aggression that it was eye-watering to watch.

"The last bout will be first to three," Lorna announced.

Watching the two best trainees fight it out in the sparring ring was a sight to behold. Their speed and precision were uncanny, and SJ knew the only person better than either was Lorna herself. They both fought with passion and confidence in their abilities. The bout reached two hits apiece.

"Fight!" Lorna shouted.

Mertylic came out of the blocks with his usual aggression, but whereas Greb had previously met him, this time, he remained where he was. As Mertylic approached, Greb launched his assault, shifting his stance slightly. SJ knew what he would do. She had seen him perform it once before. If it worked, it would be an amazing spectacle. As Mertylic moved into him, he sprang into the air like a gazelle, throwing his legs out like a whirlwind, spinning as he did. SJ saw Mertylic's eyes widen, already committed to his attack and unable to block as Greb's first foot struck him in his head, swiftly followed by his second. Greb spun so quickly before he landed back on his feet again, it reminded SJ of a Van Damme movie.

The other trainees, including SJ, jumped up excitedly, cheering. "That was awesome," SJ called.

"Fight to Greb," Lorna called.

Greb approached Mertylic, who accepted his hand with grace and composure. Mertylic whispered something to him, and Greb laughed in response.

"That's the fun over for today. Three full forms, and then you can call it a day," Lorna said. The trainees groaned as they moved to various areas of the ground and began their forms.

Another thirty minutes later, after being scolded frequently and having to restart her forms, SJ finally finished for the day. Her muscles again ached with a pleasant sensation, and tomorrow was a rest day. However, she would be back to meet Jurgen and begin claw training. Filled with excitement at the prospect, she headed back towards the Hogling Arms, the inn where she'd been staying ever since she arrived in Killic.

"I need some more Dryac. I'm nearly out," she whispered.

"You know where to go," Dave said.

The shop always seemed to have a customer whenever SJ walked past, and as she entered today, Grewlas the gnoll was busy talking to a female ratkin.

"Apply it twice daily, and it will bring the swelling down," he said, smiling at the ratkin, who turned to leave carrying a jar of some ointment.

"Hi," SJ said.

"Hi. What can I get for you?"

"I would like some Dryac, please."

"What size? I have small, medium, or large pots."

"I may as well take a large pot. Does it keep its potency?"

"Only after a year will it fade slightly."

"Excellent. I will take a large pot, then."

Grewlas walked to a shelf behind the counter and lifted down a large pot and placed it on the counter. It was four times the size of her previous purchase and should last her a great deal of time. After getting used to the exercise routine, she needed to use less Dryac as she experienced less soreness, although the Dryac aided with any discomfort.

"I need to ask. What other healing tonics or lotions do you do?"

"I have several, but I specialise in muscular ailments. You would be surprised at how many customers I see daily with strains, and purchasing healing potions is not viable for most."

"Are healing potions that expensive?"

"It depends on the grade. Prices vary based on the number of hit points they can heal. Each level doubles, if not triples, the previous price when you reach the higher-tier potions. It proves profitable for those in major cities or situated near dungeons. I prefer my peaceful life here. It gives me time to be with my family without the constant need to gather all the components."

"I'm just starting in my profession, and it's not quick to level."

"What profession are you? If you don't mind me asking."

"I'm an apprentice tailor."

SJ watched Grewlas wince. "Now, that's a tough profession to level. At least with alchemy, you can find most ingredients easily enough in the different territories. With tailoring, some materials get very difficult to find at higher levels. My father was a tailor, and there was no way I could have done what he did. He was always chasing materials."

"I am in no rush," SJ said, smiling.

"Actually, while you are here, could I ask you a favour?"

"Sure, what do you need?"

"I am running low on one of my key ingredients for Dryac. A specific mushroom grows in the caves in the next valley. I normally fetch a supply every three months but can't find the time to go with our newborn."

"When do you need it by?"

"Not that urgently, but I am almost out, so probably in the next week or so I could do with some more. I would pay you for your time."

SJ's display triggered.

Quest: Gather Sancasia Mushrooms
Sancasia mushrooms grow in moist caves throughout Amathera, where the temperature is constant. Gather a basketful for Grewlas to allow him to maintain his Dryac production.
Rewards: 240xp, 2 silver
Would you like to accept the quest? **Yes/No**

"Which valley? The one through town or on the far side of the lake?" SJ asked.

"Through town and past the meadow."

Considering SJ planned to return to check on the cottage, it would be an excellent opportunity to complete a quest simultaneously. She had been regularly checking the board in the inn, which primarily featured basic quests such as finding lost pets or exterminating rats. She did not object to these quests. Focusing on them meant gaining experience. The challenge was that her intense training kept her from questing; she wanted to get stronger and seek vengeance. The chance to earn nearly a quarter of the experience required for her next level from a single quest would provide a nice boost.

"I can do that for you," SJ said, accepting the quest.

"That would be amazing, thank you," Grewlas said.

"I will be back within the week with the mushrooms," SJ said as she collected the jar and placed it in her inventory before leaving.

"Wait!" Grewlas called as SJ turned.

"Sorry?"

"Here." Grewlas ducked beneath the counter and pulled out a basket. It was much larger than SJ had expected and reminded SJ of a baby's carrycot. "They need to be transported in this; it will keep them fresh."

"I am glad you stopped me. I forgot to ask what the mushrooms look like!" SJ said, feeling a little embarrassed.

"They are blue topped, with a white stem. Once you find them, you will know they are the only mushrooms that look like that."

"Okay. That will help rather than guessing. Thanks." SJ turned to leave again. As she went to place the basket in her inventory, her display triggered.

> This item will take up two slots. Do you wish to store the basket in your inventory? **Yes/No**

SJ selected Yes, as her inventory was virtually free. Smiling, she returned to the inn. Unsure if the skeletons required anything, she debated bringing something to the cottage.

"Dave," she whispered.

"Yep."

"Do skeletons need anything?"

"What do you mean? Such as food? Then, no."

"Clothes?"

"You will have seen Floretta wearing clothes, but I think with some skeletons it is a choice. When we met them, they wore their class gear but nothing else."

"That was probably because of the necromancer."

"Perhaps. I would ask them when you visit. After accepting the quest, I assume you plan on doing it."

"I am, but I also want to get to kata Level 6."

"If you keep working on your kata even without doing all the training you are doing, it will level, just not as quickly."

"That's good to know. I was a little worried that I may have to maintain the training level I had been doing to keep it after my kata level drop."

"No, the training is just helping with your fighting technique overall and ability to adapt. The basic kata is the skill change trigger."

Walking through the vendors in the town square, SJ noticed a stall selling various pieces of hardware and stopped to glance at its equipment. There were many hammers, mallets, rakes, brushes, etc. If she was going back to the cottage, she might take some items to make it a little more homely. After looking at the various items, she listed what she wanted to purchase. Back at the inn, she grabbed a coffee and headed to her room.

"I will need a cart or wagon to transport items to the cottage. I can't carry them all in my inventory," SJ said.

"No."

"No. What?"

"I will not allow you to buy a wagon."

"What? I didn't even mention about buying a wagon."

"You didn't have to."

"But how will I get stuff to the cottage?"

"Borrow one, perhaps, and how you just answered means you were thinking about it."

"I wasn't."

"Yes, you were. I know that tone in your voice. You get an excited little *oooo, shiny* voice."

"I do not," SJ grumbled.

"Yes, you do. Every time you spend money, you get the same tone. I think you may have a problem."

"Me? I'm not the one who attends AIGA," SJ complained.

"Now, that was a low blow. Addiction is real."

Silence.

"Sorry," SJ said eventually.

"For what this time?"

"I am trying to apologise for what I said. Don't make it seem like it's about anything else." SJ was still frustrated, knowing that Dave had hit closer to home than she would ever like to admit. She had always been a spender, being frivolous with money and running up several credit accounts back on Earth, which completely contradicted her job and role. It had always been easy to get credit.

"So, you aren't sorry, are you?"

"I am," SJ snapped.

"If you were, you wouldn't be snappy."

"But . . ." SJ stopped herself from replying and took a deep breath. "I really am sorry, Dave. I shouldn't have mentioned the AIGA meetings."

"Now, that wasn't difficult, was it?"

Biting back her immediate reply, SJ counted to ten.

"No, it wasn't," she said through gritted teeth.

"I think someone is a little tired and could use a nap," Dave said sarcastically, then burst into laughter.

"Damn you," SJ cursed.

"You forgot about buying a wagon, didn't you?" Dave chuckled.

"You can be so annoying."

"I know," Dave said smugly. "You could ask Lythonian if you could borrow the cart and Humberto."

"That isn't a bad idea. I'll grab some food and then visit him." SJ huffed.

CHAPTER 2

Cottages

After visiting Lythonian and speaking to Jurgen, SJ sorted everything to return to the cottages. She even stopped to see Gladys at the mill, asking if she needed anything taken to the cottage she and her husband, Hubert, owned near SJ's; however, Gladys declined, mentioning she would visit in a few days. Since deciding to visit the cottages, SJ had spent most of her time purchasing all the items she wanted to take with her. Even though she wasn't planning to stay, she aimed to make it homely.

Remembering what she had been told about the chimney needing repair, SJ confirmed with a stonemason, a dwarf named Husa, to visit the cottage and check the chimney. Although he wouldn't be available for at least a few days, he promised to inspect the derelict property to determine if it could be repaired. SJ informed Husa about her skeletal friends.

She packed the cart with all the essentials for setting up a new home. She didn't go as far as purchasing a mattress, but she got almost everything else that could be needed. Pots, pans, bowls, buckets, brushes, gardening equipment . . . she had bought so much. With her improved reputation in the town, she noticed that prices for items from several merchants were lower than they had been previously.

Most essential items were only coppers, so she had enough cash to hold on to the one gold coin she owned. When she discussed the costs of the items with Dave, he stated it was a norm that once your reputation increased with many traders, items would naturally become cheaper. This was also because of her Charisma, which only had a minor bonus, currently at eleven.

She would perhaps need to increase her Charisma because of the second subterfuge skill, which SJ still needed to confirm. After reviewing all the details since she had opened the sixth level of the identification skill, she leaned towards disguise. Her dress stood out too much, and at higher levels, she could be anonymous when dealing with people.

As they entered the valley, Humberto let out a neigh and came to a stop.

"What's wrong?" she asked.

"I do not know," Dave said.

"I was asking Humberto."

Humberto took a step backwards, and SJ frowned. She could see nothing causing him to back up.

"There must be something ahead," SJ said. "Let's go look."

Jumping down from the cart, SJ moved to the front, patting Humberto on his neck and stroking him as he complained. He shook his head from side to side and pushed backwards again.

"What is it, boy?" SJ said, looking ahead at the clear trail. Her senses hadn't been triggered, and she could see nothing that would cause concern. That was when the arrow struck her. The arrow lodged into her left thigh, and she cried in pain at the sudden shock of the attack. SJ's display triggered with damage notification but it was minor.

She hadn't seen where it came from.

"Left down the trail fifty metres," Dave said. "Large boulder and a single tree."

SJ hobbled back to the side of the cart, out of sight of the unknown archer.

"Damn, that hurts," she cursed.

"Pull it out. It will heal soon enough. You aren't in active combat, as it's a sneak attack," Dave said.

Grabbing hold of the arrow shaft protruding from her thigh, she gripped it tightly and pulled it outwards. The pain seared through her leg, and she grimaced, grinding her teeth as she tugged the arrow free. Thankfully, the tip was more kite-shaped than an arrowhead, so it came out easily in comparison. Dropping the arrow to the ground, she took a deep breath, calming her nerves.

"Can you see if I can get anywhere near them without them seeing me?" she asked.

"Miniature, yes. You can work around through the rocks on the left. You should be able to get near to them."

"Good," SJ said as she shrank. As soon as she was in her miniature form, she took off, easing the weight on her throbbing leg as it healed, and went straight across into the rocks by the side of the trail. Humberto was still stepping backwards, and she glanced back, seeing the cart was skewing and could tip if he backed up too far.

"Dave, can you be my eyes, please?"

"Yup. Head left twenty paces and turn right, heading down behind the rocks just over there."

"Twenty paces when flying as a fairy is not the easiest thing to judge," SJ stated.

"Rock with the two pointy bits on the left of it."

"Seen," SJ said, staying only an inch from the ground as she flew towards it.

"Now turn right, stay in this depression, and follow it until I tell you when."

Following Dave's instructions, she quickly flew down the side of the trail. The gradient was steep apart from where the trail curved along the valley's wall, and the depression, which was more like a ditch, kept her hidden from anything not looking directly up it.

"Slow down. Okay, turn right, small bush, head towards that."

Again, she moved where Dave instructed. She did not know the hostile's whereabouts.

"Stop. Right again, the large rock behind there."

Looking over, SJ could see where he was indicating and made her way towards the large boulder.

"They are round behind it," Dave whispered. SJ thought he might be a little caught up in the situation since he didn't need to whisper. In a way, it made SJ feel better. Not more than ten feet from her was the back of what had shot at her. At first, she thought it was an elf, but on closer inspection, its skin had an unusual colour. Almost a purple hue. She couldn't even ask Dave so close to it, so she equipped her claws instead. With an arrow drawn, the elf watched Humberto and the cart on the trail.

Triggering her identification skill, she grew behind it.

Dark Elf Ranger	
Level:	9
Hit points:	50
Mana Points:	50
Armour Class:	8
Attacks:	Bow
Special:	Rapid Fire

SJ was only Level 7, but her hit points were higher than its when full. The arrow she had taken in her thigh had only done eight damage, of which two had already healed. The Divine Lightning ability that drinking the dragon Bob's blood had granted through symbiosis gave her the ability to heal faster once out of combat. Preparing herself, she took the last step before striking with a vicious clawed punch directly at the neck of her attacker. Her claws struck true, and her display triggered, and as it did, she punched with her other hand into its side.

Critical strike and bleed effect has been applied.

Her blade slid farther into the back of its neck, cutting off a scream of shock, while her left fist sent claws puncturing its side. It arched its head backwards, and SJ pulled her claws back from its neck, attempting to draw them across its exposed throat.

The ranger dropped its bow and tried to pull away from the blades still stuck in its left side. Not able to move fast enough, it received a second clawed punch into the top right of its back. It let out a gurgling sound, struggling to draw air easily with the injured neck and throat and potentially punctured lungs. Taking full advantage of her surprise attack, SJ didn't hesitate and struck again, this time penetrating its lower back.

It arched its back from this last strike, and if it could have screamed, it probably would have. SJ watched the last of its hit points drop as its body fell to the ground at the base of the boulder. Although SJ's adrenaline pumped in her body, her breathing was calm and even. The training grounds had been working wonders on her cardio. Then again, the fight had lasted only ten seconds from start to finish.

Congratulations! Level 9 Dark Elf Ranger killed. 95xp awarded.

"That was easier than I expected," SJ said.

"As an assassin, you hope most fights are easy. You don't want to face many enemies."

"I know, but I was expecting a little fight."

"It still took four strikes to kill, which means your strikes were not as effective as they could have been."

"I wonder what a dark elf ranger was doing around here?"

"Another unusual sign. Dark elves usually live in the major forest regions, so I'm unsure why one would be this high in the mountains."

Bending, SJ looted its corpse.

Short Bow +1, 24 x Arrows, Dagger, Leather Armour +1, Backpack, Rations x 4, Flint and Steel, Bedroll, Blanket, Note, 32 x Copper, 2 x Silver

"Good job. I have the cart. I wouldn't be able to carry all this."

"What does the note say?" Dave asked.

SJ selected the note, and unfolding it, she looked at a script she could not recognise. The closest language she could even consider was Korean.

"I can't read this," SJ said, folding it up.

"Wait, I can. *Speak to Serj at the Wandering Ogre. He has the details of the fae target.*"

"Fae? Does that mean me?"

"You or Fran, perhaps. You are the only two fae in Killic near the Wandering Ogre."

"Why would anyone even come to find me?"

"It could be the doing of another god."

"What? How? And why?"

"You heard what Fizzlewick said about you being the talk of the gods? You may have gained more recognition than you suspect."

"Why would someone attack me?"

"That I do not know. I have said all along that this place doesn't seem right."

"Yes. But to be attacked while travelling to the cottages . . . How could they even know it's me?"

"Really! There are few beautiful faes who wear bright green dresses! Also, the elf may not even have been after you directly and just took a shot on the off chance of you being the fae it was here to target. Then again, dark elves have an abysmal reputation; few races trust them, and it could have just been attacking."

"Did you just say beautiful?"

"Is that all you picked up from that? And, er. No. Well, yes, but you know what I mean. Don't make this awkward," Dave said.

"If I didn't know better, I'd think you like me as a person," SJ said as she walked back up the trail towards Humberto. The dark elf had shot from a fair distance; it must have been over a hundred feet. Grabbing Humberto's reins, she led him down the trail. On arriving at the corpse, she looted it again and transferred the items directly into the cart, only keeping the coin, note, and rations in her inventory. Humberto was much calmer now that the dark elf was dead.

"I don't get it," SJ said.

"Get what?"

"Why would it attack me now? Also, at the range it did. It could have waited until I was much closer and hit me much more easily."

"Apart from the fact you probably would have sensed it if it had got closer. Not that it would know that, since it's all hypothetical. Humberto could probably smell it, which is why he reacted. It would have been helpful keeping it alive to ask questions, perhaps?"

"A little late now."

"It was an efficient assassination, which is great to see."

"Thanks. I still don't know why there is a random dark elf near Killic with a note about fae."

"We can investigate when we get back."

Her display triggered.

Quest: Find the Reason for the Attack
Rewards: 350xp
Would you like to accept the quest? **Yes/No**

"That's a brief description. Do they usually give out that much experience?" SJ asked.

"Experience is a little high, perhaps, but the description is possibly due to how simple the note was."

"I can't just go into the Wandering Ogre and ask people expecting to meet a dark elf if I am the target."

"It doesn't stop you from investigating, and the quest says only to find the reason for the attack, not to stop it or do anything else. I expect a secondary quest if you need to do anything further."

"I may have to find someone who can ask questions on my behalf."

"Like who?"

"Not sure yet. Setu is married, and I think Gary is too, so I wouldn't want to ask either of them. I am not sure Zej would go there, and I definitely couldn't ask Lythonian."

"I overheard some in the inn talking about it previously, but you have never spoken to them, so I'm not sure if you want to try them when we are back in town next."

"Oh. Who did you hear?"

"You know the kobold and ratkin who always sit on the stools at the end of the bar?"

"Yes. I think I know what you mean. Without knowing them, I am unsure I could get them to ask questions for me. I may speak to Niweq myself. It sounds like he is open to a deal if I can think of something he may need in exchange." She didn't relish the idea of going to him, but as the owner of the Wandering Ogre, the elf might be her best bet for information.

"Probably if you offer to dance for him."

"That will never happen."

The journey to the cottages after the dark elf attack was peaceful. No other travellers were on the road, though as it was the main route out of the mountains, it had to be used often. She heard someone shout as she moved the cart down the track to the cottages.

"Someone's coming. Be ready."

Frowning, she slowed Humberto and stopped him short of the cottages. The derelict one was in view across the field where the track wound. By the cottage's edge, a flash of white appeared, as someone or something glanced around the corner.

"Hello," SJ called. "It's SJ."

"SJ," a female voice said. Charlotte appeared from behind the derelict building. SJ moved Humberto forward.

"What's wrong?" she called as Charlotte approached. The skeletal archer was one of her three followers she allowed to live at Farleck Cottage.

"We've had some visitors over the past couple of days. A couple of orcs were snooping around."

"Oh. Has anything happened?"

"No, not yet, but we are being careful and have been keeping watch. There is no way to get to your cottage without travelling by the lake's edge, so they must use this path."

"What would orcs be coming here for?"

"No idea. Brian went out scouting, and they have set up camp on the other side of the valley. They may just be hunting and have come upon the cottages by accident, but we can't be sure. We chased them off the first day, and then Terence put the fear of god into them the second. Orcs have a problem with seeing skeletal forms of their race."

"Really. I always thought orcs were quite happy with skulls and bones."

"They are as long as they aren't orc."

SJ stopped Humberto and climbed down. "I've brought some items for the cottage to help with repairs or other things that may be needed."

"Terence is over there now while Brian and I keep watch."

"Do you think the orcs would do something here?"

"I don't think they have a clan. Clanless orcs can be a problem," Brian said, making SJ jump as he appeared right next to her.

"In what way?" SJ asked, confused.

"If they like something and are feral orcs with no home, they habitually try to take things with force."

"All the orcs I have met since I came here have been amenable and fair."

"The orcs who have integrated into a normal town or city will have given up on clan life. In contrast, the orc clans are a different story. The closest to here is a few days away, farther west, once you are out of the valley. They will readily raid villages or towns if a clan is large enough to procure their needs rather than work for them."

"I never realised the orcs were that hostile."

"It's not so much hostility as they believe they have a right to things as a senior race."

"Senior race? What do you mean?"

"History states that orcs and humans were the first two races on Amathera, and several of the orc clans still have a very strong sense of history and believe they are more deserving than others. Not all. Terence, for example, was a member of an orc clan, but their path was more established and trade oriented."

"I never knew."

"There is probably much you don't know yet about Amathera," Charlotte said.

"You say they have come twice?"

"Yes, the past two days. We hope that after Terence scared them, they may not return."

"Can you not just try to talk to them?"

"When they saw me, they immediately drew their weapons to attack," Charlotte said.

"Why? Did you do anything hostile towards them?"

"No. I was walking down the lake-side along the path from the second cottage when I saw them. They initially came after me when I turned back, and didn't stop until Brian arrived and there were two of us. The second day, when they returned, Terence was at the derelict cottage looking at stones he could use at yours. On seeing him, they turned and ran away."

"Do you think they will come again? You say there were only two of them."

"Maybe, maybe not. The fact they have been twice is what concerns us. Especially since I don't even own a bow anymore," Charlotte said.

"I can rectify that," SJ said, walking back to the cart and removing the short bow and quiver of arrows from the dark elf.

"Wow. This is a +1. Are you sure you want to give this to me?" Charlotte said, surprised, as SJ held them out.

"I do not need it."

"But you could sell this."

"I'm not worried about it. Call it a thank you for protecting the cottages."

Believing that Charlotte had smiled in response—it was hard to tell on a skeleton—SJ turned and looked at Brian. "I brought you something also if you want it?"

"What did you bring?"

SJ again went back to the cart and removed the leather armour +1. "I'm not sure if it is good for you?"

Brian took the leather armour. His armour was shabby, and the leather was in tatters. The bracers he wore were nothing compared to the set he now put on, plus a body piece, and greaves. Brian seemed happy with the gift.

"Thanks," he said, giving a look which SJ again assumed was a smile.

"I will head to the cottage and see Terence," SJ said.

"He hasn't stopped working since we got here," Charlotte said.

"Doing what?"

"You'll see when you get there," Brian said.

SJ climbed back on the cart and moved off towards her cottage.

"Are orcs that bad?" SJ asked Dave, once she was out of earshot of Brian and Charlotte.

"They can be. Again, having a dark elf tracking you down and potentially rogue orcs in a starter territory is unusual. I need to understand the code to read into things more easily. The System is not updating details for this area. It appears this part of Amathera is sandboxed."

"What does it mean to be sandboxed? I know that happened to my malware alert, and I know what it means back on Earth."

"I suppose it is possible that someone deliberately placed you in an unfamiliar area, but there were already other Legionnaires here."

"Unless they were here for a specific reason as well."

"Ummm. I will have to investigate and see what I can find out. I have a friend in the assignments department I can speak to."

"Assignments department?"

"Yes. They oversee the whole integration side and initial aspects of assignments for Legionnaires. I'm not sure how forthcoming they will be, though."

"Could you get into more trouble by doing so?"

"Meh. I am always in trouble anyway, so another black mark against my data won't make a difference."

"Yes, but you don't want the System to do anything drastic if you cause too many waves."

"I'm not the one causing waves. I am just supporting my waiver," Dave said, giggling.

SJ rolled her eyes at his comment.

"If you think you can find anything out, please do so, but if it looks like a problem, don't push," SJ said.

"Understood."

CHAPTER THREE

Homemaker

As SJ continued past Gladys and Hubert's cottage, she noticed how well-maintained the garden area looked. Charlotte had been working there, judging by how pristine everything looked in comparison to the overgrown and dishevelled state it had been in prior. She noticed some tools leaning against the side of the cottage, which she could not remember seeing before. Farleck Cottage looked as beautiful as before from a distance, and on approaching, she noticed the additional elements that hadn't existed previously. There was a picnic-style table, and benches sat out in front of the cottage. There was also a frame of wooden stakes built to one side, and draped from them was a large white sheet that created a type of gazebo.

The garden appeared immaculate, and someone had taken the time to clear the surrounding area of weeds and the odd shrub. It looked like a heavenly setting, and she would have stayed there if she hadn't had things to do.

"Hi, Terence," she called, pulling Humberto up.

"Hi, SJ," the skeletal orc said in his deep voice.

"It looks like you have been busy?"

"There is more to do yet. I am building a lean-to on the side for log storage."

SJ climbed down and joined him at the building's side. He had already built the framework and was in the process of planking the roof.

"Where did you get the tools from?" SJ asked, looking at several items lying around on the grass.

"We went back to the compound and emptied the shed. Also, Brian didn't want to leave the lizorse in the stables, so he freed them to roam."

Understanding Brian's chaotic good alignment, it made sense that he would prefer not to harm unless necessary and would protect others he deemed weaker. But imagining two random lizorse walking about in the woods didn't fill her with confidence.

"Isn't it dangerous freeing them?"

"No. They would normally stay away from beings and remain out of sight."

"Ah, that's okay. I brought tools and some items with me to equip the cottage. How has your stay been so far?"

"Great. I assume you saw Charlotte and Brian, and they told you about our recent visitors?"

"Yes. They have spoken to me about the orcs."

"If they return, we will handle them, although I doubt they will."

"I feel a little guilty. Although I gave a gift to Brian and Charlotte, I have nothing to give to a fighter."

"I am fine. I have hammers here. They are just as good as a mace for causing damage."

"Next time I come back, I will bring you something."

"That would be very kind of you."

"I'm going to put the stuff inside," SJ said, returning to the cart and unloading it.

When she walked to the door and entered, what she saw amazed her. The interior was immaculate, no cobwebs or dust to be seen. All the surfaces looked highly polished, and the old sofa even looked cleaner than it had been. Near the bed, a new bookcase stood, and Terence must have built what looked like a set of drawers. She filled the cottage with the items she had brought, emptied any unnecessary items from her inventory, and rearranged everything, moving things around until she was happy with how the room felt and looked. Apart from no mattress, there was everything needed now to set up a new home. Walking back outside, she carried over the tools and nails she had brought from town.

"Where do you want these?"

Terence turned, his eyes lighting up at the sight of nails. "Those will speed things up," he said, smiling. "Just place them there. I've built a small storage box around the back."

SJ walked past and around the rear of the cottage. Against the wall was indeed a storage box, and she lifted the lid to find it compartmented, with various items he must have recovered from the compound lying inside.

"How have you made all this stuff so quickly?" she called to Terence.

"I told you I was a carpenter, didn't I?" Terence said.

"You did. But these must take time to build."

"Not long at all. They are basic items that any novice carpenter can make. Oh, I repaired the well gears, so it works now. I need to build a new frame to replace the existing one; I noticed it was rotting slightly."

SJ was gobsmacked at the work done while she was away. It had only been a week, but they seemed to have completed at least a month's work between them.

"I don't know how you have all done so much," SJ said, walking back to where Terence was still working.

"The bonus of not needing sleep is that I can work all day, every day if I need to, and when I have wood to work with, I am doing the one thing I love more than anything else," he said with the typical skeletal smile.

"What will you do when you finish making the items?"

"There is plenty to do here. The beams can be realigned, and the thatch supports strengthened. Then there is a porch to build in front, and I thought you could even extend out the back and create a separate bedroom area. It would be wooden, obviously, because of the lack of stone, but it would be warm and dry."

"You have already done more than I could have ever expected."

"I have nothing else to do but enjoy the work, and it's in a beautiful location. I would have brought my Juki here if I were still alive."

The strangeness of speaking to already-dead skeletons did not escape SJ, and she could not imagine the life they must be leading without respite. This experience gave additional consideration to the term *eternal life*.

"Is there anything you need when I come back next time?"

"The only thing I am missing is a sharp chisel. The ones I have are blunt, making it take me longer than it should to sort things out."

"A dwarf is coming down in a few days to look at the chimney, and as long as I have been back in time, I will make sure he brings you some."

"I would appreciate that."

"I can't thank you enough for what you have done here."

"It is my pleasure. Without you, we would all still be in servitude."

SJ's display triggered.

Followership: Followers are those who have dedicated their services to you. They will do anything to support you.

"Holy freaking freaky things from freakytown," Dave spluttered.

SJ couldn't respond now, in front of Terence.

"Thanks for the work, Terence; I appreciate it. I will see Charlotte and Brian again before heading to the caves."

"Caves?"

"Yes. I need to collect some mushrooms for one of the town members."

"Which type of mushroom?"

"Sancasia. Do you know where there are any?"

"They are the blue ones, aren't they?"

"Yes."

"There are caves about a third of the way down the valley on the right side. I know some are there, but several cave networks are nearby. It may take a bit of searching to find the right one. Also, be aware that not all of them are uninhabited."

"What lives in them?"

"When we were near there, we saw several greylings."

"What are greylings?" SJ asked, never having heard of them before.

"They are dark dwellers—humanoids with long, gangly arms and legs. Cave greylings are very good at hiding in mountain areas. They mainly feed on mountain rams or hoglings, but they are not afraid to attack anything else if they think it may taste good."

"I don't fancy bumping into many of those."

"You should be fine if you don't disturb their nest. You can always tell if a cave contains greylings as they mark their territory with the skulls of their prey."

SJ shuddered at the thought of finding skulls lining the cave entrances.

"Thanks for the information, and I hope I can avoid them."

"Just remember, they don't do daylight. It burns their skin."

Terence smiled again, returning to his work. SJ turned Humberto around from where he had eaten flower heads and led him back up the path towards the lake.

"What's up, Dave?" SJ asked as soon as she was out of range.

"You have a freaking follower."

"What does it mean, exactly?"

"It means you are more than an anomaly."

"Why?" SJ frowned.

"Followers are uncommon, nearly as rare as those miniature wyvern eggs you have."

"How has it happened, though? There were no reputation gains."

"That's my point. In one jump, you went from being a nobody to Terence to him being a follower. You have someone now. If you ordered him to run into a lava pit, he would do it without asking a question."

"It can't be that bad?"

"Oh. It is. Most followers are fanatics. They support evil and will do anything their masters tell them."

"Being someone's master is not my aspiration, nor is being evil. I just want to be me and grow."

"I would say that out of all the followers you could get, an undead skeleton is a perfect match, considering how old you will probably reach."

"How or why did this happen so suddenly? I don't understand."

"Although I have heard rumours, I have never witnessed it myself. I believe it is part of the necromancer's servitude—it leaves a resonating need to serve someone. I can't guarantee exactly how it happens, but I would bet my last byte that you could leave Terence at the cottage forever, and he would keep building it and improving it."

The thought of having someone who would do anything for her was unnerving. SJ was sociable when necessary but internally identified as an introvert. She enjoyed her own space and time, as she had proven, allowing herself to be absorbed into looking through the ledgers or knitting, and she could imagine no one following her to that degree. It appeared to be another part of the new world that she would need to come to terms with.

"I will never order Terence to do anything."

"That is your choice. I have only ever worked with one other Legionnaire who received followers, and he was a half-crazed paladin. The guy was so messed up he thought he was a god. He spent his time preaching and searching for some chalice that was rumoured to give eternal life. It didn't end well for him or his fans."

"What happened?"

"He attacked the lair of a chimera, where rumours suggested the chalice was. Most chimeras in Amathera are your typical mix of a few normal breeds: big cats, birds, and other nondescript animals, but lairs can contain some rather different ones. This one contained a very strange version: a dragon, snake, and ogre mix. They could spit either acid or fire. The followers were all killed quickly during the raid, and the paladin continued alone. He did okay, but when you get your face half-melted by acid and then barbecued afterwards, you don't tend to do very well."

Having seen Bordon and Bob, SJ couldn't imagine a mixture of the two creatures, never mind adding a snake.

"I am guessing there are none around here?"

"No. Chimeras are mainly on one of the other continents. Sometimes, a flying variant that has crossed the ocean can get here."

As SJ approached the derelict cottage again, Charlotte was busy moving some of the fallen stones into a neat pile, and Brian was removing the broken door from its frame.

"I am going to head off again. It won't be long before I return. While I remember, there will be a stonemason coming to visit in a couple of days. He will look at the chimney and this place and see what can be done."

"That sounds good," Charlotte said.

"And thank you both for what you have done at the cottages. The gardens look amazing."

"Brian helped me as much as he could. He has a bit of a penchant for gardening." Charlotte smiled.

Heading towards the main trail, SJ felt pleased with the completion of the work at the cottages and couldn't wait to sort out a mattress and possibly spend a few nights there with the skeletons.

"What do you know about greylings?" SJ asked.

"They are pathetic creatures," Dave said. "They are rumoured to originate from mountain dwarves and kobolds, but no one knows for certain."

"Are they dangerous?"

"Only in large groups. I have never seen one above Level 4 before. Then again, a group of ten Level 1s could be challenging because of numbers and the potential to be swarmed."

"Are there likely any other creatures I need to know about?"

"So many could be problematic, but this is still a starter territory. Even if it's acting differently, I wouldn't expect many things that are too dangerous, as long as you are cautious, take your time, and keep your eyes open. The usual suspects are wolves; bears, perhaps, if they have young to protect; badgers; possibly wolverines; and maybe the odd puma. Of course, hoglings always seem to have nasty tempers."

"Why is it that there are so many that may attack?"

"Nature of survival. Everything is continually fighting for its place."

The trail was well-worn and smooth, and the cart moved freely. With the sun high in the sky, SJ happily listened to the birds that frequented the skies above and lived in the forest that covered much of the valley floor. The trail wound through the trees, staying on a flat gradient. She felt relaxed and free travelling along, whistling one of the bard's songs from the inn that she had enjoyed.

The cottage and her training and levelling consumed her thoughts as she day-dreamed about what she could do. She had been considering her next subterfuge skill again and thought she had made her mind up. She wanted them all for the obvious perks they brought, but considering the needs of where she was now, only one stood out as an immediate benefit to her.

"I spoke to my friend in assignments," Dave said, disturbing SJ's peace.

"What did he say?"

"He was a little cryptic in his response. This area is a test bed. They placed several Legionnaires in this area before, giving no preference to where they placed them. He said the System was revisiting territory boundaries, but he didn't expand on the details or couldn't. Because of the protocols they may have implemented, you never know with the System."

"So, it is a real sandbox, then, similar to what I know from Earth?"

"I would have to agree. It would explain the level variances and the hobs. It has made it more of an interesting start to a new life. Most starter towns are boring places with the same quest chains—rinse and repeat. The ones you have received here have added a new spice to the situation."

"I don't understand how they can assign you as administrators without briefing you fully."

"It wouldn't normally make a difference if they did. As I explained, I wouldn't usually be able to talk to you about 95 percent of the things we discuss. I couldn't have guided you to the dark elf. It is unheard of, and it's invigorating. It makes it much more exciting for me to be part of your journey than the usual rescue-a-cat-from-a-tree quests. Well, unless you are knitting or reading boring ledgers, of course."

Smiling at Dave's comment, SJ thought about how she was enjoying her new life and time with Dave.

"I forgot to thank you for your help earlier guiding me."

"Expected of rude Legionnaires taking everything for granted," he said, dripping with sarcasm.

SJ chuckled. "I am very grateful for everything you have done to help me so far."

"And I am happy to be of assistance."

They shared a moment of silence before Dave spoke again.

"I think it's the right fork up ahead over the bridge."

SJ hadn't been paying attention to the trail ahead; she was too busy musing over her thoughts. Looking up, a small stone bridge crossed a meandering river across the valley. The forest had ended, and ahead there were just open fields with small tree clusters dotted around. Where the path split, she noticed the first signpost she had seen since being on the road. Crossing the bridge, she pulled Humberto up at the fork and read the sign. It pointed straight down the trail with two names carved into the wooden sign's surface: Asterfal and Cuopi.

"Why do I recognise the name Cuopi?" SJ asked.

"It was where the elf was from—the one you saved at the necromancer compound."

"Oh yeah. I knew I had heard it before. I wonder how far down the trail it is."

"No idea. This fog of war is a pain because of my limited sight, and I can't find any maps for this area overall in the System, making me virtually as blind as you are."

"When we eventually leave this territory, does that mean you will confirm destinations more easily?"

"Yes, and no. I still have a fog of war to contend with, but if I have been in an area before, I will have a good idea of what is around."

"That's going to be helpful."

"Possibly; it depends on changes since I was last in an area."

Spurring Humberto, she turned the cart right, following the trail to where she hoped the cave systems would be.

CHAPTER FOUR

Mushroom, Mushroom

The trail continued to wind through the fields. Beyond the flat plains leading to the mouth of the valley, the visible knife-edge of its peak tapered down. The trail had become more broken, and the cart was no longer a smooth ride; SJ jostled and bounced as it travelled over the ruts.

"I think I'm going to stop here," SJ said, pulling the cart up to the side of a tree just off the path. Leading Humberto off the main trail, she pulled the cart until it was behind the tree by some bushes, and although not hidden well, it was not as obvious. She unhitched Humberto, stroked his mane, and led him towards the tree before tying him off. She didn't want him wandering away while she continued to the caves.

"I hope Humberto will be okay," SJ said.

"I have seen nothing around the area large enough to attack a horse yet."

"*Yet* sounds ominous."

"You never know what could be wandering."

Looking towards the valley side, she was probably still a few hundred metres from it. She rechecked her inventory to ensure she had everything she needed: torches, flint and steel, rations, waterskin, the basket from Grewlas, and the healing potions and anti-poison. Having left all the other items from the cart at the cottage would at least mean nothing could be stolen. It annoyed her that such a minor item as her flint and steel took up an entire slot in her inventory.

"I should have got a new belt with some pouches to carry the smaller items."

"It would have been helpful," Dave said.

She closed her inventory, happy she had what she needed but frustrated that she had only two free slots for other items apart from her tailoring slots.

"Let's go," she said, transforming into her miniature form. Taking off almost instantly, she flew along the trail. Her speed was much faster than the cart had been travelling at, and it wasn't long before the landscape changed and the slope of the wall began. Flying made travel so much easier, not having to walk up inclines. She increased her height and surveyed ahead. She was very wary of checking the skies for any sign of hungry birds.

In the rock face that presented itself, she could see several dark openings. At this distance, none of them seemed to have any distinguishing features apart from their position. Heading towards the nearest opening, she came to land by the entrance. The cave opening had enough space for a bear or a similar creature to enter, and she felt the urge to ask about them.

"Do bears live in caves?"

"Why bears?"

"Oh. No specific reason. It was always a thing back on Earth that they did."

"Bears live wherever they please. Some live in caves, others don't. The territory or region normally plays a large part, and it is warm here, so they do not need to find shelter."

"What can live in caves, then?"

"All sorts. Spiders, sometimes wolves have dens; pumas, various insects, and anything else could set up a home in one."

"Well, that isn't great, then, is it?"

"What do you mean?"

"I could be about to walk into something's home, but it may not wish for guests."

"You worry too much. You can defend yourself if there is anything."

"I am only Level 7 and still haven't got my second martial arts skill yet."

"You have already proven your ability on multiple occasions. You need to have more confidence in what you can do."

SJ felt shocked by Dave's frank and positive comment, but then smiled and gained strength and confidence from his words.

"Thanks."

Dave didn't respond, so SJ took out a torch and her flint and steel and began lighting it. Doing it in miniature form meant that the torch would give off very little light, but if she grew it, it would provide enough, judging by what it had been like inside the cave from the cocoon visit.

Once it was lit and burning well, she approached the entrance. The air inside smelt damp and stale. Slowly flying inside, she took her time and proceeded cautiously. She was keeping her eyes and ears primed for any sound. Nothing was unusual, and she hoped she wouldn't come face-to-face with anything wanting to eat her. The cave entrance went back quite a distance before opening into a cavern. She could not see the roof with the pitiful light cast from her miniature torch but could hear water dripping from the ceiling above and landing in a pool somewhere in the dark.

Her senses were calm, and she could feel no other presence or any unusual sensations that her senses had showed since her symbiosis. It was still strange when she considered that her blood flowed with that of a dragon. Her heightened senses, ability to rapidly heal, and the lifesaving precognition ability were all amazing perks. Flying around the chamber close to the floor, looking for any mushrooms that could be blue coloured, she found nothing. Eventually, she completed a full circle and still found nothing of interest. She flew back to where the bright sun streamed into the cave mouth, squinting as she flew back into the sunlight.

"One down," she said, looking farther down the cliff face of the valley. There were several, and she proceeded to the next, a couple of hundred feet away. The torch was quite awkward to fly with outside, the mild breeze blowing the thin smoke it let off back towards her, and she had to hold it out to the side to prevent the smoke from going in her eyes as she flew.

The next cave entrance was much smaller, and she wondered if a normal person could have fit inside, even though she still took the time to enter and search. It was even shorter than the first cave, and it came to an abrupt end, only being a mere tunnel rather than entering a cavern at its end.

"This could take some time," she sighed.

"You have enough," Dave said.

She spent the next hour flitting from one cave to the next with no sign of mushrooms. When she reached the seventh cave, her hopes rose. It was the first she had come across with a chilly breeze emanating from inside. Hoping that an unfamiliar environment would be what she needed to find them, she entered the mouth of the cave, which was large enough to drive a coach into and fell away on a steep incline. Flying meant that she had no concerns about moving down the passage. The tunnel wove into the earth until it reached an open cavern. She saw no signs of mushrooms in the tunnel, but as soon as she reached the cavern, she spotted a blue-coloured mushroom in the soil.

"Yes!" she said excitedly.

"Looks like you have found some at last," Dave said.

The mushroom was probably half her size in miniature form, and she could do nothing unless she grew. Once she did so, the torchlight cast into the chamber revealed clusters of blue mushrooms covering the floor. She smiled and bent down to pluck the mushroom from the loose earth on the cavern's floor. The ground was damp, and the walls had a sheen from the constant moisture. SJ removed the basket from her inventory, placing it on the ground and walked around the cavern, collecting more of the blue mushrooms to fill it.

After several minutes, her senses were triggered and she stopped looking around her. She had not even got more than several feet from the tunnel entrance; there were so many mushrooms.

"I can sense something," SJ whispered.

"I have seen nothing. Then again, the light isn't great. You should invest in a lantern at some point. They provide much better light than torches."

Rolling her eyes and not bothering to reply, she focused on the cavern's darkness. Her senses triggering were her warning sign, and she shrank down to her miniature size. The torchlight was now nothing more than a match's head in the darkness—visible but only casting light in a small sphere around her. The basket was on the floor by her side, now towering over her.

As SJ stood still, she heard a scrapping sound coming from deeper into the cave.

"There is something there," she whispered.

"I can hear it too but can't see anything," Dave said.

The sound stopped, and silence returned to the cavern, the only break being the occasional drop of water landing on the cavern floor. SJ's nerves were tingling at the unknown, and she felt a trickle of sweat run down her back. The cold sensation made her senses flare. There was something there; she knew it but did not know what.

The basket moved, and SJ almost had a heart attack as it rocked sideways. A thick, black feeler appeared over the top of it. As SJ looked upwards, an enormous insect greeted her with its open jaws.

"Ahh," she squealed, dropping the torch in fright. The sound made the creature recoil from the basket. "What's that?" she cried.

"A giant crepar. They have a toxic bite, so don't let it nip you."

SJ flew backwards across the cavern, staring at where the basket was. The tiny torch provided a minuscule amount of illumination. She watched as the insect, which looked like a massive centipede, again delved into the basket digging into its contents, removing one of the blue mushrooms. SJ watched as it picked it up in its mandibles and bit into it.

"It's stealing my mushrooms. Why doesn't it just eat the ones in the cavern?" SJ exclaimed, her initial fear now being replaced with annoyance. The creature was not paying her miniature form any attention as it grabbed another and began devouring it. SJ identified it.

Giant Crepar	
Level:	10
Hit Points:	65
Mana Points:	0
Armour Class:	35
Attacks:	Bite/Slash
Special:	Toxin

"It has a high armour class," SJ said.

"Its chitinous body provides it with natural armour."

"Do you know what its toxin does?"

"Two seconds."

Silence.

"It attacks your cells, preventing healing," Dave said.

"So, stay away from its bite," SJ said.

She flew sideways away from the creature, which was eating another of her precious collection, moving around to its side. It was difficult to make it out in the pitch black with the tiny torch's light. She could at least tell where it was, with its movement being heard easily. Several pairs of legs were visible, and its body resembled plated armour. SJ was unable to determine its true size while she was small, but she noticed that the underside did not seem as well-protected as its top.

She equipped her claws, and as she reached her full height she drove them into its softer sides. Her claws scraped against the chitinous armour that still covered its body, but aimed as low as she had and with the element of surprise, they penetrated its soft flesh. The crepar let out a hissing sound, and its body curled back on itself. The head of the creature hit SJ on her side, throwing her off balance and making her fall sideways.

Jumping back to her feet, she saw the shadowy form in the cave's darkness and moved to attack. As she did, her legs went from under her. She had not seen how long the creature's body was, and it had moved to hit her from behind.

"I need light," she stammered as she again regained her footing. The creature went to strike her again with its mandibles open. Seeing the movement late in the darkness, she only moved aside, and the creature's head missed her by millimetres. She ran to the basket, shrinking as she did. As soon as she did, she grabbed the torch and grew again, still moving away from the crepar. Another hiss and scuttling sounded behind her. With the brighter torchlight, she could see better and headed straight for the entrance tunnel.

The crepar gave chase. Running up the steep incline, she could hear its feet scraping and scratching on the tunnel's surface. Glancing backwards, she saw it wasn't very far behind her. She needed to make daylight, if possible, and fight it in the open.

"Attacking a creature in the dark is never a good idea: at least you can draw it into the light now," Dave said.

"You think!" SJ growled as she continued to run.

She turned a corner in the tunnel, seeing the bright light of day ahead; her muscles were burning from running up the incline, and she wished she had flown but needed the creature to follow, and she wasn't sure it would have bothered if she was small. As SJ broke into the light of day, momentarily blinded, she continued from the cave-mouth. Dropping the torch, she turned and waited.

The crepar's deep brown colour seemed to absorb the sun's light. Its colossal head targeted her and its mandibles snapped as it moved towards her on its unnatural legs. She stood ready, and as it neared, it reared up the front part of its long body before launching towards her.

She dived sideways out of its way, rolling across the rocky surface and wincing from the pain of the motion. Thankfully, she had only received minor damage when the creature hit her. Jumping up immediately, she turned back towards it and moved in to attack its weaker sides. She could see a green substance leaking from its wound, and its health was down to forty-two hit points after her initial assault.

That was poor considering what her blades had done against others, but knowing the creature's armour class and her level, it did not surprise her. She attacked with precision and swiftness from her training with Lorna, using her claws as extensions of her fists, striking the creature's side as it twisted its head to bite at her again. This time, being ready and aware it could easily turn towards her, SJ watched its head move and brought her claws around in defence. Its large mandibles met her blades, sounding like swords clashing as it clacked and hissed at her.

SJ stepped back, giving herself distance before again moving to its side, as she noticed its rear moving to sweep her again. Seeing it coming this time, she jumped high enough for its rear portion to miss her. As she landed, she lashed out with a sweeping claw towards its legs rather than its armoured body. Her claws cut into its legs much more easily than its armour, and it hissed, pulling away, leaving several of its lower limbs behind.

Its health was now down to thirty-three, and it tied itself almost in a knot as it twisted towards her, its mandibles clacking angrily. SJ tried to parry the blow away, but its strength overcame her defensive pose, and one of its mandibles caught her shoulder.

She grunted in pain from the hit, as her health reduced by a further six points. The creature was much faster than others she had fought, and it turned on the eye of a needle. Its body positioning was so versatile that its rear portion moved either in synchronicity or independently. It reminded SJ of a friend's pet corn-snake that had slithered around her hand as she held it as a child. She was completely terrified.

"Keep taking its legs out," Dave yelled at her.

"I'm trying." SJ grimaced as she deflected another strike from its head. It had caught her again, this time at her side. Thankfully, she had prevented it from biting her, although its mandible cut again deeply. She swung her claws rapidly, severing more of its lower limbs. The crepar let out a hiss as it withdrew again and her display triggered.

Congratulations! Bleed effect has been applied.

The crepar was now down to 50 percent health, and as it turned again to face her, she saw it tick down by another point. "I need another couple of strikes to land," she said, panting from the exertion. The fight was one of her longest so far, with the amount of dodging and weaving they were both performing. Standing with her hands high and claws extended, she ushered at the crepar to come at her again.

"You know it does not know what you're doing, right?" Dave said.

SJ growled as they attacked each other and ducked under its head, drawing her claws down the underside of its exposed abdomen. They cut into the softer armour with ease, and the crepar kept moving, jerking SJ backwards as her claws got caught. The abdominal strike had been effective, and its health had reduced to under a quarter. But with her claws caught in its carapace she got dragged underneath.

She panicked, crying out in shock.

"Remove them," Dave screamed.

She struggled to avoid the creature's many feet as it dragged her over the valley's rocky surface, before SJ successfully removed her claws. The crepar continued over her, and she felt a raw pain in her shoulder from being dragged. Immediately recalling her claws, she discovered that only the claws for her left hand appeared. That was when she noticed her right glove dangling from underneath the beast's abdomen.

"Damn," she cursed. As she climbed to her feet, it again turned on her. SJ screamed in pain and fury at the horrendous abomination of a creature, as she ran at it. She would not give it the room it needed to turn. The distance closed quickly, as she punched out towards its head with her right hand. Her blow caught it perfectly, only doing no damage, but it gave her the opening she sought to drive her clawed hand up and into the underside of its jaws. The ferocity of her strike easily pierced this time, and her blades stuck upwards into its mouth.

The bleed effect was still working, and she struggled to hold its massive head pierced on her claws. The crepar shook its whole body violently as it tried to dislodge the claws. "Hold it," Dave cried.

"I'm trying," SJ hissed as the head's movement yanked her left and right. She continued to punch it with her right fist, her blows ineffective with no claws. Her shoulder screamed at her with every punch she threw, but she was determined to defeat the mushroom thief. Its health continued to fall until it reached zero, and its body weight fell forward towards her. The sudden weight shift took her by surprise, forcing her down to her knees before she could free her claws and push its head to one side.

SJ lay sprawled on the ground gasping for breath, before letting out a victorious cry.

"Well done," Dave said cheerily.

"Well done! I lost one of my claws and tore my shoulder, never mind the slices I took to my shoulder and abdomen."

"You are alive, though, which is always a bonus, and you didn't get bitten."

SJ forced herself to her feet and moved to where its body still held her claws. Resting her foot against its corpse, she pried them free. Thankfully, the blades were undamaged, having just caught a much harder substance than she had expected. SJ removed one of the lesser healing potions from her inventory and uncorked the vial before downing it. She hadn't received too much damage. The cuts would close soon enough out of combat; it was more to ease the pain in her shoulder. The potion's effects swept through her body, removing the aches and pains, and clearing her mind.

SJ bent forward and looted the corpse.

Congratulations! Level 10 Giant Crepar killed. 110xp awarded.
5 x Chitinous Armour Plates

"All because of some damn mushrooms," SJ huffed, turning to walk back to the cave.

CHAPTER FIVE

Skill Selection

SJ had lit two torches before entering the cave to collect the basket and pick the remaining mushrooms she needed. Wedging a torch on the far side, she found the entrance from which the crepar had entered the chamber. It was a narrow tunnel with a low ceiling, and she wouldn't even attempt to investigate it. Refilling the basket where the crepar had eaten her spoils, she returned to the fresh air and afternoon sun. The day passed quickly. She had been so busy that she was looking forward to returning to town and getting a bath.

Her dress was pristine as normal, but her skin felt grime covered from being dragged along the ground and covered in crepar ichor. Placing the full basket into her inventory, she transformed into her miniature form and flew back to where she had left Humberto. Thankfully, he was fine, and she reattached him to the cart before returning to the cottages. Leaving the caves behind her and thankful she hadn't bumped into any greylings, she was quite pleased with the outcome. After all, she defeated a Level 10 creature all by herself. It was her highest solo kill to date.

As she approached the turn for the cottages, she heard a loud snapping sound, and the cart threw her sideways, causing her to land sprawled on the ground as the cartwheel broke.

"That's a new way to fly," Dave said, chuckling.

She picked herself up, ignored Dave's comment, and looked at the wheel. It was lying on its side, the pin that had kept it on the cart sheared off. The jostling of the rocky path had probably weakened it.

"Damn. I need to see if the skeletons can help me replace it. There is no way I can do it myself."

"It's a good job we are close by, then," Dave said.

Unfastening Humberto from the cart, she continued back to the cottages and waved toward two familiar faces as soon as the derelict cottage was in sight.

"Where is the cart?" Brian asked.

"The wheel fell off. It looks like the pin holding it snapped."

"That's not good. I am sure Terence can probably repair it," Charlotte said.

"Yes, but it's still up on the main trail, and I need to get it back to Lythonian at the church."

"I'm sure we can fix it. I will grab Terence," Brian said as he turned and headed towards her cottage.

A while later, the pair came into sight, walking back along the lake's edge. Terence was carrying a wooden toolbox. Reaching SJ, he smiled. She was getting used to it now.

"Where is it?" Terence asked.

"On the main trail, by the turn-off."

"Okay. Let's go see if we can fix it, then," Terence said.

The four of them headed back, and it didn't take Terence long to form a temporary repair on the cart. The most awkward part was lifting the cart enough to reattach the wheel. It weighed much more than SJ had thought. With the help of Brian and Charlotte, the three of them kept the cart and wheel in position as Terence worked. He only used a wooden pin, but he said it would last long enough to get back to town if she took it easy.

"Thank you all," SJ said as she tugged Humberto to the cart again from where he had been grazing at the roadside.

"We are here to help whenever you need it," Terence said.

The sun was dipping in the sky, and knowing how long the journey would take to get back, SJ did not fancy travelling the last part in the dark on the cart.

"I think I am going to stay at the cottage tonight and head back in the morning," SJ said.

"It will be nice to have some female company," Charlotte said, nodding towards Brian and Terence.

"What's that supposed to mean?" Brian asked.

"You two never stop talking about rubbish. That's what that means," Charlotte said, smiling at them.

"What rubbish?" Terence said defensively.

"How many times have you both told the same story now about the minotaur the master tried to reincarnate?" Charlotte said.

"Minotaur?" SJ said, taken aback.

"The story gets more elaborate each time it's told. About how bravely you both fought against it."

"You fought a minotaur?" SJ asked.

"They didn't fight it. They just think they did. You would have to hear it, which I am sure if you gave either of them half a chance, they would tell you," Charlotte said.

"That was an epic battle," Brian said, huffing.

"No. It really wasn't. You both got your asses handed to you, and the necromancer killed it," she said.

"That's not entirely true. I agree Brian did, but I didn't," Terence said.

"You both did. I remember picking bones up from both of you after he had stomped the pair of you into the ground. I was the only one of us left standing."

The two male skeletons stared at Charlotte, and neither said anything in response. Their expressionless faces made it difficult to understand their thoughts, but SJ could imagine them both having red cheeks from embarrassment.

SJ climbed back into the cart. "Come on, let's head back, and I would love to know how you both got stomped on by a minotaur," SJ said, chuckling.

The two skeletons trudged grumpily behind the cart, both muttering to each other.

The night at the cottage was very pleasant. SJ ate some of her rations and listened to an exciting rendition of the minotaur story. Terence promised he would not complete any work overnight while she slept, and she moved into the cottage as the darkness set in and settled on the sofa. The three skeletons took turns being lookout at the derelict cottage throughout the night, just in case the orcs returned, and when SJ awoke the next morning, it had been uneventful. She left the next morning, promising to come and visit again soon, and headed back to town.

On arriving at the meadow at the top of the crags, she had to move Humberto off the road as a large, covered wagon, painted blue with a golden livery on the side, was travelling on the trail. Six horses were pulling the wagon, and it looked like at least eight people could have sat comfortably inside it. As it passed, she waved to the ent who was driving, who waved back, smiling at her. Ents were probably the strangest looking of all the beings she had met in Amathera. There were few in Killic, but seeing a small tree with sprouting leaves walking through the streets was always strange.

"I wonder who was in there," SJ said as she moved Humberto back onto the trail.

"That's the usual stagecoach that runs to Asterfal twice weekly," Dave said.

"How do you know that?" SJ asked.

"Have you not seen it in town?"

"No. I have never seen it." SJ frowned.

"You were probably too busy training. I have seen it twice over at the stables."

"Oh. I had never noticed."

"If I recall correctly, the last time I saw it was when Greb taught you a lesson of manners."

"I did well against him. He is much higher level than me."

"He still taught you a lesson."

SJ could not argue with that. She felt at the side of her face instinctively where he had kicked her.

Arriving back at the church, SJ met Lythonian, who was helping the old gnome chorister plant flowers in the churchyard.

"Morning, Lythonian," SJ called as she drew up in the cart.

The draconian stood, wiping his claws off on a rag, and walked over, grinning. His cleric's robes he wore were pristine white even after working in the church grounds. "I hope Humberto behaved himself."

"He was perfect, thank you. I had a problem with the cart, though. It lost a wheel on my journey back. It has a temporary repair, but it needs fixing. I was going to take it to the wagonistas and get it fixed properly."

"Don't worry. I will speak to Katiyanna. She owes me a favour or two."

The remark made SJ wonder why the wagonista would owe Lythonian a favour, but she would not ask. "Thank you for letting me borrow it. I would have been at a loss without it."

"Did you get everything sorted you needed to?"

"Yes. I dropped everything off and collected the mushrooms for Grewlas, although I had a problem with a crepar."

"Crepar. Nasty beasties they can be. They have a tough body."

"I noticed," SJ said, chuckling. Hearing Lythonian say a word such as *beasties* made her smile. "Anyway, I need to see Grewlas, and then I am going for a nice long bath."

"No problem. I'll see you soon."

"Thanks again," SJ said as she headed onward.

Grewlas was over the moon receiving the full basket and thanked her profusely.

Quest: Gather Sancasia Mushrooms—Complete
Rewards: 336xp + 96xp bonus for reputation = 432 xp awarded, 2 x Silver

---

Back at the inn, SJ ordered a sandwich and a large coffee, missing the morning cup she had got used to. She would have to ensure she took some to the cottage the next time she went just to have a supply. Upstairs, she had poured a steaming bath with scented oils and was relaxing, soaking in the hot water, humming, when Dave interrupted her.

"I found it," Dave said excitedly.

"Found what?"

"The code gaps. I know what the crafty System did when they patched the code."

"That's great news. Can you recode it, then?"

"It will take a little longer than I initially hoped because there are over fifty layers of precursor code buried behind it, and I need to overcome two algorithm locks. Now that I know where it is, I can at least work on it."

"How long do you think before you can crack it?"

"The outcome is uncertain. It could be a day, a week, a month, or a year. It all comes down to the locks they have added. I don't know how complex they are until I work through the precursor code."

"That sounds like a foreign language to me."

"It's quite easy once you know the basics."

"I'll let you worry about that."

Disturbed from her relaxed state, SJ pulled up her character sheet to check on her experience needs for the next level and reread the details of her new skill choices.

She had spent a long time with Dave adjusting her display feature, and her character sheet now showed her a breakdown of how her attributes were calculated. Her armour class showed the points her armour granted her, along with the dexterity bonus. It was currently 17, with 10 points from her dress and boots and the other 7 from her dexterity, which added 1 extra armour class for every point she gained.

Both her hit points and mana now showed the calculation above the base levels associated with her attribute points. Hit points gave a bonus multiplier based on her constitution, gaining an extra 0.1 to the multiplier for every point she added. Her current constitution of 12 granted her a 1.3 multiplier; at 13, this would increase to 1.4, and so on. Then, it also added a flat multiplier bonus based on her level. So at level 7, it added another 0.07 to the multiplier, granting her a total multiplier of 1.37. A similar breakdown also occurred for her mana. With intelligence and wisdom both at 10, she gained 0.2 towards her multiplier. Every further point in either attribute above this would add an additional 0.01 to it.

Legionnaire 25007077			
Name:	SJ	↻ **Level: 7**	
Age:	27	**Experience:**	372 of 1000
Race:	Fae	**Hit Points:**	55 of 55 (40 * 1.37)
Class:	Assassin	**Mana Points:**	48 of 48 (40 * 1.2)
Alignment:	Neutral Good	**Armour Class:**	17 (10)(7)

Attributes	
Strength:	10
Dexterity:	17
Intelligence:	10
Wisdom:	10
Constitution:	12
Charisma:	11

Skills
Racial:
Night Vision—you have improved vision in poor light conditions.
Flight—when in miniature fae form, you can learn to fly. Flying is not available in humanoid form.
Shapeshift—you have the ability to switch between fae forms.

Class:	
Martial Arts:	Kata Level 5
Subterfuge:	Identification Level 6 (2 of 100 to Level 7)
Profession:	Tailor Level 3
Symbiosis:	
Dragon Sense—your senses (touch, hearing, smell, and sight) are heightened.	
Precognition—foreknowledge due to increased perception will allow you to evade a killing blow. (24-hour cool-down)	
Divine Lightning—your blood is combined with that of a blue dragon, increasing healing speed while out of combat.	
Malware:	Waiver (Sandboxed)
Inventory:	10 slots (10 special)
Followers:	3

"Dave," SJ said, surprised.

"What is it?"

"I have three followers?"

"Oh. It must have been all of them as a group that became followers."

"How? There was only a single notification."

"Let me check."

Silence.

"Yep. Thought so. The alert said *Followers assigned.*"

"All three of them jumped to being followers just like that."

"It makes sense—you freed them all, provided them with a place to live, and gave them equipment."

Lying in the bath, SJ was trying to contemplate that she had followers who would do anything she asked them to do. It was a scary feeling having that sort of influence over someone. "It doesn't feel right."

"Why not?"

"Having that much control over someone."

"It was their choice. No one forced them. Did you not have people back on Earth who followed people and would have done anything for them?"

"I suppose there were fans of certain famous people who probably would have, or even some politicians would have fanatic supporters, not seeing the damage they did even when they were informed."

"There you go, then. It's just a means of influence due to how you interact with people around you. Your progress has been clear, and I can see you gaining more."

"It's not exactly helpful being an assassin with followers."

"Haven't some of Earth's biggest influencers had massive followings?"

"Yes. But they have all been in the public eye doing what they do. It's not like I can advertise my class."

"Your skill tree is subterfuge, remember. Part of your choice in the future will be about how you can persuade and interact with others to get what you need from them. Before killing them, of course."

Sighing, she lowered herself in the water, allowing her head to dip beneath. Holding her breath, she counted to ten before coming back up again.

"Can I set them free?"

"You did that already."

"No, I mean release them from being followers."

"Nope. It was their choice to make."

"It makes me feel so uncomfortable."

"You'll get used to it. Anyway, once you leave the territory, you can easily leave them at the cottage, just looking after it for you. It is not as though they need to travel with you. Followership remains in place once set."

Not wanting to contemplate having three beings who would answer to her every need, she focused on her skills again.

"I've decided which skill I am going to learn."

"Weren't you waiting for Level 6 in kata before making your decision?"

"Although I was considering it, it doesn't matter since I will choose shroud."

"Great choice."

"I should have selected it sooner and wish I had. The reduced damage during the crepar fight would have helped."

"It's only thirty seconds at Level 1, remember?"

"I know, but it also doesn't need me to level an attribute to increase it further compared to the others."

"You will still need to level other attributes. Once your initial class skills increase, you'll eventually get a second skill choice."

"I meant to ask how I learn more?"

"You can assign hard points, which are earned at level stages, the first being Level 10, and then every five levels, you earn another hard point to use."

Looking at her skill tree, she selected Shroud and confirmed the details one last time before selecting it.

Shroud

As an assassin, you may hide in the shadows; when you are shrouded in darkness, damage is reduced temporarily. The skill lasts 3 seconds per level, up to 5 minutes at Level 10. (No base attribute)

Highlighting the option, she selected to learn the skill. She was a little deflated, as she felt nothing. There was no sudden rush of energy or any other feeling that allowed her to even know she had learned the skill apart from the new entry next to her Subterfuge skill on her character sheet.

Subterfuge:	Identification Level 6 (2 of 100 to Level 7), Shroud Level 1

"I selected it."

"Congratulations. You have started on your true path as an assassin now."

SJ smiled at Dave's comment.

"So then, what should we do about the note we found and the Wandering Ogre?" Dave said.

"I had forgotten about that. I suppose I can speak to Niweq."

"What if he is the one the dark elf was going to meet?"

"Do elves and dark elves usually get on?" SJ asked.

"Not normally, but Niweq is a little different. Most elves wouldn't be associated with the type of place he owns."

SJ had always imagined elves to be upright and lawful beings as most games and books portrayed them back on Earth, and she had been a little taken aback when she discovered an elf was running the local pole-dancing club. Having met several in the town since she had arrived plus creatures of many other races, she'd learned it didn't matter what race any of them were—they all had the same chance of being whatever they wished. Apart from considering direct racial influences that prevented them from picking certain classes, professions seemed an open book in comparison.

"That's it. I am going to see Niweq. I have decided. If someone is after me, I need to understand why."

"You need to be careful."

"I know, but I can't ignore a potential threat. Maybe I should speak to Fran rather than Niweq."

"That may be a more sensible option, since you are the only two fae here."

"Okay, I'll start with Fran."

"You only just decided to see Niweq?"

"A girl can change her mind, you know."

"Obviously!" Dave sarcastically replied.

CHAPTER SIX

Not Leaving Your Past Behind

Fran was not outside, so SJ greeted the goblin attendant and entered the common room of the mage apprentice training centre where Fran was head of the program. Several trainees were sitting and reading various books or manuscripts. When SJ smiled warmly at a human male who walked towards her, his sudden outburst took her aback.

"Get out," he said.

"Sorry?" SJ said.

"I said get out."

"I am here to see Mistress Francisca," SJ stammered.

"Get out. Only mages are allowed in here. It is our sacred space."

SJ stood open-mouthed, not responding for a moment. "The attendant allowed me in."

"He has no idea of the importance of what we are doing here, and you are no mage."

"How do you know what class I am?"

"It's obvious. Look at how you are dressed. You wear no robes of any order."

SJ noticed that all the other mages had now turned critical gazes at her where she stood, leaving her feeling defenceless and insecure.

"Kevin!" Fran's voice cut through the room, and his head flicked around to look at Mistress Francisca.

"Mistress. This nonmage has dared step into our world."

Fran raised her eyebrows. "Harrietta, where are you?" she bellowed, eyes scanning the room. "Come out now, or else I will visit Lythonian."

"Okay," a sulky voice replied as an apparition emerged from the side of the room. SJ jumped out of her skin at the sight.

"What the . . . !" she exclaimed.

"Now, remove the charm," Francisca said sternly.

"But—"

"Now."

"Yes, Mistress."

The apparition made a few hand gestures, and the mage, Kevin, frowned and shook his head. "What happened?" he said.

"Harrietta" was Fran's single word response.

"Not again," Kevin said, his face flushing with anger.

Harrietta shrank away into the nearby wall.

"You can't hide from me forever," he snapped.

"SJ, please come with me," Fran said.

SJ watched as Kevin searched around the room, opening cupboards and looking for Harrietta.

Once inside the office, with the door shut, SJ asked, "You have a ghost as a mage?"

"Yes. Harrietta was a mage before she died."

"Why is she here?"

"Harrietta has been my follower since long before I came to Killic."

"She is your follower?" SJ asked, stunned at the revelation.

"Yes. I freed Harrietta from the necromancer who had her in enslavement at least a century ago now."

Mouth open in astonishment, SJ stood dumbfounded.

"It's not that shocking. Many of those freed from servitude will become followers of their saviours. Harrietta likes to play pranks on the trainees. Kevin has been an unfortunate target of several of her jokes recently, and I think he is getting a little fed up with them now. I will have to speak to her about it. Anyway, what do you need? Or is it just a social call?"

SJ was trying to gather her thoughts. Fran looked to be in her twenties or thirties, yet she had just stated she had freed Harrietta over a century ago.

"I have to ask, and apologise if it's rude, but how old are you?"

"Three hundred twenty-four."

"You look no older than thirty."

Fran smiled at her comment. "Fae looks are deceiving. You will, in time, be able to judge ages more accurately. I am sure that is not why you came, though."

"No. I need to speak to you about a delicate issue." Fran's expression didn't change, but SJ sensed she was intrigued. "I recently went into the valley to collect mushrooms for Grewlas, and on my way there, I was attacked."

"I am glad you are okay."

"Yes. I am fine, but what attacked me and what I found are causing me some concern."

"Do tell."

"A Level 9 dark elf attacked me, and he was carrying a note," SJ said, calling it from her inventory and handing it to Fran.

SJ had seen Fran's eyes narrow when she mentioned a dark elf, and after reading the note, she could see the muscles in her jaw tense.

"Fran. Is everything okay?"

Fran stared at the note before scrunching it up into a tight ball in her fist. "Sorry," she said, looking up and smiling again.

"What is it?"

"It looks as though my past may be catching up with me. Sooner than I thought it might. I hoped for several decades here before moving on."

"I'm lost. Why would you have to move on?"

"It's a long story."

"I have time to listen. They say a problem shared is a problem halved, and if someone is after one of our kind, I will do what I can to help."

Fran shuffled in her chair and then sat back, leaning casually, closing her eyes. With a deep sigh, she began.

"Almost seventy years ago, I was involved in an incident between the fae council and the dark elf hierarchy. At the time, I was a junior council member working under the guidance of one of our kind's greatest leaders. Juniper was the light of the fae; she had been involved in the continuing negotiations with the dark elves for almost three centuries. Angst persists from the past war between our races. Most cooperate, but a few bear grudges.

"Juniper had been involved in settling a dispute over territory claims that date back to before the war. The territory in question is a region at Level 40–50 in the continent's west. It has some of the most beautiful forests and open plains imaginable. However, that wasn't the reason for the dispute—it was the stone ring that existed there."

"Stone ring?" SJ asked, intrigued by the start of the tale.

"The stone ring is a circle of magical power. The fae historical records date back to the time when Amathera first came to exist. It is said to hold the power of the fae in it. The dark elves believe in a similar prophecy about their race. Juniper had been involved in completing the research into the magic's origination and was close to absolute proof it was indeed of fae origin."

"Couldn't you just tell from the magic it gave off?"

"No. Fae and elven magic are very similar. The building blocks for all magic are elemental, and considering the cultural variance and positions of the stones, they lie in an area that records show was originally an elven area. It was only over time, as the elves moved farther east, expanding into the central planes and rain forests, that the fae took over the territory completely."

"So, was it originally elven?"

"No, that is the thing; the evidence that Juniper had collected and gathered proved that it was, in fact, a fae construction. She was trying to determine if the fae had originally constructed it under the duress of elven rule or whether a separate clan had created it. I visited there frequently, and the power of the circle is something to behold. I have felt nothing like it, and when in its proximity, everything has clarity. Your thoughts align, and your abilities naturally receive a boost."

"If she had evidence that it was fae, why did she not present her findings?"

"She was murdered before she finished her studies and could present them."

"Murdered. By whom?"

"A dark elf assassin named Crylik."

"How do you know?"

"Because I killed him," Fran said, stony-faced.

"Oh!"

"I had been on my way to see Juniper when she was murdered. I found the assassin still in her chambers and attacked him while he still bent over her dead body, holding a bloody dagger."

Fran's story of killing an assassin in cold blood gave SJ a completely different level of respect for the fae mage.

"What happened? Why did you leave?"

"The council didn't want to admit that the security had been so relaxed that an assassin had entered the High Council chambers. They played it down, saying it was a natural death. I wouldn't let it go, though, and it was afterwards, when I challenged the High Council during a seating with the dark elves, that I was, in simple terms, banished."

"Why would they banish you for stating the truth?"

"Peace between our races has always been on a wobbly scale. We keep it balanced most of the time, but it could tip at any moment. The High Council was happy to concede defeat over the stone circle and the death of one of their own in exchange for the return of several artefacts of power stolen during the war."

"They gave up on the circle and ignored Juniper's death?"

"Yes. They allowed the dark elves to reclaim the territory as their own."

"Why would they do that?" SJ asked, shocked.

"There are some in the council who I believe are in cahoots with the dark elves, and I believe that is how they got into the High Council and killed Juniper."

"Can you not prove it?"

"I have no proof. Only theories. The dark elves have been actively seeking me out ever since the council banished me. I have escaped with my life on several occasions over the years."

"Could you not go back and seek support from those you believe were loyal?"

"Unfortunately not. I can no longer enter the fae capital. As a banished member of the council, never mind being a fae, I would write my death sentence if I did."

The story and history lesson that SJ had just been told had been enthralling and mesmerising. Knowing that there was so much political intrigue involved in the land was amazing.

"It sounds like you have suffered because of our kind."

"I have, but I don't blame all fae. Only those who sit in the seats of power at the High Council and not all of them either."

"Can you not challenge them from outside the capital?"

Fran burst out laughing. "Sorry. No. I am a banished previous junior member of the council. I possess no power or authority over anyone or anything. Throughout years of travel, I have deliberately avoided the major cities and larger towns. I set up here in Killic as it was so quiet. Being the only fae in a starter town of mixed races meant less chance of questions being asked."

"What does all this mean now, though?"

"It means I have to find out who at the inn is passing on information, and depending on who it is, I may have to deal with them."

"We can't just walk into the inn, though, asking questions."

"No. But I know someone who can dig around."

"Who?"

"Harrietta. Show yourself."

SJ jumped out of her skin for the second time as the apparition appeared beside Fran. Gathering herself and placing her feet back on the ground where she had pulled them up onto the chair in shock, she looked at the apparition closely. Her features, although translucent, appeared to be those of a dryad.

"Harrietta. Meet SJ. SJ, Harrietta."

"Hi," SJ said with uncertainty. She had never been a fan of ghost stories as a child, and seeing one who could talk standing only ten feet away was freaking her out.

"Hello," Harrietta said, smiling.

"Have you been there the whole time?" SJ asked.

"Yes."

SJ did not know that she had been in the room with them. There was no sign, and her sense hadn't flared at all.

"That is an impressive ability to stay invisible."

"It has its perks," Harrietta said.

"I take it you were a mage in your previous life?"

"I was, yes. There are a few spells that I know."

"A few?" Fran said. "You may not level anymore, but you know more spells than most mainstream mages do."

Harrietta chuckled, and hearing such an angelic laugh from an apparition was more unnerving than hearing her speak. SJ felt goose bumps on her skin.

"I have to admit, I have never been a fan of ghosts," SJ said.

Harrietta's face turned sad, and SJ stammered a response. "I didn't mean to be rude. As a child, I was told horrible ghost stories, and they always stuck with me."

"Hopefully, I can change your opinion," Harrietta said, her smile returning.

"Harrietta, you know what I will ask you to do. Don't you?" Fran said.

"You would like me to visit the Wandering Ogre and do some snooping around," she said.

"I would, but you need to be careful. Niweq is no slouch at security, and he may have spells in place, so be careful."

"You know Niweq?" SJ asked, surprised.

"I wouldn't say I know him that well. I know who he is and what he runs. When I heard about the inn, I was initially concerned he may have been a dark elf, so I visited to find out for myself. He wasn't, but he behaves similarly to many I have known in my lifetime."

"I didn't know the place when I visited."

"It is a popular inn, as I am sure you noticed. They sell cheap beer and have scantily clad dancers, drawing many of the males in the town, as well as a few females."

"I saw. Do you want me to do anything to help?" SJ asked.

"I will let Harrietta do her work first. She has a knack for finding information."

"I am not surprised," SJ said, half-heartedly smiling at the apparition. It didn't matter how often she looked at Harrietta; she couldn't get past the fact that she was a ghost. SJ had loved watching movies and TV shows with zombies, skeletons, werewolves, and all the classic horror monsters, but something about ghosts just set her on edge.

"I am going to head off, then," SJ said. "Let me know if you find anything out or need any help. Thank you for sharing your story as well. It's the first I have heard about fae history."

"The nature of some of our kind has tarnished our history, but it remains rich with many stories that I would love to share at some point."

"That would be amazing. Maybe we can catch up at the inn at some point."

"That sounds nice. I will let you know if we find anything out. Thank you for letting me know."

SJ stood up, walked out of the office, and glanced back at Harrietta, who had turned and was talking to Fran. Shuddering, she headed toward the training grounds. She needed to check in with Jurgen and Lorna.

"What is it with you and the apparition?" Dave asked once they were back outside.

"I am not a fan of ghosts," SJ said.

"Why? Unless an apparition is a mage, they can never harm you, as they can never carry or hold anything solid, unlike skeletons, zombies, and many other undead variants."

"I can't explain it. Since I was a child, my older cousin told me stories whenever I stayed over at my Uncle Dave's, and ever since, I have been terrified of ghosts. He used to get pleasure from trying to make me cry."

"That's not very nice," Dave replied sympathetically.

"He wasn't a nice person. I never forgave him, even as an adult."

"It's a shame we can't ask Harrietta to visit him and give him a taste of his own medicine."

SJ chuckled as she walked. "That would be sweet revenge," she said.

CHAPTER SEVEN

Kata Claws

On returning to town, SJ felt more relaxed, knowing that Harrietta would scout out the Wandering Ogre. Fran's tale had been incredible, and thinking about her class and the skills she could earn, SJ only hoped that she could investigate the issues in the future. That seemed like a long way off, and considering the fact that the conflict and disagreements between the fae and dark elves had lasted for centuries, she doubted it would be resolved soon.

"Hi, Jurgen," SJ called as she reached the training ground. Jurgen was an elf fighter who aspired to be up close and personal when he fought. She had seen him practising with a sword or spear several times, but his favourites were daggers or claws, and he now wore claws.

"Hi, SJ. Are you free to train today?"

"I wish to, yes."

"Excellent. Then, come and join me, and we can chat about where we can start."

SJ followed Jurgen over to a bench at the side of the training ground.

"So, what do you know about claws?"

"Only what I have figured out myself since I found them. I use them to slash or support my punches, mainly for piercing damage."

"Those are the two fundamental aspects of claws, but they can also be strong defensive weapons when used properly."

"I have parried a couple of blows using them previously."

"Excellent, that's good to hear. In today's lesson, we will focus on form. If you can't use your claws properly, then there is no point in wearing them."

"Where do we start?"

"As you mentioned, they are extensions of your hands. The only difference is that you must get used to your arms being longer when you're wearing them."

SJ looked at him, confused. "That's pretty obvious, isn't it?" she asked.

"You would be surprised at the number of people who have tried to fight with claws and moved their hands up to block, and instead of the attack hitting their blades, it hits their wrists or forearms. It takes time and practice to adjust your movements and, ultimately, your instinct to attack and defend yourself."

With that comment, Jurgen swept his clawed fist towards SJ's side. She recoiled and instantly dropped her hands down to defend herself, receiving a nasty cut to her finger.

"Argh!" she shouted. "What was that for?"

"That was to see how you reacted, and I have to say your natural defensive movement was fine, but why did you not equip your claws?"

"I didn't expect you to attempt to cut my hands off for a start," she huffed angrily, sucking her bleeding finger.

Jurgen laughed. "And you think someone is going to walk up to you nicely and say, *Please equip your claws so that you can defend yourself as I attack you?*"

Sitting and glaring at Jurgen, she tersely replied, "No. But I also didn't expect to get attacked while discussing training."

"When do you expect to get attacked?"

"During a fight."

"And do you decide every fight?"

"No. But you would normally have an idea."

"Not always. As your class indicates, I'm sure the last thing you want is someone expecting you to attack them."

"Who told you my class?" SJ said, shocked.

"It's obvious, and to be honest, Lorna told me what you did against the mage. Unfortunately, I didn't see it myself."

SJ's finger ceased bleeding, illustrating that Jurgen had no intention of causing her significant harm. His strike had stopped on contact, and he had not swept the claws through as expected.

"Whenever you are training, you must consider that it could be the real thing. Every time you walk onto the training ground, be prepared for someone to attack and kill you. The harder you fight while training, the better chance you have of surviving an actual fight. Never let your guard down."

"I understand," SJ said. As much as the statement made common sense, she still found it annoying how he tried to get his point across. Lorna had warned her he was a taskmaster.

"Okay. Let's see your claws, then," Jurgen said.

SJ called her claws to her hands. The gloves fit perfectly, and their blades glimmered in the sun.

"Wow. They are a nice set of claws. They can't have been cheap!" Jurgen exclaimed.

"I looted them from a rare badger corpse."

"Even luckier, especially for our levels. You will see their benefits once you are more proficient in their use."

"When do we start, then?"

"Now is as good a time as any," Jurgen replied, walking over to one of the training dummies. SJ joined him.

"Let me see your basic strikes," Jurgen requested, standing to the side of the dummy.

SJ began her usual routine, which she had been practising, driving punches into the straw bodies of the dummies with intermittent slashes. She believed that her routine was well-formed and precise.

"I can see we have a lot to go over," Jurgen said, sighing.

SJ stopped and turned to look at him. "Sorry?"

"Your form is all wrong. You can't just use your kata without using the claws as your key component."

"I didn't think I was."

"Here, let me show you."

SJ stepped to one side, and Jurgen stepped in front of the dummy. Standing as if engaged in a casual conversation with someone, he unexpectedly moved. Within four strikes, the training dummy lay in tatters on the ground.

SJ stood with her mouth open at the display. Watching his swift and precise movements was frightening. "Wow."

"Your form is wrong. Your claws are your principal weapon, supported by your kata and the flexibility and positioning it allows. You are using them as knuckle dusters rather than as the weapon they are designed to be."

"I have never been trained before and didn't think I did that poorly."

"I have seen worse, don't worry, and with a few tweaks in technique, we will soon have you stripping the dummies from their stakes," he said, walking over to a fresh one. As he did, a small goblin child came onto the ground and picked up the tattered remains of the one he had just obliterated before replacing it with a new one.

"Okay. We will do it slow this time. Watch my movements closely as I prepare my strikes."

Watching how Jurgen made slight adjustments to his positioning before striking with the claws allowed SJ to understand the difference in impact and damage caused by the claws. The subtle hip twist as he struck added extra power to the movement. He also completed a shoulder pivot and wrist flick. If he had been moving at his normal speed, SJ would not even have been able to notice them.

"Did you see the difference?"

"Yes. Very subtle, but I can see the benefits it will bring."

"Great. Let us get to training, then."

The next hour was sheer hell. Every time SJ didn't perform a move correctly, Jurgen, who had procured a stick from somewhere, struck her.

Growling and wincing with each strike, she could feel her anger rising, which was supported by her determination not to get hit.

"I am impressed with your resolve," Jurgen said as he called for a rest break. Walking to the nearest water barrel, SJ grabbed a mug and took a long drink.

"Many would have given in by now, yet you show a determination I have seen in few."

It was Jurgen's first compliment, and she smiled. "At least I have one good thing going from this torture."

"Torture? I see this as more discipline. You would not be given any respite during an actual fight, and your form weaknesses would allow for an enemy to attack you. You need to be perfectly balanced and accurate. As well as being able to hit with power, it is also about the movement to ensure that your blades don't get caught."

"I have experienced that once. I had to remove my glove to stop myself from being dragged."

"Ah. Yes. It can happen often to the uninitiated. I assume you had struck across something and weren't expecting resistance?"

"Sort of. I was attacking a crepar and cut into its abdomen when my claws stuck in its body."

"To prevent that from happening, you move your wrist. If you imagine gripping something really hard for a long time, your fist begins to shake slightly because of the strain. That slight vibration that occurs can prevent such an incident. It takes time to master, though, as it feels unnatural to move a fist at the same time as punching or slashing, but it can help prevent your claws from getting caught. It is not perfect by any means, as sometimes these things just happen, but the more you can do to prevent it, the better."

SJ had clenched her fist while he spoke, and it joggled, the movement making the claws vibrate almost unnoticeably.

"I assume it means that not all the claws are applying the same pressure simultaneously?"

"Very good. Yes, it means that one side of your claws is always looser than the other. As I say, though, it is difficult to master, but with training and as your proficiency increases, you can learn it."

The next couple of hours were more of the same, with SJ usually whacked several times per minute as she continued to adapt to the adjusted techniques. Eventually, they broke for lunch, and Lorna walked over to see her.

"How's it going?" she asked.

SJ pulled the sleeve of her dress up, where the bruises were fading.

Chuckling, Lorna replied, "I told you he was a hard trainer."

"I know, but my arms feel like a freshly beaten steak."

"You have my word. I wouldn't have suggested Jurgen if I wasn't sure you would benefit from his guidance."

"I know. You could have warned me about the stick, though."

"If I were you, I would take that as a compliment. He believes you have the resolve to get past it."

"I am not sure about resolving anything. I'm becoming angrier."

"Are you going to be training again tomorrow?"

"I hope to, but I wish to do both, and only doing one day in four with claws may not be enough to improve well."

"We can always split the training. You don't have to do three days to one, but we can do a one-on-one split if that would help."

"I won't get a rest day, then, though. I thought you said we had to rest every three days?"

"If you had split the training, as I mentioned before, you could have done claws on your down day as it is not as strenuous."

"It may not be as strenuous, but it's definitely as painful, if not more so," she replied, rubbing her arms.

"The decision is yours, but I think you can continue progressing with your kata that way. Yes, it will mean you progress slower, but combining your kata with your chief weapon will benefit you more overall."

"I suppose. I wanted to reach Kata Level 6 for my next skill."

"You are nearly there anyway. The claw training still uses form, and the form adjustments will also help your kata. However, it will also throw your targets off when sparring, as they will not realise the adjustments you have made."

"Won't that impact its effectiveness?"

"No. If anything, it will enhance it. I'm not a fist weapon specialist; I only use my fists and occasionally knuckle dusters. Your claw proficiency changes everything slightly."

"It's good to know the beating has a result to it, then," SJ frowned.

Lorna turned away, laughing, leaving SJ to pick at her rations and await the next hour of torture.

The rest of the day followed a similar pattern, although as the afternoon wore on, SJ noticed Jurgen was no longer striking her as often. She hoped this was a good sign.

"That's it for today," Jurgen announced after a final whack on her forearm.

Wincing and rubbing the new bruise, she turned to look at him.

"It's a good job I heal quickly," she huffed.

"Ha. You will be fine by the morning. The bruising will have gone, the perk of being a Legionnaire."

"Do you not heal bruises as quickly?"

"Only with the use of a salve. A bruise for us is a bruise, after all. It is only your kind who have the benefits of your prolific healing. That is why I am not concerned about how many times I hit you today." He grinned.

"You were enjoying yourself, weren't you?"

"A little, perhaps," he replied, smiling slyly.

"I am not sure I enjoy being your beating post."

"You will have noticed you received many less this afternoon as your technique improved. It is amazing how much a sharp pain can make you focus."

Grumbling, SJ thanked Jurgen and promised to train with him again in two days, but she would be with Lorna tomorrow.

Walking from the training ground, Dave added to her misery by breaking out into a song, to the tune of Dinah Washington's iconic song, "What a Diff'rence a Day Makes."

What a difference a bruise makes,
Twenty-four every hour.
What the stick can cause you,
Makes you focus and glower.

"Stop already. I bet you have been working on that all day," SJ groaned. "And don't quit your day job. Your singing is terrible."

"I would never quit my day job. Watching a Legionnaire getting beaten is good fun," Dave replied hysterically.

Throughout the day, Dave had been breaking out into fits of laughter, which had only helped with her determination to succeed. Having Dave laugh at her sporadically was annoying, but no more than being hit by Jurgen's stick.

"Sometimes, it would be nice if you could understand that getting hit by something is painful. I don't suppose you have ever experienced pain."

"I have. The other day, I accidentally stubbed my toe. I turned the air blue and hopped around for ages."

"What? You have toes?" SJ said, utterly baffled.

"No. I just thought it might make you feel better."

"Grrr," SJ growled. "I'm going to see Cristy and see how she's doing."

"That will be nice," Dave replied happily.

SJ got the feeling that Dave liked Cristy. He had said nothing directly, but his tone changed when he spoke. SJ had sponsored a year of Cristy's education and had been meaning to visit her at the orphanage.

Arriving at the orphanage, SJ walked to the front desk, where a kobold attendant had half her attention on the group of children playing in the room behind the counter.

"Hi. I came to see Cristy."

"Oh. I am sorry, but Cristy isn't here."

"What?" SJ said, confused.

"Wait here a moment," the kobold replied before she walked to a closed door and knocked. Moments later, Madeline, the elderly dwarf who ran the orphanage, walked out.

"Oh. SJ. I am so glad you have called in." She grimaced. "Cristy is missing."

"What?" SJ said, shock registering on her face. "When did she go missing?"

"This morning. I reported it to the guard and sent a message to the inn, but they told me you had already left."

"Do you know where she may have gone?"

"I think she is going after the hobs. All she has been going on about since she got here is revenge. Ever since she returned from the funerals, she has spent most of her time alone in her room. It was only this morning when we went to look for her when she didn't answer the breakfast call that we discovered this." Madeline handed SJ a piece of parchment.

There was a very rough map scrawled onto it, and although the words were spelt incorrectly, it showed the town, woods, lake, and an arrow pointing to the valley where the hobs were based.

"She is definitely going after the hobs!" SJ exclaimed.

"We think so. When I arrived this morning, we found she had taken a small backpack, and the cook said the pantry had been broken into. I thought nothing of it initially, as we have had orphans help themselves at night several times."

"Has anyone gone to look for her?" SJ's heart was racing. Who allowed her to leave unnoticed?

"The guards are aware, and a druid has sent a message to his scouts to keep watch, but the scouts have not reported anything back yet."

"Damn," SJ cursed. "I'm going to speak to Captain Broadaxe. The guard must be able to do more to help." Turning on her heels, she stormed out of the orphanage and headed towards the barracks.

CHAPTER EIGHT

Missing Gnoll

SJ stormed into the barracks, her anger roiling as it had built as she walked there. The poor human member of the guard struck by the flying door staggered backwards, holding his now-bloody nose.

"Ow," the guard cried.

All the heads from those who sat at the desks in the central area turned and peered over at the dramatic entrance SJ had just made.

"I am so sorry," SJ exclaimed, seeing the blood gushing from his crooked nose. Ripping part of her sleeve off, she handed it to the guard, who stared at her with confusion and hostility.

"Be more careful next time," he said, holding the piece of cloth to his nose.

SJ's sleeve began to repair itself as the guard's eyes opened in amazement.

"Cool dress," he said, nodding his head in appreciation before continuing his journey out the door, wincing as he squeezed his nose.

SJ turned, trying to compose herself, and walked purposefully up to the front desk. The usual old orc sat behind the counter and eyed her suspiciously.

"And what brings you here so quickly that you injured one of the town guards?"

Feeling flustered now rather than angry, she said in a much meeker voice than she had intended, "I am here to see Captain Broadaxe, please."

"I am sorry—he is not in," the orc replied.

"Is there anyone I can speak to who can help me?"

"It depends on the issue. If you tell me, I can inquire about who may be best suited."

"Cristy is missing from the orphanage, and I want to know what is being done about it."

"Ah, I see. Well, that's the usual procedure for any missing being. The druids are scouting, and the guards are looking for signs."

"Has no one gone after her?"

"Go after her? She is an orphaned gnoll. Do you expect the guard to give up their duties to run after a child?"

The response sent SJ's blood boiling for an instant. "THAT IS MY EXACT POINT. SHE IS AN ORPHANED CHILD," she bellowed.

"You need to calm down. There is no need to shout. The standard missing being protocols are being followed. She hasn't been gone for more than twelve hours. Many children will return home once they get hungry. It wouldn't be the first or last time."

"You know why she has gone missing, don't you?"

"We received the report from the orphanage that she has been missing since before breakfast," the orc replied, looking at the ledger before him.

"And what about this?" SJ said, slamming the crudely drawn map onto the counter under his nose.

The orc glanced over it. "Whoever did this needs to learn how to spell."

"Cristy drew it. It was found in her room; she is heading to the hobgoblins."

The old orc scratched his head, examining the map again. "I suppose this could be the lake and the forest," he said.

"Are you for real? Her dad was killed in the latest raid, and she said to me previously that she was going to hunt them down and kill them. She has now disappeared, taking a small backpack and stealing food from the orphanage pantry. Don't you think it is all a little coincidental? Do you think saying that she will probably return this evening is acceptable?" SJ hissed furiously.

At that moment, SJ noticed Mayor Maxwell walking down the stairs from his office.

"Mayor," she called, pushing through the barrier and walking up to him as the old orc protested.

"SJ! What's wrong?" he asked, frowning deeply.

"Cristy is missing, and these buffoons aren't doing anything to find her."

"Buffoons?" the mayor responded.

"*Idiots*—is that a better word?" she snapped.

"You mean little Cristy, Henrick Dawkins's daughter?"

"Yes. She disappeared this morning and hasn't been seen since. She left this in her room," SJ said, handing the map to the mayor.

He briefly glanced at it before looking up and over at the old orc sitting at the desk. "Do you know where Alice went?"

"She went to the baker's—some dispute over flour pricing. Why?" he replied.

"Can you ask one of the guards to find her and ask her to return to see me as soon as possible?"

"Certainly, Mayor."

"Come, SJ, let's go upstairs. You look like you need a drink," the mayor said, directing her to the stairs.

SJ was pacing back and forth across the mayor's office. He had offered her a drink, but she declined, requesting coffee instead. A large bugbear entered the room carrying a tray and placed it on the cupboard at the side of the room.

"Coffee?" he asked.

"Please." He poured her a large mug and brought it to her, then sat behind his large desk. He was such a bear of a man that he even made the desk look small. He leaned over a map, studying it.

"Thank you, Karlson," he said, not looking up.

SJ stopped pacing for the first time since she had reached his office. She took the mug and sipped the hot liquid.

"If Cristy has really headed towards the valley, she won't have reached it yet," the mayor said. "Looking at the distance, I expect it to take her at least a day. Reaching the river is one thing; getting down into the valley is another. The trail by the river is difficult to traverse."

"I can't believe that nothing has been done yet," SJ fumed.

"I wouldn't say nothing. I would say that the usual protocol was followed. Until you showed me the map with her plans, no one would have expected her to go down to the valley."

"How did the guards it was reported to not ask?"

"I will find out, don't worry, but in their defence—which I know isn't very helpful now—the number of reports they receive about missing children is quite high. Parents are known to overly worry, and nearly always, the kids end up back home as expected."

"I understand that, but she is an orphan who has spoken about revenge." SJ kicked at one of the chair legs in front of the mayor's desk. The mayor raised an eyebrow.

"Sorry," she said, "I am just so angry and upset."

"As soon as Alice is here, I will ask her to send Rex out looking. He can let her other familiars know. I am sure we can find her soon enough." Alice was the mayor's second and a dryad druid.

"I hope so," SJ said, sitting in one of the chairs.

"At least you are no longer wearing out the wood on the floor," the mayor said, smiling at her.

"I just want Cristy back home and safe."

"I know, and we will find her. Don't worry."

SJ sat silently, drinking her coffee. Once she had finished the first mug, she got up and poured herself another. It wasn't much later when Alice returned to the offices.

"Mayor. You wished to see me?" she asked, looking at SJ.

"Yes. Alice, thank you for coming. I hope you resolved the issue you were looking into?" he asked.

"Yes, it's sorted out. Hubert was up to his old tricks again. Gladys has pulled him in line, thankfully."

"Ha. He tries the price scam every few months. You would think he would have tried something new by now," the mayor chuckled.

"What did you need me for so urgently?" Alice inquired.

SJ had been sitting tensely, frustrated at the general conversation, and couldn't hold back. "Cristy is missing, and we need to find her," she said bluntly.

"Cristy?" Alice asked.

"Henrick's surviving daughter. She had been staying at the orphanage and disappeared this morning," the mayor said.

"And what is unusual about that?" Alice asked, frowning.

"It appears she has given herself a quest seeking revenge," the mayor replied.

"What!" Alice exclaimed.

"Here." Mayor Maxwell held out the sheet of parchment for Alice.

She studied the map for a few moments before looking up with a shocked expression. "You think she will have gone to the hobs' village?"

"SJ does, and I am strongly inclined to support the theory. Grief can be hard to overcome without direction and guidance," he replied.

"What do you wish me to do?" Alice asked.

"Could you have Rex and your others look for her towards the valley? They would normally ignore a gnoll travelling through the woods, but she is still so young and defenceless."

"I can. I will call Rex now. It may take some time for him to get the message to the rest."

"The sooner the better."

"May I?" Alice asked.

"Please," the mayor replied.

Alice walked over to the window in the mayor's office where SJ had seen the druid's messenger bird land previously. Taking what SJ thought was a whistle from her pocket, she blew on it. No sound came out that she could hear, at least.

"I don't know how long it will take him to return. I will go and wait in my office," Alice said as she walked from the room.

"There, we have done all we can for now. The familiars will be the best option to locate her," the mayor said.

"What about getting her to return, though?" SJ asked.

"Once we locate her, we can send some guards to bring her back."

"That could take hours, though."

"Yes, it may, but what other option do we have? There is no guarantee that she stayed on the main path in the woods."

"I can't just sit around here and wait," SJ said. "I am going to go and start heading towards the valley on the off chance she is still on the path."

"I can't stop you from doing what you think is best . . . Just be careful; there have been reports of increasing activity in the woods over the past few days."

"What activity?"

"Wolves. There is a suspicion that a dire wolf may have led a pack onto the plateau. There have been several sightings."

"That is even more reason to be out there looking," SJ said in shock.

"We still don't know if she has gone that way. I would wait until we get the reports back."

"I am not going to leave it on the off chance that she didn't go that way," SJ stated flatly, frustration building in her again. Standing, she walked to the tray and placed the mug down. "Thank you for your help, Mayor."

"Be careful," he replied with a genuine look of concern on his face.

As she walked out of the barracks, SJ swore under her breath.

"Why are they not sending guards?" she hissed.

"I can see both sides," Dave replied. "If there is a dire wolf in the area, they need to be careful whatever they do."

"And what about Cristy?"

"I know it's difficult to understand, but the mayor was right. We don't know if she has headed that way."

"I am not leaving it to chance," SJ said.

She marched straight back to the inn and ignored the usual patrons she shared pleasantries with, proceeding instead upstairs to her wardrobe. She selected the few items she wanted to take before returning through the common area. Fhyliss, a gnome whose mother, Kerys, owned the Hogling Arms, called to SJ as she walked out of the inn, but she did not respond. As she stalked through town, she drew several looks with the scowl on her face.

"Why am I walking!" she hissed, transforming into her miniature size and beginning to zip through the streets. Several townsfolk looked startled at her miniature form whistling by them. When she reached the edge of town, she flew straight out over the field where she had battled the hobs and into the forest. The path was well-worn, and staying a few feet above it, she was making good time. It had been late afternoon when she had gone to the barracks, and by the time Alice had returned and spoken to them both, the evening was drawing in.

SJ couldn't stop thinking how scared Cristy would be in the forest at night. She flew as fast as she could down the trail, hoping that the young gnoll had stayed on it. SJ had got lost as a small child in the Trafford Centre in Manchester and remembered how she had felt then even with people around her—never mind being alone.

Dave, who'd been quiet since she had set off, said, "Three o'clock."

SJ glanced sideways and noticed a pair of glowing eyes in the trees off the side of the trail. She raised herself farther from the ground, ignoring whatever it was, and continued her journey.

"What was it?"

"A wolf," Dave said.

"I haven't got time for them now."

"No, but if you find Cristy, you will have to consider it when you return. If a dire wolf is up here, they will have a pack with them."

"And I will kill anything that gets in my way or dares to try to harm Cristy."

"Valiant words, but until you know their levels, that may be easier said than done."

"Anything, I said. I don't care who or what they are." The intensity in SJ's voice startled even Dave.

"Understood," he replied sincerely.

The trail twisted and turned through the forest, and at her current speed, she was covering it much faster than her initial visit to the town. The difference between her flying speed and her average walking speed was phenomenal. She had seen no signs of anything unusual and ploughed through the forest as fast as she could. Knowing how long Cristy had been gone, she thought she could easily have travelled most of the way, if not to the river by now.

The light faded as she flew, but her improved vision allowed her to see still as she whipped down the trail. Nothing had come near her, and she thought nothing ground based could, even if they wished to, at the height and speed she moved. As she reached a break in the forest, recognising a gnarled old tree she had passed around the lake, she slowed down. She knew just up ahead, the forest ended and the river fell to the valley. As she neared, she could hear the running water cascading down the mountainside.

Shuddering as she reached the area where a raven had plucked her from the sky not so long ago, she landed for the first time since she had set off. Her breathing was perfectly normal, and although her wing muscles ached a little from the long flight, they did not hamper her. Growing to her humanoid size, she stood looking down the river's edge towards the valley bottom. Far below, she could see speckles of orange and yellow, which were likely fires or lanterns from the hobgoblin village.

After taking a moment to drink from her waterskin and eat some of her rations, she shrank again to her miniature form before taking off. Staying on the left side of the river, she began to track it down much more slowly, keeping an eye out for any signs. Not knowing if or even how far exactly Cristy could have gone, she was worried that she may have passed her, especially if the gnoll had moved off the trail to find shelter as it had started to get dark.

Her senses flared, and she stopped dead, spinning around in the air.

"There is something in the woods," she whispered.

"Can't see anything," Dave replied.

Moving up so that she was nearer the height of the branches of the trees that accompanied the river path, she edged towards them. She heard a voice as she neared.

"Boss will like this one. He has always had a thing for gnoll," a voice said.

"Little small, though," another replied.

"Placed on a sandwich with some fresh fish, I bet he would love it," the first voice replied to a round of laughter from several others.

"That has to be Cristy they are talking about," SJ whispered.

"Possibly. I haven't seen anything yet," Dave said.

Edging forward into the branches, SJ glimpsed a fire not too far ahead. She wove through the treetops until she came to the edge of a clearing. Sitting in the clearing was a group of eight hobgoblins, and by the side of the largest one was a small sack. As SJ watched, she noticed the sack move.

The hob next to it thumped it. "I said don't move," it said. An audible groan came from the contents of the bag.

None of the hobgoblins appeared to be dressed like magic users, and SJ took the chance to use identification.

Hobgoblin Lead Scout	
Level:	11
Hit Points:	60
Mana Points:	55
Armour Class:	12
Attacks:	Pierce, Slash
Special:	Hide

Hobgoblin Scout	
Level:	8
Hit Points:	45
Mana Points:	45
Armour Class:	9
Attacks:	Pierce, Slash
Special:	Nil

6 x Hobgoblin Fighters	
Level:	7
Hit Points:	50
Mana Points:	40
Armour Class:	8
Attacks:	Stab, Slash
Special:	Nil

There was no way she could take them on, eight versus one, and with the levels they had, it didn't matter how anger-filled she now was; it would be a hopeless fight. Frustration built inside her as she looked at what she assumed was the small, helpless form of Cristy inside the sack. Turning back away from the makeshift camp they had set up, she moved back away towards the river. Under the sound of the rushing water, she now spoke to Dave.

"I need to do something," SJ whispered.

"What? You can't possibly be thinking of fighting that many alone."

"I have to do something, though."

"Wait until they are asleep, or at least some of them are. I am assuming they will have a guard posted."

"I know I'm an assassin, but I can't do enough damage in one hit to kill them. Which means they could wake the others."

"If you slit a person's throat while they are sleeping, they are going to receive maximum damage plus critical as incapacitated."

"That's still asking a lot. As they bleed out, they could disturb the others."

"True. Although being awoken in the middle of the night with a friend bleeding out with a slit throat would scare them half to death."

"I will keep watching them and see what happens. If they do post a guard, I may be able to do something, or I may even get a chance to grab Cristy and run instead of facing them."

"A good plan, but there is no way you can do that in miniature form. You may escape, but those hob scouts would track Cristy easily, and there is one huge assumption that you are still making."

"What?"

"That it definitely is Cristy."

"It has to be. How many other small gnolls would you expect to find out here?"

"Oh, I agree that it is more than likely her, but it's still an assumption."

SJ didn't respond as she tried to think of a way to free the gnoll, whether or not it was Cristy.

"SJ."

"Yes?"

"I have an idea. A completely insane and stupid idea, but an idea."

"Go on."

"You know that wolf we passed back in the forest?"

SJ thought she knew where this was going and wasn't happy with the direction.

"Yes."

"What if you drew them here?"

"How did I know you were going to say that?"

"If there is a dire wolf, then there will be a pack, and a pack of wolves, even if lower level than the hobs, would cause mayhem."

"But how would I draw them here without being the prime bait myself?"

"I haven't quite thought about that part yet."

"I'm just going to go back and watch them for now and see what they do."

Taking off from the branch she had landed on, she returned to the campfire and stopped on a high branch of a tree overlooking the clearing. Even with night vision, there was no way they would see her six-inch-high form hidden in the canopy. The hobs had been cooking, and as she watched, they packed up. To her surprise, they kicked dirt over the fire, extinguishing it, and packed up the few belongings they had, and the highest-level scout picked up the sack and, without care, threw it over his shoulder.

"Come on, let's go. We will be back before the first light. The next patrol will already be on its way."

The hobs followed the group leader as he moved through the tree-line, paralleling the river. SJ tracked them, keeping her distance from high in the canopy. The fading light gave her night vision an ethereal glow as it dimmed. They followed what must have been an animal track through the forest and eventually descended towards the valley floor. The slope was steep, and the trees looked as though they clung to the soil with only a few roots, giving the impression that they could topple over at any moment.

Following the hobs still at a distance, she came to the edge of the forest. A sharply declining path wove down the remaining side where scree had taken over from the trees. It even looked as though rough steps had been cut into parts of the path leading to the valley. SJ moved out and high above the hobs, following their continuing descent with the leader at the front of the group of eight. There was nothing she could do.

"Stop wriggling," the lead scout growled as it deliberately jostled the sack on its back.

SJ was feeling panic rise in her chest. She could not attack them, but she had to do something to stop them. Looking back up the steep slope, she saw an opportunity and flew towards it. An enormous boulder was perched precariously off the hob's path, but if she could get it to fall . . .

She landed behind it, at least a hundred feet above where the hobs were, before she grew to her full size and pushed her weight against the boulder. Gravity would do the rest if only she could get it to move. Hoping this wasn't as stupid an idea as she thought it might be, she strained against the boulder. The scree it sat on shifted slightly, and she pushed again with all her strength. Again, it moved ever so slightly, scraping. The hobs were now nearly directly below it. Leaning against it, bracing her feet against the valley side, she pushed again, grunting from the effort, and then it gave.

The boulder crept at first, sliding on the scree side, and then it rolled as its mass pulled it downwards. As it picked up speed, it crashed into the loose scree, that also fell, sliding like a stone avalanche under the persuasion of the boulder. The sound was horrendous, and SJ shrank to her miniature form and took off as it careered towards the party of hobs. Screams of panic erupted from them as they sprinted back or forward to get out of the way of the stone avalanche.

The boulder reached them first, crashing into one of the hobs, while it tried to scramble back to its feet from where it had slid off the trail. Its body was catapulted out from the valley's side, and it fell screaming down the rocky face and landed with a sickening crunch, then slid. In the meantime, the smaller rocks and scree had arrived, pelting the remaining hobs with hundreds of stone missiles. None of them were the size of the boulder, but the amount the single movement had set free was a sight to behold.

The rockslide took out three and carried them farther down the valley's side. A thick cloud of dust had been kicked up with the passing of the stones, and SJ flew towards the leader, who still carried the sack. He had kept moving forward with one fighter, while the remaining two now stood on the other side of a thirty-foot-wide deadly scree field. The path had been obliterated by the falling rocks.

They were calling to each other and down at their colleagues, only two of whom SJ heard weakly calling back.

"Go get them," the lead hob shouted.

SJ watched as the one with the leader and the other two cautiously worked their way onto the loose stone and approached their fallen comrades. One of them slipped, sending a fresh cascade of rocks into the midst of those below and causing further shouts and screams.

This was going to be the best chance SJ would have. Flying over to where the lead scout stood shouting orders, she silently landed and grew.

CHAPTER NINE

Oooo Shiny

The lead scout had dropped the sack unceremoniously onto the ground, where it wriggled. SJ reached full size as the scout screamed at his comrades below.

Knowing this would not be an easy kill and having to ensure she got the most from the surprise attack, SJ steadied herself, glancing over its armour-clad body to see where the gaps were. It was a split-second decision, but along with its open neck and head, its shoulders and arms were unprotected. It was waving and pointing down the slopes where the other hobs were.

At that moment, she struck using the skills from her single-day training from Jurgen, still fresh in her mind. She tensed her fists and, with two fast, clean punches, struck it in its neck and then upwards into its armpit. It shrieked in pain as its neck was pierced, but with the continuing chaos below and the rocks still rolling by in a lesser number, she didn't care. Her upward strike under its armpit also struck true, and she saw the tips of her blade pierce through its shoulder.

Surprise Attack—your surprise attack has triggered a critical strike.

SJ watched in astonishment, as the hob's health plummeted. It had sixty hit points to start with and, after both hits, now sat on eighteen. The criticality and surprise leant significant boosts over her basic damage capability. The hob spun towards her, its left arm not functioning properly as it hung limply at its side, the claws having severed something critical. She was no doctor, so she couldn't name what it may have been.

Shock registered on its face.

"You," it hissed as a short sword appeared in its right hand, swinging towards her in a slashing motion. The slope was uneven, and she stepped back as the sword swung towards her, the hob's incapacitated arm flopping about. The speed with which the scout had reacted had taken her by surprise, and its blade cut into her abdomen as she stepped backwards trying to maintain her balance.

Grimacing from the cut she felt across her stomach, she stepped in as its arm continued its unbalanced slash at her. Stabbing out with her left, she jabbed into its right arm. The hob, without the use of its left arm, was very unsure on the scree, and it staggered and ended up moving out of the way of her punch. She followed with a front kick to the hob, bringing its sword arm back across as she did. The abdominal hit had removed twelve hit points, and her foot connected with the hob's stomach as the blade of its short sword connected with her outstretched leg. The hob staggered backwards farther, beginning to fall onto the scree, losing its sword as SJ also lost her balance, falling sideways, and began to slide.

The hob's eyes went wide as it flailed its good arm, trying to stay upright as SJ fell sideways, crashing hard onto the stones. She received another eleven damage, meaning the hob had almost reduced her to half hit points in two hits, neither of which had been clean strikes. She slid towards the hob, and as she did, she pivoted and brought her claws around to face it. The hob had slid backwards, now trying to right itself, scrambling at the rocks to gain purchase. She wasn't bothering, allowing the momentum of the slide to bring her in range again.

Although she couldn't strike at it properly, she could hit its arm by leaning into the slope and swinging her claws around in a vicious stroke. With its left arm flopping uselessly at its side and having dropped its sword as it had fallen, the hob couldn't defend itself, and she raked her claws across its right arm. It screamed in pain again, and this time, it didn't stay crouched.

As it came crashing down onto her upper body, she only just turned one of her hands upwards in time. Her claws penetrated its good arm. It was now half covering her as they both picked up speed over the rocky terrain. The hob screamed in anger and pain, both its arms virtually disabled. The abrasion damage and the weight of the hob on top of her pushed SJ against the harsh surface, taking her health down.

SJ could only think of one thing, and rather than try to fight, she shrank.

"What are you doing?" Dave screamed.

She had noticed where her feet were compared to the hob, and as she shrank, she pried her blades free and was drawn away from under it. The hob was only on the top half of her body and wasn't able to grab her; she broke free from its weight. It stank awful, and its odour permeated her nostrils. The sliding scree looked huge in her miniature form, and the small pebbles were more like catapult ammunition. As soon as her body was free, she pushed herself up and jumped, beating her wings as fast as possible.

SJ lifted from the rock surface in her miniature form, flying up and away from the continuing bombardment of stone and dust. The hob stared at her with pure anger as she rose, as it continued to slide. In an instant, she had taken off and escaped danger. The hob collided with a lone tree that clung onto the valley wall, letting out a wail as it bounced off the trunk. SJ watched its health being reduced as it disappeared to the other side of the tree and went out of sight.

She flew after it before realising the valley side became sheer, and as she gained sight, the hob disappeared over the cliff edge screaming before landing on its back on a rock ledge thirty feet below. It only had five hit points left now, and SJ would not let it survive. She flew straight down towards it, where it lay with its broken body struggling to move. SJ reached full size as her knee crashed into its stomach, slamming her claws into its chest. Its eyes opened in shock, agony, and disbelief as it lost its life.

She panted heavily, as if she'd run a marathon, covered in grime and bleeding from injuries. The remaining hobs were still a fair distance away, and with the injuries several had sustained, they could not get near to where she now was quickly or easily. Curses were hurled at her as her display triggered.

Congratulations! Hobgoblin Scout Level 11 killed. 120xp awarded.

She looted the corpse, shrank, and took off.

3 x dry rations, 1 x small waterskin, 78 x copper

Straight back up where their initial brawl had started, she found the sack still lying where it had been covered in a layer of dust from the rocks. In her humanoid form, she bent down, grabbed the top of the bag, and using her claws, cut the top from it. The relief she felt on seeing the wide, terrified eyes of Cristy was immeasurable.

"Are you okay to move? We need to get out of here," she said.

"SJ?" the little gnoll replied in shock.

"Yes. Can you move?"

"Yes," Cristy replied as she wiggled out of the remainder of the sack, trying to look around and get her bearings.

Two of the hobs were trying to edge their way back across the slope towards them, struggling on the loose surface.

"I will find us a route. We need to reach safer ground," SJ said, shrinking again. Switching between forms at will was unbelievably advantageous. She took off and looked back up the slope from where they had come. The route looked terrible, but the ground looked sturdier and less loose than below. Also, with Cristy's much lither and nimble form, she would hopefully not struggle on the loose rocks to the same degree.

"Follow my instructions," SJ called from where she flew a few feet above the slope.

Cristy looked at her with wide-eyed terror, then glanced back at the hobs, who were still trying to fight their way up the slope to where she stood.

"Now, Cristy. Move."

Cristy moved. Following SJ's instructions, she picked her way up the rocky slope. A tree-line began approximately fifty feet above where they were, and the ground levelled slightly and the rocks gave way. SJ flew towards it, looking back. Even though Cristy was small, she still threw up the odd stone that toppled towards the hobgoblins, who were gaining ground on her position.

"Quicker," SJ called.

"I'm trying," Cristy cried, her small face fear-stricken. She had never expected what had happened to her, and she was terrified from being captured. The hobgoblins eventually made it back to the area where the lead scout had dropped Cristy. They were still a hundred feet behind her now.

"Twenty feet," SJ called.

Cristy continued to scramble until she eventually made the trees. The ground became firmer, allowing her to grip and proceed much faster. The tree coverage was still sparse compared to the forests at the top of the ridge and didn't offer many areas to find cover or hide from the hobs that were angrily calling after them.

SJ looked up ahead from her height, and in the moonlight that now filled the sky and with her night vision, she saw what appeared to be a cave entrance. Calling down to Cristy, she directed her towards it. SJ flew ahead, and as she neared it, it only looked large enough to fit a small child into the entrance or, in her case, a miniature fae. Cristy was approaching behind her as she landed by the small cave-mouth.

"In here," SJ called to Cristy as she moved inside.

When she moved out of the natural light, her assisted vision went, and she was soon in total darkness. Cursing, she stopped and called a torch from her inventory and her flint and steel before fumbling in the dark to light it. She heard Cristy panting behind her.

"SJ," Cristy called.

"I'm in here. Come in. The hobs can't fit."

"It's dark," Cristy called back nervously.

SJ continued to strike the flint, creating sparks and lighting the tunnel for the briefest of moments.

"What scares you more, the hobs or the dark?" SJ shouted back from where she struggled to light the torch.

"Hobs."

SJ could hear the nervous tension in Cristy's breathless voice as she moved into the tunnel. The torch eventually lit, but its match-sized glow did little to improve her vision in the tunnel. "I don't know how long this tunnel is, but we need to keep going," SJ said.

Turning, SJ could see Cristy just a few feet behind her, and she walked forward again. The tunnel shrank slightly, and SJ worried it might get too small even for Cristy. She pushed on, though, and after a further ten feet, it widened again, and the height increased to the point where SJ could no longer make out the tunnel ceiling in the light cast by the torch.

"Can you reach the tunnel ceiling?" SJ asked.

"No," replied Cristy, who was now standing up in the tunnel. She was only about two feet tall, and SJ was unsure how high the ceiling was. Taking a chance, she crouched down and grew. As her size increased, so did the torch's brightness, and her eyes were met with the wonders inside the cavern they had entered. It wasn't huge, but SJ could see bright silvery-blue veins running through the rock's surface. The veins drew a cobweb of patterns, and SJ gawped in amazement at their beauty being reflected.

"I wonder what this is?" SJ asked, more to herself. Little Cristy now stood by her side.

"It's a mithril vein," Dave replied with amazement in his voice, "and I do not know what it is doing here. Mithril is a high-level material and should be nowhere near this area. I doubt there are even any miners who would have the skills to mine it. Dwarven miners would go crazy if they knew this was here."

"I don't know," Cristy replied, standing open-mouthed and admiring the ore's beautiful reflections.

"Sorry, Cristy. I didn't expect you to. I was talking aloud to myself. It's mesmerising."

"It is very pretty," Cristy replied.

Standing in the chamber, SJ could hear the voices of two of the hobs. They must have made it to the cave and seen them enter.

"I can't fit in there," she heard one of them say angrily.

"Try. You're smaller than me."

"You must be joking."

"You think the ogre will joke if we go back empty-handed?"

"What do you mean *empty-handed*? We weren't even meant to bring anything back. It was pure luck that the gnoll walked into us, and the rockslide wasn't our fault."

"Did you see her, though? It was the one who attacked the mage and has now killed Svert. The boss is going to be fuming."

"Still not our fault."

"His temper won't see it that way."

"We need to get Creti and Kouli from the rocks. They are still trapped."

"I suppose."

Their voices trailed off as they moved farther from the mouth of the cave.

"I think we should stay here for the night and head back in the morning," SJ said. She had brought a blanket, which she grabbed from her inventory and handed to Cristy. "Here, take this."

"Thank you," Cristy said. "I'm sorry for getting you into trouble."

SJ didn't have the heart to be angry at Cristy for running off. She would speak to her about how stupid she had been at some point, but not now. They still weren't safe yet. SJ took another torch from her inventory and lit it, placing it into the ground of the cavern so it bathed the area in light. "Wait here. I will see how far this cavern goes back." SJ walked through the cavern, remembering the crepar from the last cave she visited. She equipped her claws. After checking the entire area for other entrances, she discovered none, meaning the only way in or out was the way they had come.

"There is no other way out. In the morning, we will head back out and up onto the ridge back to town," SJ said as she returned to Cristy, who was sitting on the cavern floor with her legs hunched up and the blanket over her. Taking her water-skin from her inventory, SJ handed it to Cristy, who eagerly took a long pull before handing it back. SJ did the same and then put it away again. The cavern floor was quite smooth and had more of a sandy texture than rocky, and she settled herself down, lying on her back with her hands behind her head.

"Try to get some sleep," SJ said.

Cristy didn't respond but settled down. SJ was just drifting off when she felt Cristy move next to her. She instinctively put her arm out, and she rested her head on SJ's shoulder cuddling into her side. SJ pulled the blanket around her small form to cover them both, before laying as still as she could, listening to Cristy's breathing. As it slowed, she began to snore gently. Smiling, SJ stroked the small gnoll on her head and closed her eyes again. It wasn't long before sleep took her.

CHAPTER TEN

Homeward Bound!

SJ removed her arm from around Cristy, not wishing to awaken her yet. Cristy made a soft grumbling sound before curling up in a tight ball. Leaning over, SJ placed the blanket over her tiny form. SJ stood and stretched, then grabbed and ignited another torch from her inventory, replacing last night's, which had almost burnt out. She moved quietly back towards the cave entrance.

Shrinking down to her miniature form, she walked back along the tunnel until she saw the bright light of the morning sun at the cave's mouth. According to her display, it was only seven. As expected, she had fully healed overnight, and her dress was pristine again. She could feel a mild ache in her wing muscles, which must have been because of the speed she had flown when searching for Cristy.

"Morning, Dave," she whispered as she approached the entrance.

"Morning," he replied cheerily.

"I need to get Cristy back to town."

Reaching the entrance, she dropped the torch, stood on it to extinguish it fully, and peered out of the cave-mouth. She could hear nothing apart from the calls of early morning birds. In the warmth of the sun, SJ closed her eyes and rotated her shoulders a few times, helping to ease the stiffness in her back.

"I wish I had brought my Dryac with me," SJ said.

"Next time, remember it, then," Dave replied, chuckling.

"You think!"

She crept from the mouth of the cave, not wishing to fly just yet; she grew to her full size. Picking her way down the valley's side, she reached the break where the trees gave way as the steepness increased and the ground became scree. The sight in the daylight put a whole new perspective on what the boulder she had released had caused.

A clear path was running down the slope where the triggered rockslide had torn its way down the side. She could see below where the steps had been cut in and that the path the hobgoblins had been using had been obliterated. There were no visible signs of anyone around, and peering into the distant valley, she could see smoke rising down at the village. It must have still been a couple of kilometres, if not farther, from where she now stood.

"I can't believe they live so close to the town," SJ said.

"It is unusual, as I have said before, but with the sandbox's potential, it all makes sense. I am trying to discover if the town has implemented the same level starter cap, but my department friend has not replied since my last enquiry. I am unsure, but I may have got him into trouble."

"I told you to be careful."

"I was. The System can get a little grumpy."

"You know, I'm still confused about who the System is and where it originates."

"Oof. No one knows. That has been a question since the first AI was born when Amathera was created."

"I wonder how it interacts with Earth, though."

"Again, no one has any idea. It is like the term you use on Earth when you ask what the meaning of life is. It is just as apparent here. Why was I created? What is my exact purpose? Is there anything else beyond this existence? The same questions with the same multiple answers, none of which anyone has ever managed to confirm or deny."

"It starts to get philosophical and deep when you consider it all. The fact that there is a second chance at life from an accidental death means to me that maybe the System has control over Earth as well."

"Would that then not make it the god that many people of Earth believe in?"

"Perhaps," SJ said, musing over the thought.

Several moments passed before SJ spoke again. "Okay. Let's get back to town and get Cristy safe."

"Agreed," Dave said.

Making her way back to the cave entrance, SJ shrank again and walked inside, not worrying about lighting another torch. She edged her way along until the torch's light from the chamber became visible. Walking in, she grew again. Cristy's tiny form was still asleep under the blanket. SJ bent down next to her, stroking her head.

"Cristy. Time to get up."

Cristy began to mumble, "Dad."

SJ's heart sank. She couldn't imagine what Cristy must have gone through and still was.

"Cristy. It's SJ. It's time to get up. We need to get back to town."

Cristy opened her eyes, sat up, and rubbed them with her small, balled-up fists. Blinking, she looked at SJ bent down next to her.

"Morning," SJ said, smiling.

"Morning," Cristy replied, yawning.

"We need to get back to town and get you safe."

"Okay."

SJ called some rations from her inventory and handed them to Cristy, who began eating ravenously. She did the same with the waterskin. Once she had eaten too, SJ put them away before packing the blanket away as well.

"Come on, let's go. I will check ahead as we move. Okay?"

"Sure," Cristy replied.

After collecting the torch, SJ led them back up the tunnel, shrinking to her miniature form. The bright sun made them squint as they stepped from the cave-mouth, the sun's warmth washing away Cristy's weariness.

"I'm not sure of the route from here, so I will need to check," SJ said as she took off. "Wait here for a minute."

It was the first time SJ had flown since yesterday, and she felt the difference. Her back muscles were achy, but she wouldn't let a little discomfort stop her. Moving higher and looking ahead, she found a path leading through the sparse trees, which looked easier to traverse until it reached the main forest line on the ridge. She returned to Cristy and began directing her where to go. It didn't take them too long before they had managed to make it back up to the top on even ground.

The forest in front of them was thick, the trees close together, and there was no sign of a path. "I think we just push through," SJ said, growing to her full size and forcing through the thick underbrush. Cristy followed close on her heels, and SJ felt her reach out and take hold of the back of her dress. She didn't want to be separated.

They continued through the brush for a while before eventually coming to an animal track, which SJ turned and followed. Although it wasn't easy, she could roughly tell how they needed to go. The track wound through the trees, weaving in and out of the thick trunks. There were sounds of life all around, and on more than one occasion, SJ stopped to check. Dave hadn't spoken, and she knew he would scan the area for them. It was strange how he had become her third eye after their initial meeting, but she knew deep down that she could trust Dave with her life.

The realisation that she was willing to place her life in the hands of another was something she had never experienced before. She had had close relationships, and at one time, she had been engaged, but never had she felt the same level of trust as she now did with an AI she had known for less time than any other relationship she had been in. She couldn't explain the reasoning behind it.

They had continued for nearly an hour when the trail came to a small pond area. There were tracks surrounding the pond in the soft earth, and it was seem-ingly frequented often. SJ cautiously stepped out, but she could see nothing there. Working around the pond, they found another trail that continued into the forest, which, if her bearings were right, turned towards the west. Not being sure, she said, "I wish I had a map to confirm which direction we need to go."

Dave's voice replied, "Don't worry. I will tell you if you are heading off track. This area is still covered in fog of war, but based on the larger map, you aren't too far from the trail you originally came down. Just keep following this one."

"We aren't lost, are we?" Cristy said nervously.

"No," SJ said, reassured by Dave's words. "We just need to keep going this way. It would just be easier with a map."

It took another twenty minutes to follow the new trail with no signs of danger, and SJ's senses had not triggered once before they broke out onto the main trail. The trail was worn, and SJ recognised it straight away, as it curved back to the northeast around the side of the lake towards the town.

"Now we are on the path. It shouldn't take long," SJ said, smiling down at Cristy, who had moved to her side and held her hand. At that instant, her senses were triggered.

Dragging Cristy, she moved to the side of the trail and into some bushes at the base of a tree. "Shh," she said.

Cristy looked at her with terrified eyes.

SJ placed her finger to her lips and indicated that Cristy should stay where she was hidden in the thick bush, then she shrank to her miniature form. Sneaking out to the edge, she took off, flying straight up into the branches directly above before coming to a rest. From this vantage point, she could see up and down the track.

"See anything?" she whispered.

"Nothing. I guess you sensed something?" Dave asked.

"Yeah," SJ said, still scanning the trail. Sitting silently, it was several moments before Dave spoke.

"Movement to the right. The far edge of the trail. There is something just off the trail in the tree-line."

"Damn," SJ cursed.

SJ intently watched the area Dave had indicated and soon saw a very slight movement in the bushes.

"I need Cristy off the ground," SJ whispered, taking off and dropping back down.

Cristy had been staring up at her virtually the whole time, and on reaching her, SJ whispered, "Can you climb the tree?"

Cristy looked at the tree they were next to and held out her paws with a nervous grin, which had rather sharp-looking claws on their ends.

"Good. Then climb up to the branch I was sitting on."

Cristy didn't respond but began to reach and dig her claws into the tree's bark and climb. Thankfully, she hardly made a sound, and after a minute, she was fifteen feet off the ground and crouched on the branch. SJ returned and landed next to her again, looking back onto the trail. That was when she heard talking.

"If the path hadn't been destroyed, we would have been there by now," the voice grumbled.

"Stop complaining. You know we are due back in a couple of days. We need to keep reporting," another replied.

SJ saw the group coming from the southern part of the trail. Something had triggered her senses on the northern side, and now, on the south, she counted five hobgoblins. Looking at them, she triggered her identification skill.

Hobgoblin Scout	
Level:	10
Hit Points:	55
Mana Points:	50
Armour Class:	7
Attacks:	Pierce, Slash
Special:	Hide

4 x Hobgoblin Archers	
Level:	6
Hit Points:	35
Mana Points:	35
Armour Class:	4
Attacks:	Pierce, Slash
Special:	Nil

The party was weaker than the last group of hobs, and they were all lightly armoured. They were only equipped with bracers and greaves, and there was no chest protection she could see. Two of the four archers carried short bows, and two carried crossbows. The scout had what SJ thought was a long bow across its back. They all also carried either short swords or daggers on their belts.

The party continued up the trail, nearly parallel to where SJ and Cristy were hidden on the branch, when the bushes exploded from the other side of the trail. The size of the beast that leapt out was significant. This was a monster compared to the grey wolf SJ had fought when she first arrived. Its fur was blue-black with a white mark between its shoulder blades. It stood almost four feet at its shoulder, and its maw was huge, yellowed fangs dripping with saliva as it landed on its first target.

The poor hob it had chosen screamed as the giant wolf's jaws clamped down around its throat, violently ripping and then turning on another. The hobs, screaming and drawing their weapons, tried to defend themselves. That was when four more wolves appeared from where the monstrous one had come. SJ again triggered her skill. Three of the wolves looked very similar to the one she had fought. The fourth was jet-black, and its fur seemed to gleam in the sunlight bathing the trail.

Dire Wolf	
Level:	14
Hit Points:	105
Mana Points:	25
Armour Class:	21

Attacks:	Bite, Claw
Special:	Howl

3 x Grey Wolves	
Level:	6
Hit Points:	55
Mana Points:	0
Armour Class:	9
Attacks:	Bite, Claw
Special:	Nil

Black Wolf	
Level:	8
Hit Points:	70
Mana Points:	0
Armour Class:	11
Attacks:	Bite, Claw
Special:	Nil

As the fight developed, the hobs dropped into a circle, their backs to each other, looking out at the beasts that were now prowling around them. The dire wolf stood back from the other four and let out a howl. It was one of the most terrifying sounds SJ had ever heard, and the forest went silent in response. Even the hobs and wolves seemed to flinch.

The wolves began attacking the hobs, moving in and back away again, trying to find an opening to strike cleanly. SJ was impressed by the hobs' organisation as they held their ground steadfastly. The wolves were biding their time. Due to the risk of leaving themselves vulnerable to attack, the hobs refrained from launching an attack of their own.

The circling, snapping, and slashing continued until one wolf made its first mistake. It had dived in towards a hob to snap at its arm and, on doing so, left itself open to be attacked on its flank. The hob next to its target swung with a short sword, catching it cleanly on its side. The wolf yelped as a large cut was opened, and shrank away. The dire wolf had seen enough and pounced. With no consideration of the other hobs, it wouldn't let its pack member be injured, and ploughed straight into the four of them as though they were bowling pins. The screams and chaos that ensued were absolute mayhem.

Once the dire wolf had scattered the other hobs, it made them targetable by the rest of the pack, and they reacted, snapping and biting at the hobs who tried to fight them off. The wolves had the advantage of five against four since the dire wolf's initial target would never see another day, its corpse lying where it had initially been attacked.

SJ watched as the wolves systematically used their advantage to attack the hobs and placed bites on them, wearing them down. The dire wolf soon made a meal of the one he had ploughed into. The struggle continued; two of the wolves were seriously injured, one lying on its side with a vicious abdominal wound and another staggered, its front paw bleeding heavily. However, the second-to-last hobgoblin fell to the black wolf, and only the scout hobgoblin remained.

Its chest had scratch marks on it, and SJ had seen it defend at least two attacks with its bracers, but there were no visible bite marks on them. The two remaining wolves and the dire wolf now stalked towards it. It cursed and hissed, swinging its blade in front of itself wildly as it tried to get in a position to attack. It didn't take long; the scout was lucky enough to disable another wolf but had opened its flank for the dire wolf, who seized the opportunity and dived in, grabbing its outstretched arm carrying its sword, and clamped down, then shook its head from side to side like a dog with a toy.

The hobgoblin was jostled and thrown off balance, tripping. As it did, the other wolf dived in as well. SJ watched in horrified amazement.

"That was brutal," Dave said.

SJ didn't respond, still watching the display, when she realised that Cristy had moved.

"Where's Cristy?" SJ whispered as she saw her nearly at the base of the tree. She hadn't paid her any attention, being too focused on the fight below.

As the dire wolf stepped back from the hob scout, it sat back on its haunches and howled. The forest again fell silent in its aftermath. SJ had hissed down at Cristy for her to stop, but the gnoll hadn't slowed, and she reached the ground and walked onto the path before SJ could even take off and get down there.

"No," SJ shouted, no longer trying to hide where she was. The wolves turned at her cry, and the dire wolf tilted its head and looked in her direction. It growled, and a deep, unearthly sound left its throat. There was nothing SJ could do; she could not take on that dire wolf, especially with the other able-bodied wolves nearby. Cristy, showing no signs of fear, walked out onto the trail.

One of the wolves snarled, baring its teeth, and stalked towards her. They were probably thirty feet from her and could be on her instantly at the speed at which they moved. SJ, panicking, took off and flew down to where she was.

"Cristy, run, climb a tree now!" she screamed only inches from her ear.

Cristy paid her no heed and stood there looking at the dire wolf, not taking her eyes off it. The snarling wolf came closer, snapped its jaws, and growled. The second wolf stopped, turned its head, and looked back. SJ was waiting for the pounce and could see the tension building in the dire wolf's haunches, where it was still sitting after howling. It bolted. SJ screamed as the beastly creature hurtled towards where Cristy stood. SJ flew up and turned away, not wanting to watch Cristy get eaten.

CHAPTER ELEVEN

Friends of the Forest

When SJ heard nothing, no scream, no cry, no growl, she turned back and looked down. The scene made her eyes pop as if they were going to fly from her face. The dire wolf stood directly before Cristy, where it had landed from its pounce. It hadn't attacked, and SJ heard Cristy giggle as she reached her hand to the underside of the giant wolf's head. The wolf allowed Cristy to stroke the side of its enormous head with her tiny, outstretched paw.

Amazed, shocked, and awestruck, SJ had no words as the dire wolf lay down on the ground in front of Cristy. She walked to the side of it, continuing to stroke it.

SJ lowered herself from where she hovered until she was nearly at the level of the wolves. One of the others growled towards her, saliva dripping from its mouth. SJ was ready to fly in an instant and watched it warily.

"Cristy, what are you doing?" SJ said, her voice returning but filled with nervous wonder.

"This is Patch," Cristy replied.

"Sorry?" SJ said, shock registering on her face.

"Holy troll's snot!" Dave exclaimed.

"Patch," Cristy repeated, stroking the wolf's head. The dire wolf tilted its head so Cristy could reach behind its ear more easily, and she began to scratch it. This made the dire wolf's rear leg twitch. The wolf was probably six times her size, if not more. It stood four feet at the shoulder, and its jaws looked like they were large enough to fit Cristy inside.

"How do you know him? I assume it is he?" SJ said.

"I've known Patch since he was a pup. I used to feed him," she said.

"What?" was all SJ could reply.

"Patch was a cub when my dad saved him. A mountain bear had killed his mummy, and we found him suckling next to her. This was about three years ago. I went out with my dad when he was only collecting traps and not hunting, and that's when we found Patch. He has grown a lot since the last time I saw him," she said.

The tiny form of the gnoll standing next to the monstrous dire wolf was unimaginable, and if SJ hadn't seen it with her own eyes, she never would have believed anyone telling her the story.

"Patch is your friend," SJ said.

"We are more than friends; we are family," Cristy replied, a tear forming in her eye. "He is the only family I have left now."

Confused beyond all expectations, SJ just stood up and watched the continuing interaction. Once Patch was happy with his ear being scratched, he flopped his body onto its side and rolled so that she could then scratch his belly. This did not differ from the hundreds of interactions SJ had seen between friends of hers and their pet dogs.

"I think he came to the ridge looking for me," Cristy said.

"Looking for you?"

"My dad used to see him every couple of days. He lives on the far side of the lake with his pack. That was where Dad used to go trapping. We would take a boat over the lake."

"So, because your dad hadn't been over, Patch has come around looking for him."

"Yes. I think so."

Cristy looked at Patch, who was busy enjoying his belly rub, his tongue dangling from his mouth in pleasure. "Dad's dead," Cristy said, tears filling her eyes, and she burst into tears.

Patch reacted, turning his head, and SJ was sure he had understood every word being spoken. At the words from Cristy, he shot up again, sat back, tilted his head up to the sky, and howled. This howl was different. It was not like his previous victorious howl. It seemed to carry meaning and grief and hit SJ like a train. The other wolves did the same; all of them could howl. The cacophony of noise was not fear-inducing but tear-jerking. They were calling for a lost soul. SJ just knew it.

They howled for several moments before Patch again stood and placed his head next to Cristy, and SJ saw a tear in the wolf's eye. It was not crying; it was just a single tear. SJ watched as Cristy looked at the beast's head and gently brushed it away with her tiny paw.

"He won't attack you," Cristy said, turning her tear-streaked face to look at SJ.

SJ lowered herself to the ground, standing still in her miniature form. The remaining wolves didn't back away, none made a sound or moved towards her. Her senses told her to flee, but somehow, she knew she was safe, and she grew to her humanoid size. Cristy ran over to her and flung her arms around her leg, a fresh round of sobs coming from her. SJ looked at the dire wolf, who stood there looking back at her as she soothed Cristy and stroked her hair.

This continued for several minutes until, eventually, Cristy ran out of tears and, hiccupping, looked up at SJ.

"I miss him," she said. Patch then walked over. No menace, no threat. He just walked over and nudged Cristy on her shoulder with his head. She released SJ's leg and looked at him again.

"I know you miss him too," Cristy said.

"Every day, something new is happening in your life that I have never seen before," Dave said, his voice betraying him with emotion and surprise.

"We really should get back to town, Cristy," SJ said. "We need to let them know you are safe."

"Can Patch come?" Cristy asked.

"I'm not sure the town would allow him. I heard they had reports of a dire wolf in the area already, so the guard will look for him and his pack."

"But his friends are injured."

For the first time, SJ fully took in the scene. The five hobs lay dead, and the two injured wolves were amongst them. One wolf looked in a bad way, and another one had walked over to it, nudging it and licking at the horrible-looking wound down its flank. Knowing that animals didn't fully heal naturally, SJ was unsure what to do. The doe she had saved previously and had met again still maintained a limp and she doubted a wolf would be much good to the pack with an injury.

"I wonder if my potions will help," she said aloud deliberately for Dave's benefit.

"It may do if you can get it to drink it. They are weak potions, though," Dave replied.

"I am going to see if this helps," SJ said, calling one of her lesser potions to her hand. She uncorked the small vial and walked towards the wolf injured the worst, unable to stand with its deep flank injury. The black wolf beside it let out a warning growl as she stepped closer. SJ put her hand out in a placating gesture and moved forward. The dire wolf let out a low growl of its own, and the black wolf looked at it and then took a step back.

SJ bent down by the head of the grey wolf. The wound was oozing blood, and it looked deep. SJ placed her hand on the head of the wolf, who looked at her with sad eyes, their bright yellow as faded as the wolf itself. Gently lifting its head from the ground, she tipped a small amount of the potion onto its tongue. It licked instinctively, swallowing it. She repeated the process until the whole vial was empty. As she watched, she saw the wound begin to heal; the blood stopped flowing initially, and then the wound closed.

The potion wasn't enough to heal it fully, but it would hopefully keep it alive at least. The other injured wolf could stand weakly but could not put weight on its front leg and had to hop to move. SJ knew that both injured wolves would be unlikely to survive in the wild. Nature was cruel. Then the black wolf growled, turning, and its hackles rose as it looked down the trail to the north. The dire wolf growled, and the three uninjured wolves lined up facing the same way. SJ stood and looked down the trail. She couldn't see anything, but then she heard it. Footsteps running down the trail, multiple pairs.

"I hope it's not more hobs," SJ said.

"I don't think so," Dave said.

The sound got louder, and then they came into view. Charging around the corner came a large orc. She recognised several other town guard members and the white-haired paladin who had healed her after the battle.

"Charge," Gary, the orc, screamed as he swung his axe in front of him.

"STOP!" SJ screamed, running to get in front of the wolves, who were all tensed and ready for the fight to come.

SJ threw her arms out wide as Gary and the others stopped.

"SJ? What do you think you're doing? Get out of the way," Gary shouted.

"No. They are friendly," SJ called back. There were only twenty feet between the groups now, and the three wolves stared at the guard force, who stared back in reply, all brandishing weapons.

"What do you mean *friendly*?" Gary said, confusion on his face.

"The dire wolf is a friend of Cristy's," SJ said. At the mention of this, Patch turned to look at SJ, and Cristy, who had been standing behind him, walked to his side.

All the guards stood with their mouths open in shock.

"He is my family," Cristy said as she stroked Patch on his foreleg.

"But they are wolves," Gary replied in shock.

"Please put your weapons down, and I will explain," SJ said.

Gary looked around, taking in the scene of the recent fight, the hobgoblin corpses, and the fact that SJ and Cristy were standing amongst the wolves with no signs of aggression being shown. He lowered his axe. He glanced at the rest of the guard force and told them to stand down. The guard members lowered their weapons with uncertainty, before eventually sheathing their swords.

SJ then explained the history of Cristy and Patch to them. It didn't take long, and although the guards were as confused as she had been at the revelation, they accepted it, especially as the young gnoll stood stroking the huge dire wolf as though it was her pet dog.

SJ couldn't remember the paladin's name, so she approached him.

"I am sorry. Can you heal animals?" she asked.

"I can heal anything that doesn't have an evil alignment," he responded.

"Could you please try to heal the wolves that are injured?"

The paladin looked over at Gary, who appeared to be in charge of the group, and then shrugged, nodding. As he walked towards the injured wolves, the others growled at him. SJ walked by his side. "He is going to try to heal your friends," she said.

Stepping to the side, the wolves let them pass, and the paladin leaned over the wolf that SJ had given the potionto. Saying a few words, he placed his hand on its side. A bright flash of white occurred, and SJ watched in amazement as the wound closed and the colour returned to the wolf's eyes.

"That's that one healed," the paladin said, turning to the one with an injured leg.

It hopped backwards initially until it saw the one that had been on its side start to get back to its feet. It stopped and lowered its head towards the paladin. The paladin again placed his hand on the wolf, and another bright flash of white occurred as the wound on the wolf's foreleg healed.

"Thank you," SJ said to the paladin. He nodded in response.

"We got the message you were in the forest. Rex informed Alice this morning, and we set off straight away," Gary said, turning to look at SJ. "With the recent wolf sightings, we thought we had better come and check, which now seems unnecessary."

"If you hadn't come, I doubt the two injured wolves would have survived," SJ said.

Patch walked towards the paladin, who was still near the second wolf. On nearing, he dropped his head as he had done towards Cristy.

"I think he is saying thank you," SJ said, looking into the paladin's fear-filled eyes. The paladin stood weaponless, mere inches from the beast.

"That's okay," he replied rather nervously.

Patch turned back away, returning to Cristy's side.

"Can they come back?" Cristy said.

"Back?" Gary asked, looking at her.

"Back to town," she said.

"I don't think so. People would not be happy with a dire wolf near the town," Gary said.

"They won't harm anyone."

"And how could you be sure? They are wolves."

Cristy's little face scrunched up in annoyance. "Patch is my family," she shouted.

"Patch?" Gary said with a confused look.

"Patch is the dire wolf," SJ answered.

"Look, we need to get you back to the orphanage. Miss Madeline has been worried sick about you since you disappeared," Gary said.

"I'm not going. Not unless Patch comes with me."

"He can't come back with you."

"Well, I'll stay here with him, then."

"Cristy," SJ said.

"What?" she said, huffing.

"Patch can walk back with us, but he just can't come into the town. I am sure he can stay nearby, though, and as long as he and his pack don't attack any of the town, I'm sure they will be fine in the woods."

Gary looked at SJ. "They can't be anywhere near town. I know we have healed them today, but the wolves are renowned for the damage they cause, and the hunters can earn a living off them."

"Do the hunters hunt on this side of town?" SJ asked.

Gary stood and scratched his head for a moment, thinking. "Well, no, because of the hob scouting parties, like this one lying dead around us."

"Exactly," SJ said.

"What do you mean?" Gary asked, frowning.

"Patch and his pack on this side of the town will act as another line of defence and deterrent against the hobs, especially the scouting parties."

After briefly considering SJ's comments, Gary replied, "I suppose it makes sense, but I can't give them permission to be near town. Only the mayor could do that."

"Well, I suggest we get back to town and see the mayor, then," SJ said, smiling at Gary.

Gary frowned, looking at her and scratching his chin again. "Sven. What do you think?" he asked, directing the question to the paladin.

"I tend to lean towards what SJ just said. A pack of wolves on this side of town would act as a deterrent for the scout parties. It won't affect if they come to raid, but it could cause them issues at least," Sven said. Gary grumbled, mumbling under his breath before he spoke again. "Okay. They can walk back with us but must stay in the forest. They are not allowed to enter the fields leading to town. We can then see the mayor and get his opinion on it."

"Are you okay with that?" SJ asked Cristy.

Cristy looked from Patch to SJ to Gary before replying. "I suppose."

"Good. Then, let us get back. Jaslow, Brin, can you check the hobs, please?"

Two of the accompanying guards moved to where the dead hobs lay and looted their corpses before picking them up and moving them into the tree-line off the main track. Soon, the only signs of any fracas were the marks on the ground and the darkened patches, which had soaked up blood.

"Right, come on. It's a long way back yet. We need to get moving," Gary said.

Cristy was whispering to Patch, and SJ could not hear what she said. A moment later, Patch lay on the ground, and Cristy began climbing onto his back.

"What are you doing?" SJ asked.

"Riding Patch," Cristy replied, smiling as she sat with her legs over the dire wolf's back. Patch stood again, lifting Cristy into the air and making her let out a shout of glee.

Gary turned, and the party of guards followed him as they returned to town. That was until there was noise off to the right of the track. Stopping, they all turned and drew their weapons. In amazement, SJ watched as five more wolves appeared from the tree-line. They were all smaller than the others, and three small cubs followed them. The leader of the wolves from the tree-line and the largest was a brilliant white colour, and it walked up to Patch and nudged his face.

"It looks like Patch has a girlfriend," Cristy said, smiling.

CHAPTER TWELVE

Monsters and Mithril

A couple of hours later, the group eventually reached the forest's edge. Cristy climbed down from Patch's back, and after talking to him for a while, she eventually left him standing with his pack while she continued with SJ and the rest back across the field to town. On the group's return, several townsfolk stopped and looked at SJ walking along, holding Cristy's small paw in her hand.

The group walked straight to the barracks, several accompanying guards peeling off to the training grounds, and Gary, Sven, SJ, and Cristy entered. The usual orc sat at the desk, and SJ was unsure if he ever stopped working or slept.

"Is the mayor in?" Gary asked, approaching the barrier.

"Yes. He is in his office," the old orc replied, glancing at SJ, then staring at Cristy.

"Thanks," Gary replied.

Upstairs, they passed the table holding the model of the town. Cristy's eyes turned in amazement.

"That looks amazing," she said as she walked past, receiving a smile from a gnome busily making updates. It was like a live model, and SJ didn't think they ever stopped working on it with all the required building adjustments.

"Mayor Maxwell," Gary said as he approached the mayor's open door. The mayor looked up from his desk and saw SJ walking with little Cristy. A broad grin appeared on his face.

"Thank Amathera. You are both okay," the mayor said.

"It was an interesting night," SJ said.

"Thank you, Gary, for escorting them back safely. I don't wish to take up any more of your time," the mayor said.

"There is something we need to discuss first," Gary replied.

"What's that?" the mayor asked.

"We have ended up bringing some guests back with us."

"Guests? What sort?"

"The kind I am not sure you will be very happy about," Gary said, looking a little sheepish.

The mayor stood from behind his desk. "Don't tell me the hobs are behind you?"

"No. No," Gary replied quickly.

The mayor sighed deeply. "That's one good thing, then. So what guests are you referring to?"

SJ had been allowing Gary to talk, but jumped into the conversation.

"Actually, Mayor, they are not guests. They are Cristy's family," she interjected.

"Family?" the mayor replied, frowning.

"Yes. It's a bit more complicated than you may imagine, so I would ask for your patience while I explain," SJ said.

SJ spent the next few minutes explaining what had happened to her and Cristy before eventually coming around to the fight between the wolves and the hobs. The mayor looked enthralled, listening to her tale and her battle description.

"That sounds quite intense," he said when she finished.

"That's not the main part," SJ said. "The main part is that the dire wolf is Cristy's family."

"What!" the mayor exclaimed, gasping at her comment. SJ even heard the gnome working on the miniature town gasp behind her. She thought he must have heard most of what got discussed in the mayor's office and must be trusted.

"Yes. Patch is the name of the dire wolf." SJ then talked through how Cristy knew Patch and what had since happened. "So, in conclusion, I believe that if they are allowed to stay at the forest edge outside of the town's border, they will help in two ways: They will prevent hob scout parties and allow Cristy to visit as she wishes."

After the revelation, the mayor sat heavily in his chair, looking perplexed. "You want me to authorise a pack of wolves to live just outside town?"

"Yes. In the simplest terms," SJ said.

The mayor scratched his thick beard, contemplating the news from SJ. Gary and Sven had just stood listening to SJ's tale, having already heard what had happened on their return, and now both stared at the mayor, awaiting his response. Cristy took it upon herself to let go of SJ's hand, where she had been standing quietly as the grown-ups spoke, and walked around the mayor's desk. She looked up at him. Smiling, he turned to look down at her.

"Please," Cristy said, her eyes wide like saucers. Her face had the power to warm even the coldest heart.

The mayor looked at her momentarily, and SJ saw his demeanour change slightly.

"Oh, Cristy. I'm not sure allowing a pack of wolves to live so close to town is a good idea. What if they start attacking the livestock or venture into town?"

"I promise they won't do any of that. They will only do what Patch tells them. He's their leader," Cristy replied.

For Cristy's age, SJ was impressed with her communication ability.

"Why don't you come and meet Patch?" Cristy said.

"You want me to meet him?" the mayor replied, raising an eyebrow.

"Yes. I think he would like you," Cristy said, smiling.

The mayor looked over at Gary and Sven, who just shrugged, and SJ smiled.

"I suppose I could meet him," the mayor replied. "Alice?" he called.

Alice came walking through from the adjoining office. "Yes, Mayor?"

"I assume you just heard all that was discussed?"

"I did."

"What are your thoughts?" he asked.

"As a druid, I have no problems with animals near town as long as they are not evilly aligned. I have no experience with dire wolves, so I cannot advise. I know they are supposed to be highly intelligent creatures, and if their trust is gained, they will die for you."

"Really!" the mayor replied, surprised.

"Yes. Some druids seek them out because of their intelligence and undying loyalty. I have never met a druid who had one as a familiar, and I think this Patch would be too old now to attempt to bond with, but there is no harm in visiting him."

The mayor looked again down at Cristy. "Okay. We will visit him. Depending upon how the visit goes, I will then decide."

"Yay," Cristy cheered, smiling at the mayor with the biggest grin she could muster. "You really will like him, I promise."

"We will see," he replied.

"Come on, then," Cristy said, taking hold of the mayor's giant-sized hand.

The mayor looked at her hand in his and smiled warmly at her again. "Okay. Let's visit Patch."

An hour later, the group had returned to the barracks. Patch had been the perfect dire wolf—if there were rules or manners for dire wolves. There had been no growling or anything that may have caused any concern for the mayor, and he had decided before returning to the town that the wolf pack could stay on a trial basis for two weeks, and then after that time, he would make a final decision. Cristy initially objected until SJ assured her that if Patch and his pack behaved, stayed away from the town, and didn't attack anyone, they should be fine. Cristy was still unhappy with the trial but eventually succumbed to persuasion.

"We need to get you back to the orphanage," Gary said as they all stood outside the barracks.

Cristy turned and looked at SJ. "Do I have to? Can I not stay with you? I have no friends there."

SJ wanted to say yes to Cristy but couldn't commit to full time care. "I always have to leave and go away, and I don't have a home. I stay at the inn."

"You have a cottage," Dave said.

Cristy looked forlornly at SJ, and the gnoll's wide, small eyes made SJ's chest hurt. "Gary. Could you tell Miss Madeline I will let Cristy stay with me tonight?" SJ said.

Gary smiled at them both. "Of course," he replied as he set off to the orphanage.

Just as the mayor was about to head in, SJ remembered.

"Oh. Mayor."

"Yes?"

"I found something you may be interested in," SJ said.

"Really? What have you found?"

"I believe that mithril is valuable?"

"Exceedingly. It is only found in the higher territories. Why?"

"I found some," SJ said.

"You will do well when you sell it. I bet Zej would be interested in using mithril bars."

"No, you misunderstand me. I haven't found a bar of mithril. I have found a mithril vein."

"WHAT?" the mayor spluttered in amazement.

"Where we stopped last night, there is a cave with a mithril vein running through it. The reflected light it cast was beautiful."

"You are serious, aren't you?"

"Yes," SJ said.

"Has it not been claimed by anyone? Had it been mined?"

"No. It was only accessible by a small entrance. Cristy and I could fit through, but anyone or thing larger than Cristy could never access it."

"How large was the area?" the mayor replied, unable to keep the excitement from his voice.

"The cavern was probably sixty feet by forty feet and twenty high. Running throughout the walls and ceiling were veins."

The mayor stood dumbfounded. "You realise how much that mine would be worth if there really is that much there?"

"I have an idea. Yes," SJ said, lying; she did not know its value beyond what Dave had told her. She knew from games she had played back on Earth that mithril was always one of the higher-value ores, renowned in dwarven and elven black-smithing. When considering Amathera as a different world, it was amazing how stereotypical some aspects were in relation to Earth's fantasy worlds.

The mayor's eyes were lit up at the thought of the mithril, and SJ could see him performing mental calculations. "A mithril vein here, so near to town, would bring in so much income. It would guarantee jobs and livelihoods for so many."

"There is one problem."

"What?" the mayor asked.

"It is near the hobgoblin village—not too close, but close enough that they could see a group near it, and it is not easily accessible either."

"Damn. We need to confirm the area and see what we can do. Would you be willing to show Shelly where the mine is?"

"Who is Shelly?" SJ asked.

"Shelly is our mining lead; we mine our stone from the mountain to the west of town. She would be the best bet to confirm the details."

"I can do that, but unless everyone is the size of Cristy or my miniature form, they won't be able to enter the cavern."

"Shelly can mine through the stone in no time. I am sure she can get to the cavern."

"The area is near the route the hobs use to traverse from the valley's floor."

The mayor swore under his breath. "I must send a scouting party to check the cave's location. Would you be able to go with them?"

SJ's display triggered.

Quest: Escort the Scouts
Show the scouts the cave's location and the hobgoblin village's locality.
Rewards: 300xp
Would you like to accept the quest? **Yes/No**

"Nice xp boost," Dave said.

SJ regarded the mayor for a few moments. "I can escort them to the cave and show them where it is, but what is in it for me?"

The mayor's eyebrows raised at the comment. "What do you mean?"

"If I show you where the cave and the mithril vein are located, and you can mine it, then the town will make a significant amount of money, from what you indicated. Therefore, I could just not show anyone and then mine it myself."

"You are no miner!" the mayor exclaimed.

"Not yet. But I could be," SJ said.

The mayor stood looking back, his eyes narrowing before returning to their usual appearance. "Until we can verify the cavern's contents, we do not know how much it is worth."

"And unless I show you where it is, you won't ever have any idea what it is worth anyway," SJ said frankly.

"Mithril is highly sought after," Dave said. "The veins in the cavern were high volume. I do not know how much precisely they could mine, but based on the cavern size and considering the structure of normal mithril veins and the width of the channels you found, I would expect there to be at least eight tonnes, and that is not considering how wide the vein field might be."

SJ received no response as the mayor looked back.

"What if I said there was nearly, if not over, eight tonnes of mithril, not including how far the vein actually runs in the surrounding rock?" SJ said.

The straight face the mayor had been attempting to keep was lost in the statement. "Eight tonnes of mithril," he gasped.

"I would guess, if not more, considering the vein width, the only thing I can't be sure on is the depth and distance the field stretches," SJ added.

"How do you know?" the mayor frowned.

"I am a Legionnaire," she said, smiling.

The mayor stayed silent for a few moments. "If the vein is as large as you say . . ." The mayor paused as he completed some mental calculations. "How does one percent sound?"

"One percent of what?" SJ asked.

"Mined mithril sales," the mayor replied.

"Ask him if he means refined bars or raw ore," Dave said.

"Refined or raw ore?" SJ asked.

"I am not sure we have anyone who can refine the ore," the mayor answered.

"I bet Zej can," Dave said. If Dave thought Killic's dwarven blacksmith was capable, then SJ agreed.

"I am sure Zej can refine the ore," SJ said.

"If we can refine it, I would agree to one and a half percent," the mayor said.

SJ could tell he was used to negotiating contracts. There was no way he would give up on the potential profit the town could make from such a find. They were still standing outside the barracks, and Cristy still held SJ's hand as she spoke. At a tugging on her hand, SJ looked down. "What is it?" she asked.

"I'm hungry," Cristy said.

SJ smiled at the gnoll. After what had happened over the last few hours with Patch and the pack, SJ had completely forgotten how young Cristy was. "I am going to get Cristy some food. I will consider your offer and let you know. In the meantime, it should allow you to speak to Shelly and sort out a scouting party. The cave is not going anywhere, so there is no rush."

The mayor looked down at the tiny gnoll, who only just reached the height of his knee. He was so tall in comparison. "Where will you be?" he asked.

"I am going to take Cristy back to the inn," SJ said. "Come on, Cristy. Let's get something to eat."

Cristy grinned at SJ as her stomach let out a grumbling sound. Her little cheeks coloured, which was a feat for her small fur-covered face. Chuckling, SJ turned back to the mayor.

"Speak soon," she said, smiling.

CHAPTER THIRTEEN

An Idea, Perhaps?

As SJ led Cristy back through town towards the inn, Dave talked.

"Okay. The market value of mithril fluctuates, but if you consider some of the average prices and the fact that you don't have auction house access to sell ore or bars to other Legionnaires, then getting the town to do the work and taking a cut from the top is a great idea. I know the latest sales prices, although my data may be a little outdated as they change regularly: 1 kilogram of raw mithril ore sells for 3.1, and 1 kilogram refined is about 11.3.

"Eight tonnes of raw ore would be refined to about four tonnes of pure mithril, depending on the smithy's and miners' skills. I have picked lower-end values to make my assumptions. Eight tonnes of raw ore at 3.1 equals 24,800, so 1 percent is 248. Four tonnes at 11.3 equates to 45,200, and 1.5 percent is 678. This all depends on demand and market prices.

"The vein size will determine actual potential, but the profits could be much higher, considering that eight tonnes is the minimum expected haul. The income from that mine would boost the town's value and potential by a considerable degree. The larger cities fight over mithril mine rights; several skirmishes and battles have been fought."

"Silver?" SJ said.

"Pardon?" Cristy asked, looking up at SJ.

"Oh, sorry. I was just thinking aloud again," she said, smiling. Looking at Cristy, she noticed how dishevelled she looked in the clothes she had worn on her adventure. "We need to get you some new clothes," she said.

"No. Not silver. Gold," Dave replied.

SJ gasped.

"Are you okay?" Cristy asked.

"Yes. Sorry, I just remembered something, that's all. Let's go to the tailor's," SJ said.

Distracted from SJ's reaction, Cristy's face showed a broad grin, and SJ redirected them to Fizzlewick's.

Fortunately, the shop was open. Fizzlewick carefully measured and confirmed sizes, then presented some lovely clothes for Cristy to try on. SJ smiled at the god disguised as a quarterling as he fussed over Cristy in his broken speech, making her feel she was royalty. By the time they left, SJ filled her tailoring inventory with three new outfits, with boots or shoes to match each. It only came to sixty-five coppers, which SJ was sure differed from what it should have cost. Thanking Fizzlewick, the pair continued their journey to the inn. Cristy's stomach had growled loudly as they finished in the shop, and she needed food.

At the inn, the lunchtime crowd was in. Several patrons exchanged pleasantries as SJ walked to the bar, leading Cristy.

Kerys smiled broadly at them. "Hello again," she said to Cristy.

"Hello," Cristy replied.

"Hi, Kerys. Cristy is going to be staying tonight if that's okay?" SJ asked.

"Of course."

"I am going to clean up, but could I order two lunch specials?"

"No problem. Would you like them in your room?"

"That would be great, if you don't mind."

"Sure. I will ask Fhyliss to bring them up when they're done."

Leading Cristy upstairs to her room, SJ prioritised sorting a bath out for her while they waited for their food. Only minutes later, Fhyliss knocked on the door carrying a tray.

"Hi, Fhyliss," SJ said as she answered the door, stepping aside to let her in.

"Hello, and you must be Cristy," Fhyliss said, smiling at the small gnoll.

"Hi," Cristy replied.

Fhyliss carried the fully loaded tray to the table and placed it down. The tray overflowed with delicious cuts of hogling, salad, and thick unsliced bread, plus a small pot of butter. Floretta, the skeleton who ran the kitchen, was an amazing cook, and the food was beautifully laid out and looked divine. Also, for SJ's pleasure, there was a large steaming pot of coffee. Floretta had even included a small milk jug and glass for Cristy.

"This looks amazing, thank you. And thank you for the coffee," SJ smiled, picking up the pot and pouring a large mug.

"Our pleasure as always," Fhyliss replied.

"How much?"

"You can sort it later when you come down."

"Thanks," SJ said.

Fhyliss left them to it, and they both sat down and wolfed down the food.

"I am so jealous," Dave said sulkily as SJ bit into a thick chunk of bread smothered in butter, deliberately smacking her lips to annoy him further.

Cristy giggled at the sound, not knowing its true meaning.

Once they had eaten and SJ had finished filling the bath, Cristy got in. SJ had filled it with the scented oils, and Cristy looked tiny in the large tub. Cristy stayed there, splashing and sighing, for quite a while. Eventually, once cleaned and dry, which was no mean feat for a fur-covered gnoll, SJ learned, Cristy got dressed in a set of her new clothes. It comprised a pair of black baggy trousers, a matching baggy top, and black boots, similar to what SJ would have classed as combats back on Earth. It reminded SJ of a grunge style; she looked so cute. SJ couldn't stop smiling. It gave Cristy a look of attitude. Cristy loved the outfit and spun around, showing it off.

The afternoon disappeared quickly, with SJ and Cristy playing various games that SJ remembered from Earth. They stood looking out the window playing I spy, which was Cristy's favourite, although she was terrible at it. SJ allowed her to win and kept giving up to make her feel better. She even sat with Cristy, drawing in her notebook from Fhyliss, and taught Cristy how to write her letters more clearly.

SJ had nipped downstairs briefly to return the tray and order some food for dinner, and it was only when Cristy yawned loudly that SJ realised how late it had got. Looking at her display, it was nearly twenty, and the time passed quickly. She had spent days at friends' houses with their kids and had forgotten how much fun it was to watch them as they learned something new and played.

"I think it is time to get you to bed," SJ said after Cristy's third successive yawn.

"I'm not tired," she said, yawning again.

"Yes. You are. Come on now, let's get you tucked in."

SJ took her through to the enormous bed and eventually settled her down.

"Can you tell me a story?" Cristy asked sleepily.

"I could. Let me see what story I can tell you. Umm," she mused. "I think I will tell you about Cinderella."

"Who is Cinderella?"

"She was a poor, bullied sister who became a beautiful princess," SJ began the story. She didn't get far before Cristy's breathing grew heavy and her eyes closed. Carefully getting up from the bed, SJ bent and kissed the small gnoll on her head, stroking her hair and pulling the blanket up to cover her.

"Night, Mummy," Cristy mumbled.

On hearing the words, tears formed in SJ's eyes, and she stayed stroking Cristy's head until she snored lightly.

Walking back out to the main room and sitting down, she dabbed the tears from her eyes.

"You would make a wonderful mother one day," Dave said sincerely.

SJ had never even considered the potential to have a relationship in Amathera, and the thought gave her a fresh round of emotions she had not considered since arriving. "Do Legionnaires have relationships?" she asked quietly.

"Some do," Dave replied.

"I had never considered it."

"You may in time, but for now, we have priorities: reaching Level 10, upgrading your skill to Level 6, and completing your tailoring quest," Dave said before adding, "which you have neglected recently."

SJ flushed a little, knowing she had been putting off making the gloves. She had read the recipe but had not even attempted to make any yet.

"Well, I may as well start now. I can't go anywhere with Cristy sleeping here."

"Good idea and we can also discuss mining and money," Dave cackled maniacally.

SJ awoke the next morning with the small form of Cristy cuddled up to her side again. Slowly extricating herself, she climbed off the bed and went to the other room.

"Morning," Dave said.

"Morning," SJ yawned, checking her display. It was only six, and the sun was already high in the sky.

"Are you ready for negotiations today?" Dave asked.

As they had discussed the mining and potential income last night, they had agreed that the percentages offered for the mithril mine were too low. Dave explained all the aspects involved with mining, including labour, resource needs, smelting, et cetera. The list was quite substantial, but it was nothing that SJ wouldn't have expected. He then gave rough costs for everything and concluded that the town would profit at least 50 percent from the ore, never mind if it was smelted into bars. SJ would see the mayor today and request 5 percent and 7.5 percent accordingly for ore or bars. She had low expectations, but she wouldn't settle for the initial offer. It was time to use her Charisma.

"Once I have dropped Cristy back off at the orphanage, I will see the mayor again."

"Sounds like a plan. You are going to miss her," Dave said.

They had spoken about it the previous evening, and SJ had thoroughly enjoyed yesterday with Cristy. Under different circumstances, she would have loved to have taken her on, acting as her guardian, but she couldn't justify it. Her life and future were uncertain, and it would be unfair to drag Cristy around everywhere. She had thought about the cottage and allowing Cristy to stay there but was worried about her eating properly, even if she spoke to Charlotte, Brian, and Terence about it. It could be an option if they could supply food and look after her.

"I need to speak to Husa and grab some chisels for Terence from the market," SJ said, remembering that the stonemason was due to travel to the cottages soon.

SJ got ready and then woke Cristy up. After eating breakfast downstairs, SJ took Cristy back to the orphanage. Madeline was thrilled to see Cristy, and SJ handed over Cristy's new outfits she had bought for her. Cristy promised not to leave town alone again, and SJ agreed to take her to see Patch in a few days. As she walked through town, SJ stopped at a shop selling tools and bought a set of chisels before locating Husa. He was busy building a new home on the western edge of the town, and SJ handed over the chisels, asking him if he could drop them off. After ensuring his team's progress on the new build, he agreed and promised to be free in a day or so to go down.

"Time to see the mayor," SJ whispered.

"I can't wait to see his face when you ask for the new amounts." Dave giggled.

The barracks were the usual hub of activity, and several townsfolk were busy talking at the various desks, which served different purposes for the township. SJ had read several of the desk plates, which listed the departments. There was virtually everything you would expect within any town hall. A large bugbear complained about refuse collection, and the ratkin desk clerk scribbled down notes about his complaint. The normality of the town and how everything operated still amazed SJ.

After waiting for her turn at the front desk, she was informed that the mayor was unavailable. He was apparently at a council meeting. SJ did not know they even had a town council, but it made sense, considering how everything was set up.

"Do you know when it will finish?" SJ asked.

"It depends. They can last an hour to several, depending upon the topics," the orc replied.

"Where do they meet?"

"Upstairs, the next floor up. It's not open to the public."

"Okay. I will come back later, then."

SJ was just about to leave when she heard her name being called. Turning, she saw Alice coming down the stairs.

"Alice," SJ said as the druid approached.

"Hi, SJ. Would you be willing to join me? The mayor sent me to find you; thankfully, you are here anyway. He would like you to address the council."

"Me. Why?" SJ said, confused.

"He would like you to explain what you found in the cave. He has made a statement, and the council questions its validity."

"Validity?"

"Orik is the dwarven representative and oversees all dwarven issues in the town, but he doesn't believe a mithril vein can exist in this area. The mayor would like you to describe what you saw."

"Okay. Sure."

As Alice led her up to the floor where the mayor's office was, SJ followed closely. However, instead of going inside, Alice took a turn down the corridor. SJ had never been there before, and another flight of stairs led upwards. They lacked the grandeur of the set leading to the first floor. At the top of the stairs, she was met with an enormous set of double doors. Alice knocked on the door, and they opened. She led SJ inside. Two large orcs stood on either side of the door, and once she entered, the doors were closed again behind her.

Representatives from each of the township's dominant races—twelve in total—sat around a huge oval table, and the mayor's colossal form sat at the head of the table.

"That was quick, Alice," the mayor said. "Thank you for coming, SJ."

With all eyes on her, SJ felt a little nervous. "I was coming to see you anyway, so it's fortunate."

"Excellent. I have mentioned your discovery, but my esteemed colleague Orik would like to clarify what you found. Without further details, he is unwilling to release Shelly from her duties at the mine."

"No problem," SJ answered as Alice led her to a chair near the table's end. Slowly sitting, SJ felt even more nervous. "What would you like to know?"

A large, elderly dwarf sat on the left of the table. He had a long, thick grey beard that rested on the table which wiggled when he spoke. "You say you have discovered mithril?"

"I have, yes."

"How do you know it is mithril?" Orik asked.

SJ could not answer that it was what her AI had told her, so thinking on her feet, she came up with what she hoped was a plausible story. Being aware that the usual townsfolk also had the same levelling and skill progression systems, she used that for an answer.

"We are given certain information when we are reborn as Legionnaires. This includes the knowledge of base materials within Amathera," SJ said, knowing that no one could confirm it unless another Legionnaire came to town, and as far as she was aware, no others had turned up since Darjey's and Malcolm's deaths.

"I see. Can you explain what you saw exactly? The mayor did tell us, but can you please explain in your own words?"

"On entering the cavern under torchlight, the walls were covered in silvery-blue veins of ore streaking across the walls and ceiling. The light reflecting from them was mesmerising and beautiful."

"Was it more silver or blue in colour?"

"Silver. Why?" SJ said.

"There are several ores that have a silvery-blue colour, and many false claims of mithril have been made over the centuries," Orik replied as he coughed. Picking up a tankard from the table, he took a drink before he continued. "These claims have led to many issues and conflicts. People fighting over an area only to discover that the claim is false."

"Unless you have someone small enough to fit in the cave to confirm that it is mithril, which I am 100 percent sure it is, the only way you will reach it will require mining the entrance, which can't be done currently because of the proximity to the hobgoblins," SJ said.

Everyone present murmured around the table, and SJ realised the mayor must not have mentioned the hobgoblins to them. "Calm down, everyone," the mayor said.

Several moments passed before quiet returned. Many faces were now etched with annoyance, and several even looked fearful.

"We are not going to do anything until we have scouted the area properly and checked the chances of anything being discovered if we did proceed," the mayor said. "Our problem is that we will not know for sure without widening the entrance. If it is mithril and we don't take this opportunity as a town, we would be stupid. You are all aware of the town's finances and that we can't continue to sustain the natural population growth without another source of income."

This revelation about the town's finances shocked SJ. She had believed that the town operated on a closed economy, but understood with an increase in population that it would become unsustainable. SJ sat thinking momentarily, and murmurs and conversations began from those around the table.

"Have you ever considered attacking the hobgoblins in their own village?" SJ asked, raising her voice to be heard above the conversations.

The comment caused immediate silence at the table, and all eyes, including the mayor's, turned back to her.

"What are you suggesting?"

"Why do you keep waiting for the hobs to come and raid the town? I have seen how many are available to defend the town, and your numbers at least match or are greater than the hobs'. So why wait for them to attack you? Why do you not attack them and clear them from the valley?" SJ asked.

A fresh round of muttering began around the table, and the mayor sat scratching his beard as he mused over the comment. "We have never attacked them because they would see us coming from such a distance. When we reach the village, they will know that we are coming and be set up to defend. This advantage could easily sway the outcome of a fight. Like how we block our roads with wagons, they could be ready for any assault. An assault on a heavily defended position is likely to suffer significant losses. As the hobs do every time they try to attack here."

"Maybe there is something you can do to stop that," SJ said.

"What would that be?" the mayor replied, frowning.

"I mentioned the path the hobs use to traverse the valley wall. It is a perfect place to perform an ambush, and if the hob army travels up the path, they cannot move quickly and will be spread out along the route. This would give you a tremendous advantage and allow you to pick them off."

"How do you plan to prepare the township force for such a situation? We cannot just sit out there waiting for them to march."

"Can you not draw them into an attack?"

Another round of chattering started, and this time, they didn't stop when the mayor requested silence. It took several minutes before quiet settled around the table again.

"It is a thought, but I am unsure how to draw them out to attack," the mayor eventually replied.

"Well, we need to scout the location before we do anything drastic," SJ said.

After a while, the conversation ended, and SJ confirmed she would meet a scouting party later that afternoon to return to the location. The reason was that as light faded, they would be less likely to be spotted.

Upon leaving the meeting room, Dave immediately started talking about an idea to attract hobgoblins.

"Are you insane?" SJ whispered as she made her way back down the stairs.

CHAPTER FOURTEEN

Insanity

I t makes perfect sense," Dave said defensively.

"To you, maybe," SJ said as they left the barracks.

"Well, it does. If you speak to Fran and see if Harrietta can help, we can get underway once we know."

"This is madness you are talking about, and you are not the one who will be in danger."

"True. Although neither will you, initially."

"Initially being my point exactly," SJ retorted.

"Well, don't say I didn't try to give you some advice," Dave sulked.

"I appreciate it. I honestly do. I just don't think it's feasible."

"We will never know unless we at least try."

"Look, I will speak to Fran, okay? See what she thinks."

Dave's plan was absolutely insane, considering the danger it might put her in. Although it could easily cause Bordon and his hobgoblin followers to attack, she wouldn't even consider it until she had spoken to Fran.

SJ had decided she would train for the rest of the morning and walked around the side of the barracks to the training ground. Lorna was nowhere to be seen, so she walked to the training circles and began practising her kata. She had practised her forms for half an hour when a friendly face appeared.

"Hello, SJ," Greb said as he approached.

"Hi, Greb," SJ said, smiling. The kobold was always friendly and happy whenever she saw him, and looking at him, you never would have thought he was so skilled in martial arts.

"I see you are getting stuck on the last move," he said.

"Am I?" SJ questioned as she finished.

"Yes. Your poise is wrong. Here, let me assist. Take your stance three moves prior."

SJ stepped through the actions in her mind before getting to the point Greb had mentioned and took the pose. It was at the point of a straight punch, and she stood with her arm out as expected on completing the move.

"Okay. Hold the position. I am going to touch you," he said.

Greb walked to her side and gently placed his clawed hands on her shoulder and wrist of her outstretched arm. "You are overstretching. See here," he said, pulling her shoulder back to position it for her.

"When you perform the last punch before the kick, imagine that your shoulder is frozen and doesn't move. Any slight movement will put you off balance for the sweep, and you will end up overcompensating."

SJ could feel the difference. It was subtle, and as she tried to perform the final sweep motion followed by the last punch, she noticed the difference in the transition.

"Wow. That really made a difference; it's so much easier and more natural," SJ said, smiling.

"Now try doing it at your normal speed. It takes a little getting used to, but you will get the hang of it."

SJ restarted her kata again, and as she got to the last moves, she knew again that she had done it wrong and cursed as she became unbalanced on the sweep.

"Argh," she said, kicking at the sand.

Greb chuckled. "It just takes some more practice, that's all. Try again."

SJ worked through her kata a few times slowly, ensuring she locked her shoulder until she was happy with her body position.

"Okay. Here goes again," she said.

Greb watched intently as she worked through the kata. It was three stages, transitioning from an initial defensive form to recreating two attacking forms. As she neared the last moves, she focused on her shoulder positioning and threw the punch before the sweep, locking her shoulder. The fluidity was perfect, and her sweep came naturally, followed by her last punch. "Yes!" she shouted, smiling as her display triggered.

> Congratulations! Kata Level 6 achieved. You may now select your secondary skill.

SJ shouted an even more elated *yes* and ran to Greb, hugging him. Greb was taken aback by her sudden action and stood with his arms by his sides. SJ released him. "Sorry," she said, blushing. "I just levelled."

"Oh," Greb replied, smiling. "If it were just perfecting a form, I would train you more often if I got hugs like that."

SJ felt her cheeks go even hotter.

"What choices do you have?" Greb asked.

SJ looked at him. "Aren't all choices the same for everyone?"

"Not always with martial arts. We train in Amar Ti, but there are other forms that some races use, and they have different skill options. You mentioned you had a defensive style initially, so you may have something related to that."

"Oh. Let me see," SJ said, opening her skills sheet.

Martial Arts
Leg Sweep—on successfully performing a sweeping kick, you can cause the target to lose balance, leaving them prone. (Base attribute Dexterity; counter Strength)
Wheel Kick—you can jump and perform two rotations before landing. (No base attribute)
Palm Strike—successfully inflicting a palm strike can incapacitate a target as you strike. (Base attribute Strength; counter Constitution)
Clawed Avenger—when wearing claws, your damage is increased by +5 per level up to a maximum of +50. (No base attribute)
Claws of the Storm—chance to inflict lightning damage on an opponent. Successful strike may cause the victim to be incapacitated for five seconds per level up to a maximum of fifty seconds. (Base attribute Dexterity; counter Constitution)
Improved Guard—you can block one attack, allowing an instant strike back. (2-minute cool-down. No base attribute)

"There are some nice skills for first-tier selections," Dave said.

"Did you get anything interesting?" Greb asked.

"I am not sure what you would classify as interesting," SJ said.

"Well, you have seen the kick I did in the sparring. That is my first-tier skill." Greb smiled.

"Is that called a wheel kick?"

"Yeah, that's the one. That's a superb skill to acquire. What else do you have to choose from?"

"Leg sweep, wheel kick, palm strike, clawed avenger, claws of the storm, and improved guard."

"Two claw skill offers, that's unusual. I guess they are your primary weapons?"

"Yes."

"I don't know anything about those. All the other four are standard skill offerings for Amar Ti. Since I don't use weapons, I had six skills dedicated purely to Amar Ti," Greb said.

"Do you have a tier-two skill yet?" SJ asked.

"No. I am not Level 10 kata yet. I am still only Level 9. I get my second option then."

"I assumed you were higher than that."

"Ha. No, I don't train hard enough, personally. I know I have seen you here most days on and off, but I usually only train twice a week. If I wanted to advance to Level 10, I would need to train more frequently. I will get there one day."

"Thank you for your help today. I can't believe I reached Level 6."

"It was my pleasure. It is nice to see someone as dedicated as you are. I should really follow your example," Greb chuckled.

Walking from the training ground, SJ was elated that she had unlocked her next skill. Whispering to Dave, she returned to the inn to get food and asked him for his advice.

"What should I select?"

"All are nice, but with your claws, I would select one of those. The claws of storm is a high tier-one skill; it is not very often given out as an option. Your problem is that it is a percentage-based success, whereas clawed avenger is a basic damage bonus. If I were you, considering your class basis of being an assassin and wishing to inflict maximum damage from a surprise attack, I would select the latter," Dave replied.

"Would my Dexterity base not mean my success rate would be improved with claws of storm?"

"Yes, but like our discussion about the subterfuge skills, your target impacts the basis. The claws of storm have a counter of Constitution. Take this into consideration against someone like Bordon as an example. As an ogre, he will have an insanely high basic Constitution. You can see that from his hit points when you identified him. Therefore, the chances of your skill ever activating would be virtually zero. Well, 1 percent actually, as that is the lowest it can ever reach as a minimum to trigger a skill successfully."

"I see what you mean. Its benefits would be good on lower or potentially equivalent levels but not on others."

"Not exactly. You will have noticed that some creatures have higher hit points than standard races for equivalent levels. That means that their basic Constitution is higher. So, if you fought even a Level 8 ogre, the chances of your skill still triggering would be very low because of its high base at low skill levels. Higher skill levels can obviously help significantly, but it takes time to get the skills points needed."

"Fair enough. Levels are not the only consideration."

"Nope."

SJ took Dave's advice and selected Clawed Avenger.

Congratulations! You have learned Clawed Avenger Level 1: +5 base damage to every attack.

Smiling at the message, SJ opened her damage charts and added the adjustment bonus. It moved her claws to sit within the top 3 percent of her current weapon level. She looked at the badger's blades details again. The badger's blades' base damage was 5–9 +3, then +7 for her Dexterity adjustment, and then +5 for her new skill, before considering any potential target attributes and armour class. The +5 was a significant advantage, moving her to a minimum of twenty damage and supporting her ability to inflict damage against higher armour classes.

SJ grabbed some lunch at the Hogling Arms; it was still early enough before she had been asked to go back to the barracks to meet the scouting party, so she decided to see Fran. Arriving sometime later, several mages were in the yard, and it looked like two of them were sparring with each other. She watched for a few minutes as they cast spells at each other. It was interesting to see what they cast, and both mages had a basic elemental attack and shields they could trigger.

When Harrietta appeared beside SJ, saying hello, she nearly had a heart attack. Squealing exceedingly loudly, she jumped, drawing the attention of one of the mages who was fighting. That meant he didn't see the streaking red fireball thrown at him, and his very loud and obscene outburst deafened SJ's scream of terror as his robes caught fire. A water mage began dousing him and putting them out. SJ's cheeks reddened with embarrassment, and she turned, heading inside to find Fran without acknowledging Harrietta.

"Fran," SJ said angrily when she saw her in the common room talking to another mage.

Fran turned, noting the tone of SJ's voice. "What's wrong?" she asked, frowning deeply.

"Harrietta just tried to kill me."

"What?"

"She just appeared at my side saying *Hello*."

Fran's frown turned into a smile. "Did she make you jump?"

"Jump. I almost had a heart attack," SJ huffed in response.

Fran couldn't help but start laughing. "You get used to it eventually," she said, smiling.

"I will never get used to an apparition appearing out of nowhere; it's unnatural."

"She is unnatural. She is undead," Fran chuckled.

"Not funny," SJ said.

"What do you need?"

"I wanted to catch up on certain things," SJ said cryptically.

"Sure, give me two minutes. Go and help yourself to a coffee; there is a pot in my office."

SJ turned and glared at Harrietta. If she had not already been dead, she probably would have been from SJ's look. Her face was thunderous. Storming to Fran's office, she walked in and helped herself to a coffee, then sat in a chair. Harrietta had again followed her and was stood on the far side of the room, watching her intently.

SJ kept turning her head and looking in another direction, and within moments, Harrietta would reappear in her eyeline. "Please stop," SJ said.

"Why? Am I not beautiful still?" Harrietta replied.

SJ turned and looked at her again. Harrietta had the typical beautiful features of a dryad and would have been beautiful in her previous life, but SJ could not see it as she was now. Not wishing to antagonise her, she said, "Yes, but it doesn't give you the right to scare people."

"I didn't mean to," Harrietta replied defensively. "I was only saying hello."

"Next time, don't sneak up on someone and do it," SJ snapped.

Fran walked into the office and noticed the tension between them. "Are you two not friends now?" she said, smiling.

"I am not sure we ever will be," SJ responded.

"I hope you will be," Fran said.

"So do I," Harrietta added.

SJ turned and glared at Harrietta again.

"What did you need?" Fran asked.

"First, how did you get on at the Wandering Ogre?" SJ asked.

"I need to go back. I think I found out who it may be, but I can't confirm yet," Harrietta responded.

"Oh. Who?"

"I have my suspicions that it may be a halfling. There is one who has only recently been going there, and he has not been in the town long. In the conversations I overheard, he was asking a lot of questions about fae and various other people from the town."

SJ remembered the halfling she had spoken to the first time she had visited the Wandering Ogre and asked for directions. "He doesn't smoke a pipe, does he?"

"That is not an identifying trait for a halfling; nearly all smoke pipes."

"I wasn't aware."

"I need another couple of nights watching before I should be able to confirm," Harrietta said.

"That wasn't difficult. You both just had a civil conversation," Fran said.

"Hmph," SJ said.

"So, what else was there?" Fran asked.

"I have had an idea. And before you answer, hear me out fully, as it is a little insane."

"Go on, do tell." Fran was now intrigued as she sat in her chair and leaned forward, resting on her elbows.

"I have been speaking to the mayor, and I know you speak to him often."

"I do."

"Well, I want to try to guarantee a hobgoblin raid."

"What?" Fran said, sitting back with a shocked look.

"Let me explain. The route to the valley follows a very steep path cut into the valley's side. It is not accessible by more than two abreast at the most. I want to trigger Bordon's group so they move to attack the town, and as they proceed up the valley side, we can ambush them."

"That doesn't sound too insane."

"No, the insanity bit is how I trigger it, and that is where I need Harrietta's help." SJ turned to look at the apparition.

Harrietta opened her eyes wide now. "Mine?" she said.

"Yes. I wondered if you could scout the village and see where the ogre keeps his club."

"His club? Why would you want to know that?" Harrietta said.

"I know that it's magical." SJ noticed Fran nodding in agreement. "My plan is to sneak in there and steal it. If I can, we can virtually guarantee that the ogre will send the hobs to attack to get it back. That way, we will lead them directly into a trap."

Fran's shocked expression said it all. It took her a few moments to gather her thoughts before she said, "I have to agree that is insane."

"It is a little, but if it works, it could allow the town to drive the hobs from the village once and for all. If we can reduce their numbers enough, they can no longer raid the town."

"It is very risky. We do not know what defences the village has."

"That is why I was hoping that Harrietta may help," SJ said, turning to look at Harrietta again. "With your ability, you should be able to sneak in and scout."

"I could. It is what I'm good at," Harrietta smiled.

"Are you willing to at least scout the village so that I can confirm the details before I present my idea to the town council?" SJ asked.

Harrietta turned and looked at Fran. Fran shrugged before turning back to SJ.

"As long as Harrietta is happy with doing it, I have no objections. Harrietta?" Fran asked.

"It sounds fun," Harrietta said.

"Thank you so much. When do you think you may do it?" SJ asked.

"I can head to the village anytime; it is not as though I am time-bound," Harrietta replied.

"I am travelling to the valley later this afternoon, and we will scout out a mine nearby. Would you like to accompany us?" SJ said.

"No, it's fine. I can head down there now and see what's what. Going somewhere new will be interesting; I haven't been out of town for a long time now," Harrietta said.

"Amazing. I will see you later, then, if that is okay?" SJ asked.

"I am sure I will find you easily enough later."

"Just please don't scare me," SJ pleaded.

"I promise to try not to scare you," Harrietta said with a wicked smile.

The statement did not inspire confidence in SJ, and as she left the academy, a sense of foreboding crept up on her.

Returning to town, she called in at a vendor's stall, resupplied with rations and refilled her waterskin, then headed to the barracks to meet the scouts she would escort to the cave.

CHAPTER FIFTEEN

What's a Borzie?

The party that had been formed only comprised four, and SJ was thrilled to see that she knew two of them, Greb and Gary. "It's great to see you two here," SJ said as they stood in Captain Broadaxe's office in the barracks.

"As soon as they heard you were heading to the valley to scout, they both volunteered," the dwarven captain said. "Remember, all this is just a scouting trip. Do not interact in any way with the hobs. If you see any, if possible, hide up and stay out of their way. Only if it is a life-or-death situation are you to attack. We don't want them getting any ideas as we rarely send scouting parties out."

"Understood, sir," the four assembled guards said in unison.

"SJ is leading the way as she knows the cave's location. Gary, you are leading the overall party. Rex will follow you and return to Alice if there are any problems. Leaving now, we expect that you will arrive just as it gets dark. Once the area is scouted, I need you to return straight away."

"Yes, sir," they all replied.

SJ was impressed with the four of them and their professional attitude. They left the captain's office, and Gary led them through a rear door to an area SJ had never seen. Walking down a short corridor, they arrived at a caged door.

"What's this?" SJ asked.

"The armoury," Gary said, smiling.

"Oh. I didn't realise you had one."

"Where do you think we get all the town's defence weapons from?"

"I thought you all owned your weapons."

"We do, but we can also sign out other weapons as needed, and since this is a scouting mission, I want something quieter," Gary replied as he knocked on the metal cage door.

A halfling appeared, and climbing a small step, he opened the hatch in the door. There was a small metal shelf, and it reminded SJ of the police armouries she had seen in American TV shows.

"Hi, Gary. What do you need today?" the halfling asked.

"Hi, Bowie," he said, turning to SJ. "Have you ever fired a crossbow before?"

"No," SJ said, shaking her head.

"In that case, can I get four crossbows and bolts? Also, five cloaks, please."

"Sure, give me a few minutes," the halfling replied, climbing back down and disappearing behind a wall. Several minutes passed, and SJ could hear a lot of grunting and groaning from within the room before he eventually returned, balancing the four crossbows, four sets of bolts, and five cloaks precariously. SJ did not know how he had even picked them up. He placed them on a table at the side of the door and then climbed back up the step before leaning down and lifting them through. Each one he handed out: he made the recipient sign for. This took several more minutes, and once they were fully supplied, they all thanked him and left.

Gary handed SJ a cloak as they left the barrack's main entrance. "Here, put this on." It was a deep, mottled green colour and looked like the camouflage patterns she would have expected on military uniforms back on Earth.

"Thanks," SJ said.

"It will cover your dress at least," Gary replied, smiling.

SJ took the cloak and pulled it on. It was made of thin, soft fleece-like material that didn't hamper her movement.

"That goes well with your dress," Dave said.

The party began towards the valley. SJ learned the names of the two others in the party: Joplin, a human rogue, and Rach, an elf ranger. Joplin had been a guard member for several years, and Rach had only recently joined after finishing training as a new ranger. As they made their way along the forest path, they heard the howl of a wolf. Joplin and Rach lifted their crossbows.

"It's okay," SJ said. "That will be one of the pack."

"What pack?" Rach asked nervously.

"Have you not all been told?" SJ asked.

"I hadn't briefed them yet," Gary said, coughing nervously. "We don't normally come out this side of town."

"Ah," SJ said.

Gary spent the next few minutes informing the other three about the pack of wolves that now lived between the town and the valley. Joplin's eyes widened in awe as he discovered the existence of a friendly wolf pack. Greb took it in his stride; the howl did not make him react. The more SJ got to know Greb, the more stoic she realized he was in nature. Even when training, he rarely showed emotions.

It was getting dark as they neared the trail's end, and they slowed their approach, not wanting to walk into a hobgoblin scouting party. SJ had informed them the hobs seemed to be permanently out in the forest at the top of the ridge. Joplin scouted ahead as they approached, and the others followed him as he indicated they were all clear. SJ directed them down the river's edge until she reached the area she had cut into the forest, where the hobs had been with Cristy. Now making her way through the underbrush, she found the small clearing and the animal trail the hobs had used.

Unhindered, they reached the top of the steep slope where the steps began. It took SJ a few moments to gather her bearings, and then they began the more arduous and slower task of working through the tree-line until they reached where SJ knew the cave-mouth was. The gradient increased, leading them down the side of the slope into the thinning trees until they reached the entrance.

"The village can be seen from here if you just move over through the trees there; it is clear in daylight," SJ said quietly.

Gary nodded and signalled to Greb, who made his way towards it. Gary looked at the cave-mouth, but there was no way any of them in the party could ever squeeze through the tunnel. They then moved over to where Greb was crouched by a tree, looking out into the valley below.

"You see the fresh rockslide?" SJ whispered to Gary, the freshly disturbed stone clearly visible in the moon's bright light.

"Yeah. I can also see the path you mentioned. That is not an easy climb to get up here."

"I am surprised you have never been out here before."

"We haven't been required to for a long time now, and my rota is normally around town. I wouldn't usually be involved in scouting missions, but I had to volunteer when I heard we would escort you." Gary smiled.

"No one has ever scouted the hobs before?"

"It is normally left to the druids and their familiars, such as Rex."

"I suppose it keeps people out of harm's way." SJ couldn't fully appreciate the interaction between the druids and their familiars and did not know if they could communicate in a way that allowed them to describe things they had seen.

Looking down into the valley, they could see the fires and torchlights of the enclave. There were at least two dozen patches of light in the now-encompassing darkness. They stayed watching for a few minutes before Joplin whispered harshly as he pointed towards the left of the village, "Can you see that?"

Their eyes panned left, and they saw a line of torches in the distance. Because of the ground's undulation, the lights were not easily noticeable as they appeared and disappeared again, but something was moving across the left side of the valley. It must have been of significant size, as the line grew as it got nearer. Turning back to look at the village, they watched as more torches were lit and shouting began.

"What's happening?" Rach said quietly.

Travelling across from the valley's floor they could hear shouting; they were too far away to make out anything being said, but they could see a hive of activity in the village. Gary stared into the distance, his eyes scrunched, trying to work out what it was. At that point, the four of them all jumped out of their skins as a voice sounded just in front of them. Rach let out a squeal of surprise and clamped her hand to her mouth—she had pulled the trigger on her crossbow with a soft thunking sound, sending her bolt harmlessly down the valley side.

"I will go look," the voice said.

Thankfully, there was too much commotion below for Rach's squeal to be heard. SJ gathered her wits before the others, looking around wide-eyed, wondering where the voice had come from, and spoke first. "Harrietta. What did I tell you about scaring people?" she hissed quietly.

"Sorry," Harrietta said as she appeared before them.

Joplin scrambled backwards at the apparition's appearance. Rach and Gary both had eyes like saucers. Only Greb, who had still jumped, had regained his composure.

"It's a good job they are making noise down there, or we may have been heard," SJ said sharply.

"I said sorry," Harrietta huffed.

"I thought you said you would check the village out already?"

"I thought it easier just to accompany you."

"Have you been with us the whole time?"

"Yes."

SJ rolled her eyes. "You could have at least let me know."

"You know now," she smiled. "I am going to find out what is going on. I'll be back soon." The apparition disappeared again.

Joplin turned and looked at SJ; his face was white as a sheet. "That was a talking ghost, right?"

"Yes. I thought you would know about her. She is Mistress Francisca's follower."

"I did not know," Joplin replied.

The other three shook their heads, indicating they didn't know either.

"I'm sorry. She was going to scout for me, but I didn't know she would be with us. I thought she had gone ahead already."

Continuing shouts could be heard as the group watched from the cover of the sparse tree-line. They watched as the line approaching from the left spread further into one long, extended line facing the village. The village now also had a line of torches that were facing them. There was still a substantial distance between them, and the left line worked forward until it stopped facing them. From seeing the area in daylight, SJ knew it was a huge open plain below in the valley with little if no cover.

"They look like battle-lines," Gary whispered.

"Battle-lines? Who would be attacking the hobs?" Greb asked.

"I do not know. I have seen formations like that before, in my clan days. Suppose you look at how the torch lights are positioned on the left group, the spacing, and how they stagger slightly. I think they are orcs," Gary said.

"Why would an orc clan be marching on a hob village?" SJ asked.

"This is unheard of. There is no way that a battle should be forming near a starter town," Dave said urgently. "This sandbox feature that has been implemented has amended the entire structure of the land. At no point in the history of Amathera have I ever known such a thing to occur. I need to do some digging."

"An orc clan will march on anything it believes it has a right to," Gary replied. SJ noticed a sneer on his face. She would have to ask him about his past; she had not known he had originated from a clan.

"It is an orc clan, and they mean business. That is a full assault group," Dave said.

"If they are just about to fight, this would be the prime time to take advantage and hit them," SJ said.

"It would, but it would take time to get the guard here. Never mind down into the valley."

"Gary. Should we send Rex back anyway to tell Alice?" Greb said.

Gary looked at him, frowning momentarily, making his mind up before removing a small whistle from his pocket. It looked just like the one Alice had used in the office, and SJ heard no sound. Within moments, the form of Rex swooped down from above on the ridge. Gary removed a pencil and paper and scribbled a note. Folding it, he placed it into a small cylindrical tube on Rex's leg. "Go, Rex, as fast as you can," Gary said. Without making a sound, Rex took off and flew back toward town.

The companions watched the proceedings below; the left line, which Gary had said was orcs, had stopped some distance from the hobgoblin line along the village edge. Nothing seemed to happen as the time passed. A shimmering began in front of the group, and Harrietta appeared down the valley before approaching. This time she gave them a chance to be aware she was there and not all jump at her sudden appearance.

"There is an orc army approaching. I managed to get near the ogre as he spoke to his mage. They have been at ends for months. The orcs believe this valley is theirs, but it is their first time marching on the hobgoblins. Flying the lines briefly, I'd say there are probably about two hundred fifty hobs and a hundred fifty orcs."

"That seems slightly smaller than the last group that attacked the town," SJ said.

"The ogre had sent a group off to go away with the female hobs and their young, and several male hobs accompanied them. They have just kept their main fighters behind."

Having never considered that there would be young down in the village, SJ gained a new perspective on the situation.

"This will be interesting," Dave said.

As they watched, the beating of drums echoed through the valley.

"Orc war drums," Gary said.

"Should we get closer?" Greb said.

"No," Gary replied. "We will wait. I doubt the clan will attack at night; they will probably wait until daybreak, so we have hours. They will keep the war drums going all night to disturb the hobs, to keep them awake and on edge. I was born with war drums beating and can sleep like a baby through them."

The night ticked by. None of them could take their eyes from the torchlight as they listened to the ominous sound of the drums beating. It was terrifying for SJ to imagine scenes from many old films back on Earth. Even though she had been a part of the raid on Killic, the fact that two bodies of beings were lined up against each other, just waiting for that call to charge, was nerve-racking and fear-inducing, making her skin tingly with anticipation.

"Whoever wins this fight will still be a problem for the town," Gary said to SJ.

"Why's that?" SJ asked.

"Clans think they can take what they like. If they win here today, they will attack the town soon enough. If the hobs win, at least they will be weakened."

Eventually, the sun's first light appeared as its soft glow lit the sky; with the break of dawn, the drum beat upped its tempo. From their vantage point, they heard the cries and roars begin along the orc's line. This was returned by the hobs, who began shouting and roaring back. SJ then noticed the huge imposing form of Bordon standing at the centre of the mass of hobs. She could feel the nervous tension in the air and was not even amongst the masses below.

A small group of orcs separated in the centre of their line, and a mounted orc stepped forward and in front of the line.

"No!" Gary exclaimed. "It can't be." Shock etched his face.

"What?" Greb asked.

"That is my old clan. I'd recognise that mount anywhere."

"I can't tell what it is from here," Greb replied.

"It's a horrible thing. No one knows how he ever tamed it."

"What is it?" SJ asked.

"A borzie. They are foul beasts. Imagine a hogling in a permanent frenzy and you may be close. What confuses me is why they are here. I was born two territories away in a Level 20–30 capped area. Many of those orcs will be much higher levels than the hobs they face, so they are not worried about having a smaller force."

"I am going to get closer," SJ said.

Gary looked at her with a concerned look.

"Don't worry, I will be miniature." SJ removed her cloak and shrank down. "Harrietta, are you still here?"

"Yes," the ethereal voice replied.

"Will you join me?" SJ asked.

"Of course," Harrietta said with a happy lilt.

"Be careful," Greb said as SJ took off.

She flew down the valley side, staying close to the ground in the early light of daybreak, SJ just hoped no one would see her. She tried to stay out of view of the two lines of combatants as much as possible, hoping they would all be otherwise engaged. It didn't take her long to reach the plains. "Harrietta."

"Yes?" Harrietta replied.

"Sorry. I just wanted to check you were still with me."

"I would have said if I couldn't keep up with you."

"Good."

They were probably only a few hundred metres from the village now, and the sound of the war drums being struck echoed all around. Up by the ridge, it had sounded ominous, but nothing like being this close. She flitted through the grasses of the plain, finding the main path that the hobs had created over time, running to the base of the valley's side. Staying to its edge and low, she approached.

The buildings were ramshackle; she could see they had not been maintained. The area was disgusting, with rubbish and filth everywhere. The hobs were not concerned about personal hygiene based on the state of the place. There was evidence of various animal skeletons lying around. Not seeing any movement on this side of the village, SJ flew to the nearest building.

Pausing briefly at the entrance, which hung open, she peeked inside quickly, checking it was clear. The stench that hit her nostrils was horrendous, and she recoiled from it. The floor was littered with blankets, and it looked like over twenty hobs probably slept in it usually. Scattered on the floor were what SJ could only guess may have been some children's toys. She couldn't fathom living in these squalid conditions and could understand why they sought to take the town.

The sun peeked above the mountainside, and the war drums stopped as the first full ray of morning light bathed the valley floor. SJ froze at the sudden silence. She whirled around and checked that nothing was near. All she could hear was the occasional sound of movement.

"They are meeting in the middle," Harrietta whispered.

"Where are you?"

"Looking through the ceiling." SJ looked up, and Harrietta's face smiled down at her before disappearing again up through the roof.

"I am coming up," SJ whispered. Moving to the roof, SJ landed gently. She was so glad her wings were virtually silent. Cautiously, she moved forward in her miniature form, until she reached a broken and decrepit chimney that looked like it might collapse at any moment. Peering around the stone side, she took in her first clear sight of the battle-lines.

With the morning light streaking between the lines as it continued to creep above the mountainside, the massive form of Bordon strode out towards the centre while from the far side, a huge orc stepped forward on the largest boar SJ had ever seen. The orc was massive, much larger than Gary, and Gary wasn't small, but the boar was monstrous. She wasn't surprised they could tell it was a mount from the treeline. It had four huge tusks protruding from its lower jaw and was at least the size of a large rhino back on Earth. It was covered in chain-mail, and running down its snout was plate armour. A skull crest and red flail were painted on the front of the armour between its eyes.

The huge orc pulled the mount to a halt, almost at eye level with Bordon. The orc wore scale mail, from what SJ remembered of her gaming days, and carried a large round shield painted a blood-red colour with the same crest. In its other hand, it carried a vicious-looking flail, whose chains dangled down the side of his mount with three huge, spiked metal balls attached.

Bordon stood there in the attire he had worn at the township—minus his damaged breastplate—after his battle with Zigferd: skin trousers, bare feet, and now a bare upper body. His muscles, no longer hidden under a breastplate, were huge and rippled across his shoulders as he flexed. He held his huge club in a monstrous hand, bouncing the massive head in his open palm with a steady rhythm. "What do you think you're doing, Bordon?" the orc called. The pair was still about forty feet apart. "You know you can't beat my clan."

Bordon laughed, a deep, resounding sound.

CHAPTER SIXTEEN

Amatherean Standoff

Your clan is weak and pitiful. The elves ran you from your home, and now you try to muscle in where you are not wanted," Bordon said. It was the first time SJ had heard the ogre talk in the common tongue, and it was a broken, unnatural sound. "I have already told you I will not give up the valley."

"Your rights? You are the scum of Amathera, you and your kind. No morals, no standards; look at the state you have made of this village. I remember visiting here years ago. It was a beautiful area, and you and your group have devastated it since your arrival." The words from the orc were more eloquent than SJ expected, and his reply sounded educated.

"The valley is ours, and soon the town will be ours. Your kind are not welcome here. You have been warned before about entering."

"It's not yours; it belongs to the orcs. We are the oldest race of Amathera. Whatever land we choose to reside in belongs to us by rights of age," the orc called.

"I will give you ten minutes to start moving from the valley, Jabrey, or it will be the last thing you ever do," Bordon threatened, growling deeply. The hobgoblin line cheered his comment.

Jabrey waited for silence to return before replying, "I will, therefore, offer you the same. Ten minutes to leave the village. You may head west over the mountains and find yourselves a new home." At his response, the war drums began again.

SJ hadn't seen the hobgoblin mage, she was so transfixed on the two leaders talking, but now remembering, she scanned for where Iratu was. Bordon returned to his line, not worried he had turned his back on Jabrey. The orc leader spat on the ground before turning his mount and trotting back.

"Have you seen the mage?" SJ whispered.

"No," Harrietta whispered in response. It was still freaking SJ out she was talking to an invisible ghost who could easily be sat cross-legged just watching everything unfold without a care in the word.

"I need to find him," SJ said. As Bordon returned to the hob ranks, SJ watched them part and allow him to go through. Many of the hobs were carrying crude spears and swords. The hobgoblin archers were spaced out along the line. Most of the orcs appeared to be wearing scale mail compared to the hobgoblin's leather armour, and several were bare-chested and had the clan emblem painted on their chests. They were all wearing war paint, whether stripes of red across their faces or markings on their clothing or armour. The force looked fierce and formidable.

As the drums continued to beat and the hobs began shouting back, SJ worked toward the roof's edge. Bordon walked towards a building and stooped to enter the doorway. An old, battered sign was hanging from a post at the door. A picture of a wolf's head could still be seen on it amongst what looked like several axe strikes. The building must have been the village inn in its old life. Now decorating either side of the door were two animal skulls. SJ thought they might have been bears, although they looked much larger than any bear she had ever seen. Gathering her steel and looking at the lines of chanting drumming enemies, she flew straight to the inn's roof.

Assuming she was safe since no one called and her senses hadn't triggered, SJ landed on the roof and edged to where a chimney had once stood. It was now just open to the elements, and peering down, she saw the hunched form of Iratu and another hob. SJ could not see Bordon from where she was positioned. Beneath the opening was a cauldron, and within a putrid purple liquid formed thick bubbles before they burst, releasing small clouds of vapour.

Bordon spoke in the tongue she had heard on her last encounter with them; she didn't know what was said or the reply.

"He asked if the poison was ready," Dave put in. "The mage and rogue confirmed it was. They have cooked up something not just poisonous but alchemical between them."

SJ nodded, not knowing if Dave would even realise, but guessed he would. She needed to ask him about how he viewed the world. It had never really entered her mind before. She assumed it was like a third-person view but would check when in a position to speak openly.

SJ waited for Dave to interpret as the group spoke.

"The rogue is going to start distributing it to the hobs. They have been cooking it up all night since they noticed the orcs' approach."

SJ was thinking about what she could do. Yes, the orcs were problematic, but compared to the hobs, they seemed civilised. She wished Gary was here so she could find out more about them. She thought through her options before removing a healing potion from her inventory. Steam was rising from the cauldron, and the mage and rogue were now off to one side, collecting some vials. SJ opened her own and poured the liquid into the cauldron without further consideration.

The red liquid landed on the surface, seeming to float, before sinking slowly, dispersing in the mixture. The rogue returned to the cauldron and picked up a ladle resting against its side. The reaction began as he moved to scoop some of the cauldron's liquid. The already-boiling liquid became more violent, the bubbles forming more rapidly on its surface. SJ stared down as more steam erupted from the cauldron, and a thick mist rolled over its sides. It reminded SJ of the smoke in nightclubs she had visited when they flooded the dance floors.

The rogue drew back and shouted something to the mage, who turned with a startled look on his face, and then it happened. The cauldron exploded. SJ pulled back from the hole in the roof just in time as a spout of purple liquid, light, and smoke erupted. Below her, she heard the scream of the rogue and mage. SJ moved to the flat edge, which was not visible from the assembled lines because of the roof shape, as the mage staggered out of the inn. The explosion had caused most to turn and look, including Bordon, who had returned to the line. The mage coughed and spluttered as he escaped the vapours and mist that followed him out the door, his robes covered in the liquid, and he pulled them off as the material corroded.

"That was a mental thing to do. You realise you could have just blown the whole village up? Messing with alchemical reactions like that can be and is very dangerous, but man, did that look good shooting out of the hole in the roof like that," Dave chuckled.

"I had to do something," SJ whispered.

Two hobs came running over to the mage to assist him, and he struck out at them and screamed in rage, continuing to remove his robes.

"Now, that was foul language indeed. What had that kobold ever done wrong?" Dave tutted.

SJ could imagine what he had said. The mage's robes were ruined and now lay on the ground, and underneath his robes, he was wearing regular clothing, a pair of trousers and a loose-fitting shirt, with several marks on them where the liquid had eaten into them. The robes made him appear imposing, but he looked much scrawnier and less intimidating without them. In her last meeting with Iratu, she had struggled to damage him, and without his robes, she hoped it might be different. Bordon called to him, and Iratu screamed back, pointing back into the inn.

"He just blamed the rogue," Dave giggled.

The purple vapour and mist cleared, and as it did, the tempo of the war drums increased. Bordon was facing the enemy line, waiting, tapping his club into his huge palm in time with the orcs' drum beat. Then silence enveloped the lines, and the drums stopped all at once. It hung in the air for several moments as Bordon cried out. The hobs chanted and took a step forward.

As this happened, the drums began again, and the beat was much faster. SJ stared across at the orcs as cries erupted, and they banged their weapons against their shields in time with the drum beat. It was a sight to behold. The orcs stepped forward, and then a second step picked up speed. The hobs did the same.

Bordon began increasing his speed as he ran across the battlefield, aiming directly for Jabrey on his mount. He screamed in rage. His club was held high above his head. Because of his size, he reached the centre before anyone else, and three orcs moved to intercept him as he attempted to approach Jabrey, whose mount was still standing stationary, awaiting an order to charge.

One of the unfortunate orcs received the full power of Bordon's club as he swung it like a polo player would from horseback, catapulting the orc backwards, and its helmet went flying. She wasn't sure if its head was still in it as Bordon ploughed through the other two, knocking them aside like bowling pins. Jabrey still sat there, not moving, and it was only as Bordon closed to within thirty feet that he moved. The borzie went from stationary to a speed SJ struggled to keep track of, and the two powerful beasts met with a sound like thunder.

As the two leaders clashed, the hobs and orcs reached each other. Some fired crossbows before dropping them and switching to mêlée weapons. Several bolts hit their marks, and a few staggered from initial wounds. Utter chaos had begun as a vicious mêlée got underway. As this happened, SJ looked down and saw the mage pick up his ruined robes. He screamed in anger at them before throwing them to the ground again. Looking out towards the battle, Iratu snarled and stepped into the gap between the buildings. Flourishing his hands, he conjured a red ball and released it with an angry scream. The fireball he had created flew across the field, taking an unsuspecting orc completely by surprise. It was hit square in its face, and it screamed, throwing its hands up and grasping its now-blackened face as two of the hobs then pierced it with their spears.

Orcs screamed, and hobgoblins cried as the violence ensued between the two sides. Bordon was viciously striking at the mount of Jabrey. He was not trying to hit the orc himself but trying to disable his mount. The giant borzie swung its huge head and tusks in defence. Jabrey swung his flail, the metal spiked balls having a significant reach on them, and they smashed into Bordon's side. Although Bordon staggered from the blow, he received no physical damage, and SJ was sure she noticed Jabrey's eyes widen in realisation. The mage must have cast his invulnerability spell on him already.

The orcs would not stand a chance of winning if Bordon remained invulnerable, and SJ knew what she had to do.

"Harrietta?" SJ whispered.

"Yes?" she said, right by SJ's ear.

"Can you help me attack the mage?"

"If you wish. What would you like me to do?"

"Have you not fought before?"

"Nope. Fran doesn't allow me to fight, and before I was turned into what I am now, I didn't know many combat spells. I know a few now, but they are not high level."

"Can you think of anything that can help? He normally has a shield, which takes time to break down."

"I can cast dispel magic and see if that helps. I only learned it the other day. Give me a minute to prepare."

"I am heading down. Can you cast it, please?"

"Sure, but I will be visible when I do. I can't do magic while hidden."

"Just cast it, then fly away. I don't want you getting hurt."

"Unless there is a cleric or paladin here, I very much doubt they have anything that can affect me."

"Okay. Wait for me to grow."

SJ took off, flew to the other side, and dropped by the side of the wall. There was no way anyone was paying her any attention, not with the carnage unfolding on the plain.

Iratu had his back to her, casting another fireball, screaming as he hurled it at two orcs. SJ equipped her claws and grew. Standing next to the building, she looked up and saw Harrietta appear as she closed her eyes and, with a flourish of her hands, cast a rainbow-coloured stream of light at the mage. The light met with the shield surrounding Iratu and crackled over its surface. Iratu turned and looked up where the stream was coming from, screaming again and throwing a dark bolt at Harrietta. Harrietta didn't even flinch as the bolt passed through her harmlessly. The rainbow skittered across the shield's surface, making it visible, and as SJ watched, the shield broke down. As soon as it was open, she ran.

Iratu didn't notice SJ off behind and to the side, and it was only when she reached him and triggered her identification skill that he noticed and turned.

Iratu the Mad	
Race:	Hobgoblin Mage
Level:	18
Hit Points:	71 of 105
Mana Points:	185 of 270
Armour Class:	10
Attacks:	Magic
Special:	Invulnerability

She noticed the reduced armour class and hit points from the damage he had sustained from the cauldron blast just as her claws tore into Iratu, raking his side. The reduced armour class and surprise attack allowed her to hit easily. His health dropped by a further twenty-one. SJ's heart leapt at the increase in damage. If she could land a few strikes, she could finish him. Iratu spun, screaming in rage, swinging his arm out violently. SJ was not expecting the blow, and it caught her across her face. She tasted blood in her mouth as her vision blurred for an instant.

He may have looked weak, but he was still a Level 18 mage compared to her Level 7. Taking precautions, she stepped away and readied herself. The mage flashed his hands in action as a black bolt appeared. Just as SJ thought it would fly at her, a blue bolt of light struck the mage on his side, distracting him, and it fizzled out.

"Get him, SJ," Harrietta screamed from the roof where she now floated, clearly visible.

Iratu's hit points had not reduced from the blue bolt, but it had been enough to make him turn and glare at Harrietta, and that was the only opening SJ needed. Using her latest kata form, she attacked. The mage was fast, and on turning back, he blocked her strikes with his arms, parrying her forearms so as not to injure himself on the claws. The black dagger appeared in his hand again, and SJ knew it was poisonous. As he went to slash out at her, SJ dropped to a sweeping kick, bringing her shin around to impact the side of his ankle as the blade swept over where she had just been stood.

Taking another step back immediately, she faced him again. As she watched, a second blade appeared in his other hand. SJ knew this was going to get dangerous. There were no healers nearby who could help her if she got poisoned; she still had the antidote from Gladys but wasn't sure how strong a poison from the mage might be. Iratu moved at her. It was obvious that, though a mage, he also practised with blades as she fended off his attacks with her claws. She triggered her shroud skill, to at least offset any damage received. Remembering the conversation with Jurgen as she did, she ensured not to overextend, allowing her blades to meet those of the daggers.

Another flash of light, and this time, an orange lance hit Iratu. He groaned from the impact, but it again did little damage. Harrietta was trying to help in any way she could. SJ stepped in as a follow-up to the strike, and with Iratu off balance, she plunged her claws into his abdomen. Again, they penetrated easily with his reduced armour class, and another twenty-three hit points fell. With the minor damage from the magic and her kick, he only had twenty-two remaining.

"Get him," Dave screamed in her head excitedly.

"Watch it," Dave and Harrietta cried in unison as a hob attacked her.

She hadn't noticed the hob that had moved back to support Iratu, and only when its mace caught her in the side did she realise, a moment too late. Her senses were already heightened because of the fight so had not registered the new threat. Her health took a dive, reducing by a third; thankfully her shroud was still active or it could have been much worse, and she staggered sideways from the blow. Wincing in pain, she turned to face her new threat as Iratu stepped back from the mêlée.

She didn't even bother identifying the hob. Filled with rage, she launched an attack. She moved with a speed and surety that she had never had before. Her moves felt natural and precise, her adrenaline pumping. The hob backed off, a look of fear in its eyes at her savageness. She slashed, jabbed, and kicked out at her new foe. It backed away, trying to keep its distance and use its mace to block her blows as best as possible. As it backed into the wall of the inn and had nowhere else to go, she hit home, piercing it in its chest and performing a claw strike straight across its face. Imagining it was one of the straw training dummies, she performed her repeated strikes. Its health dropped quickly, and SJ stepped back, panting as its body fell to the ground. She spun to look for Iratu, who had disappeared from the side of the building.

"Where is he?" SJ screamed.

"He went left," Harrietta called.

SJ glanced at the ensuing battle; she could not tell who was winning, but she would not let Iratu escape this time. She ran around the corner of the building, and her senses went into overdrive. She dived forward as, once again, her dragon blood saved her from certain death. The ball that passed her was not a fireball but seemed to absorb the very light as it passed by.

"That was an arcane death spell. It has a cool-down of twenty-four hours. He will have just used up his mana with that," Dave said.

The ball continued past where SJ had stood and out into the battlefield. Two hobs and an orc were busy fighting when it struck them. The screams they let out pierced the whole battlefield's sounds. Their bodies disintegrated as it ate into them. SJ stood and looked at Iratu. His shoulders sagged, and she could tell the spell must have taken a lot out of him as she pounced. As she sprinted down the alley towards him, he moved his hands in a flourish again, and as another bolt began to form, the strain was clear on his face. Harrietta stepped in again, throwing another blue bolt at him, disturbing his cast and giving SJ the time to reach him. Leaping at him, she thrust both her sets of claws out as she jumped, punching them both forward and piercing him in his chest.

Her momentum carried them forward, and Iratu toppled backwards as she landed on top of him. Her claws buried deep into his skin. Staring at her with wide eyes of disbelief, the hobgoblin mage said one word in an accented common tongue. "How?"

CHAPTER SEVENTEEN

Charge

As the life left Iratu's eyes, SJ's display triggered. She didn't even bother looting the corpse before shrinking and flying back up to the roof of the nearest building. Harrietta approached her from the other rooftop, vanishing as she did. SJ read her notifications.

Congratulations! Iratu the Mad killed. 210xp, shared = 105xp awarded.

Quest: Vengeance—Update
You have witnessed the heartache and torment caused by the evil that resides in Amathera. You may seek vengeance on those guilty of crimes against the town.
Kill Bordon the Brandisher: 1000xp
Kill Iratu the Mad: 700xp—Complete
Prevent any further hobgoblin raids on Killic.
Rewards: 1500xp, reputation with Killic. Usual level kill experience awards apply.

Rewards: 700xp + 140xp bonus = 840xp awarded

Congratulations on reaching Level 8
You have been awarded the following:
5 hit points
5 mana points
+1 Dexterity
+2 free points to distribute as you wish

SJ opened her character sheet.

Legionnaire 25007077			
Name:	SJ		↻ **Level: 8**
Age:	27	**Experience:**	882 of 1200
Race:	Fae	**Hit Points:**	62 of 62 (45 * 1.38)

Class:	Assassin	Mana Points:	54 of 54 (45 * 1.2)
Alignment:	Neutral Good	Armour Class:	18 (10)(8)

Attributes	
Strength:	10
Dexterity:	18
Intelligence:	10
Wisdom:	10
Constitution:	12
Charisma:	11

Skills	
Racial:	
Night Vision—you have improved vision in poor light conditions.	
Flight—when in miniature fae form, you can learn to fly. Flying is not available in humanoid form.	
Shapeshift—you have the ability to switch between fae forms.	
Class:	
Martial Arts:	Kata Level 6, Clawed Avenger Level 1
Subterfuge:	Identification Level 6 (10 of 100 to reach Level 7), Shroud Level 1
Profession:	Tailor Level 3
Symbiosis:	
Dragon Sense—your senses (touch, hearing, smell, and sight) are heightened.	
Precognition—foreknowledge due to increased perception will allow you to evade a killing blow. (24-hour cool-down)	
Divine Lightning—your blood is combined with that of a blue dragon, increasing healing speed while out of combat.	
Malware:	Waiver (Sandboxed)
Inventory:	10 slots (10 special)
Followers:	3

In one interaction, she had almost increased two levels. If she could kill Bordon, she would be well on her way to Level 10.

"That was amazing. Well done," Harrietta said.

SJ didn't even flinch this time. "Thanks for the support. I couldn't have taken him out without your help."

SJ quickly added two free points to her Constitution, increasing her health by the base increase it gave, adding a further 50 percent. Her health increased to seventy-one from its base of forty-five at Level 8, and she could understand how Bordon could easily have the hit points he had, considering his potential constitution and the multipliers. Though, she didn't know if the bonuses were race specific.

Looking at the continuing battle, she noticed that the numbers on both sides had decreased. Bodies lay everywhere, and it didn't appear either side had dedicated healers available. This meant they were seriously limited in their capabilities. Looking out to the main showpiece, Bordon and Jabrey continued their individual fight. SJ could see blood flowing down the side of Bordon, meaning that his invulnerability had been broken. The borzie appeared to be struggling as Bordon continued to beat on it. SJ watched as Jabrey swung his flail out again at Bordon. Bordon caught the strike on his club and the flail chains wrapped around it. Tugging violently, Jabrey was dragged from his mount as he fought to keep a hold of his weapon.

As Jabrey slipped off his mount and fell to the ground, the borzie took advantage, now more agile without its rider. It almost instantly charged from only ten feet away, and it smashed into Bordon's legs. Bordon's cry was heard across the battlefield as its tusks gouged deeply. Bordon ripped his club back, dragging the flail from Jabrey's hand, and with the flail still tangled around his club, he swung it violently at the borzie. It caught the borzie on the side of its head, and it staggered from the blow.

Jabrey had sprung back to his feet, and his diminutive form compared to Bordon now appeared with a two-handed sword. He was still considerably taller than others on the field, which Bordon made look like mice in comparison. The ogre defended himself using his club as a shield, deflecting Jabrey's vicious blows. It was actually better for Jabrey now that he was unmounted, as Bordon had to defend against two sides. As the battle continued, they exchanged blows, the occasional one finding their way through each defensive move. The borzie had backed off again and went to charge again. Bordon gripped his club with two hands, swung it down like a sledgehammer, and smashed it on the top of the borzie's head with his considerable strength.

SJ winced at the blow and saw the borzie drop on its front legs. It struggled to stand, and Jabrey let out an unearthly scream as he lunged forward, plunging his two-handed sword straight into Bordon's abdomen. The ogre bellowed in rage, and SJ saw his form change. Bordon was bleeding from various wounds he had taken, and the sword now plunged into him sent him into a frenzy. Gripping the blade in his free hand, he pulled it back out as Jabrey tried to push it deeper. Watching in amazement, SJ watched Bordon's skin colour change. His grey tones went red—and it wasn't because of the blood that covered him—as he triggered his rage skill.

Bordon swung his club at Jabrey again as the borzie struggled to get back to its feet, staggering sideways and falling on its side. SJ had completely forgotten throughout the events to trigger her identification skill but did now, focusing on the three in battle.

Borzie Mount	
Level:	25
Hit Points:	64 of 298
Mana Points:	0
Attacks:	Gore
Special:	Charge

Jabrey Xiquist	
Level:	27
Hit Points:	143 of 335
Mana Points:	55
Armour Class:	34
Attacks:	Flail, Stab, Slash
Special:	Thick Skin

Bordon the Brandisher	
Level:	23
Hit Points:	211 of 480
Mana Points:	55
Armour Class:	28
Attacks:	Bash, Charge
Special:	Rage

SJ's jaw dropped in awe as she read the remaining hit points. Each was under half its starting value, and the borzie was at less than a quarter. She was also astounded at Jabrey's level. A Level 27 orc so close to the town . . . As they continued to fight, she looked across the battlefield and again triggered her skill, readying herself for the flood of information she would be hit with. As her display triggered, she closed her eyes, allowing the sensation to pass, before opening them again.

63 x Orc Warrior—Levels 9–17
9 x Orc Berserker—Levels 11–18
93 x Hobgoblin Fighter—Levels 6–13

4 x Hobgoblin Berserker—Levels 8–15
19 x Hobgoblin Archer—Levels 6–11
Congratulations! You have reached Identification Level 7.

She checked her skills quickly.

Subterfuge:	Identification Level 7 (98 of 200 to reach Level 8), Shroud Level 1

Both armies were reduced by half or more, and the battle had raged for a while.

"Look left," Dave said.

SJ looked left. Her sense hadn't triggered, and as she wasn't in active combat at the moment, her health was replenishing with the influence of the dragon blood. Across towards the valley side, she saw them approaching. The mixture of colours and varying beings meant one thing: The town guard had arrived. They had descended the valley side, which meant they moved slowly over the steps and the rockslide that had restricted it, but they were on their way and currently unnoticed by those fighting already.

"Yes," SJ said excitedly.

"Yes?" Harrietta said questioningly.

"The guards are coming," SJ said.

"Oh," Harrietta replied.

Not going to chance her luck until the others arrived, SJ stayed on the rooftop of the building. She had been considering attacking a few stragglers nearer the back, but her health had not recovered fully yet, and she was only a Level 8. As the fight continued, the guard arrived at the valley floor. SJ watched them wait to form into a group before proceeding towards the village.

"I am going to tell them Iratu is dead," SJ said, taking off and flying straight over towards them as they approached. No one was looking at her or paying her attention. The combatants were too busy in their fights for survival. At the front of the group, Mayor Maxwell led with Captain Broadaxe and Lorna at his sides. As SJ approached, the mayor and Lorna both transformed. Though SJ had seen the mayor's other form, she'd never seen Lorna in her tigress form, and the size of the tiger alongside the massive bear was a vision of wonder. As the guards got within a hundred metres, they began to run.

SJ reached the mayor, flying by his side as he lumbered forward at a considerable speed, for his size.

"Iratu is dead," SJ called.

The mayor didn't reply but acknowledged her statement with a nod of his head.

A guard member blew a horn, and its blaring supported the guards' battle cries as they sprinted towards the fight. Many of the orc drums had been silenced by now, and the horn cut across the battlefield, making several heads turn and look at the town's forces as they arrived. As they got within fifty metres of the orcs and hobgoblins, a barrage of bolts and arrows flew, beginning their parabolic flight towards their targets. As they rained down on those fighting, fresh cries of pain could be heard as several were struck. The town guard must have comprised nearly a hundred twenty. SJ saw several amongst the group that she knew but also several who were not regular guards from what she could see. Lorna cut right and aimed her run at a hob and an orc fighting; neither expected the flash of orange and black that tore into them. Lorna slashed with her claws and bit with her fangs. Captain Broadaxe wheeled to the left, and a group of guards followed.

"Attack," he screamed as they reached twenty metres from the main group. The mages from the town stopped, keeping their distance from the combatants. The first spells flew towards the combined enemy forces. The mayor continued towards Bordon, knocking an orc flying as he ignored its weak attempted swing, and SJ stayed with him as the others joined the mêlée.

As the mayor roared, SJ flew upwards above the battleground, and the mayor threw himself at the ogre. He careered into Bordon back, and SJ was not even sure the ogre knew he was there. His rage had taken over any form of sanity the ogre may have had as he continued to fight Jabrey, who was valiantly trying to defend himself, duel-wielding two short swords after having dropped his two-handed sword.

SJ saw a hob and orc fighting to one side, and she dropped to the ground as she grew to her full size. The adrenaline coursed through her as she entered the fray. Her claws were still equipped, and she flew at the hobgoblin closest to her. The hob shrieked as her claws pierced its side, and the orc it had been fighting took advantage, swinging its sword across its enemy's throat. The hob silenced and fell to the ground. SJ pulled back, shrinking again. She sprinted away and took off again before the orc could compose itself to attack her.

Picking areas that allowed for easy entry and exit from the fight, she repeated the same process several times. She was lucky to escape being struck a few times. Her sudden appearance as she grew and then shrank took most of her opponents off guard, and she triggered her shroud skill when she could. It was on the fifth attempt of the same tactic that she was hit. As she landed, a hob threw an axe and smashed into her shoulder, sending her staggering off balance and rolling to the floor.

Thankfully, its blade had not struck her, but the force of the strike was enough to reduce her by ten hit points. Wincing from the pain in her shoulder, she sprang back to her feet. Now equipped with a sword, the hob ran at her as she rose. Throwing her blades up in defence, she parried the strike. The hob was in a wild frenzy and swung at her backwards and forwards with a slashing motion. She backed away, parrying what she could. Its attack was so ferocious that she couldn't even consider finding an opening to strike back. That was when she heard the roar and an orc ran towards her.

Seeing the orc in her peripheral vision, she tried to step out of its way as it swung its sword.

"Duck," it screamed.

"Now," screamed Dave.

SJ instinctively did as she was told, and the orc's blade swung over where she had been and connected across the chest of the hob. The hob was thrown backwards from the blow, and the orc stepped over it and plunged its blade into the hob's chest. That was the moment SJ realised it was Gary.

Another orc ran towards them, and Gary shouted, "Hargrit, you're mine," and screamed as he charged at the orc. SJ looked around, shrinking again and taking off. As she flew over the battlefield, she scanned the unfolding situation. The orcs' and hobs' numbers were dropping rapidly now the town had arrived. As she saw the flashes of white from healers, the mages bombarded the enemy with spells. The entire area was bathed in a myriad of colours from the spells. It was absolute mayhem from where she now flew fifty feet above the battle as the three forces battled each other.

Many of those SJ now classed as friends were involved heavily in the battle. SJ watched as Captain Broadaxe severed an orc's legs from under it with his great axe and, wearing his shining armour, strode casually with his axe over his shoulder towards his next target. SJ spotted Lythonian, mace and shield in hand, combatting two orcs simultaneously, parrying and striking them, wearing them down. Gary fought Hargit. Fran was casting spells from a safer distance. SJ could see the flash of Zej's war hammer appear above the mass of bodies he was fighting. Lorna fought with a hob, having switched back to her humanoid form and now performing her martial arts skills for all to see. She was lethal and precise.

SJ looked at Bordon. His health was down to a quarter now, and Jabrey was not far behind him, limping from a wound he had received to his leg. SJ had never identified the mayor, so she did not know what health he had remaining, but he had a nasty cut on his side. The three monstrous foes stood in a triangle, staring at each other as a brief standoff took place before Bordon roared and swung for Jabrey. Jabrey ducked, and as he did, the mayor swiped at Bordon's leg, tearing a fresh stripe of claw marks across his calf. It was a brutal display of strength and stamina. No foe should be able to withstand the damage that both Bordon and Jabrey had and still were. The borzie was lying on its side. Still, it wasn't dead, as SJ could see its chest moving, but it was immobile.

SJ spotted Rach as an orc loomed over her. She had been knocked to the ground, and she held a short sword in front of her body to protect herself. SJ swooped down towards them. The orc brought its sword down, and Rach blocked it, holding the flat of her blade and its hilt as it pulled back to strike at her again. The next strike went for her head, and again, she blocked it, but her palm slipped from the blade's handle, and she struggled to move it back up in time as the orc went to strike again. SJ was still in the air when she transformed and, plummeting the final few feet, she crashed into the orc's side.

It was not pretty, but it had the desired effect, sending the orc sprawling and SJ alike onto the ground, the wind knocked out of her. She had taken damage from the impact against the orc's solid form and could not position her claws to strike it. It grunted as it went to stand up and, seeing SJ the closest, swung at her, missing wildly. Following that, the orc tried to attack Rach, but she swiftly defended herself by plunging her short sword into its midriff. It froze with its arms in the air with a look of confusion on its face before it toppled over.

"Thanks," Rach said, gasping and standing up.

SJ climbed to her feet and shrank again, nodding in response. Her breathing was laboured from where she had just winded herself. Taking off, she began controlling her breathing until it returned to normal. She was looking for weak areas to strike or people who needed support. Most of the fights seemed to go favourably for the town, with the orc and hob numbers decreasing every minute.

Glancing back at the leaders, she watched as Bordon hit Jabrey in his face, sending him sprawling, blood and spit flying from his mouth like a boxer. He fell to one knee, and Bordon swung his club towards the mayor. One of his huge paws was lifted to block the blow. It wasn't enough, and the club smashed into his foreleg. The mayor let out a deafening roar of pain, collapsing to the ground, not able to support his body. SJ reacted.

Swooping down, she flew behind Bordon, anger flaring at seeing the mayor injured. Bordon stood twelve feet tall, and landing to attack would be pointless as she could not strike him easily apart from his legs, so she repeated what she had just done for Rach. This time as she transformed, she ensured she held her claws out perfectly before her, falling at an angle and speeding towards his back. Bordon didn't see her coming, as he wasn't expecting anything to attack from the air, and she crashed into his solid form. He only took a slight step from the impact, but her claws dug in deeply, penetrating his muscular form. The impact felt like hitting a cliff face, and she had seriously dazed herself. She now dangled by her claws protruding from his back. Bordon hissed and screamed, beginning to spin and jostle SJ. With breaths coming in gasps and her head reeling from the impact, she found herself in a helpless state. She was flung about like a rag doll until one, then the second claw came free, and she flopped to the ground.

Falling squarely onto her face, she then rolled onto her back, overwhelmed by weakness, her body battered and bruised. Reduced to a mere quarter of her health by the assault and the fall, she found herself unable to move. Lying prone, her senses spun out of control in the face of imminent danger. With her precognition ability spent and lacking the energy or awareness to evade, she could only watch as Bordon's colossal club descended upon her.

"See you soon," Dave's sad words rang in her groggy mind.

Dave watched on in dismay as the club swung down towards SJ. If he had a heart, he knew it would have been breaking at this moment. He was just finishing his weekly report as the scene unfolded before him.

Legionnaire Weekly Status Updates
Legionnaire Number: 25007077
Reporting Administrator: GF87UJ43Lvq18IO
Legionnaire Level: 8
Continent: Axynllrewam
Location: Territory 8-TF4W
Nearest Settlement: Killic

Report Findings:
At the time of the report, Legionnaire 25007077 (known as SJ) had continued to develop and grow her reputation across the starter territory. She has been selflessly committed to protecting the town and its inhabitants. At no point has she sought recompense, only performing what she believed was right. As of this moment, she is being killed.

Thankfully, she will be ready to return to the white room for reassignment because of her unique status of not being under the Terms and Conditions.

I am unsure what the mental impact will be on her during this second reincarnation, so I will monitor her progress carefully.

Personal Recommendations:
I would normally advise that, because of the unique factors surrounding this territory, it would be a suitable location for her to be reborn into again. The issue with this is the fact that she will have lost all her standing within the local populace as part of the process. Because of this I would suggest that she is reincarnated in a differing starter zone to prevent unnecessary confusion for the local populace of Killic, many of whom are her friends.

It was strange for Dave to be writing about a future recommendation for a respawn location. The single life of other Legionnaires who were reincarnated in Amathera never afforded them the unique opportunity that SJ would be presented with. He really had been enjoying his time with SJ in Killic. It was much more fun than any other Legionnaire he had worked with, but he wasn't looking forward to going through the basics again. It seemed to be a time-wasting exercise when she would know what she needed to do.

He didn't know how long the System would take to perform the reincarnation. It could be instant, or might take days or weeks. He might have to get in touch with Maria and talk to her. She had been a little off with him recently. He had been seeing her for a while now, and their relationship had seemed to get quite serious at one point. She had been talking about them creating an AI together, but over the past few weeks, she seemed distracted by the new project she was working on.

Dave didn't know the details precisely. Apparently, it was top secret, and the System had completely restricted her from discussing it. The problem was that whenever he spoke to her now, she always spoke about one particular subject: Tom.

He supposed he was just as bad as he always sent her regular updates about how SJ was doing.

It was strange how his data files seemed to have aligned with SJ, and he was even thinking about speaking to her about Maria and seeking advice. This was definitely the strongest alignment he had ever felt. He was even beginning to suspect that due to how close they were becoming, he was interpreting her neural transmissions and understanding her thoughts before she even spoke to him.

He hit send on his report, sighing deeply, anger filling him as he considered what she must be going through as she died. In all his years he had never felt this way before about another Legionnaire. She really had become his best friend, and he had feelings for her. Not those feelings, but the feelings of someone you cared for and respected deeply. Sadness seeped into every byte of his data, and the club's movement appeared in slow motion as it fell.

"See you soon," he said.

CHAPTER EIGHTEEN

Legionnaire

Darren sat in the office of Master Fretun. The man was nasty, horrible, and manipulative. The problem was that he was by far the best alchemist in Asterfal and had agreed to take Darren on as his apprentice. Darren did not know why he had taken him on. He had been drunk in the Bugbears when he had met Master Fretun and started talking. The Bugbears was one of the less reputable inns in Asterfal. It catered to a particular type of clientele. Darren had stumbled into it one of his first nights there, after he had jumped in a wagon from the last town he'd been staying at. The repetitive quests had got boring, and he needed something new to do after reaching Level 20. He had fallen in love with Asterfal since arriving. He rented a room above the bar and had been spending his coin recently frequenting downstairs too often.

Asterfal had been the closest city, as well as the unnamed capital of the southern region, and was an amazing city compared to the village he had started in. He had spent the first few days walking the streets and discovering more about the place. On the surface, Asterfal was a beautiful city with pristine stone buildings beautifully sculpted. Most of the population had seemed friendly enough, but as with any city, there was always an undertone that he had yet to work out entirely.

He had found the Bugbears by chance, and the lively music and singing had drawn him inside. Since he had been there, there was always something going on, and the clientele varied. He had been in several of the inns since his arrival to get food, and although the Bugbears wasn't the best by far, its atmosphere had attracted him most. They regularly had live music, whether a local bard or sometimes even groups. It was a hive of activity and never a dull moment. The occasional fight broke out, but he had seen that in all the inns he had visited. It was a culture shock from the serenity of the starting village to be amongst such a packed and diverse population again.

He had originally hailed from Bristol, and the Bugbears reminded him of many student bars he frequented. He had been on Amathera now for sixteen months, ever since he had been struck by lighting where he had been performing and woke up in the white room naked. The strange voice that had spoken to him at the time had been robotic and monotone, and thankfully, it rarely spoke. Only infrequently did it say anything related to the stages he had reached as he had developed. He had chosen to become a half elf and was content with how he looked.

After choosing ranger as his class, it took him weeks to learn how to fire his short bow, having never tried archery before. When he levelled, he had invested all his earned points into his Dexterity, making him quite proficient. The elven trainer he had worked under had been an expert, and his skills had improved once he had grasped the basics well enough. He had spent the first few weeks hunting, shooting anything that would allow him to earn experience and grow more. Rabbits, squirrels, hoglings, wolves; you name it, he had hunted it.

The quests he had completed had become very dull, and he had repeated several just to earn the experience needed to level as quickly as possible. The village had been quaint and picturesque. It was set in a forest, which had always reminded Darren of New Forest in the south of England, where his parents had always taken them on holiday. When he had reached Level 10, he moved from the village to one of the close towns, and that is when everything changed. He was no longer considered something special but more a nuisance by many. He had tried to earn a reputation as best as he could and had struggled with many. Outside of the village, everyone seemed to have their own agenda, and to many, he was just another being.

He had also realised that many outside of starter areas didn't trust Legionnaires, and they shunned him. Level 20 had allowed him to pick his second profession. His primary profession had been as a tanner, which aligned with his ranger class, given the number of skins he had collected.

One thing he had struggled with since his arrival was the ability to heal well. His Constitution was still low, and he usually stayed at a distance when fighting if he was able. He rarely used his short sword in combat, and his weapon proficiency in its use was much lower than that of his bow. The problem was that recovering from any injuries took time. Yes, as a Legionnaire, he healed over time, but his Constitution was now impacting him, and he would soon have to sacrifice improving his Dexterity and start adding points to it. This led him to choose his secondary profession, alchemy.

With alchemy as his choice, he would at least be able to make healing potions. He had initially been buying them, but the prices were ridiculous and had become too costly. He had been spending his coin a little too freely since arriving in Asterfal and needed to pick up some work soon, having spent too many nights drinking in the Bugbears.

That was when luck had fallen in his lap. Master Fretun had appeared in the Bugbears one evening and, by chance, ended up sitting at his table. They had spent the evening talking freely over ale, and Master Fretun eventually offered Darren the opportunity to become his apprentice. Darren had jumped at the chance. Master Fretun worked for the chancellor and was highly esteemed in Asterfal. Darren had only been working for the alchemist for a couple of weeks, and this morning, Master Fretun had called him to his office to see him.

"Yes, Master," Darren had said.

"Ah. Darren, good, good. Take a seat."

Now Darren sat in one of the plush, ostentatious chairs by Master Fretun's desk.

"What do you need?" Darren asked.

"I have a task for you. I have some components that must be transferred to one of the starter towns to a Master Rui."

"Could a courier not just deliver them?" Darren asked, frowning.

"No, unfortunately not. They are alchemical and are rather time sensitive and can't be mixed until you arrive at the destination, as the potion loses its strength very quickly. I was hoping you might be up for the task. I have written a set of instructions, and the small chest contains the components. You would be required to mix them the night before you deliver them to Master Rui. Are you up for the challenge?"

Darren's display triggered.

Quest: Alchemical Expression
Master Fretun has asked that you travel to Killic to deliver Master Rui a new alchemical mix to cure his ailments.
Rewards: 4000xp
Would you like to accept the quest? **Yes/No**

"That's a nice reward for a courier quest," Darren said.

"We all know how hard it gets to level as we grow. We will help with quests when we can." Master Fretun smiled. His smile contained no warmth.

Darren accepted the quest. Picking the sheet of paper up from the desk, he read the instructions.

> *On arrival, the components are to be mixed. Because of their nature and sensitivity, you must mix them at midnight. Their unique properties will not react and combine otherwise. Once mixed, the potion must be delivered for consumption within twelve hours.*
>
> *The Santine (yellow liquid) must be mixed with the Plerus (brown liquid).*
>
> *Pour the Santine into the Plerus and stir rapidly for 15 seconds to trigger the reaction.*
>
> *Once triggered, you will see the colour change and may leave it to diffuse fully.*
>
> *Once the liquid clears, you must apply the stopper, which may take several minutes.*

"The instructions are precise?" Darren said.

"Yes. This is something very new that we have been working on recently. It has taken some of the best alchemists in Asterfal to confirm the process, allowing it to succeed."

"Why does the potion have such a restricted timescale on it?"

"Because of its mixture requirements, its consumption requirements are also limited. After it is mixed, if it is to work, it must be consumed within twelve hours. I have already forewarned Master Rui that someone will bring the delivery, so he expects it five days from now. The journey to Killic will take you four days by wagon. On arrival, as I say, you are booked into the Hogling Arms. You are to mix the contents at midnight and then deliver them the morning of the fifth day."

"It sounds easy enough. I am not sure why it needs to be me. I had been hoping to reach Level 3 in alchemy in the next few days, and this will knock me back, but I won't turn down the easy experience."

Since he had reached Level 20, his experience needs had increased substantially, and the thought of 4000xp for doing nothing was too good an option to refuse.

"You will have plenty of time to catch up on your alchemical studies on your return, and Master Rui is a dear old friend of mine." Master Fretun smiled again.

"No problem, Master. I will head off in the morning. You said he is expecting my arrival?"

"Not yours specifically, but I promised him he would receive it in five days. He has been very ill recently, and this will hopefully assist with his return to full health." Master Fretun picked up a small pouch from his desk drawer and handed it over to Darren. "For expenses."

Darren dropped it into his inventory before replying. "Thanks, I will get going then." He stood, collected the chest into his inventory, and placed the instructions in his pocket.

"Good luck and I will see you on your return," Master Fretun said as he left his office.

Darren smiled to himself as he headed out of the Asterfal council chambers. He had counted the contents of the pouch as he left, and it contained fifteen silver. That was a vast sum to pay expenses, but he wasn't complaining. Nine days away all expenses paid—he really had landed on his feet this time. He headed back to the Bugbears to grab his gear before setting off.

CHAPTER NINETEEN

Second Chance

The three-way battle continued, with the orcs, hobgoblins, and town guard fighting in a violent and frenzied mêlée. Only the guards had any magic users, and their spells continued to light up the battlefield with their colourful displays. SJ had tried to attack Bordon, and although the attack was successful, the aftermath was less than desired.

Lying in her battered state, she was amazed by how fast her mind worked as the club came hurtling down at her. She reflected on what she had achieved during this first outing to Amathera. The friends she had made, the progress, the challenges she had overcome. It had been a wonderful experience, and she only hoped her next would be the same. Closing her eyes, she waited for the end.

The roar that erupted across the battlefield was ear-splitting as the mayor flung his body forward, even with the pain he must have felt from Bordon's blows. His colossal head smashed into the ogre at the last moment, forcing Bordon's strike wide of its target. Even the faintest graze of the club as it thudded into the ground at her side reduced her health further, leaving her with only three hit points and a health icon on her display flashing wildly. But it was nothing compared to what it would have done if the club had struck her fully. The ogre roared with a ferocity that portrayed his annoyance at his blow being deflected and turned on the mayor, hammering his club onto his exposed side. The mayor lay prone now, not moving, only the shallow rise and fall of his chest showing life remained.

SJ could no longer see what was happening. Her mind was so foggy from crashing into Bordon from her aerial assault.

"MOVE," Dave shouted. "GET UP NOW, YOU USELESS PIECE OF KOBOLD DUNG."

Dave's words screamed inside her mind. Slowly, with uncertainty, SJ rolled onto her hands and knees and crawled away. A hand grabbed her under her arm, drawing her to her feet. Stumbling, she saw Sven, the paladin who had healed her and the wolves. His white hair and beard were covered with red stains. She felt a wash of energy rush into her body and saw a bright flash as his healing embraced her.

SJ's health increased rapidly, and the healing stopped when she reached about three-quarters of her maximum. "Come on, move away now," Sven said, urging her to get a distance from the battling monsters.

"Thank you." SJ coughed, trying to control her breathing. She shrank to her miniature size and took off. The mayor lay on his side now, injured and helpless. Jabrey was continuing his struggle against Bordon. In his enraged state, the ogre seemed unstoppable.

Jabrey backed away, avoiding the ogre's powerful and wild swings. A hobgoblin who had been at odds with a guard stepped too close as Bordon swung, and he caught it, sending it sailing through the air like a batter hitting a baseball.

The movement of Jabrey drawing Bordon away allowed Sven to reach the mayor. With both hands on him, a brilliant light, brighter than any she had seen, erupted from his hands. His body shuddered violently as the energy poured through him. The mayor stood again. Although in a weakened state, there was still hope. As the pulse of light faded, Sven collapsed to his knees. Sven was spent, and SJ swooped down as she grew, this time supporting him as she helped him away from the battle.

"You saved the mayor," SJ said as she helped him.

"Thank you. That took everything I had left," Sven panted.

The numbers decreased as more hobs and orcs fell to the guard or each other. SJ glanced around, moving from the immediate combat until she allowed Sven to drop to the ground. Sitting, he called a blue potion from his inventory and drank.

"It will take me a while to recover," he said, smiling at her. "Don't do anything else stupid. I saw what you did to Bordon." He laughed weakly.

SJ didn't respond again, shrinking and taking off. Surveying the continuing battle, she identified targets and again continued her dive-bombing attacks, making sure that her feet were on the ground before reaching full size, not wanting to repeat her two flawed aerial assaults.

A sniff resounded in her mind. "I honestly thought you were gone. The way the mayor sacrificed his own safety was amazing. I have never seen an Amatherean do that for a Legionnaire before."

"He was amazing," SJ said.

She currently hovered above the field again. The number of active fighters was dwindling because of injury, death, or exhaustion taking over. The fight had been all-consuming of both time and energy.

Turning, SJ looked at Bordon again. Jabrey and the mayor, despite their injuries, continued to fight with determination. They were working together, making the ogre switch from one to the next as they closed in on him, clawing, snapping, or slashing with blades. Bordon's health drained as he continued to swing his massive club in response. The ogre's skin colour had changed back to its original grey, losing the red hue it had taken. The rage skill must have faded. Standing on his hind legs, the mayor threw himself at the ogre's back. His jaws clamped onto the top of his shoulder, tearing into his flesh.

Bordon let out a scream of agony, reaching his hand up, trying to paw the mayor's huge maw from his throat. It was in vain, though, as the mayor was not letting go. Bordon fell to his knees, and as he did, Jabrey attacked, thrusting both his blades deep into the ogre's chest. Bordon's massive form fell forward, crashing to the broken and bloodied ground. The mayor stood over his dead body and roared in victory. He turned to look at Jabrey, who now leaned on his knee, gasping.

The remaining hobgoblins who witnessed their leader fall began to run, both the orcs and guards cutting them down as they did. Several broke from the field and began heading to the west. The orcs and guards continued to fight until Jabrey's cry brought gradual silence.

"STOP," he called.

"That has to be one of the most epic battles I have witnessed," Dave said.

SJ didn't reply as she landed near the mayor, who was talking to Jabrey.

"If you leave now and promise not to return, I will allow your remaining forces to go freely. If you ever return here or take up arms near the town again, you will break this oath."

SJ had missed part of the conversation as it concluded on her arrival. As SJ watched, the mayor transformed into his large human form. He was only a little shorter than Jabrey and walked forward, offering his hand. Jabrey looked at him before they grasped each other's forearms.

"I swear by the gods this oath will not be broken," Jabrey uttered.

Their giant forms were bathed in a blue light.

"An Oath of Agreement. I haven't witnessed one of those for a very long time," Dave said.

"What does it mean?" SJ whispered.

"Jabrey has agreed to the mayor's terms and will leave the valley. His forces are reduced by too many, and he knows he can't beat the guard with what he has remaining."

SJ could see only forty orcs still standing. Many were wounded, but if the battle had continued, with the size of the remaining guard force still being nearer a hundred, they would not have survived. Captain Broadaxe strode to the pair, his great axe casually resting on his shoulder.

"Jabrey," the dwarf said as he stopped beside the mayor.

"Ballentine." The orc nodded at him respectfully. "I had heard rumours you were here, but now I see it is true. I can see what this town may have."

SJ had never known Captain Broadaxe's first name before now.

"Ha. It has been a long time since we last met," Ballentine said.

"You know each other?" the mayor asked, a little surprised.

"We fought alongside each other once during the gnoll rising," Ballentine replied.

"I see," the mayor replied. "I will give you time to tend to your wounded and bury your dead as you wish, but I expect you to leave the valley within the week."

"It will not take long to confirm our fallen," Jabrey replied.

"Then, good. Let us not get in each other's way. I will remove our injured and dead and leave a small force to observe," the mayor said.

"Understood," Jabrey replied. He turned to a large orc standing nearby and spoke to him in a guttural language SJ had never heard. The orc shouted orders to the remaining orcs, and they all placed their weapons away and began the thankless and painful task of working through those on the field. Jurgen shouted to the guard to do the same.

SJ had never witnessed a true battle before. At close hand, many took out healing potions, handing them around, while the clerics, including Lythonian, moved across the field, drinking their blue mana potions and healing those injured. SJ could see Lythonian bend down next to a member of the guard who she had seen in town frequently. Lythonian rolled his hand over his eyes. Unfortunately, some would not be returning to the town.

Jabrey moved off and talked to a berserker orc, and the mayor turned and addressed SJ.

"Without your support today, the town would again have lost many," he said.

"I only did what I could to help," SJ said, feeling she didn't deserve praise. She had fought no braver than others in the town.

"You killed the mage. We would not have taken Bordon if that mage had still been alive when we arrived. Even with Jabrey's help."

"I only did what I thought best to do."

"And again, it has meaning. You are a very strange Legionnaire, SJ. Never have I met one who sacrifices themself for those of Amathera as willingly as you do."

"I am sure many have. Maybe you just haven't met them."

"Nope. Never to the degree you have, and I think I know why," Dave chirped in her ear. "You are selfless because you care. You have made friends and have people you care about, whether you see it or not. Your interactions and commitment to others, such as Cristy, are unheard of within Legionnaires."

SJ didn't respond to Dave and stood a little dumbfounded. She had considered none of Dave's comments. She was just doing what she had always done in her life, helping and supporting those around her when she could.

"Maybe they have. I have yet to meet one, though," the mayor said.

He looked across the field at the carnage the battle had left behind.

"Lorna?" he called.

"Yes, Mayor?" Lorna replied.

"Send scouts after the escaped hobs. I want to make sure they leave the valley completely. If we find signs of them stopping in the valley, we will send a patrol after them."

"Yes, Mayor," she said as she moved off and began speaking to a few guards.

SJ's display triggered.

Congratulations! Your selfless acts to support the town of Killic have increased your reputation to Revered.

SJ stood open-mouthed, shock registered on her face. She had just jumped three levels of reputation in one go.

"Wow," Dave chirped.

The mayor turned away to talk to Ballentine, and SJ searched for Gary. She eventually found him tending to another orc, who had a nasty-looking gash across his abdomen.

"I am sure one of them will heal you, eventually. Once they have finished tending to ours," Gary said.

"I hope so," the orc replied.

"Gary," SJ called as she neared.

"SJ," he said, grinning.

"Thank you for saving me," SJ said.

"Saving you. I am sure you would have gotten the upper hand eventually," he replied.

"I am not so sure," she said. Looking at the orc on the ground, she noticed the garb and red stripes of Jabrey's clan.

"Oh. SJ, meet my elder brother Gruik," Gary said.

"Oh," SJ said.

"Gruik, this is SJ, our local fae saviour," Gary said.

"I am no saviour," she retorted.

"You have just received revered status with the town. That doesn't happen without reason."

"You know that?" Confusion etched her face.

"We all receive updates when members' statuses change. How do you think traders adjust prices without knowing people's status?"

This comment threw SJ. "So, everyone knows I am revered with the town now?"

"Yes. All those who have taken the oath."

"What oath?"

"As you saw between Jabrey and the mayor, all those who work for the town have taken an oath to be citizens. We are held to it unless we leave the territory. If you do, then it resets. Many have done so over the years, then returned and never taken it again, but many still do and have. It is not mandatory but does have perks with discounts."

This was another additional consideration, and SJ was not in the mood to fully understand it.

"There is so much I don't know." SJ shook her head.

"There is still a lot to learn," Dave agreed. "You will over time. What you have done in this town since you joined is beyond any starter town's expectations, and what is happening here is not normal, as we have discussed before. Oaths and allegiances are something that would not normally be considered at your level, and it would normally be unlikely that you would ever even know about them or need to know about them. I have never known Legionnaires to take oaths unless to a guild charter, as part of their membership process, and that is only once you reach Level 20."

SJ looked down at Gary's brother. "I hope they heal you soon," she said as she turned to walk away. She would have to question Gary about his brother and his previous life, but she needed some space for now. All this was a little much for her now that her adrenaline had withdrawn. Shrinking, she took off and flew over the village to the far side of the river. She needed some time to think.

Walking through the tall grasses, breathing deeply, SJ tried to calm her mind, which was still racing from the battle. She could hear the occasional cry or call for help as another wounded person was discovered.

"Are you okay?" Dave asked.

"I'm not sure. I've never witnessed anything like that before and did not expect ever to be involved in such a battle. The raid on the town was nothing compared to the violence today."

"It is not something I would expect you to witness at such a low level, but what you have achieved will go into the AI archives."

"What?"

"When I file my report."

"Your report?"

"Yes. I have said before that we must feed back to the System. There is a weekly report that I must submit. Yours have been interesting to write and submit so far. Much better than many boring and mundane ones I have had in the past."

"We seriously need to talk much more about Amathera at some point."

"Yes. Although most of the bits are not relevant until you progress further."

SJ sat heavily in the grass.

"I think you need to go through your notifications," Dave said.

SJ sighed. She had been ignoring anything that flashed on her display, and when she looked, she saw there were many. As she read through them, her excitement grew.

Quest: Vengeance—Complete
You have sought revenge against the evil surrounding Killic.
Kill Bordon the Brandisher: 1000 xp—Complete
Kill Iratu the Mad: 700 xp—Complete
Prevent any further hobgoblin raids on Killic.
Rewards: 1500xp, reputation with Killic. Usual level kill experience awards apply—Complete

---

Rewards: 2500xp + 50% = 3750xp awarded

Combined xp for assisting with multiple targets: 640xp awarded

SJ was astonished. She had earned 4390xp in total.

Congratulations on reaching Level 9
You have been awarded the following:
5 hit points
5 mana points
+1 Dexterity
+2 free points to distribute as you wish

Congratulations! You have reached Clawed Avenger Level 2, earned through the rigours of combat.

Congratulations on reaching Level 10
You have been awarded the following:
5 hit points
5 mana points
+1 Dexterity
+2 free points to distribute as you wish

On reaching Level 10, you also have one skill point to distribute.

Congratulations, navigation has been unlocked.

Upon reaching Level 10, you achieved your first growth target in Amathera.
You may select one of the following rewards:
N/A
N/A
N/A

Congratulations on reaching Level 11
You have been awarded the following:
5 hit points
5 mana points
+1 Dexterity
+2 free points to distribute as you wish

On reaching Level 11, you also have one skill point to distribute.

"Level 11!" SJ exclaimed.

CHAPTER TWENTY

Sandboxes and Sandcastles

I did not realise that the clawed avenger could level through combat?" SJ said, surprised.

"Yes. All skills can improve with time, as does your kata with training. You have used your claws very efficiently today with your hit-and-run tactics," Dave said.

"I don't know what this N/A part is and why I haven't been given anything for reaching Level 10."

"I do not know. In the beginning, there is no information pertaining to what it means, as it's not usually offered."

"Could you raise a ticket again?"

"Give me a few minutes. I can't guarantee response times. You know how long it took them last time."

SJ had six stat points and two skill points she could allocate. Opening her character sheet, she decided on what to increase. Her Dexterity naturally increased with her levels. She added two to Constitution and Charisma and then one each to Wisdom and Intelligence. The decisions were based on her understanding of the skills she had been offered, what the main attribute bonuses aligned to, and that the counter for some of her skills was Wisdom and Intelligence. Thinking logically, she didn't want to fall foul of someone with her own skill base.

Legionnaire 25007077			
Name:	SJ	↻ Level: 11	
Age:	27	**Experience:**	322 of 3000
Race:	Fae	**Hit Points:**	100 of 100 (55 * 1.81)
Class:	Assassin	**Mana Points:**	67 of 67 (55 * 1.22)
Alignment:	Neutral Good	**Armour Class:**	21 (10)(11)

Attributes	
Strength:	10
Dexterity:	21
Intelligence:	11

Wisdom:	11
Constitution:	16
Charisma:	13

Skills	
Racial:	
Night Vision—you have improved vision in poor light conditions.	
Flight—when in miniature fae form, you can learn to fly. Flying is not available in humanoid form.	
Shapeshift—you have the ability to switch between fae forms.	
Class:	
Martial Arts:	Kata Level 6, Clawed Avenger Level 3
Subterfuge:	Identification Level 7 (98 of 200 to Level 8), Shroud Level 2
Profession:	Tailor Level 3
Symbiosis:	
Dragon Sense—your senses (touch, hearing, smell, and sight) are heightened.	
Precognition—foreknowledge due to increased perception will allow you to evade a killing blow. (24-hour cool-down)	
Divine Lightning—your blood is combined with that of a blue dragon, increasing healing speed while out of combat.	
Malware:	Waiver (Sandboxed)
Inventory:	10 slots (10 special)
Followers:	3

"Excellent choices. I am pleasantly surprised," Dave said sarcastically.

Rolling her eyes at his comment, SJ checked out her damage ratings. With her increased Dexterity and skill progression in her clawed avenger to Level 3, she did an additional 26 damage per strike above the base weapon damage, gaining +1 for each Dexterity above 10 and +15 for the clawed avenger. The significant damage increase would help with any surprise attacks she performed.

Smiling broadly, SJ lay back in the grasses for a few minutes, letting herself digest the sudden growth.

"Now I am above Level 10. I guess I'll need to move on soon," SJ said.

"Erm. There may be a slight problem," Dave said shyly.

"What problem?" SJ asked, frowning, concerned at his reply.

"I'm not sure yet, but the sandbox the System uses is a little strange in handling the growth changes. The more I've dug into it, the more I realise that you were placed here because the area was already being sandboxed as a precautionary measure."

"What do you mean? The System went against its promise of no repercussions, then?"

"No, it hasn't, that's the thing. It was already trialling it, but I believe it deliberately placed you here so you aren't sandboxed. You have just been placed in the sandbox. Which may be in your favour or against. Normally, once you reach Level 10, you just jump in a wagon and move to the next territory or the nearest larger town or city, and hey presto, carry on questing and growing. The problem is with what the System seems to have activated. This is not necessary."

"Not necessary, why? Have I been trapped here?"

"No. It's even stranger than that. Open your map feature."

SJ did as Dave said, and her vision was flooded with a new screen. Most of it was blacked out, which she assumed was the fog of war. Near the bottom left of the page was a tiny area with colour. Focusing on it, she could zoom in. As she did, she saw more detail, with marked territory borders in a faint outline and broad open areas, which she guessed must be the seas or oceans that separated the continents. They contained respective numbers, which she believed were level-based for gaining experience.

As she zoomed in further, she eventually reached where she could read *Killic*.

"So, what am I looking for?" SJ asked.

"Can you see the territory boundary?"

"Yes. It stretches quite far by its looks."

"As soon as you reached Level 10, it adjusted."

"What do you mean *adjusted*?"

"The territory has expanded to accommodate the surrounding territories, which were basically suitable for Level 10–20 Legionnaires and Amathereans."

"That's good, then, isn't it?"

"It is . . . yes and no. This means that borders gradually increase as you gain levels. I don't think this has anything to do with you being an anomaly. It is more about what the System was testing. I can't be certain, but I think it had hoped either Malcolm or Darjey would reach Level 10 to trigger it previously."

"So, why is it possibly not a good thing, then?"

"You have already seen that some beings in the area are at much higher levels than I told you to expect."

"Yes."

"Well, it has now increased the level variance even further. You can't see it on your map, but the territory borders are now open to all beings up to and including Level 40."

"But Bob came here at Level 88."

"Bob is not classed as a normal being. He also had no intention of doing anything; I am pretty sure if he had tried to cause problems, the System would have prevented it. When I talk about beings, I'm talking about those that may be problematic to the territory or the area. We had already seen Jabrey come from a 20–30 area to take the village. This means that others can do the same all the way up to Level 40. It increases the chance of higher-level monsters, creatures, or beings entering the area. The territory to the left contains some violent races. There are savage gnoll tribes in the desert region further south. wyverns, ogre clans, draconian hoards, et cetera. With this area now being opened to many, they may start to come and investigate."

"The System is allowing everything to become amalgamated, then?"

"It looks like it may do that. That means we may end up with all territories open and no restrictions. Many tribes or groups may wish to come to a region, and a town like Killic becomes a nice prize for some, particularly now that mithril has been identified in the region. The whole resource balance has been adjusted as well."

"I am at a loss. Can you not see what the System has planned as an administrator?"

"No. Since the emergency patch, I have lost the same access since my coding has been adjusted. I am still trying to break through the layering they added. Now I cannot interrogate the details, and I keep getting 500 errors."

"500 errors? What are those?"

"That is the issue. Nobody knows what they are. I have been speaking to other AIs that have lost their Legionnaires since, and they have been experiencing the same. There are several starter towns on this continent alone, and they are all apparently undergoing the same phased transition."

"Why would higher levels come here, though? It's not as if they can level from the surroundings."

"Imagine being restricted to never being able to leave an area, or only ever increasing in difficulty through territory progression, and then suddenly the floodgates are opened. Some territories fight for survival against other tribes or creatures daily. Suddenly having the freedom to move and settle in a new territory like here? There is the potential that a weaker clan from a higher region may move here to escape their usual issues, which may not be good for the town. Killic and the surrounding area would normally be untouched or inaccessible to them."

"I thought you said that Amathereans could level normally. Can't they just progress as needed?"

"They can, but many, like Lorna, Zej, Gary, or Lythonian, for example, would have originally been from nearby higher-level territories and moved here for safety or peace. As I say, some other territories are not as pleasant or organised as here. It is also much more dangerous and difficult for Amathereans to level as they don't get the same bonuses Legionnaires do. Their growth is massively restricted, like their restricted healing and regeneration ability; otherwise in time everything would need to be a Level 100-plus territory."

"That means the town is at threat, then, and maybe even more so than before?" SJ asked with concern.

"Potentially. I don't think many will come, but there is a chance they will over time. Then, once one arrives, others are likely to follow. I think this is what happened with Bordon and Jabrey. I think Bordon came here to find an easier home to live in, and Jabrey followed, seeing the benefits. Anything or anyone can normally cross territory boundaries, but the System normally prevents actions from being performed by higher-level beings. Otherwise, a Level 100 could enter the lower territories and slaughter everyone."

"I need to speak to the mayor and let him know."

"I am sure he will work it out for himself once he looks at the details."

"I'll speak to him."

The revelations from Dave were concerning. SJ was torn—rather than supporting Killic, she may have just painted a target on its back.

"I am going to find the mayor," SJ said resolutely.

SJ found him quickly, but he was too busy supporting and directing the clean-up operation to speak. It took several hours for the battle scene to be cleared of the dead hobgoblins, who were laid on a pyre before the mage set them alight. The twelve who had fallen from the town were to be taken back, and stretchers were made to carry them home. The fact that so few had been lost in the battle was a testament to the healers and the wonders they did. SJ found Sven and thanked him again for saving her. He looked dishevelled and still drained from the spell he had cast to save the mayor.

By the time the procession returned to town, it was late afternoon. The guard force that had remained behind was awaiting their return, and calls erupted as they were seen coming from the forest. The townsfolk lined the streets, and several ran out onto the field to meet their loved ones or, sometimes, the deceased. It was a mixed emotional journey for all those involved.

They had stopped before entering the town's main road, and the mayor addressed the crowd, making them aware of what had occurred and that the hobs were no longer a threat, with the death of Bordon and his tribe being ousted from the village. The orcs were discussed, but relief swept the gathering with the confirmation of the oath that Jabrey, their leader, had taken. SJ was still unaware, but oaths seemed to hold significant power.

The mayor wanted SJ to come to the barracks and meet with the council immediately, as they would gather to discuss the next steps, but she kindly refused. She was exhausted and needed to eat, bathe, and sleep. Lorna had remained at the village with a group of ten to watch the orcs. Jabrey had agreed that he would bury the orcs away from the village as they didn't believe in cremation.

Opening the inn door, SJ was met with the faces of those she had got to know and recognise, even if not as friends, at least as acquaintances. Fhyliss saw her and came running over, flinging her arms around her. Her four-foot-tall frame looked more like that of a child.

"Thank you," Fhyliss said.

SJ just looked down wearily, not having the energy to reply.

Fhyliss stepped away and, grabbing her hand, dragged her over to a chair by the bar. SJ didn't resist, and she sat down heavily.

"Food. You need food. Floretta, please get SJ the best meal you can—energy boosting, preferably. She looks terrible," Fhyliss yelled into the kitchen.

"Will do," Floretta replied.

Kerys noticed SJ as she returned from the cellar with Bert and came straight over to her. The inn's troll bouncer always made an impressive sight.

"SJ, are you okay? You look terrible," Kerys said.

"Thanks," SJ said, laughing.

"Sorry. I just mean you look exhausted, and your face looks drawn."

"The aftermath of the battle is a little draining, that's all," SJ smiled weakly.

"I have something that may help. Wait here," Kerys said as she disappeared behind the bar back down to the cellar. A few minutes later, she returned carrying a bottle and a glass.

"Here," she said, removing a cork with a loud pop and pouring a fizzy yellow liquid into the glass.

"I really don't want any alcohol," SJ protested as she handed it to her.

"It isn't alcohol," Kerys said, smiling.

SJ took the glass, which smelt of lavender and honey infused together.

"Drink it," Kerys urged her.

SJ raised the glass and sipped the liquid. It tasted sweet, like honey, but the bitterness of lemon hit her taste-buds.

"Gahh, what is this?" SJ asked, pulling her face at the taste.

"Something special," Kerys chuckled. "Drink up."

SJ knocked back the rest of the small glass, scrunching her nose at the bitter aftertaste it left. It was nothing like its initial smell or taste. As she sat there, she could feel the liquid travel into her stomach, and it was the strangest sensation in the world. It felt as though every inch of her insides was being infused. Her muscles tingled, and her skin felt alive, as though something was crawling all over. She couldn't figure out whether it was a pleasant sensation. When it reached her head, it felt as though her hair was standing on end, and she lifted her hand to check it wasn't.

As the sensations subsided, her body felt alive, the weariness in her muscles had gone, the tiredness from her mind cleared, and her eyes were wide as though she had just awoken from the best night's sleep ever, feeling rested and refreshed.

"What was that?" SJ said in amazement.

"It's rejuvinatus. It's a very old and secret recipe that has been passed down between the brewers in my family for generations. How do you think Fhyliss and I keep this place running all day and night between the two of us?" she said, laughing.

Her laugh was light-hearted and bright, making SJ smile warmly. The weariness of battle seemed to have been pushed back from the front of her mind, and she felt as though she could fight again at a moment's notice.

"That is amazing," SJ said.

"If you ever need a little pick-me-up, let me know. I rarely share it, but with your status change, I believe you deserve some." Kerys smiled fondly at her.

SJ had forgotten about her revered status and wondered if that was why so many had smiled at her when she walked back through the town. It was strange to consider the way the reputational gains worked. Floretta came from the kitchen area carrying a large tray of food and placed it down on the table in front of SJ. It was a full spread of cut meats, salad, and thick sliced bread with butter. Her mouth watered at the sight.

"Thank you, Floretta. This looks lovely," SJ said.

"No. Thank you for what you did today," she said, smiling. It was still strange to see skeletons smile.

SJ spent the next thirty minutes giving a rendition of the battle to Fhyliss and Kerys, who both oohed and ahed. Fhyliss asked many questions, and Kerys eventually ushered her off, telling her to let SJ rest now. Kerys told SJ that although the brew revitalised you, she still needed to rest; otherwise, the effects would eventually reverse if you relied on it too much.

SJ eventually headed upstairs to her room. On entering, she was amazed to find that her bath had been drawn, and a giant bunch of freshly picked flowers sat on the table. A small card with a painting of the waterfall from the mountain was resting against it. Turning it over, there was one word: *Thanks.*

SJ knew it was from Fhyliss as she had seen a similar painting in her room when she had been given the pencil and notebook. SJ felt refreshed but a nice tired, not the drained she had felt. She undressed and climbed into the bath. The scent of the oils and the warmth of the bath made her feel sleepy. She rested her head on the rear of the large tub and closed her eyes. It had been an unusual day.

CHAPTER TWENTY-ONE

Future Remembrance

Wake up, lazy," Dave said.

"What? Do I have to?" SJ groaned, rolling over in her bed. The festivities of the night before had a resounding effect inside her head.

"Yes. We have things to do and people to see, and you must sew some more gloves. You aren't even at Level 5 tailoring yet and still need to open your dress starter bonuses. You really are being lazy, you know," Dave said.

"Lazy! I was in a huge battle yesterday, got kept up until all hours this morning, and now you want me up and sewing, never mind everything else you just mentioned."

"There we go—you're awake now, aren't you?" Dave said happily. "May as well get up now, and wow, do you snore badly after you drink?"

"I don't!" SJ said.

"And you know because . . . ? No one has ever mentioned it to you before now?"

"No, never."

"Maybe they didn't want to hurt your feelings. You nearly woke the whole town up at one point."

By this point, SJ was sitting upright in bed, her head throbbing, and she did not want to argue with Dave so early. Grumpily, she climbed from the bed and walked through to wash her face and clean her teeth. Her mouth felt terrible this morning. She needed to speak to Zej when she saw him next because one of the last things she could remember was drinking some of his dwarven brandy.

"My head," she moaned.

"You did put it away last night," Dave said. "It's quite impressive, really. Well, until you fell asleep in your chair and Bert carried you back upstairs to your room."

SJ realised she was fully clothed still. After having her bath and a sleep, she woke up early in the evening and went down to the bar, where the crowds had already gathered, as they had after the raid, and the feast had begun. It had been an emotional evening. The drinks had begun, and the music had started. There was one thing the town knew how to do well: celebrate the lives of those who were lost. The funerals for the dead were going to be this afternoon, and she had promised she would be in attendance, but before then, she had things to do.

Feeling a little more refreshed, she made her way downstairs. The tables were all back to normal after the previous evening. SJ smiled at Kerys and then frowned deeply. As SJ walked to the bar, Kerys shook her head.

"Here," she said, placing a small glass of yellow liquid on the bar. "You look like you need it again." She tutted and turned to grab the coffee pot.

SJ downed the liquid, again pulling her face, but within moments, the throbbing disappeared and she felt right as rain. "Thanks," SJ said sheepishly. "I hope I didn't cause a scene last night. I drank a little too much."

"No," Kerys said, laughing. "Once you fell asleep in your chair, I asked Bert to carry you upstairs. Apparently, you were very polite to him, saying how grateful you were, and he was your knight in shining armour."

SJ's cheeks flushed in embarrassment. "Did I!" she exclaimed.

"Ha. Bert has dealt with much more than being given a compliment before. I think you made his night."

"Urgh. Sorry."

Kerys placed a large mug of coffee on the bar, and SJ picked it up, savouring the smell.

"Oh. I remember the mayor asked me to remind you that the meeting is at ten today at the barracks, and he asked for you to be there."

"Okay. Thanks." SJ checked her display. It was only eight thirty, so she had time. "I will grab breakfast, please, if that's okay."

"Sure," Kerys said as she walked to the kitchen.

After eating, SJ headed over to the meadow. She hadn't been in a few days and enjoyed spending some time doing her katas before walking over to the barracks. As she walked through the town, most people passed pleasantries with her, and compared to the initial arrival when she had walked through unnoticed, everyone now seemed to smile politely or nod their heads in recognition.

At the barracks, she was ushered upstairs by the usual old orc at the desk. The mayor was sitting in his office, and she walked through to see him.

"Morning, Mayor," she said.

"I really wish you would call me Zigferd. You don't work for the town," he replied, smiling at her.

"Zigferd. How are you this morning?" she asked.

"I will be happier when today is over and we properly say goodbye to our friends. How's your head?"

SJ blushed. "Fine, thanks. Kerys fixed me up with something to help."

"Ahhh. Yes. I have had some of that myself before. It was wonderful stuff. I have told her she should sell it, but she won't."

"I bet she would make a lot of money if she did. Drink until you drop, then top up and go again. I can't believe how well it makes you feel."

"Ha," Zigferd chuckled. "Anyway, we need to talk. You mentioned yesterday that you had things to discuss."

"Yes, I do," SJ said, and she relayed the details she was now aware of from her map opening. Zigferd listened intently and looked at his own maps and those he had drawn, marking out the new border areas.

"This is concerning," Zigferd said.

"I know, and I think I may have triggered it."

"You aren't the System. We all live under its remit. If it is changing things, then we must adapt."

"How? Many in the town are at low levels."

"Yes, but now they can level higher with the open borders. We can train and increase beyond our previous limits and still have our town as our central point without moving territories to progress. I am only the level I am because I moved here from other territories and had given up the chase on levelling further. If the System changes the rules, then we must adjust. Amathera is not an easy land for many to live in."

"I have heard that, and I thought many didn't want to level beyond the territory boundaries."

"Some won't, but with the expansion of the borders, many will have little choice. Some will pursue basic progression without forcing themselves to level through training as the level cap has risen. Others will take the opportunity that is presented."

"How will you go about it?"

"I will add it to the agenda for the meeting today."

As the mayor finished speaking, an announcement from the mages filled the building.

"TODAY'S SERVICE WILL BE HELD OUTSIDE IN THE CHURCH'S GROUNDS TO SAY GOODBYE TO OUR FALLEN HEROES AT FOURTEEN HUNDRED HOURS. PLEASE BE PROMPT."

SJ sat silently after the message finished. The fact that they would bury twelve of the town today was a horrendous thought.

"I am so sorry for the town's losses," she eventually said.

"You have nothing to be sorry for. The conflict had been happening for months. If anything, you emphasised dealing with it once and for all. That alone will hopefully save many future lives."

"It doesn't feel like it. It only feels as though things have got worse since I arrived."

"No. They have improved. Let me explain. You were present in the meeting when I mentioned the town's finances and its ability to sustain its continuing growth. If you had not discovered the potential mithril, I'm not sure what we were going to do. We rarely receive Legionnaires, and considering what you have described, I am not surprised, as I think the System is only allowing a few to experience the changes."

SJ was amazed at the mayor's understanding of the System.

"Orik still won't believe that vein is really mithril until he sees it, stubborn old goat that he is. But I believe it. It'll provide the income to allow us to expand and to improve the current living conditions for some of the town's members. I am sure you have noticed that not everywhere is as well off as other areas. We have tried our best to provide for all, but it has been challenging."

The information the mayor shared eased SJ's mind slightly, but she still felt foreboding uncertainty about the changes.

"The priority after today will be to confirm the mine," Zigferd continued. "Then we can start to plan and implement the next steps. It will take time, but I plan to expand our borders to the village in the valley. That would mean it would become our first line of defence against intruders entering the area. It'll also allow us to use the natural defences of the valley wall. We wish we had done this sooner, but no one ever expected Bordon to arrive in the village, and by the time he did, it was too late. The main benefit will be ensuring better defences to our west, as some territories in that direction are quite severe. The northern route running through the crags to Asterfal is a much calmer area, and I wouldn't expect many issues, but again, I think I will consider pushing out to the crags to provide a border guard.

"Then, once the village and the crags are fully secured, we can expand within those areas, develop new buildings, and even build a mine and bring in outside facilities to allow for growth. The mine will make money, but several invest in mining operations, especially within the dwarven factions. This would be long-term, though, and not something that would be done until everything was established. We would not want to advertise the mine until we have protective measures."

The considerations that the mayor had already taken impressed SJ. She had never been one for town building in games, preferring the crafting side and personal growth instead.

"It sounds like you have everything worked out already."

"Not everything, and there will be a lot of hurdles along the way. Expanding the town's borders will take time because of the requirements. Financially, we will be tied until we can start to sell the mithril."

"Could I not help with that?"

"How would you be able to help?" Zigferd asked, tilting his head.

"If you didn't want to have the town's name associated with the mithril, I could trade on the town's behalf. I am sure I am likely to draw less attention as a Legionnaire, no?"

"Perhaps. But anyone of our level suddenly starting to sell or trade in mithril would cause questions whatever happens. The lowest-level territories mithril is normally found in are above Level 50."

"I am sure something can be planned. Also, when you have time, I wanted to speak to you about the potential percentage earnings from the mine."

"Of course, but we now must go upstairs to the meeting. If you will accompany me," Zigferd said, standing.

SJ stood and followed the mayor upstairs to the council meeting chamber. The same representatives were there, along with a few SJ had not seen before. One was a female dwarf who wore a leather apron. She looked out of place compared to the others who sat in what SJ would deem smart attire.

SJ stood next to the dwarf. "Hi," she said, smiling.

"Hello. You are the one who has had me dragged from the mine?" she said.

"Oh. You must be Shelly. Hi. I am SJ."

SJ held out her hand, and Shelly took it. Her hand was like a vice as she smiled at her.

SJ flexed her hand on letting go to return its feeling.

"I still don't know why I am here," Shelly said. "I was told Orik wanted me to be present. We were supposed to start a new tunnel today, which will be delayed now."

"Hopefully, you will be pleasantly surprised," SJ said.

As the mayor took his place at the top of the table, the conversations died off until they all turned to listen to him.

"Thank you all for coming today. We don't have long as we all still require to be ready for this afternoon's farewell to our fallen."

Several around the table nodded, and one of the elven representatives wiped a tear from his eye.

"I have a few issues to address and then some new information to cover, which was not on the agenda. First, I would like to thank SJ for what she has done for the town since her arrival."

SJ's cheeks flushed with embarrassment as everyone around the table turned to look at her, smiling, and several clapped in appreciation. She had never felt so embarrassed before.

"Thank you," she stammered.

"Now, the next point. Orik, I see you brought Shelly today. Would you like to explain why she is here?"

Orik grumbled into his beard as Shelly whispered under her breath, "Brought me. I was ordered to be here, or he would find a new lead at the mine. Miserable old goat he is."

SJ had to stifle a laugh at her comment.

"Yes. Shelly will investigate this preposterous proposition that mithril is in the area," Orik said.

Shelly's mouth dropped open. "What?" she said much louder than she meant, and it was her time to turn beetroot red as everyone turned to look at her. "Sorry," she blurted.

Orik glared across the table at her where she stood.

Zigferd continued since it appeared that was all Orik would say on the matter. "You haven't briefed Shelly, I see. SJ here believes that there is a mithril vein towards the west valley. We know the cave's location but require it to be excavated to confirm that it is mithril. Because of this, Shelly, we will require your assistance to open the tunnel and check. I assume that will be okay?" Zigferd said, looking at Orik, who again grumbled and didn't reply.

Shelly couldn't help herself. "You really think we have a mithril vein," she said, her eyes still wide in amazement, turning to SJ.

"Yes. It is mithril," SJ said, smiling.

"This is the news any dwarf dreams of. Where is the location? I need to check," Shelly said excitedly.

"There is enough time, Shelly; do not worry," the mayor replied, chuckling at her enthusiasm. "I remember when you used to be like that, Orik," he finished as several around the table chuckled, and Orik's frown deepened.

The meeting continued, and many other aspects were discussed before they reached the topic of expansion. As soon as it was mentioned, some gasped and looked concerned, while others looked excited at the opportunities it might bring. SJ didn't speak again while she stood listening and taking in the discussions. As her display showed her it was approaching thirteen, the mayor stood.

"Dear all, thank you for attending, but we must close for now. We can continue tomorrow if necessary."

Several muttered it was necessary, and Zigferd confirmed they would reconvene again at ten the next day.

SJ left the room with Shelly chattering away at her, trying to get the details of the mine and what she had seen. She explained everything she knew so far as they walked out of the barracks. Shelly was thrilled with the information and couldn't wait to investigate. Shelly was apparently staying at the inn while in town, as she usually lived at the mine. Apparently, they had accommodation there as the mine had been there for many years.

As they returned to the inn, SJ made her excuses and went upstairs to freshen up before attending the service.

When SJ arrived, the churchyard was beautiful. The altar and pews had been brought outside, and the volunteers must have spent all morning preparing for the service. The surrounding grounds were perfect. The grass looked as though it had been freshly mown. Not a blade of grass appeared out of place. SJ wondered how they did such things so efficiently until she noticed a dryad standing by a flowerpot.

"Earth magic," Dave said.

SJ watched in amazement as flowers sprouted from the pot. Picking it up, the dryad handed it to the old gnome SJ recognised as the lead chorister, who placed it by the altar. SJ had arrived quite early, but just before the service was due to start, it appeared that the whole town was present. She noticed Kerys, Fhyliss, and Bert standing at the back and politely nodded to them. They nodded back in acknowledgement, and not long after, the service began.

Thankfully, SJ was not at the front this time, as she had been with Cristy, and didn't feel as exposed. The service was again a poignant and moving affair. Stories of heroism were given about those who had fallen, immortalising them in the memories of those in attendance.

Eventually, they moved over to the graveyard to lay the fallen to rest. It lasted three hours, filled with the heartfelt renditions offered by so many. It was the largest single tragedy the town had ever suffered. All those in attendance felt the sorrow.

Once the funerals were concluded, everyone made their way back to the inn. The town square had been transformed. Tables and chairs were all laid outside, and the inn doors were wide open, extending how many the inn could hold.

SJ found Kerys inside, busying away as the crowds arrived. "Do you need a hand today?" she asked.

Kerys turned and grinned at her. "That would be great if you are able. Have you ever poured tankards before?" Kerys asked.

"Yes," SJ said. During her university days, she used to bartend to earn extra money to cover her living expenses, and she soon felt at home working behind the bar as the crowds picked up. The bard, whose name she still didn't know, performed from a small stage set up outside. The sun shone brightly, and his renditions brought tears and joy as the afternoon became the evening. By the time the crowds eventually cleared the inn, it was past midnight.

"Thanks for your help today," Kerys said, smiling at SJ.

"It was a worthy cause," SJ said, then went upstairs to bed. It had been an emotionally draining day, and SJ now felt exhausted. It didn't take her long to fall into a deep sleep.

CHAPTER TWENTY-TWO

What Mana?

It had been several days since the funerals of the fallen, and slowly, the town had returned to normal. The vendors were all out as usual, their bright stalls and wares on display as SJ walked through the square heading to the training ground. Lorna had returned to town the previous day, confirming that Jabrey and his remaining clan members had all left the valley. A scout detail had been left at the village, and there was a clean-up operation in progress to clear out all the signs of the hobgoblins' presence.

The mayor decreed the village would be flattened, and new structures would be built once it was purged. The damage and filth from their occupancy could never be cleaned from the buildings. A building crew and several mages had been assigned to undertake the work and begin the rebuilding process. They were also informed to consider planning for a wall to be built to encompass the path leading up towards the town from the valley floor.

The valley only had three easily accessible routes into it: the west side, where the hobgoblins and orcs had returned through; the path to the ridge where the town was situated; and a southern tunnel network, which apparently led through to the far side of the mountains and was not usually travelled. On the far side of the mountains was the border to the desert territory that had been mentioned, and with the potential movement of tribes or similar, Zigferd wished to ensure that the tunnel was guarded and secured.

The amount of work that the town now had to complete was significant.

Over the past few days, SJ had been working on her tailoring and had finished the last pair of gloves. She was so excited to complete the quest that she had scared Dave half to death when she screamed, and her display triggered, congratulating her.

Congratulations! Tailoring Apprentice Level 4 completed.

Quest: Tailoring Apprentice—Level 5
Learn the secrets of enchantments.
Would you like to accept the quest? **Yes/No**

"Enchantments?" SJ said.

"Ah. Yes. Now you have learned the basics, the next stage is understanding how enchantment slots work. You will have to see Fizzlewick, and he can explain it to you, but as you increase further now, you can start to add slots to your items. It's a long process and very tricky, but it must be completed early. The number of slots you can add to an item depends on your ranking. As an Apprentice rank, you may only add one, and then at each successive rank, it increases by a further one."

"I thought an enchanter, not a tailor, would complete that?" SJ asked.

"The enchantments are, but if the item is not produced with the available slots, how do you believe they are enchanted? Otherwise, enchanters could randomly enchant an item with hundreds of differing enchantments if not specific to the professions."

"Once I reach Master, as an example, could I add five slots to items?"

"Yes. That is another reason your dress is unique: it will eventually have seven slots available on it since a Grand Master created it."

"It currently doesn't have any, though."

"No, and I don't think it will open until you finish the training needed for Apprentice Level 5. I think it may also be the same for all your other eventual slots for the dress."

"So, to get all seven slots, I would need to be Grand Master myself, then."

"Yes. I believe this will be the case," Dave said. "Exciting, isn't it?'

"It has taken me so long to make the gloves, never mind reaching Skilled or Journeyman status within the profession."

"Tailoring is difficult, but you have more of a purpose to succeed and progress than most ever do. Your dress alone should be enough to give you focus."

"It does, and I want to. But there are so many other things that I also need to do. My claws and kata training are going well, but it all takes so long to level."

"You could always consider completing more quests."

"I will have to, yes. I can't stay at Level 11 forever."

"You will have plenty of opportunities, my YLF."

SJ chuckled at Dave's endearment, which he hadn't called her in a while.

"How is your coding doing?"

"Meh. I managed to get through two further layers, but this next one is a right doozy. It's very complex."

"I am sure you will get it sorted soon."

"I am not sure about soon, but I have my quest to complete as you do yours."

"Ha," SJ laughed. "What experience and rewards do you get?"

"Oh, I will decide nearer the time, although I am at least considering giving myself an official title."

The inane and senseless conversations that Dave and SJ frequently had made her feel like they had known each other for years. They were so comfortable talking.

"Right. I need to go and find Fizzlewick, then," SJ said, standing and stretching. She had been hunched over at the table sewing the gloves for too long again.

"Oh. I just had a response to the quest query about reaching Level 10."

"What have they said?"

"It was apparently a feature that the System decided to implement when it did its original planning phase. Then since it commenced, it never implemented the feature."

"Then why was I told?"

"Why do you think?"

"Because of the waiver," SJ answered.

"Yep. It appeared for you due to you waiving the terms and conditions. The System was apparently a little upset when the admin team discussed it, as they thought it had been removed."

"What's the outcome, then?"

"Since you were offered a quest with no reward and still had a target, they are agreeing to a one-time offer," Dave said excitedly.

"Don't leave me in suspense. What is the offer?"

"They will give you one of two choices. The first is the ability to increase one of your attributes by three points permanently. The other will permanently increase one of your skills by one rank."

"That's great," SJ said excitedly. "What should I do? Let's see." SJ reviewed her character sheet. The points were a nice addition to either option. "I am going to add it to my shroud skill. If I get that to Level 3, that gives me ninety seconds of reduced damage, which would make a tremendous difference, and since I already get additional attribute points, they are not as necessary."

"A very sensible option," Dave agreed.

SJ updated her skill.

Subterfuge:	Identification Level 7 (98 of 200 to Level 8), Shroud Level 3

"Thanks, Dave. Okay, let's see Fizzlewick." SJ smiled.

As SJ walked by the barracks, she spotted Shelly jumping up and down, very animated. She and Orik, the grumpy old dwarf, were standing with another dwarf SJ did not recognise.

"Morning," SJ said as she walked near.

"SJ," Shelly said, turning with a huge grin on her face.

"Hi, Shelly," she smiled back.

"We broke through last night," she beamed, unable to stop her enthusiasm.

"So, you have confirmed it, then?"

"That's why I'm here now."

"These are council matters, not for general discussion," Orik interjected.

"And I am placing a vote to have SJ added to the council," the mayor said as he walked out from the barracks.

SJ's jaw nearly hit the floor. Why on Amathera would he be considering adding her to the council? She was no one of importance.

"Reputation can bring benefits beyond experience bonuses," Dave said, obviously understanding SJ's expression.

"I heard what you said, Shelly. That is excellent news. When do you think we may start operations?" Zigferd asked.

"A lot of prep work is needed first. Mithril is difficult to mine. My uncle has messaged his cousin, who is travelling here from Asterfal to help with operations."

"Nevik?" the mayor replied, a little shocked.

"Yes," Shelly replied.

"I haven't seen Nevik in several years. It will be nice to see the old goat again." Zigferd smiled.

"He should be arriving later today, I believe," Shelly replied.

"When he arrives, please ask him to stop by."

"I will, Mayor."

"Now, Orik, we have a meeting to attend, and since you are here, SJ, I would also like you to join us."

"I was going to the tailor's," SJ said, still shocked by Zigferd's comment.

"Fine, then. Can you join us later once you are finished? I have a few things I wish to discuss with you. I will be casting the vote this morning and hoped you would be in attendance."

Not understanding why he would even want her to be part of the council, SJ didn't respond.

"Look, I know it may be a bit of a shock to you, but with the changes we have discussed, I think it would benefit us all to have someone of your stature and potential on our side. I know you may not understand, but I am sure you will in time."

Zigferd had invited SJ to take part in recent discussions because of her revered status and the importance of the mithril mine, but she had never expected to be considered an integral part of the town to such a degree.

"I will call in as soon as I am done there," SJ said.

When she arrived at Fizzlewick's, the shop door was open, and the wagon was parked out the front. Several large crates were being loaded into the back of it. Fizzlewick's quarterling persona stood by the doorway, calling instructions.

"'Areful. Evrytin' is 'olded neatly," he said to the two ratkin moving the boxes.

"Morning," SJ called.

"'Orning." Fizzlewick smiled and winked at her.

"You look busy,"

"Order 'ipment."

"If you are too busy, I can call back later?"

"No. Go in, be done 'oon."

"Thanks," SJ said, smiling as she swerved around the ratkin walking out the door with another crate of goods. SJ stepped into the back room, pushing the beads to one side. She could hear a clunk and sliding sound as she did, and the two looms she had seen before were busy weaving cloth. One was producing a bright blue material and the other a golden material.

SJ watched the looms perform their tasks. Having visited old cotton mills back on Earth and learned how the looms worked, it was amazing to see them automated, the mechanisms moving under their own duress. It had to be magical. There was no other way to perform the actions without manual intervention.

She heard the bell tinkle as the store door closed, and moments later, Fizzlewick walked through in his human form.

"Hello, SJ. I see you reached Level 4 and now need to learn enchantments," he said, smiling.

"Yes."

"Excellent. Then, please follow me."

"What are you making?" SJ asked, looking at the looms again.

"I have just shipped the first part of an order, and this material is for the second half. I could just conjure it up, but I love the process and time involved with making the materials, and it's much more pleasing."

"That is a large order."

"Ah, yes. It is the new uniform for the Asterfal city guard. The newly appointed chancellor there wished to change it to his house colours."

"Chancellor?"

"Yes. A chancellor rules Asterfal. All cities have chancellors or someone similar to oversee the day-to-day running of things."

"How often do they change?"

"Not very, unless there has been a dispute or similar situation that causes them to. Asterfal's new chancellor was only recently appointed after the untimely death of his predecessor."

"Oh."

"Yes. Chancellor Alequi of the dryad enclave died several months ago, and only recently did the new chancellor, Santic of the kobold council, take over."

"I didn't realise that the political landscape was so varied. I assumed the cities were all run by lords or similar."

"No. Most cities have pledged an oath to the emperor, but several don't and class themselves as freeholders. Asterfal is one of these. It has a very diverse population. Some cities are more racially bound in comparison. There are also all the race capitals and territories to consider."

"So how does a kobold become a chancellor?"

"I have never met Santic personally, but I have heard he is very charming. He can convince many and has previously influenced the outcome of several high-value contracts between Asterfal and some larger cities."

SJ followed Fizzlewick downstairs, and as normal, he called two large, comfy armchairs for them to sit in.

"Let's get to it, then. Apprentice Level 5 training is not like your normal training for tailoring. It is all about state of mind."

"Please explain."

"Adding enchantment slots to clothing items requires a combination of factors. One is the item quality. If the item quality is not good enough, then it doesn't matter how much time and effort you spend. It will never work. Second, it is your mental state. For enchantment slots to be successfully added, you must be in a tranquil meditation as you complete the task. If you aren't, then again, it will fail."

"I used to practise meditation back home," SJ said.

"Hopefully, then, you will have an advantage. Many Amathereans do not know what meditation is, unless they are in one of certain classes, such as monks, clerics, or paladins."

"Don't mages meditate as well?"

"No. A mage's mind is like a chaotic whirlpool. Very few mages can successfully meditate on enchantment slots."

"So, what must I do?"

Fizzlewick explained the meditation process required to enchant materials. The requirements did not differ from her other meditation sessions when she practised yoga back on Earth.

"Sit comfortably, relax, close your eyes, and control your breathing. You need to be calm and at peace with your thoughts. Once you are done, you need to picture or imagine the materials you are working with. Hold the material you wish to enchant and slowly push your mana into it."

"Mana? I have never used anything that requires mana before. How will I know if I'm doing it right?"

"You will feel it. Once your mana starts to flow, your pool will drop. Enchantment slots can be applied to any material with the correct tailoring levels. The material must absorb fifty mana for every slot you wish to create, and at the Apprentice level, you may only create one enchantment slot. If you break from the meditation or stop pushing the mana into the material at any point, it will fail, and you will have to start over."

"I need some cloth to practise with."

Fizzlewick summoned a bundle of cloth, which appeared on the small table.

"I warn you, it is not as easy as it may sound. The speed at which you release your mana will determine success. Too quick or too slow, and it will fail. Eventually you'll be able to find it and feel its flow."

SJ placed the bundle on her lap, holding it. Sitting upright in the chair, she relaxed. She went through the steps she had completed many times before and felt her body relax and her breathing slow. Once she felt at peace, she focused on her mana, and nothing happened. Not knowing *what* it would even feel like didn't help.

"What is it supposed to feel like?" SJ asked.

"It's hard to explain, but I suppose if you have ever felt a lurching sensation in your stomach, then it's along those lines, or at least it is for me." Now that SJ had a vague idea of what she might experience, she tried again, but nothing. She repeated the same exercises several more times before cursing, "Why is it not working?"

"As I said, it takes time. Your basic state seems fine, but you are not relaxed because you continually think about the mana. You need to allow it to flow naturally."

"How, though?"

"I would spend time practising. I can't really explain how you feel when you do it, apart from the sensation I get, as I do not know myself."

"How do you add slots, then?"

"Ha. I am a god."

"Dave. Any ideas?"

"Nope, no idea how it feels or is supposed to feel, so I can't explain, sorry," Dave replied.

"Gah. This is stupid." SJ put the cloth back down on the table.

"It will happen. You just have to find your own path to release your mana. Learning the technique normally takes no more than a year."

"A year!" SJ exclaimed.

"Yes, usually for the first time, beings take about a year to succeed."

"I am stuck as a Level 4 tailor until I can do this," SJ said with annoyance.

After a while longer, SJ gave up. "This is impossible."

"As I have explained, you are not clearing your mind fully. Keep practising, and it will happen soon enough. I am sure."

SJ checked her display. Given the time she had spent trying to manipulate her mana, it had been over two hours since she arrived at the tailor shop. "I must go. I promised I would see the mayor and town council."

"Please do as you need. I will be here when you are ready. I may just add that it will be nice to stay here for a while. There are some lovely members of the township."

"Stay here for a while?" SJ asked, frowning.

"Well, yes. Now the borders have changed. There is no rush to move on so soon, and I am enjoying my time here," Fizzlewick replied, smiling.

"You are enjoying yourself?"

"Oh, yes. I enjoy doing the mundane daily tasks of a shopkeeper. It is quite therapeutic, and it is a pleasant change from being involved in continual political scandals."

SJ remembered the story about the naked emperor but couldn't fathom any level of interaction with individuals so high in position. She was astounded by how she had been treated so far in the town, and that the mayor wished her to join the council filled her with trepidation.

"Thank you for teaching me, Fizzlewick. I will be back as soon as I complete the quest."

"No problem at all, and enjoy your new position." The god winked.

SJ opened her eyes in amazement. She knew Fizzlewick was a god, but he seemed to know every little detail about what was happening to her each time they spoke. Leaving the shop, she made her way to the barracks.

"I wish I could understand the mana flow better," she huffed back on the street.

"Speak to Fran when you get a chance. I am sure she can assist and explain it better than I ever could. I know what it relates to but wouldn't know how it feels or what you need to do to utilise it. Mages are taught about mana flow from the start. It is their initial skill, and they must learn it before they can even start to learn spells."

"I will once I have finished at the barracks. I also need to see Cristy. I promised I would take her to see Patch."

"I like Cristy," Dave said cheerily.

It was strange how Dave always seemed happier when Cristy was around and SJ thought he might have paternal feelings towards her.

"You are always much nicer when Cristy is around," SJ said.

"What do you mean *much nicer*? I am always nice."

"Really," SJ said as she arrived at the barracks entrance.

CHAPTER TWENTY-THREE

Council

SJ went straight upstairs and, seeing that the mayor wasn't in his office, continued to the council chamber. When she knocked on the door, one of the burly orc guards opened it and ushered her inside. The table was in a heated discussion, and SJ stood quietly by the entrance, not wishing to interrupt the proceedings.

"I have told you already." A large ent was speaking. "We can't allow the valley to remain undefended. We need to expand our reach, as the mayor stated. Without the expansion, we will be open to worse threats than the orcs or hobgoblins in the future."

SJ had not seen him before, and he was an imposing figure. He had a thick-barrelled chest (or maybe trunk; SJ was unsure how to describe his anatomy), which had at least four branch-like arms that animatedly followed his current conversation, supporting his argument.

"We do not have a large enough force," a goblin SJ recognised as a regular member replied. "It will stretch the guard too thin to cover the expansion. Without recruitment and increasing our size, expanding would be pointless."

The arguments carried on with one aspect or another being considered, accepted, or rejected by all around the table. SJ was amazed at the level of chaos that unfolded.

"I don't suppose they normally have much to talk about apart from the most recent garbage collection," Dave said. "It's quite entertaining, though."

After several more minutes, the mayor had obviously had enough as his voice cut over those sitting around him.

"SILENCE," he called.

Slowly, the discussions lessened until quiet fell in the chamber.

"Thank you. It seems we are currently at an impasse over how to proceed for the betterment of the town. Considering this, I propose that all parties here today write their thoughts and expectations and deliver them for consideration at our next meeting. We will not confirm the outcomes today. Once we have everyone's thoughts, I will ask for them to be transcribed for distribution and confirmation before voting on the proposals I have presented today. At the start, I knew this would be an emotive conversation, so please consider your audience when you give feedback."

Several around the table nodded in agreement with the mayor's words, but SJ noticed a few didn't and still carried scowls on their faces. Seeing the lack of coherence was surprising. Every previous interaction showed they were a civilised and agreeable council, but this was obviously not the case in certain aspects.

"Ah, SJ," Zigferd said, smiling. "Please come and join me."

The sudden address startled SJ, who slowly proceeded to Zigferd's seat at the head of the table.

"Now, all. I have one final agenda item before we part for today," he said, pausing and looking around at all the faces of those present. "I have an unusual proposal to make, and it has never to my knowledge been done before, but with the changes we are seeing across the land, with the amendment of territory boundaries and various other considerations around our town growth potential . . ." Again he paused, awaiting appreciative nods of acknowledgement. "I am proposing we add a new member to our council."

SJ watched Orik roll his eyes while others frowned, looking confused and shocked. The council already comprised representatives from all the town's dominant races.

"Who are you referring to?" a gnome asked.

"I thought that would be obvious by her presence here today," Zigferd replied.

There were several audible gasps, and immediate chatter began again. SJ heard one comment over any other, making her scowl in frustration.

"You want a fae on the council!"

"Now, this will be interesting," Dave said. "Fae are known for their problems, as I explained in the past, and I think for some, even though you have done nothing to support those expectations, several will hold a grudge. In relation to Legionnaires, they are seen in various positions across Amathera, and there have been some over the years who have risen to rule, but these are infrequent. Many do not wish to be involved in the political landscape and what it entails, preferring to just fight and grow. Your inclusion within a council at a starter town would be considered another unique opportunity."

"Calm down, calm down," Zigferd stated before the complete chaos of before could ensue. Silence gradually returned to the table. "This is a proposition only and will be voted on as per standard, but I believe with SJ's abilities, she may become a very useful member of the town in the future, and her experiences that we do not know may very well support our development. I can understand some of your reactions to including a fae, but you all know Mistress Francisca and what she has previously done to support the town, and I believe that SJ here is of the same mould."

SJ stood a little shocked, not fully appreciating or understanding what he was referring to.

"I think he means as your class grows. I think he is already considering what you may bring to them as a future option, not just your interactions so far," Dave said. "That's very clever of him."

SJ couldn't respond but had so many questions she wanted to ask. She hadn't expected to be thrown into it without being able to discuss the proposal first.

"Again, with this information I have given, please consider the proposal. The details are not yet discussed nor confirmed, and I didn't wish to throw this on you without allowing you to think it through, as I know this will be amending the way we have worked before within the council. I propose we reconvene in three days, giving everyone enough time to discuss the expansion and additional member proposals and present any thoughts. With that, I bring the meeting to a close today."

Council members stood and filed out of the chamber while the ent moved to confer with Zigferd. SJ felt out of place, and rather than just standing there, she left. She also needed to speak to Zigferd and find out what he really wanted from her. Walking downstairs, she went through his office area, where Alice was having a discussion with the gnomes who oversaw the model updates.

"So, you want a new model?" one of the gnomes asked.

"Yes. We will require one that allows for boundary expansion but still require this one to be maintained," Alice said.

"And where are we going to start building this one? Also, we would require further help."

"I understand. The mayor proposes that the new model be built in the council chambers so it can be discussed and planned directly."

"What level of detail?"

"Enough to show elevations and locations so that the lay of the land can be seen from it. I believe he also asked for primary structures, such as walls and such."

"Umm. This will be an interesting project. I have not created landscapes for many a year now, but I would rather enjoy them."

"That is fantastic news. Who else do you need to help you?"

"A young ratkin has recently shown interest in my creations and started to tinker. I think I can use him for basic construction. He doesn't have the skill to complete the finer detailed work but can at least commence it."

"That's wonderful. Could you speak to him today?"

"Of course. He usually works at the stables, but I believe he is wasted there."

SJ wondered if he meant Little Stuart. She knew he worked at the stables and collected bellpops for Floretta, but this job could be better in the long run, as it would support his family. "Are you referring to Little Stuart?" SJ asked.

"Yes. That's him," the gnome replied.

SJ smiled at the thought of the young ratkin working with the gnome.

Zigferd walked into the room behind SJ. "I think we need to talk," she said.

"We do indeed. Please." He indicated with his hand.

SJ walked into his office and took a seat. Before the mayor sat down, he closed his office doors. It was the first time she had seen the door closed and silence enveloped the room.

"Now we have some peace without interruptions." Zigferd smiled.

"It would have been nice to discuss your proposition before you announced it to the council," SJ said.

"I understand. I am sure you feel a little uncertain and maybe a little shocked by it."

"I am, yes."

"It is simple, really. You are a Legionnaire. You are also a specific class and will eventually have specific skills, from what I have been made aware of," he replied, smiling knowingly. "Amathera is not the place you may believe it to be so far, and even today, you will have noticed a different side to the council that you won't have seen before."

SJ couldn't argue and nodded in agreement.

"I believe—and it is for selfish reasons, I'm not going to lie—that if we can get you to join the council now as the borders expand and the diplomatic issues arise, you can be a very useful tool."

"I am just a tool, then?"

"No. Not in that manner, but we all must have a purpose to play, and you bring a different aspect to our town we have never had before. Your outlook, commitment, selfless acts—you fight for what you believe in, and I believe you will continue to do so. If you fight for Killic, then Killic will be a much stronger and better place for it in the future."

"You do wish to use me as a tool, then?" SJ said defensively, folding her arms. She was not happy with being considered a pawn to be used. She had always been frustrated with how senior management at her firm back on Earth had used people beneath them for their own benefit.

"No. Please don't misunderstand my proposition. I believe that you will bring influence and continuity to the council."

"How will I achieve that? I do not even know the members."

"But you would in time. You have a very persuasive nature."

"Persuasive?" SJ frowned.

"Yes. The way you interact with people gets them to open up to you. I have heard from many you have spoken to, and they hold you in high esteem."

"I don't even know that many townsfolk."

"You would be surprised what helping at the inn does for someone in this town. It is its hub, after all."

"I have only helped on a couple of occasions."

"Yes, I know, that is my point. If you can influence so many by doing so little, what do you think you can achieve in the longer term?"

SJ had never considered her interactions with people that way. Her ethos had always been to be friendly and kind, even back on Earth, unless someone went against her, and then the claws came out. On Amathera, that now had a completely new meaning.

"I am not sure I like being in the spotlight to that degree," SJ said uncertainly.

"It's a great opportunity," Dave said. "Consider how it will allow you to get involved in the long term."

"You wouldn't be in the light so much," Zigferd said. "You would be a racial representative, as we have for all the other races in town. It is just unheard of for a fae to be a town or city council member. Many see your race choice as problematic, but thankfully, you and Mistress Francisca have brought an increasingly improved view of fae."

"I need to think about it," SJ said, still not happy about the racial biases that many had shown, especially the reaction in the chamber.

"Please do. It would be appreciated if you could confirm as soon as you can. I ask that you consider the long-term goals of the town."

Thanking Zigferd for his time, SJ got up and left his office. As she went downstairs, she was met with a wide-eyed ratkin she recognised. Little Stuart was being shown into the barracks by the gnome who had been speaking to Alice. He was covered in bits of hay from, presumably, the stables.

SJ smiled as she walked from the barracks, hoping that this might be the break that Little Stuart needed for his family.

"Time to take Cristy to see Patch," SJ said.

Walking across the field with Cristy, SJ was surprised to see a line of carts heading past them back towards town. It was the most traffic she had ever seen, particularly on this side of town. Recognising Shelly sat by the driver of one cart, she waved.

"How is it going?" SJ called over the clatter of hooves and squeaking wheels as she and Cristy stood off to the side, allowing them to pass.

"Good. We should be able to start in a few more days. We are just finishing the entrance and path to it," Shelly called.

"I will have to come and look soon," SJ called back.

"Please do." Shelly smiled broadly as the cart trundled past.

As soon as they entered the forest path, Cristy called out. It didn't take long for there to be a howl in response, and several minutes later, the gigantic form of Patch came bounding from the forest straight up to Cristy.

Seeing the pair interact was like watching an owner and their pet dog. Patch, rolling on his back, allowed Cristy to scratch and rub it for him. The playful interaction continued for a while until another howl broke the silence. Patch stood back on his feet and snarled, looking into the forest.

"What is it?" Cristy asked.

SJ was worried about the behaviour Patch had just shown.

Patch turned and looked at Cristy before turning back, and he disappeared into the forest.

"Something isn't right?" SJ asked, concern etched on her face.

"We should go check," Cristy said.

"We don't know where he has gone or what it is, and I don't want you in danger."

"I am a big gnoll now."

SJ smiled. "You are indeed very brave, but unless we know what is going on, I'm not willing to take you towards danger. You experienced enough when you were kidnapped."

"Kidnapped?" Cristy said, frowning.

"The hobs took you. Stay here, and I'll check. If it's safe, I will come and get you, okay?"

Cristy huffed, "I suppose."

SJ shrank to her miniature form, taking off. The path that Patch had left in his wake as he bounded through the underbrush was easy to follow, and she didn't have to fly very far before reaching a clearing. The clearing was not very large, and a small mound was off to one end; standing in its opening was the white wolf she had seen previously. There was no sign of Patch or the others.

"That must be their den," Dave said.

"It looks like it," SJ said. "But where have they gone?" That was when she heard the howls deeper into the forest. At this end of the ridged valley she had never ventured into, it took her a while to pinpoint the location of the howl. As she neared, she could hear snarling and growling. The forest had thinned as she ventured farther, and she was surprised that it opened into a flat plain that appeared to fall off a cliff.

Stood in a line facing out from the forest were the wolves: Patch and the four she had originally seen in the woods. The creature that stood before them SJ had never seen the likes of before. Resembling a combination of an armadillo and a mole, it stood nearly five feet tall with its back appearing plated. Flying above, SJ observed the creature's front feet, which were supported by some very large, seriously sharp-looking claws, and large-looking incisors. It stood facing down the wolves snarling at it.

"It's a rock gobbler. They can dig through solid stone with those claws, and this one looks hungry, upset, and large," Dave said.

SJ triggered her identification skill.

Rock Gobbler	
Level:	13
Hit Points:	180 of 180
Mana Points:	0
Armour Class:	35
Attacks:	Bite, Claw
Special:	Coil

"It has a lot of hit points for a Level 13, and that armour class is crazy," SJ said.

"You won't be able to hit it easily. Their armour plates are very strong, and if they use their special, you may as well just walk away and leave it."

"What does it do?"

"It triples its armour class when in its balled form. The things become virtually untouchable, even lower-level rock gobblers. Your chance to even scratch its scales would be virtually nothing."

"The wolves are unlikely to damage it either, then?"

"If it coils, they won't touch it, nor could you. Wolves, though, are pack hunters, and against single prey, they will surround it and work together. The problem is they are low level, and even Patch will struggle to damage it as a dire wolf."

SJ watched as the standoff continued. The rock gobbler snarled but didn't close in, and neither did the wolves. Slowly, the wolves spread out to form a semicircle. The creature turned its head, tracking them. It hissed and snarled again and took a step backwards.

SJ noticed a large hole in the ground a couple hundred feet from where it was. "It must have dug through," she said.

"Seems like it," Dave remarked. "It will need dealing with. They have a specific favourite rock they like to devour."

"They actually eat rock?" SJ asked, amazed.

"Yes. They can break down anything, their stomach is so acidic, and they particularly like the taste of mithril. They are a common pest in mithril mines. Although this one is pretty large."

SJ's display triggered.

Quest: Save the Mine
You have discovered that a rock gobbler has appeared in the area. If this creature is not killed, the prosperity of Killic and your future income will be threatened.
Rewards: 320xp
Would you like to accept the quest? **Yes/No**

CHAPTER TWENTY-FOUR

Gobbler

That's great. You said you wanted to do some more quests," Dave said cheerily.

"Not against something like this. I doubt I can even get through its armour, and I know the wolves won't, considering their low levels. Any advice?"

"Don't get hit by the claws."

"Really. That is all?" SJ said sarcastically.

"Well, you can allow yourself to be hit if you wish, but I really wouldn't advise it," Dave replied flippantly.

"Any helpful advice would be appreciated."

"They are slow, and their eyesight is very poor, so you should have enough notification of an attack."

A wolf sprang towards its left side, and as it did, the rock gobbler snapped its jaws towards it. On doing so another wolf on the right moved in to snap at it. The rock gobbler moved its front leg to strike, and SJ noticed how slow it was compared to most things she had fought so far. The wolf easily dodged its attempted bite and claw attack as the other snapped at its side. The wolf that struck it didn't do any damage; it remained at full health.

"This is not going to be fun," SJ said as she flew behind the creature. The armour plating seemed to come down and cover virtually all its body as though it wore a scale shirt. Where its stubby tail joined its body, it looked as though it had less armour plating.

SJ lowered slowly, with the bulk of the creature between herself and its head. She had not flown low and doubted it had even perceived her as a threat. Landing, she grew, equipping her claws and approaching the rear of it, then stabbed into the gap in its armour. SJ had not been expecting its reaction to the attack, and it jumped forward as if launched from a cannon. Patch bounded out of the way as it landed where he had been some thirty feet away. She had penetrated its body but only did eight points of damage.

"That thing can move," SJ said in surprise.

"Its legs, although short, are ridiculously strong as it pushes against stone when burrowing, and don't even bother trying to attack its head. It may not look armoured, but it's harder than steel."

This was going to be a long fight. As the wolves continued to snap at it, holding its attention, SJ continued to shrink and grow, performing attacks at its rear. It could not twist, and she could imagine it performing a ten-point turn on a road in the UK, it was so inflexible with its sideways movement. It was designed for one job only: to dig and move forward to its next source of food. With its stubby legs, it was slow, and it lumbered forward trying to strike at any wolves that came in front of it, occasionally launching to attack.

After almost ten minutes of fighting, it was still had over a hundred hit points remaining.

"This is ridiculous. There must be something that can damage it more easily," SJ said as she flew to its rear again.

"Only if you have a lightning or fire spell or similar," Dave replied.

"SJ!" The small form of Cristy had appeared at the edge of the forest, crying her name.

"Cristy, stay back," SJ called on seeing the small gnoll.

Cristy mustn't have heard her response, as she wandered farther from the treeline, staring at the creature the wolves continued to fight.

"Cristy!" SJ bellowed, trying to be heard above the snarling, growling, and hissing of the creatures.

Still, she didn't respond, and SJ flew straight towards her. "Get back in the treeline now!" she screamed at the small gnoll as she neared her.

Cristy looked at her with shock on her face; it was the first time SJ had ever said anything with anger in her voice and it obviously had impact. After standing for a moment looking at her, Cristy turned and ran, tears running down her cheeks.

"Argh," SJ screamed in frustration. She hadn't meant to shout at Cristy; she just didn't want her getting hurt by the ridiculously armoured creature. "I need to go follow her. I can't have her running off."

"The wolves will keep it busy," Dave said.

SJ followed Cristy and could hear as she ran through the brush of the forest on all fours. She was quick, and SJ struggled to keep up even flying, having to dart in and around the trees. Eventually Cristy slowed, and SJ caught up with her. Cristy came to a stop and curled up in a ball at the base of an immense tree, sobbing.

SJ landed gently and grew. "Cristy," she said softly.

Cristy didn't look at her and buried her head into her arms, further covering her face. The dress she had been wearing was all torn and tattered from being caught in the brush.

"Cristy. I am sorry. I didn't mean to shout at you. I was scared you might get hurt, that was all."

Cristy sobbed as she responded. "I thought you were my friend."

"I am your friend. You know I am. That creature could have hurt you if you had got any closer than you did."

"I just wanted to help. I was worried when you had been gone so long." She turned to look at SJ. Streaks covered her little face and her eyes glistened.

SJ could feel a tear in her own eye. "I know you did, and I am sorry I didn't come back straight away. I was helping the wolves. That creature is too heavily armoured. It isn't like attacking a hogling or a hobgoblin."

SJ bent down next to her and held her arms out, and Cristy moved over until SJ could envelop her in a hug, stroking her head gently. "I'm sorry," Cristy continued to sob, and SJ felt terrible. After a minute the sobbing lessened, and Cristy pushed away to look at her.

"I need to go back and check on the wolves, but I don't know where they are now," SJ said, looking around, lost after chasing Cristy.

"I can lead you. I can smell them," Cristy replied, her little face wide-eyed.

"Only if you promise to stay in the trees and not go into the open. Whatever happens," SJ said.

"I promise."

"Come on, then. Show me which way."

Cristy moved back through the trees. It took them much longer walking back than the mad dash Cristy had made, and SJ could hear the fighting was still going on when they returned. "Now, stay here, please," SJ said.

"I will," Cristy replied, nodding her head.

SJ shrank and flew back onto the plain. The rock gobbler had only lost a further two hit points in all the time she had been gone. The wolves were flagging, their movements less fluid, and the beast almost hit one of the grey wolves, which only narrowly bounded from its path.

"I need to do something different," SJ hissed.

"I have an idea," Dave said.

"What idea?" SJ said hopefully.

"You need to try to lead it away from the woods towards the cliff's edge."

"And do what?"

"Make it launch at you and over the side. Their vision is poor. It won't know where it is. You have seen how far it can jump when it tries to attack, so you can try to get positioned so it jumps too far."

"It won't go for me when I'm small."

"No. That's the problem," Dave chuckled nervously.

The cliff's edge was probably a couple hundred feet from where they fought, and SJ began the slow process of trying to make it turn around to face her. The creature was worse than a heavy goods vehicle, and SJ got into a routine of landing and growing in front of it and running as it tried to launch its attack. It jumped nearly thirty feet each time, and eventually after several minutes, it faced towards the cliff.

"Now lead it straight," Dave said.

Two of the wolves had moved back from the fray, heavily panting, and SJ believed they must have been exhausted. She didn't have the luxury to be tired—she needed to get rid of this thing. Landing fifty feet from its front, she grew again and called at it and screamed to get its attention. The wolves were also now on the same side of the creature as SJ, giving it four creatures to choose from to attack.

It leapt towards a wolf, thankfully still moving closer to the cliff edge. The wolf this time was not fast enough, and one of the gobbler's enormous claws caught it on its flank. The wolf yelped in pain as it crashed to the ground, unable to land properly, and whimpered. SJ rushed forward and struck at the face of the gobbler in anger. The gobbler's head turned as she did, knocking into her, and sent her sprawling sideways. It felt like being hit by a sledgehammer, and this close its teeth looked like huge razor blades. SJ had swept her claws down the side of its face to no effect. SJ back-pedalled, realising how stupid she had been getting so close. Considering this thing ate rocks, why she had even thought about going near its head she did not know. Dave had warned her how hard it was.

She had drawn its attention, and as she moved backwards, she noticed the tension in its limbs. The unsightly beast was like a coiled spring being released when it jumped, an instant movement. SJ turned and ran. She was probably twenty feet away, trying to run at an angle. It landed with a deafening thud, missing her by inches. She glanced back as it got ready to jump again.

The only bonus was that because of the size of it, its mobility and time between attacks was slow, and she made it another thirty feet before it sprang again. Still out of range, she carried on towards the cliff as it coiled again. The wolves had withdrawn. Patch stood by the side of the injured wolf with the others as they watched the fight, howling and growling.

"Nearly there," Dave shouted.

SJ could see that the cliff's edge was only fifty feet from them and continued to draw the gobbler towards the edge. The next jump caught her off guard as she stumbled on the uneven ground approaching the cliff edge, where it had eroded and pitted over time. Catching her foot in a hole, she squealed as she tripped, sprawling onto the ground, and stood again. She was only ten feet from the edge when the creature leapt again. She hadn't been able to move far enough, and as the creature hurtled towards her with its claws extended and jaws open, she knew it was going to hit her.

It wasn't a clean strike thankfully, but it was still like being hit by a cannonball. The wind was knocked from her and the impact threw her backwards, reducing her hit points by half. She realised she hadn't landed—they were in free fall.

"Shrink!" Dave screamed.

SJ was already in the process, and as she shrank, she opened her wings. The friction buffeted her, but she worked into a glide, opening her body wide like a parachutist. The rock gobbler shrieked, still plummeting towards the base of the cliff nearly a thousand feet below. As she glided, she spiralled and followed its descent until it eventually met with the cliff's rocky bottom. Far below, it looked like a water bomb had just exploded, leaving a wet patch on the surface.

As SJ's speed continued to decrease, she could begin using her wings. It was a much more successful landing than off the mages' wind spell powering the windmill. As she got control of her descent, the shock of the free fall and the exploding creature subsided. At the base of the cliff was the start of some grassland with sparsely dotted trees, and it reminded SJ of pictures she had seen of the savannahs in Africa. The bit that amazed her was the vast expanse of sand that started not long after. It stretched off into the horizon.

"That's the next territory," Dave said. His responses lately seemed to come in answer to her thoughts, without her even having to speak. "Desert region, 10–20 base monsters initially. The far desert area increases to 20–30, and several nasty tribes live there. There is a town, but it's not on the map and I am not sure which direction or how far it is from here."

"I didn't realise it was so close and how fast the territory areas change. It's like just crossing a line," SJ said, staring at the sudden environmental change.

"It's even more dramatic between an ice and desert region," Dave replied.

SJ struggled to imagine an immediate transition from desert to ice. "I better head back up but want to see if the rock gobbler has any loot first."

"Possibly—you sometimes get ore from them for the obvious reasons as they eat so much."

SJ's display had triggered when the rock gobbler hit the ground, exploding into the glutinous mass that now covered the cliff's base. The shared experience between the wolves had only granted her 25xp, which for such a long, hard fight seemed ridiculous. The quest completion was a little nicer, though.

Quest: Save the Mine—Complete
The rock gobbler has been thwarted, and you have removed the current threat to your potential future income.
Rewards: 320xp + 100% reputation bonus = 640xp awarded

Her improved reputation with Killic was a massive boost, but SJ had noticed the significant difference in experience needs between levels now. To reach Level 11 from 10, it had increased from requiring 1500xp to requiring 2250xp, and for Level 11 to 12, she now needed 3000xp. The reputation increases would really help going forward with the increase for each level. She checked out her new total.

Experience:	987 of 3000

Landing by the remains—there really wasn't much of a body left after the impact—she looted the rock gobbler.

---

6 x Armour Plates of the Rock Gobbler, 1 x Vial of Intestinal Acid

"Oooo. Be very careful with that vial," Dave said. "The contents can be sold for a nice price, but if you get it on yourself, expect severe pain. When I say that acid is strong, I mean insanely strong. The armour plates are great for smithies with the knowledge to reshape them. I would advise to go to see Zej. I don't know if he will be able to use them or not. Reshaping animal and insect armour is a specialist skill that not many smiths have."

"You said before that as an assassin I can't wear armour."

"Yes. Until Level 20; then you can wear leather, and at 40, chain-mail."

"What about animal skins or components?"

SJ could sense Dave frowning when he responded. "You do know where leather comes from, don't you?" His reply dripped with sarcasm.

"Of course, but these plates are not leather. What do they count as?"

"Erm . . . I have absolutely no idea. No one has ever even considered that before. Their armour class is equivalent to decent scale mail if not weak chain-mail. Umm, I need to check, be right back."

SJ began her climb back to the top of the cliff, and as she neared, she could see the small and panic-stricken face of Cristy looking down. Dave started chatting excitedly.

"It's unlisted."

"What's unlisted?"

"The armour plates of the rock gobbler."

"What does that mean?" SJ asked, frowning at his response.

"It means they are not identified as a type of armour, which theoretically means you could get away with wearing them. I am not sure what the System would do if or when it found out, but there is absolutely nothing in the rules about the use of the armour plates. All standard animal hides including crepar chitinous plates are listed, but these aren't."

"I will need to get them to Zej, then, to see if he can do anything with them."

"Yes. Definitely," Dave said, his voice buzzing with excitement.

"SJ," Cristy called as she neared the top.

"I'm okay," SJ called back, landing.

Tear streaks again were clearly visible on Cristy's face. "I thought you were dead," she said, throwing herself at SJ once she reached her full size.

"No, I'm good! How is the injured wolf?" SJ said, as she looked over to where they were still standing around it.

"I don't think it's good," Cristy said tearfully, and SJ felt her body slacken against her.

"Let's see. Maybe we can help," SJ said as she hurried towards the wolves.

The black wolf turned and growled as she approached but didn't step in her way as she knelt next to the injured grey. Its side was torn severely from the claws of the gobbler.

"We need a healer," SJ said. "Cristy, can you wait here with Patch while I fly back to town?"

"Yes," Cristy replied, now sitting by the grey's head and stroking it. The grey was whimpering quietly, and SJ wasn't sure how long it would survive.

"I'll be back as soon as I can," she said, as she shrank and took off. Raising above the treetops, she could see the town in the distance and headed straight towards it as fast as she could.

CHAPTER TWENTY-FIVE

Professional Opportunity

Alice was the first person SJ had seen on returning to town, and she followed SJ as soon as she heard about the injured wolf. As a druid, she could heal animals, which SJ had not even considered previously, although it made perfect sense; she'd only been thinking of clerics and paladins. On returning to the southern edge, the wolves had initially not taken kindly to Alice appearing, and had prevented her from getting near the grey. It was only after Cristy intervened that they stepped aside begrudgingly.

"I have no influence over these wolves at all," Alice said as she knelt at the injured wolf's side. Looking at the wound, she placed her hand on the ground and then her other hand on the wolf's head. Mesmerised, SJ watched as green tendrils of energy appeared from the ground and snaked towards the wolf. It was like watching surgery, the way the tendrils began to knit and repair the wound, sewing it back together. The wolf was almost dead when they arrived back, and when Alice finished healing, she took a small vial from her inventory, gently lifted the wolf's head, and poured it into its mouth.

Its eyes had become cloudy yellow, but as the liquid was absorbed, they returned to their previous vibrancy.

"He should be okay now. He's lucky—another few minutes and he wouldn't have made it," Alice said.

"Thank you," SJ said.

"What damaged him that badly?"

"A rock gobbler," SJ said, turning and pointing at the hole in the ground where it had dug through.

"There was a rock gobbler this close to town?" Alice said in surprise.

"Yes. I had never seen one before."

"They are a nuisance. We have had the odd one in the stone mine over the years. It's strange that it came to the surface, though. They usually remain underground all the time. How big was it?"

"About four feet high, Level 13."

"Level 13, and you managed to kill it?"

"I cheated a little. I made it jump off the cliff."

"Wow. You're lucky."

"Thankfully, the wolves helped."

Patch reacted to the comment and let out a howl. SJ turned and smiled at the dire wolf.

"You'll be okay now," Cristy said, stroking the recovering wolf on its head again. It licked her hand lovingly.

"I need to get back to town. I was supposed to be confirming some orders," Alice said.

"We are heading back now as well and will accompany you. Thank you for your help," SJ said.

"No problem."

As they walked back to town, SJ chatted to Alice. It was the first time they had ever had a personal conversation, and it was interesting to find out exactly what Alice did for the mayor. SJ knew she worked like a personal assistant, but it was more than that. She was basically the town's second, which SJ hadn't realised before.

The wolves parted ways with them at their den, and in Killic, SJ said farewell to Alice and then escorted Cristy back to the orphanage. Since the wolves had moved closer, there had been no incidents, and many had now even forgotten that they lived there, apart from the occasional howl that could be heard.

"Dave?" SJ said as she walked down the street past the open shopfronts and vendors calling for customers.

"Yes."

"You remember previously you mentioned portals? That was from Level 10, wasn't it?"

"Oh. I had completely forgotten about them. Yes, from Level 10 you can assign one. Why? What are you thinking?"

"I was thinking of adding one at the cottages and just wondered how you went about it. I have seen no display announcements or anything that would give me the ability."

"No, they don't appear as an ability. You remember I mentioned that you required a deed to a property."

"Yes."

"Well, the deed will have been updated to allow a portal to be placed at a specific location. Once it is, it will appear on your map."

"So the deed controls it?"

"Yes. If a deed is owned, the rights become visible if the property has been visited. You can't just borrow a deed from someone to remove the fog of war. If a deed changes hands, any portal present is removed so that a new owner may position one if they wish."

"The deed is back at the inn. I should go and collect it."

Once the deed was in hand, SJ turned her steps toward Fran. She really wanted to understand more about mana. Looking at the deed as she walked along, she read the information again. At the bottom was a small symbol on the parchment that had not been there previously. "Is that the portal function?" SJ asked, pointing at it.

"It's not a function. You don't press on it and it magically works. It's not like your display that you select through thought. Now that you have reached Level 10 and the symbol is present, it just means that it can have a portal added at that location."

"How?"

SJ was excited about creating her first portal and detoured to an open field area rather than going directly to the academy, and sat down in the luscious grass. Now that she had remembered about it, she wanted to get this sorted.

"First thing. Open your navigation screen. Once you have it open, you will see the position of the cottage."

"Yes. I can see it."

"Zoom in on the cottage. Like most menus, it has three dots."

"Yep. Got it," SJ said, selecting it.

"Don't select it under any circumstances."

"What?" SJ said, panicking. "I just did. Does that mean I've broken it?"

"No. Only joking, of course you select it," Dave chuckled.

SJ rolled her eyes. "Don't do that to me. I thought I had just stopped it from working."

"Now, on your new menu, there should be an option to add a portal."

"Yes. There is!"

"Now you can decide where near the property you wish it to be. Keep zooming in closer, and then you can pick a location. It must be outside the building, within a radius of two hundred feet."

A glowing ring had appeared on the map. Zooming in, she could see the various areas around the cottage. Knowing where the open space was, she selected it.

"Amazing. So how do I activate it?"

"Now that the position is on your map, all you need to do is confirm that you wish for a portal to be placed there. Once you confirm it, the symbol changes to green."

SJ confirmed her selection, and the icon was changed to a green cross inside a circle. "Okay. Done. So, I did need to press a button," SJ said.

Dave huffed. "You didn't press it though, did you? Urgh, sometimes working with Legionnaires is such a drag."

SJ chuckled at Dave's response. "Can it be removed?"

"If you ever want to remove it, you can basically do the reverse and cancel its placement."

"If I place a portal, is it one-way?"

"Unless you have a permanent residence where you can apply a soul stone, then yes."

"What's a soul stone?"

"It will trap some of your life essence in a certain area and allow you to return to it as required. Mages can produce them if they are skilled enough. If you ask Fran when we see her, she may have the knowledge needed."

"If it's just a stone, though, what if someone stole it?"

"They are called soul stones, but they aren't exactly stones. They are magical anomalies. Fran would be required to cast the spell, if she is able, at the location where you wish it to be locked to."

"There is something new to learn about every day."

"There is," Dave agreed.

When SJ arrived at the academy, Fran was outside directing some trainees. She was overseeing what must have been an earth mage moving boulders from one location to another.

"Easy. Easy," Fran said as she monitored the mage, who was levitating the large boulder. The mage's face looked strained, and he had beads of sweat on his brow. Eventually, he moved it to above a pile of neatly placed boulders and released it, gasping at the exertion. It dropped onto the boulders with a thud, rocking before coming to a rest.

"Well done. You just need to keep practising so that you can lower it slowly. To assist with construction, you must be able to manipulate the materials with accuracy and care."

"Hi, Fran," SJ said when Fran turned from the student.

"Hi," Fran said, smiling on seeing her. "We have some things I would like to discuss."

"I came to see you about a few things as well," SJ said, returning her smile.

Fran led her inside to her office. "Coffee?"

"Yes, please," SJ said.

Fran poured two mugs and then took a seat in one of the comfy chairs.

"Would you like to start, or should I?" Fran said.

"You can," SJ said.

"First, Harrietta believes she has identified the culprit for the messages that drew the dark elf."

"Oh. Who is it?"

"She believes it is a kobold who works at the Wandering Ogre."

"A kobold? I thought she had suspected a halfling originally?"

"She did but has since been back on several occasions, and it appears that the halfling just has an infatuation with fae and is a general busybody wanting to know everyone's business. The kobold, on the other hand—Harrietta believes not just that he works for Niweq, but that he's also associated with Asterfal."

"Why would he be associated with Asterfal and working at the Wandering Ogre?"

"I think Asterfal has had someone near Killic for some time monitoring and spying on the town. It makes sense, as many cities will monitor towns or have people keep an eye on them, and with what we recently achieved over our unwanted guests, it is likely to have already been fed back to whomever they report to. Even if not by them, the news will soon spread to Asterfal. It was no secret that the town had been suffering raids."

"I heard that Asterfal has a new chancellor."

"It does," Fran nodded, pleased with SJ's knowledge. "He is also a member of the kobold council. The suspected kobold at the Wandering Ogre has only been in Killic for a few months, which ties in with the sudden changes."

"But why would they have even mentioned or ever suspected you? How would they know about your history?"

"If he is a spy, they will have access to many of the reports that have been filed over the years. I have not always led a clean and peaceful life as I do now. Having fought several dark elves previously can leave a mark and a trail, especially in the circles of power."

"If we know who it is, can't they be dealt with?"

"They could be. The problem is that if they are also working for the Asterfal chancellor and suddenly disappear, suspicion may be directed our way."

"That is if they even know what he may have done. He could be working independently."

"There is that chance. I know the dark elves have a reward on my head, and if he has the contacts, he could very well know that."

"If you don't mind me asking, how much is the reward?"

"The last time I was aware, it was twelve gold."

"Wow!" SJ exclaimed. "That's a lot. I'm not surprised that someone would report you."

"Exactly. Now, we have a plan, but it's something that will require your support."

"What do you need me to do?"

"Kill him."

"SORRY?" SJ gasped.

"As a Legionnaire, if you kill him and are caught, it won't be as problematic. Whereas if I kill him, then suspicion will just grow."

"But I am also fae, and couldn't Harrietta do it for you?"

"Yes, you are, but you are a fae assassin who was hit on by a drunken kobold, which you took offence to and took your revenge for. Unfortunately, Harrietta cannot kill directly. She can defend and support but not kill outright. Her alignment prevents her from doing so."

"If I get known as an assassin, that will damage my reputation."

"Not with the town. You would have to do something severe to lose revered status. Such as kill the mayor."

"Well, that's never going to happen."

"Also, the Wandering Ogre is outside the town's jurisdiction, which means it doesn't come under the town's protective rights."

"I meant to ask the mayor about that. If the borders change, would that not bring the Wandering Ogre into the town's jurisdiction?"

"Only if Niweq granted it. The mayor can't just force it on him without his consent. He can expand the town's borders to surround it but not include it without Niweq's permission. Otherwise, people could just go around continually expanding borders until they controlled the whole of Amathera. Only rulers can instigate forced amendments to ownership, and they only do this infrequently as it can cause severe backlash from affected parties. Especially if they suddenly find they are subject to taxes."

SJ knew all about taxes and how the system operated, many times, for the rich over the poor. She wondered if the same format was in play in Amathera.

"I assume there are allegiances, and taxes are paid as part of that?"

"Killic falls under the protection of Asterfal. However, we have seen no support since the raids began. I think that has been an ongoing issue the mayor was trying to address, and he had begun to withhold tax payments."

"Why would a town like Killic pay Asterfal? What benefits do they present to the town?"

"I do not know the details. That is a conversation you would need to have with the mayor."

"In simple terms, then, you wish me to dispose of this potential kobold spy."

"If you are able. Yes."

SJ's display triggered.

Quest: Find the Reason for the Attack—Complete
The reason behind the dark elf attack has been confirmed because of a spy in Niweq's ranks at the Wandering Ogre.
Rewards 350xp + 100% reputation bonus = 700xp awarded

Taking her to 1687 of 3000 experience to Level 12.

Quest: Eye Spy
Remove the threat of the eyes on Killic and prevent any further issues for Mistress Francisca.
Rewards: 400xp
Would you like to accept the quest? **Yes/No**

"Nice experience again," Dave said.

"What else did you want to discuss with me?" SJ asked.

"You have been asked to join the town council."

"I have. Is there a problem?"

"It's not a problem. If anything, it is an opportunity. You are aware of the reputation fae have and that many of us are untrusted because of our mischievous antics.

The fact that you have already reached such high esteem in the town and have the chance to be part of the council is a significant boost—not just for yourself but for our kind."

"How can I, being a council member, have anything to do with the fae race?"

"It won't happen immediately, but I am sure you will begin to influence things in time. You seem to have a knack for doing it even if you don't mean to."

"So you think I should accept the position, then."

"Yes, absolutely. It is an honour and a privilege to even be considered. Many in the town would love to join the council."

"I will consider your thoughts. I still have not decided either way yet."

"I would urge you to accept," Fran said, smiling. "Anyway, you said you wished to speak to me, too?"

"Yes. What can you tell me about portals and mana?"

"I can tell you everything I know. What specifically do you need to know?"

"I have just begun my Level 5 profession skill, and I can't push mana into the material to allow for enchantment slots."

"Ahh. That's because you are thinking about it."

"What do you mean?"

"Mana is all around us. You won't realise, being a non-magic-user, but in simple terms, everything we do affects mana and its distribution. It fluctuates constantly."

"If it is all around us, why do mages suffer from mana exhaustion?"

"It is not just as easy as syphoning it. It's how you manipulate it that counts. Mana regeneration is a tricky skill to master. It takes time and considerable effort to become good at it and increase your recharge rates outside of using mana potions."

"So, how do I go about using the mana I have? I am not worried about recharging it as I am guessing it naturally does recharge?"

"It does, yes. The recharge rate is affected by your Intelligence and Wisdom attributes. Use your mana the way you wish. First, you must understand what it really is and how it affects everything. It's not just as simple as pushing it. It is more as though you accept that it is there and that it is part of the bigger picture that makes up Amathera. There are areas where the mana generation is much purer. The stone circle that we discussed previously is a prime example. The mana there is one of the purest forms I have ever known."

"If I accept what mana is, then I can manipulate it?" SJ frowned.

"Basically, yes. It's the acceptance that is difficult for many to comprehend. Many a mage apprentice has failed at the first hurdle by not being able to open their minds up enough to accept its function in everything."

"I just need to consider it the same as atoms, then."

"Atoms?"

"Sorry. Atoms are the basic particles that make everything back where I am from. Everything contains atoms, like what you are saying about mana."

"I suppose it is a comparison. I have never heard the word *atoms* before, though."

"It's a science term."

"Science?" Fran was frowning deeply now.

"It's hard to explain. Like there is magic in Amathera, where I come from, originally, everything is based around science. It is not as wonderful as magic but quite amazing."

"I see. So, does this science help?"

"Yes. Very much so. It makes up the building blocks of most things, as you say mana does."

"And do you accept these atoms as existing in their entirety?"

"I do. I had not considered mana to be the same, though, and had been focusing on it being this, well, I don't know what exactly. Now you have explained it as you have, it makes a lot more sense."

"Interesting." Fran cupped her cheek, thinking. "I wonder if what you know about science can be used here?"

"I am no scientist, unfortunately, and not an expert. I only know basic concepts."

"That is a shame."

"If I can focus on mana being just particles rather than magic, I may get this to work," SJ said, smiling.

CHAPTER TWENTY-SIX

Acquaintances

After nearly an hour of attempting to use her mana again, SJ gave up with a frustrated scream. Fran chuckled. "Don't be so disheartened. Even focusing on their skill, an apprentice mage can take days, if not weeks, to learn to manipulate mana."

"I know. According to what I have been told, it could take up to a year. I just want to progress in my profession, and this is preventing me from doing so," SJ said.

"You're still attempting to force it to happen. Every time I watch you, your face scrunches up. It must flow naturally. Here, watch my demonstration again." Fran sat perfectly still and then moved her hands in front of her. "Now, as I am channelling mana, I can still hold a conversation. I am not pushing it. I allow it to manipulate what I am doing as though it is a part of me."

SJ watched as a small ball of water formed in her hand as she spoke.

"I know you can't see what I am doing exactly, but I am not forcing anything. I am just thinking about what I want to create, and it is doing it by itself. It is a strange sensation. I suppose there must be things you do without thinking about them, allowing your subconscious to control your actions. Like walking downstairs. Do you look at every step? Or do you know what to expect because you have walked down them previously? So do it naturally, without thought."

SJ tilted her head as she listened to Fran's recital. It was an interesting way to consider it. Instead of fixating on pushing the mana, she solely needed to concentrate on the result and let her body react naturally.

"One last attempt," SJ said, taking a deep, calming breath as she centred herself again. Closing her eyes, she controlled her breathing and reopened them once she felt her body relax. Looking at Fran, she held the cloth in her hands and talked to her.

"I know you are an enchanter, and I wonder what enchantments you can provide," she said.

"Oh. There are several that I have available to me. I had been learning the lightning protection one after we discovered it helped against the orc mage, but since he is no more, I have switched to a mend enchantment."

"I have that on my dress already. It's amazing."

"Your dress is fabulous. I would love to know what the enchantment is that it has."

"I think it is called self-repair."

"Ah. That is like mend but in an improved form. Mend repairs tears in clothing, whereas self-repair replaces burned or damaged items as if they were new again. I could not afford the spell for that."

"Do you have any that are combat focused?"

"I have several that could be considered combat focused but not offensive. I have only ever really focused on defensive spells. That is one of the reasons we had been training so much to fight the hobs."

"That makes sense. I would . . ."

Fran cut SJ off. "There we go," she said, smiling.

"What?" SJ said.

"Your mana."

SJ realised her mana pool was dropping, so she shouted excitedly, stopping it. "Yes! It worked." SJ had not even thought about the process while talking to Fran, meaning the enchantment process had begun naturally. The only thing she now needed to do was complete it at will and focus on the speed at which she pushed her mana. Not understanding what the basis was that was needed was annoying.

"Your mana was flowing, yes. Now you have done it once, you should be able to trigger it again. I told you that you were trying to force it."

Her pool had dropped by seven. She did not know how long it had been reduced because she had not paid it any attention. "I need to control the speed, though, as it feeds into the material, from what I was told."

"Yes. You can't just push the mana in, or it breaks the material's capability. It is the same for all professions, smithing, et cetera."

"I also was told that the quality matters?"

"Yes. Higher quality items are more susceptible to receiving enchantment slots."

"If an item has an enchantment slot, I assume it can be enchanted with anything?"

"No. Unfortunately not. The enchantments themselves are also dependent upon the material quality. The prime example is what we just discussed between mend and self-repair. Self-repair must be applied to a higher quality material for it to take."

"I see. So, once an enchantment is placed on an item, it is permanent, isn't it?"

"Yes. Until replaced."

"You can replace them. That is good to know."

"Replacing enchantments is a costly process, though, as there is always a possibility that it may damage the original item by removing the enchantment slot that it was placed in."

"Can they be replaced again?"

"They can, again, though unless you are of the profession, there is a premium you pay for the facility. You have seen yourself how difficult it can be to even add one enchantment slot. A high-level item with four slots, if it lost one, would require someone with a high profession level to replace the slot."

"It is profitable, then, once you become a higher level?"

"It can be. In larger cities, several focus only on that part of their profession rather than producing items. As I say, they charge a premium."

"I will just have to level myself, then, so I don't need to pay for it," SJ smiled.

"Definitely the best way to be."

"I have another question before I leave today."

"What did you need to know?" Fran asked.

"Can you make soul stones?"

Fran raised her eyebrows in response, staring at SJ for a moment before responding.

"You can create a portal, can't you? Which means you are now at Level 10. If so, why have you not yet jumped in a wagon to Asterfal?"

"I will be staying for a while. I am not sure what you have heard about the changes, but I don't need to leave straight away to continue growing."

Although SJ trusted Fran, she really didn't want to be talking about her level openly.

"I have not made a soul stone for many years. Amathereans do not get the ability to locate portals. Not without being part of a high council with specialist mages who can construct them. However, the mages and councils are controlled by the capital and have very restricted access to them, usually they will only ever be permitted between specific locations. The closest portal I am aware of is in a city called Lisofill. It is a dryad city in the east, over the far side of the mountains. There is no direct route from here without heading towards Asterfal first. Unless you wish to try and use the cave system, which isn't advisable."

"Could you create a soul stone, then?"

"I could try to cast it. As I say, it has been years since I last performed the spell. Do you have everything you need for it?"

"Everything I need?" SJ asked, frowning.

"Yes. There are components to casting a soul stone. It is not just casting a spell. You need specific items. First, and most importantly, you need a deed to a property."

"I have that."

Fran raised her eyebrows again. "Second, you need a trusted location to place the soul stone."

"I haven't confirmed yet, but I do not see that being a problem."

"Finally, you must give me permission to split your soul."

SJ gasped. "Sorry?"

"That is what a soul stone is. You take part of the person's soul to use as the essence gate for the portal. You can leave your portal where it is, but if you are after a soul stone spell, then you wish to return through it, and the only way is by tying part of your soul to it."

"Does it harm me in any way?"

"Not harm, no, but it does utilise your health."

"My hit points are affected?"

"Yes. It will cost 5 percent of your total hit points for every portal you place. That is not recalculated at 5 percent each time. It is 5 percent of your starting amount. If you have one hundred hit points, you will have ninety-five available. Creating a second soul stone would remove another 5 percent, leaving you with ninety."

"How do city ones work, then?"

"Direct city links are permanent portals that cities charge for their use, depending upon where they are linked to. If an individual wishes to create a soul stone to one, which they may do, they require authorisation from the portal's owner or controller, and they have to have been confirmed through bonding prior. The politics start to get a little complex."

"It is possible for Amathereans to have soul stone links to various portals, then?"

"It is, but it is very expensive, and they are rare. The only ones I ever created previously were for the High Council members in the fae capital."

"Well, I have everything needed to allow one to be created. One final question. When you use a portal, is there a cool-down before you can reuse it?"

"Yes. After using any portal, you must wait at least eight hours. The strain it puts on your body is severe, and if you tried prior, you would likely never arrive at the other end and would just join the mana clouds in the sky." Fran smiled.

"Thanks for all the information. It has been helpful. If it is okay with you, I will think about it and get back to you."

"Of course, just come and see me when you decide."

"I should really go now. I have taken up too much of your time already today."

"It's fine. I enjoyed our conversation, and as I mentioned, please consider the mayor's offer to join the council. It would still require votes, but I believe you would have the backing with your recent accomplishments. Also, the kobold needs to go," Fran stated.

"I will think about it." SJ frowned. She hadn't accepted the quest offer yet but was still considering what to do. To assassinate the kobold would require careful planning, and she wanted to investigate things before considering accepting it. Fran had seemed quite nonchalant in relation to the task, but it was SJ's future and the impact the action may have that concerned her. "The next meeting isn't for three days, so I have time," SJ said, standing. SJ glanced around the room. "Where is Harrietta?"

"She's still at the Wandering Ogre. She spends every day there and calls back in the evenings to update me on what she has discovered. I have been told some good old tales about clients who visit." Fran grinned.

"Ha. I bet you have. Anything you would like to share?" SJ smirked.

"I will keep things anonymous for now, but when I see certain members of the town next, I may have to drop a subtle hint that I know something."

SJ laughed at the thought of the potential poor husbands who may not wish to know what Fran was now privy to.

"I better go now, thanks again," SJ said as she left Fran's office.

As SJ returned toward the Hogling Arms, she mused over what to do.

"Dave?"

"Yep."

"I have been thinking about the offers."

"That's dangerous."

"What is?" SJ frowned.

"Thinking," Dave chuckled.

Rolling her eyes, SJ continued, "I have been trying to consider a way that I could interact with the Wandering Ogre without drawing unnecessary attention."

"Go on."

"Well, if the town expands its borders, Niweq will need to have a conversation about the potential of the Wandering Ogre coming within its jurisdiction."

"Or not. He could just reject the offer, of course."

"I know, and I understand that, but what I am thinking is that it's an opportunity to kill two birds with one stone. No pun intended."

"But I like puns."

Sighing, SJ continued, "If I were a member of the town council, and I mean if, and if I then suggested that I speak to Niweq on behalf of the town, I could visit without drawing any attention to myself in doing so."

"That is an excellent idea. But to what aim? You can't just walk in there and kill a kobold who works for him."

"No. Although I may at least meet them and start a conversation with them, ideally, I would want them away from the Wandering Ogre if I was going to do anything, anyway. It would be too suspicious to kill them on the site."

"You could always consider a more sinister plan."

"More sinister than planning to kill someone?"

"Okay. Maybe not more sinister but more . . ." He paused. "What's the word to describe it? Creative plan."

"What's that, then?"

"Disposing of the kobold does not necessarily have to be by your hand, does it? The quest doesn't mention anything about the actual method of death. It doesn't state you must assassinate the threat. It just states to remove the threat."

"And how would you expect me to do that?"

"Your secondary class is subterfuge, and I know you don't have the skills open yet for various elements of it, but you could always try to persuade Niweq of the kobold's reputation and have him removed. Anyone getting removed from the Wandering Ogre is never going to be accepted in Killic, and news travels fast."

"That would prevent having to kill someone when theoretically they may not be the right person. I know Harrietta has observed them, but assassinating someone with no due consideration or confirming the facts myself feels a little off."

"It's not Earth, remember. Assassins are always hired to remove targets or threats for many reasons. Jealousy, trade, et cetera. There is no one specific reason."

"I will never kill targets without purpose, though. I have said that since the start."

"I know, but if needs must, you may need to widen your narrow-minded thought process."

"Narrow-minded?" SJ said, startled at his comment.

"Yes. You are restricting your development by only pursuing one specific angle in relation to your chosen method of career progression."

"I wouldn't say that it is narrow-minded. It is moralistic, yes, but not narrow-minded."

"However you view it, you have placed a restriction on yourself that no other assassin that I have ever heard of has—or none in their right mind—"

"Hey," SJ bit out.

"—would ever do," Dave concluded.

"I won't just kill people for the sake of it unless they have done something wrong that deserves it. You know my feelings on this."

"I know, and I appreciate them. I really do. I am just stating a fact."

SJ fumed over Dave's comment and didn't speak again until she had returned to her room.

"So, what are your thoughts outside of my narrow-minded, messed-up considerations?" she huffed.

"Like I say, I think the idea has potential. You would need to first speak to the mayor and then consider some schmoozing."

"Schmoozing with who?"

"The town councillors. You said you don't know them, and if it is going to be a vote, you want to make sure there is enough support on your side."

SJ sat, considering. "That makes sense, although I am not sure how I can just walk up to many of these people and start talking to them without having something in common."

"There you go, then. There is your next mission. Find out about the members."

"I suppose I can, not that two days is a great deal of time to get to know people."

"No, but it's a start, at least."

"I agree. Okay, it's time to go and find out where they work when they're not in the meetings, and I think I know the best person to ask," SJ said, standing back up with conviction.

"Let's go," Dave said enthusiastically.

Late in the evening, SJ was returning to the inn for a much-needed dinner. It had been the busiest day since SJ had arrived in Amathera, and although tired, she was proud of how much she had accomplished.

"Well, that wasn't too bad a day, was it? You've started to make some good inroads with several of the council members," Dave said.

"I'm shattered and I still have many more to find and speak to tomorrow, and I also need to speak to the mayor."

"The ent made me laugh when you visited him," Dave chuckled.

When SJ had left her room in the late afternoon, she went downstairs to speak to Kerys, the fountain of local knowledge. Kerys had been more than happy to share details about the various council members, even giving her some prewarning about some of their foibles. SJ had learned that there were twenty-five town council members, which was more than she had realised, never having seen them all present at once in the chamber.

SJ had discovered that the ent was a butcher when he wasn't representing his kind within the town, and she had visited him in his shop. As soon as she walked in, he approached her and busied himself around her, asking how she was and what he could do for her. His name was Earleqious, and he had been the ents' council member for over a century, long before the mayor even came to Killic. He had told her stories about Killic's growth and the troubles he had witnessed. He stopped talking only when a customer walked in, and he continued as soon as they left.

The strangest thing was seeing him work. Having four arms, he was a dab hand at butchering, able to work wonders with his knives using two at once. SJ had stared in amazement as he chopped and stripped the carcasses of several hoglings while she visited. She was also privy to a delivery of fresh hoglings from one of the hunting parties and watched the interactions. There were apparently two butchers in the town, and he had a rivalry with the other and would pay extra to ensure he got the best carcasses.

It wasn't just hoglings that he butchered, although they seemed to be a staple food of most townsfolk. There were all different cuts of meat from various creatures, many SJ didn't recognise, and several fowl strung up by their feet on the bars that lined the shop. Earleqious had even tried to get her to have a go and butcher one of the hoglings, which she had kindly refused.

"I don't think you will have a problem getting his vote," Dave had said as they left.

"He was nice, but he just doesn't stop talking."

She had also visited one of the gnomes and one of the elven representatives and was building up a picture of their relationships. Over the next two days she planned on visiting a human, dryad, dwarven, gnoll, kobold, ratkin, draconian, orc, and bugbear council member. She wanted to speak to at least one of each party since each race appeared to have two members. The only races she knew of that didn't have permanent representatives were the trolls, lycanthropes, halflings, quarterlings, and undead.

Apparently, as the presiding mayor was a lycanthrope, they only held one vote. That meant there was always an odd number of votes, and they could never be deadlocked. SJ had originally thought that Alice was one of the dryad council members but learned that she was just the deputy mayor and held no voting power, although she had mayoral authority. The complexity of the politics just in a town this size was substantial. To consider what it might be like within a large city was mind-numbing.

SJ's work was cut out for her, getting around them all, especially if any of them talked as much as Earleqious had. She took out her notebook and pencil and made notes about each she had met. The elven representative she had spoken to had been the most off with her, not wishing to talk outside of just passing initial pleasantries. She had felt quite uncomfortable and ended up leaving after a short period. The gnome had been much friendlier and had spoken openly but was too busy to chat.

"If they add me to the council, I wonder what position I should take."

"What do you mean *position?*"

"All the members, from what Kerys said earlier, are not just racial representatives but also hold specific roles within the council. It's not as if I can just join and say, *Hey, I'm an assassin, I can kill whoever you wish*, is it?"

"Well, you could do that, but you are not really skilled enough yet to sell your profession."

"I was being sarcastic," SJ said, shaking her head.

"Really!" Dave replied, his own voice dripping in sarcasm.

"Okay. It's time for a late dinner and a good sleep. I have a lot of people to see," SJ said.

CHAPTER TWENTY-SEVEN

Proposal

I have told you before that I will not put up with those excuses," Zigferd bellowed as SJ reached the top of the stairs leading to his office. A bugbear came hurrying past, nearly bowling her over.

"Yes, Mayor," it called, not slowing as it headed downstairs.

SJ walked over to the mayor's office, where he was sitting at his desk, holding his head in his hands and mumbling to himself.

"Zigferd. Are you okay?" SJ asked from the doorway.

Looking up, the mayor smiled. "I'm sorry, SJ. This is just some bad news again."

"Anything that I can help with?" SJ asked.

"Unless you can find the funds to repair the bridge to the dock, then no."

"What? How has the bridge been damaged?" SJ had crossed the bridge on several occasions; it was a solid structure.

"Some idiot decided to try to transport a whole wagon of stone over in one go for a new storehouse being built. Trying to save on costs. But the load was too heavy for the structure. The bridge collapsed, and the wagon sank, dragging the horses in with it."

"The horses drowned?" SJ said, shocked.

"No. Thankfully, the driver jumped in and cut the reins, allowing them to swim to the shoreline. The problem is that the bridge needs repairing as a matter of urgency, and this month, the funds are already low after the compensation from the battle."

"Can you not get it repaired and then pay afterwards? I am sure the town members realise the importance of the bridge?"

"They do, and they would. The problem is that we have been eating into the town's reserves for months. With no additional income, and without the mithril mine operational yet, we are nearly broke."

"Is there no way of increasing the town's income?" SJ asked, taking a seat before the mayor's desk. "Is there nothing that you can export to surrounding towns or villages? I am not sure what's around here geographically."

"Several smaller towns and villages exist, but many feel the pinch themselves. The new chancellor at Asterfal has increased the taxes on everyone since he took over, focusing on Asterfal's well-being only. I haven't paid over the past two months and have been issued a writ for monies owed."

"How can you be paying Asterfal? Not even a single person came to help with the hobs."

"They did initially. When the hobs first appeared, they funded the increase in the guard force. That is all they did, though, so after we recruited more guards, they cut any more coin or failed to provide any other support. This now means that we have a larger guard than we need. Although since we're considering expansion in the future, we will need an even larger guard eventually, especially with the open avenues across the territories."

"You are in a catch-22, then."

"Sorry?" Zigferd replied, scrunching his face in confusion.

"It's a term from where I am from. You need growth, but you can't afford it, and without growth, you can't increase your income. So, you can't do right for doing wrong."

"Basically, yes. The council are split on how to proceed. I have suggested increasing town taxes, but that reduces the viable funding within the town itself."

"I had started to think that the town was self-sufficient financially."

"It is. Our exports are limited. Mining and fishing are our main income streams, but these are limited because of the surrounding areas not having the coin themselves.

"Anyway, that is enough about my problems. What can I do for you?"

SJ sat silently for a moment. "If I am voted in, I will provisionally accept your invitation to the council."

"That is fantastic news," Zigferd replied with a huge grin.

"I have a few questions, though, and need to understand some things."

"Of course. What would you like to ask?"

"Voting. I am aware there are currently twenty-five members, including yourself. If I joined the council, there would be twenty-six. That could mean split votes in the future. I would like to propose that you also invite Fran to the council. That way, we have two racial representatives like the other races, and voting would remain freely abled."

Zigferd raised his eyebrow, considering, before he replied, "I could offer Mistress Francisca a position, but I doubt she would take it. She has never shown interest outside of general support for the town—by that I mean in relation to the council."

"If you don't ask, you will never know."

"That is true, and I will take it as an idea. There is another option to consider."

"What is that?"

"If you are voted in, which I am sure you will be, I suggest you join as a non-voting member. That way, the balance remains the same, and you can be impartial over future decisions. It also means that you will not be tied up in as many meetings or problems that require discussion, as I know you will still have your own growth to focus on."

"That sounds like a great option," Dave said.

Considering his comments, SJ had to agree. Being a member of the council without the restrictions around voting would be more of an advisory function, which sounded more suited to her.

"I like the non-voting option."

"If you agree, it will be added to the proposal before the vote. If anyone is against your joining, this might sway them."

SJ was nervous because the decision over her joining the council would be based on a vote of confidence. "I spent last night and most of the day today meeting with the council's race representatives, and most were quite amenable. The only one who seemed to have any major problems was Orik."

"Hahahahaha. Orik likes you. You have no problem with Orik's vote."

"Really? That is not the impression I get," SJ said, shocked.

"Once you get to know Orik, you will realise that the grumpier he is towards you, the more you are in his favour. He has always been the same in his relationships and interactions with others. He holds Shelly in such high regard but will never tell her to her face."

"Has anyone ever mentioned it to her? She has a real issue with him."

"I'm not sure, but it also does no harm to Orik as he normally gets what he needs to from the dwarven community without any arguments. I can virtually always guarantee his support."

"Talking about the mines, I need to see how they have been progressing."

"Apparently, very well. The infrastructure is nearly complete. From the last report I received, they were apparently finishing building the rails to bring the ore to the ridge from the entrance."

"When do you think they will commence mining and smelting?"

"Mining is hoped to commence within the week. Smelting is something else entirely. Nevik arrived the other day and is currently discussing the smelter's location. He wants it close to the mine, which means we will have to clear some of the forest, but we don't want it too close to the valley edge. Advertising that a smelter has suddenly appeared could draw unnecessary attention."

"Will that matter if the wall gets built in the valley?"

"No. Long-term, it won't, but we can't build the wall until we start making money. Selling raw mithril ore is just not as profitable as selling smelted ore. We also need to find a way to get it to market."

"I am not sure, but I may know about that. I can't guarantee it yet, but there is a possibility that I know someone who could help. If it doesn't go against their standing, I am sure they would also wish for a cut."

"If you know anyone, please speak to them and let me know. I am willing to offer a percentage cut of profit if it means that we can get the materials onto the market safely and securely. I must add—without drawing attention to the town. I could go to the dwarven miners' guilds, who I am sure would snap my hand off to be involved, but then it would become general news, and that's when we are likely to start seeing issues from people coming here. Ideally, I would like it to remain unnoticed for as long as possible."

"Are you not concerned about people in the town talking about it?" SJ asked.

"No. All those aware are sworn under the oath to secrecy regarding town matters. They couldn't openly discuss it unless they wished to break their oath, and if they did, then more fool them."

The consideration of oaths intrigued SJ more than anything else now. "If I join the council, I assume I must take an oath?"

"You would be asked to be a standard part of the enrolment ceremony."

"Okay. I will speak to my friends and see what they think about whether they can help or not, and I'll let you know. I was also unaware of the oath requirement until you mentioned it, so it is something else to consider."

"I'm sorry. I didn't even think to mention it. It's part of the standard working of any town."

"That's fine, but let me consider it a little first. As things stand, I am willing to accept the position, with the caveat that I'm still considering the oath requirement."

"That is understood. Thank you for coming to see me, and I hope it won't prevent your acceptance. I believe you have much to bring to Killic over the years."

SJ reeled a little at the comment. She hadn't really thought through how long the term would last.

"No problem. Thanks for your time. If I can think of anything to help with the finances, I'll let you know. I am a dab hand at working with numbers."

As she left the barracks, ideas ran through her mind.

"You have that look on your face again," Dave said.

"Which look?"

"The one where you are thinking. Either that or you have constipation."

SJ snorted, drawing a strange look from a female orc walking with her child.

"Sorry. I just remembered a joke," she said, smiling at the scowling face. "Don't make me laugh," she whispered.

"So, what are you thinking?"

"I think we both know someone who may or may not help."

"Fizzlewick?"

"Yes."

"It's a consideration, I suppose, but I am unsure how the System would react."

"Did you not say he has been an advisor in a capital of all places?"

"Well, yes, he has. I am unsure whether he will be allowed to get involved at this level."

"What does the level matter? If he has helped a capital before, why could he not have helped a town? He even said himself that he was enjoying it here. I also want to let him know I have more of an idea about my mana now."

Before SJ had set out on the day to meet more council members, she had spent time practicing her mana use again. It was a strange sensation when it triggered, and she wanted to confirm the speed and mana use to create the slots now. She burst into the tailor's shop enthusiastically, throwing the door open a little too hard and losing a grip on the handle. The door flew inwards and collided with a mannequin displaying some clothes, sending it flying across the shop floor.

The three customers standing inside at the time turned around at the crashing door and dummy.

"Sorry," SJ said sheepishly, feeling her cheeks get very hot. She bent over, picked the mannequin up, and placed it back where it should have been. The customers turned back to the counter, and SJ saw the quizzical look of the quarterling from around the side of the counter.

SJ made herself busy browsing the clothes on display and even picked up a couple of items she really liked the look of. She didn't need to wear her dress all the time and thought it was about time to upgrade her wardrobe. As Fizzlewick finished serving the last customer, she waited patiently in line. As soon as they were gone, he locked the door and flicked the closed sign, closing the shutters.

"What has brought you here in such a hurry and so excited?" he asked as he changed to his human form.

"Two things. First, I have managed to start controlling my mana."

"That is very fast. You continue to impress me, and what else?"

"I need to ask you a specific question about whether or not you are willing to help."

The god raised an eyebrow, and half smirked. "I'm willing to help. I see. Well, unless you let me know what you are wondering about, I can't confirm either way."

"Okay. The second question is first, then. You are aware of the mithril mine?"

"Of course, yes."

"The town is looking to smelt and sell the ore."

"Understandable, as smelting will get a better price."

"They don't want to appear as a seller on the market suddenly, and I was wondering if you had any ideas or thoughts on how it may be achieved?"

Fizzlewick continued to smirk. "You are asking if I can help?"

"Well, not directly but yes."

"What exactly did you have in mind?"

"Dave told me you have been an advisor for a capital before."

"Yes."

"Would you be in a position to advise and support the town?"

"And how would I be doing this?"

SJ could feel her nerves tingling as she asked a god if he could help, but it was strange how she saw him. Even though he was a god, he always seemed more like a grandfatherly figure.

"If Killic suddenly went to market selling mithril, it would draw a huge amount of unwanted attention and questions. Is there anything you could do to assist in the distribution of the mithril that would not draw the attention of the rest of the continent towards Killic? I am aware of the territory restrictions normally imposed on mithril, and if they did go to market, it would very likely draw the wrong kind of attention."

"I see. Well, then, let me consider the question. You are asking if I can somehow influence the distribution of the mithril into the market so that no one will know where it came from?"

"Basically, yes."

"If I were to undertake such an activity, how would this transactional process benefit me? I am a god and do not require Amatherean possessions, after all."

"What would you wish for if you could in any way support the distribution of the mithril?"

"Now, that is a tricky question. There is nothing I need, although the proposition to be involved in the town's influence as this new approach is taken is quite intriguing."

"New approach?"

"We are aware of the boundaries and the adjustments just like you are. We were conferred with before they were implemented. That is one of the exciting aspects about your involvement in them with your status."

SJ opened her eyes wide. "So, you know about the sandbox?"

"I know enough. But unfortunately, I cannot say what I know. Suffice to say that things are only just getting started." He smiled.

"So, could you help?"

"I may be in a position to provide some guidance and influence regarding distributing mithril, yes."

"That is amazing," SJ said excitedly.

"But . . ." Fizzlewick said, pausing.

"But what?" SJ asked, her excitement disappearing immediately.

"But I would like to meet with the mayor in person. Although I have seen him, I have never met the man, and I would like to fully understand who I am supporting. I know that you trust him and that they trust you, as your reputation shows. It doesn't mean that I trust him, though."

"You want to meet him as yourself?" The request shocked SJ.

"I said in person. I never said as who or what." Fizzlewick smiled.

"Can you not already tell what he is like?" SJ asked.

"If you mean can I get involved and see what is happening? Well, yes, if I wished to, I could. I like looking into a being's eyes when I talk business. I don't bother getting involved with the day-to-day lives of most, as their choices are their own. I have my followers that I need to look after. You would be amazed at the number of prayers I receive each day to help with the specifics of tailoring tasks."

The thought of the thousands of prayers that a god might receive daily was mind-blowing.

"How do you do it?"

"Do what?"

"Answer all the prayers."

"Oh. Well, it is a little complex to explain, but every prayer received carries a rating via the System; the higher the rating, the more influence the individual is using, therefore the more astral essence that I am given. This astral essence is then used as part of the process of supporting the wider tailoring profession. The intricacies and details are a little complex, but overall, as long as input remains higher than output then the coffers stay full, and influence remains. It is a continual function of a god. One of my siblings once didn't bother responding to any of his prayers and he soon came unstuck, his astral pool shrank, and he was left high and dry. After that, it took him a long time to regain his astral pool."

"It sounds more like a business than anything else."

"I suppose it is, really, when you consider it."

"I thought you gained your essence from items that are made?"

"The majority I do. But I do still receive prayers as well."

"When would you be able to meet the mayor?"

"I can be free whenever needed."

"I am confused how you are going to present yourself to him, though."

"It won't be as you see me now."

SJ felt nervous about introducing Zigferd to Fizzlewick. "What name would you go by? I can't just say Fizzlewick, as he may know of your past, and I can't use Haber, as surely he's heard of the God of Tailoring."

"Umm. I think I will use my elven form. He uses the name Nexis. Would you like to see him?"

"Yes, please," SJ said. It was amazing seeing a god change forms so easily.

In moments, Fizzlewick's facial features changed, and his body shape adjusted, growing in height by several inches. Once he had finished transforming, the elf that stood before her, almost six feet tall, with finely sculptured olive skin and vibrant green eyes, was a being of beauty.

SJ gasped in amazement at the transformation. "Is there anything you can't transform into?"

The voice that responded was different and now held a youthful musical lilt. "Unfortunately, I am restricted to bipedal forms. Becoming a dragon would have been great, but we can't."

"You look stunning," SJ said, un able to take her eyes off him. He was wearing a beautifully cut outfit that clung to his frame, accentuating his athletic appearance, and SJ could imagine him being the star model at a Paris Fashion Week.

"Why thank you," Nexis replied, smiling, which added another layer to his beauty.

"You may be a little intimidating, though."

"What makes you think that?" he asked quizzically.

"You look like a perfect specimen." SJ thought the Charisma of this persona must be nearly one hundred.

"This form does have its benefits, and I usually use it for negotiations." He smiled.

"I am sure it does," SJ said, feeling a little starstruck. Her stomach was in knots. She remembered feeling the same way when she had been to watch her favourite band in concert as a teenager and one of them had looked at her during their performance. "I will speak to the mayor and arrange the best time. There is a council meeting tomorrow, so it won't be until after that."

"Ah. Yes. The votes."

"You know about them?"

"I know most things. Just because I have not been to or met many of these people in person doesn't mean I don't know what is happening where I am currently choosing to reside."

Reeling from the transformation and the god's cryptic undertone, SJ remembered the other reason she came to visit him.

"Before I forget again. What speed do I need to push mana for the enchantment slots?"

"Ideally it will be a natural speed. It can vary for everyone, but it should never be forced or held back. Unfortunately, that is the only advice I can give. There is no right or wrong, it is what your body decides is best when in a meditative state, and the only way you will know is when you can achieve the result. Then it is the case of repeating it as you need to. Which is where the challenge comes in. Many have managed it once or twice but then struggled again, and they give up on slot enchantments. That is why those who are skilled can make themselves very wealthy."

What he said was tied to the information that Fran had given her. "I will keep trying, then, and hope that it works. Also, I was practising on a cloth bundle. I wanted to ask as I am a little uncertain, but when creating a slot, should I not be practising on a completed item?"

"No. For practice, there is no point. If you fail when trying to enchant an item, you can reduce its quality. On a raw material, it doesn't affect it."

"Can I then use the material to make something, and it gets the slot when made?"

"No. That would be great if you could, because then you would never fail against an item, but unfortunately again, it's not allowed. Once you use the material, it loses anything added to it."

"Can I practice on the same cloth bundle multiple times?"

"Yes. As a raw material, it can be enchanted as much as you wish with no restrictions, as it holds no benefit and could never actually take an enchantment."

"I see. That is useful to know. I better go now, but thank you so much for agreeing to meet the mayor, and I will let you know when it can be arranged."

"No problem at all. It has been a pleasure, as always, SJ. Keep up the good work. I see a bright future in you." Nexis smiled.

"If I got additional data storage every time you are involved in something I have not witnessed before in Amathera," Dave said as she got back to the inn, "I would soon have more storage than the System."

SJ smiled and whispered, "I need to consider how to arrange the meeting. I can't just have him suddenly arrive without any prior warning. It would be strange if someone looking like Nexis suddenly appeared in the town and no one had seen him before."

"That is an excellent point. Although do you know and see everyone in the town?"

"Not daily, no, of course not, but an elf with his looks would have been noticed, believe me."

"Really? I thought he was a little mediocre."

"Mediocre? Are you kidding me? He was beautiful."

"Have you fallen for your deity?" Dave asked sarcastically.

SJ could feel her cheeks heating. "No, I don't mean it that way," she said, flustered.

"Sure, sure. I believe you," Dave said, chuckling.

CHAPTER TWENTY-EIGHT

Votes Count

The next morning, SJ got up early and felt very nervous about what was expected to be undertaken that day. The council meeting was set for ten, and her stomach was already tied in knots. She had struggled to fall asleep the previous evening with the turmoil going through her mind. She had never even expected to be in this position, and initially, although astounded by the offer, it had not really felt real. Now that it was about to happen, it was entirely different.

"How are you this morning?" Dave asked.

"Nervous," SJ said as she stood looking in her mirror, straightening her dress and fiddling with her choker.

"Why? You have nothing to be nervous about."

"Nothing. Are you kidding me? They will vote today whether they want me as part of the council."

"And?"

"And? What do you think? I never expected it to happen."

"Meh. It doesn't affect you either way. If they wish you to be part of it, all is well and good. If not, you just continue as a normal Legionnaire would, causing mayhem and chaos."

SJ sighed. "A little moral support wouldn't go amiss."

"I do support you. If they don't accept you as a member, they are making a stupid mistake, but that is what it is. You can't change fate. Look at you. You got squished by a tree."

"I'm not sure I class this as fate."

"What would you class it as, then?"

"Judgement."

"No one is judging you, though, are they?"

"Of course they are. They are voting whether they believe I am good enough to join the council, even as a non-voting member."

"But it isn't you, is it? The real you, I mean. It is only the persona you have shown so far."

"What is that supposed to mean?"

"Have you been truthful to yourself?"

"Yes." SJ's brow furrowed at his comment.

"Really truthful?"

"Yes. Always since I arrived."

"Okay. Then they are judging you," Dave replied cheerily.

"Urgh. Way to calm a girl down."

"Sorry. I was being agreeable."

"Sometimes it is much better to be less agreeable and more diplomatic in your replies."

"I will consider that for next time. I am a little excited myself, though. The last time I had a Legionnaire in any position of authority was in a guild, and I had never been in a township or city before. It will open a new world of interesting things as time progresses."

The realisation of what she was potentially getting involved with was not unknown to her, and she could feel panic rising in her chest as she stood there. "Why do I feel as though I need a drink?"

"I don't know, why do you?" Dave replied.

"Again, not helpful."

"Sorry. I just want to see you succeed and do what is best for you," Dave said sincerely.

SJ paused, staring at herself in the mirror. Sometimes, she wished she could see Dave. Looking into her own eyes, she said, "Thank you."

Downstairs, the inn had the usual morning crowd for breakfast. Since Floretta had begun including mushrooms, it had become more popular, and SJ had mentioned to Floretta that adding tomatoes and baked beans would be beneficial. Floretta had been completely thrown by the term *baked beans*, and SJ had had to have a long conversation about what they were. Floretta was unsure she had anything similar but said she would consider the additions. She liked the sound of adding fried tomatoes, though.

Sitting at a table after ordering breakfast, SJ was drinking a coffee when the inn door came flying open. Everyone turned to stare as a cloaked figure came striding into the inn. The cloak was pale purple, and the clothes beneath it looked pristine. The figure walked straight to the bar before removing his hood. SJ nearly fell out of her seat. It was Nexis.

"Good morning. Could I please have breakfast and a glass of honey wine?" he asked in his melodic voice.

The whole inn stared at him, and Fhyliss, who was working behind the bar, stammered a reply: "O-o-of course."

"Thank you. I will be sat with the young fae over there," Nexis replied, pointing to SJ.

If she hadn't been flustered before, she was now, as Nexis, walked over and sat at the table with her. "Morning," he said, beaming.

SJ had frozen with a fork full of food halfway to her mouth, and snapping out of her trance, she put it down. "Morning," she said, her eyes like saucers. "What are you doing here?" she whispered.

All the eyes in the inn were still on her and the elf.

"I thought it best to be seen in town if I am going to be meeting the mayor soon. I didn't want to be a stranger."

"Did you listen in on a conversation I had with Dave?" she questioned.

"Whatever would give you that idea?" he replied, grinning.

"I have the meeting this morning. So I am not available."

"I am well aware. I thought I would just wish you good luck, that is all."

"How can I explain that you arrived so soon after discussing the issue? It takes days to reach Asterfal."

"Here," Nexis replied, placing his hand in his pocket and removing a small flat gem. It was opaque, and SJ frowned.

"What is that?"

"It's a messenger stone. It allows parties who hold linked stones the ability to communicate."

"Oh!" SJ exclaimed, shocked at the information and ability to communicate over a long distance. She had thought it must be possible, having experienced and listened to previous conversations in the inn, but had never had any confirmation.

"How do I use it?"

"You can't. It's fake but will give you the cover you need if anyone asks how I arrived in such a timely manner."

"Thanks," SJ said, pocketing the small stone.

Fhyliss came rushing over, almost tripping as she delivered the plate of steaming food and large glass of honey wine to Nexis.

"Here you go, sir," she said.

"Please don't call me sir. My name is Nexis, and I am a friend of SJ's. She has said wonderful things about you," Nexis replied. The charm oozing off him was palpable, and SJ saw Fhyliss physically shudder.

SJ glanced around the room, and most eyes were still fixed on Nexis.

"Thank you. That's so kind of you, SJ," Fhyliss said shyly, smiling at her.

"And what about your wonderful mother as well? Kerys, isn't it?"

"Yes. She is sleeping now. She will be working this afternoon."

"Excellent. While visiting town, I could also do with a room. Do you have any space currently?"

SJ knew a wagon had arrived from Asterfal yesterday, and several new patrons were now in the inn.

"We have a room left, but it isn't very special. It's more of a store cupboard than a room."

"As long as it has a bed where I can rest my head, that is all that matters."

"Of course, I will get the key for you. Nexis, wasn't it?"

"Yes, my dear, Nexis. Thank you," he said, turning to look back at SJ. Fhyliss stumbled back away from the table. SJ saw a female dryad grab her arm as she went past, whispering to her.

News of his arrival was going to travel fast. Nexis removed a small, beautifully crafted knife from a sheath on his belt and began to eat the food. He picked up one of the plump, juicy, fried delicacies of a mushroom and placed it in his mouth. "Ummm. Delicious."

SJ closed her mouth, which had hung open again, and picked up her fork. After eating another couple of mouthfuls of food, she looked back over at the god. He was paying no attention to anything around him, focused purely on the plate of food in front of him.

"Did you have to make such a scene?" SJ whispered towards him.

"If I am going to play my part as an auction trader, then I have a part to play," he replied, smiling.

"So, you have decided how you will do it?"

"Oh. Yes. I will explain the details fully when we meet with the mayor and I have had a chance to see into his eyes."

SJ gulped at the thought of Nexis meeting the towering and imposing form of Zigferd.

"What about the shop?"

"It is in excellent hands, don't worry," he replied.

"But how, when you are here?"

"I can multitask, you know."

SJ knew she was in an alternate reality already, but it now seemed like she had entered an entirely new one. She sat in silence for the remainder of her breakfast. When she had finished, she asked for another coffee, which Fhyliss brought over, shaking still. She poured her a cup, nearly sloshing it everywhere. Nexis just sat and smiled at her.

"Please thank the cook for me. The food was delightful," Nexis said.

"I will," Fhyliss replied. Her cheeks could not have been more flushed. "Oh, and here is the key to the room. It's at the top of the stairs, the first door on the right. It's small but has a bed, and it's clean."

"Thank you again," he said.

"So, you are staying here?" SJ asked once Fhyliss left.

"No. Of course not. I stay home normally, but it is nice to get out and about and interact occasionally."

"Home? Where is that?"

"It's a long way from here. It doesn't take more than an instant to travel, though. The benefits of my kind are that we are our own soul stones, so we can come and go as we please."

"How many of you are there?"

"One, of course."

"No, I mean variants of you."

"Currently just the two you know."

"Why when Bob came did you close the shop, then?"

"Out of respect for Bob. I wished him to know he had my full attention when I spoke to him. He is a very dear friend."

Baffled beyond belief, SJ drank her coffee. "I need to head off to the meeting," she said, standing.

"No problem. I am going to hang around here for a while. May have a nap. A walk around town. Haven't quite decided yet. But I will have another honey wine—this is a very fine year."

SJ shook her head. Turning, she saw many eyes were still transfixed on their table. "I will see you later then, Nexis," she said at a normal volume.

"Indeed, SJ. I will see you this afternoon. I hope it goes well."

"Thanks," she said, and left the inn.

SJ walked down the street, lost for words or thoughts, for that matter. She realised she no longer felt nervous about the vote being due within the hour.

"Well, that was interesting," Dave's chipper voice said, bounding into her mind and disturbing her thoughtless thoughts.

"Confusing perhaps."

"I think it was very genuine of him. His role-play is amazing. You must compliment him when you see him. He had Fhyliss eating out of his hand."

"That wasn't role-play. I don't know his Charisma level, but that is pure charm."

"Still impressive to see. Especially how fickle people are."

"Fickle?"

"Yes. Just because he is a good-looking elf in that form and plays a role doesn't mean that he is a good person. People fall for those sorts of people all the time. It is a common misconception. Good looks do not mean someone is a good person. Otherwise, charlatan and charmer wouldn't be a profession choice for some."

"Very philosophical this morning, aren't you?"

"I do try to keep my philosophical side open to development," Dave replied.

His statement was accurate, though. Nexis's looks and charm meant nothing, especially since SJ knew it was an act by a god.

The chamber was packed when SJ arrived. She had never seen all the representatives in attendance before, and walking inside the room with its dark wooden beams and stately furnishings, which she hadn't really noticed previously, made SJ feel minuscule and insignificant. Apart from the council members, a human sat with parchment and quill.

"SJ, welcome. Please come and take a seat." Zigferd indicated to a chair next to his own at the head of the table.

SJ self-consciously walked around the table to where Zigferd stood. The other council members now all stood, waiting for the meeting to begin.

"Am I late?" SJ asked as she reached the table head.

"No. We had other matters to discuss prior to your attendance today." Zigferd smiled. "Please, everyone, be seated."

The group all began to sit and adjust themselves in their chairs. SJ had gone to sit too, but Zigferd looked at her subtly, raising his eyebrows to signify she should remain standing. Once quiet settled in the chamber, Zigferd began.

"Dear all, I know we have already gone through the formalities of today's meeting, and I thank you for your time and commitment to Killic." Several people around the chamber banged the table with their hands. "We now have a rather unique and important vote to hold. You are all aware of the reason for this vote and the conditions related to the information I gave you all prior to the meeting.

"Today, as the presiding mayor of Killic who has held office for fifty-two years, I am proposing that we amend our town charter. This will be the first amendment of its kind since the charter was written, and that is why today I invited scribe Artorian to be in attendance to make and seal the changes if this is voted upon."

Several banged on the table again, and SJ could feel the sweat on her back from being in the spotlight.

"It is with great honour and the privilege that you have granted me as your mayor that I propose the addition of the town council's first non-voting and first fae member. Since her arrival in Killic, SJ has been one of the most impressive new starters we have ever had the privilege of knowing. Because of her selfless commitment and approach to the town and its people with her caring and supportive nature, she has changed the opinion of many in relation to the unfortunate habits many of her kind portray.

"Because of this, I would ask you to consider all the supporting information, and we will cast a vote. The vote will be a hidden ballot, so those who may feel uncertain can vote accordingly without due concern. I will now break the meeting for fifteen minutes to allow votes to be cast. Please drop them in the chest on Artorian's desk."

Zigferd stood there, and silence remained for a few moments until chairs scraped and several stood. Small groups broke off, and conversations broke out between the various race representatives around the room. "That's it, then; we just wait now," Zigferd said, turning to SJ with a smile.

"I have never felt so nervous before," SJ answered. She had met with several people in attendance over the past few days, and most of her meetings were amicable. Many kept turning and looking at her as she stood there as though awaiting the hangman's noose.

A bugbear entered the chamber carrying a tray of drinks and walked over to SJ. "Drink?" he asked,

"I would love a coffee if you have one?" SJ said.

"I can get you a coffee, yes," the bugbear replied.

"Thank you," SJ said.

A few minutes later he returned carrying a pot and mug for her. She took a nervous gulp. Several had walked up and placed their cards in the chest, and as the fifteen minutes ticked along, more did so, until there were only a couple who hadn't.

"Time," Zigferd called.

Once he did, the members retook their seats. "Please sit, SJ," he said.

It was the first time she had sat since entering the room, and her legs felt like jelly. The relief was welcome. Artorian, the scribe, opened the chest and read through the inserted cards, creating piles in front of him. SJ watched the process with trepidation, and the air could have been cut with a knife as they awaited the count.

Artorian finished and then turned, nodding to Zigferd. SJ could feel a trickle of sweat on her back, and her palms felt clammy as she sat there nervously.

"Please, Artorian, if you would be so kind." Zigferd gestured toward him.

The scribe stood and walked to the far end of the table opposite where Zigferd and SJ sat.

Coughing, he cleared his throat. "The results of the vote are as follows. This was a two-stage vote as described in the town manifest. Item one addresses whether to include a fae on the council as a non-voting member. Those in favour: fifteen. Those against: eight. Abstained: two."

SJ felt her stomach lurch when she learned eight had opposed the addition of a fae to the council.

"Now to the second part of the vote. As item one passed, this is to vote on whether SJ will be accepted as a non-voting town council member. The voting is unanimous with those in favour being twenty-three; again two have abstained."

Banging began on the table, a few cheered for the vote's success. SJ sat in shock; they had just amended their long-standing town charter to include the addition of a fae. The amazing fact was that twenty-three out of twenty-five had voted for her, irrespective of her being fae, and two abstained, probably people she had never spoken to or met before.

Zigferd stood up. "Artorian. Thank you so much for your time. Please amend the town charter as soon as possible so that all council members can re-sign. Also, can we please have the officiate's seal for SJ as her representative on the council?"

"Of course, Mayor. I will have the amendment to the charter done momentarily. It can be signed before the meeting ends today. The same applies to SJ's seal," Artorian replied.

"SJ. Please stand." Zigferd ushered towards her.

SJ stood nervously.

"Will you take the Oath of Killic and swear your allegiance?" Zigferd asked.

"I will."

"Then please read the following." Zigferd handed SJ a piece of parchment, which she unrolled and read.

"I, SJ, do swear by the gods that I will truly serve the town of Killic in the office of the council, and I will do right to many people after the laws and usages of this town, without fear or favour, affection or ill will."

As SJ finished speaking, a bright blue light encased her before it dissipated again.

"SJ, would you like to say anything else?" Zigferd asked.

"I did not know I would need to," SJ said, turning to Zigferd. Looking back to the table, she addressed them. "Thank you all for your vote of confidence in my position on the council. I know I am a non-voting member, but I will do what I can through my actions to support the continuing growth and prosperity of Killic as we enter this new System age."

"Here, here," several cheered, banging the table again.

"Again, thank you, and I hope to get to know you all better soon."

More cheers erupted and SJ felt her cheeks redden under the intense scrutiny.

"Okay. We still have matters to address yet in relation to the expansion of the borders. We will break for ten minutes and then continue if that is okay with everyone."

Again, the members stood and mingled. SJ was unsure what to do until several council members came up and started speaking to her. Many congratulated her. The largest shock was when Orik, the grumpy old dwarf, walked up to her. He stared at her with his usual criticising gaze. She shrank away until he threw his arms around her and gave her a hug. "Welcome to the council," he said warmly. It was fleeting but the most heartfelt of the congratulations she was given.

The meeting soon got back underway again.

CHAPTER TWENTY-NINE

Who, What, Why

The meeting had continued for much longer than SJ had expected, and the discussions amongst the members had become very heated on occasion. The conflict over the expansion, structures, and suggestions over border locations was considerable. The resounding consideration that everyone had, even those in full support, was the ability for the town to financially cover the costs involved.

The meeting concluded again with no formal decision or vote being carried, with a significant split in opinion over the best way to proceed. SJ had listened to all the conversations but not put her opinion across, as she could understand both sides of the argument. Expanding the town was hugely beneficial and would improve their standing within the territory. The risks associated with expansion, though, could initially outweigh any benefits as they were likely to be targeted if they displayed renewed prosperity. Walking down the stairs afterwards, Zigferd asked her if she was free to talk.

"I have some time, although I do need to go and complete some training today. I have been a little remiss due to the meeting," SJ said.

"Excellent," Zigferd replied, leading her back to his office. "Alice. Will you join us please?"

Alice had been ahead of them and, on hearing her name, turned and smiled. "Of course."

Once the three of them were sat in the mayor's office, Zigferd began. "Well, firstly thank you both dearly. Alice, without your continuing support and provisions you provide to the town daily, we would not be as strong as we are. SJ. Thank you for accepting the role as a member of the town council."

SJ could again feel her cheeks heating. "Thank you for the opportunity," she said.

"I have a couple of things that I would like to discuss. The main one being the position I hope to see you take on the council," Zigferd said, looking at SJ.

"Oh. What position?"

"Alice and I have already discussed the role, and we believe that you have the most suited skill set to achieve the desired results."

"What skill set? And what results?" SJ asked.

"We believe that you would make the perfect ambassador for Killic."

"Ambassador? Is that not going a little too far? I am a fae, and I am well aware of the mistrust that is shown towards us."

"I can understand your initial reservations, but we believe that you can overcome the fractious attitude of many."

"I thank you for your words, but I am not sure I am the right person to be an ambassador."

"I think you will fit the role perfectly," Alice interjected.

"How so?"

"You have a natural charisma and charm that has not gone unnoticed in the town. It is an uncanny ability to bring ease to so many, yet still be such a stalwart fighter. You show both strength and caring combined. That is an unusual balance," Alice said.

SJ blushed from the comment. "I am just me."

"And that you are is why we believe you will fit the role perfectly. There are several key aspects we would like you to consider over the coming weeks, if you would take on the role."

SJ knew that being an ambassador might mean travel and diplomacy requirements. It would also hopefully give her the angle to speak to Niweq at the Wandering Ogre. "If you believe I am suited, then I can only try."

"That is excellent news. I will ask that Artorian entitles your role as such."

"Who is the current ambassador?"

"We have not required one before, but with the territory borders opening, we believe that it is important that we now have the role and function."

"I see. Does this have to be voted on?"

"No. Assignment of council functions is between me and Alice. We are both in complete agreement over this."

"That's amazing," Dave said. "As an ambassador you will get to travel, see the wider world, meet so many interesting—and potentially not-so-interesting—people."

"You mentioned a couple of things?" SJ said.

"Yes. Second, we would like to offer you a residence."

"Sorry?" SJ was shocked.

"A residence. You can't stay living in the inn now that you are an integral part of the town," Zigferd replied.

Flabbergasted, SJ said, "I hadn't even considered it. I suppose it would make sense, although I am not sure if I can afford a property. I don't know their cost."

"Don't worry about cost for now. It's just a place that you will call home, and eventually, if you wished to purchase or build something yourself, you could do so in time.

"Alice has spent some time already considering various locations and options, and she would like to show you them today. You don't have to decide straight away obviously, but the offer and opportunity is there."

The thought of having her own place in town was appealing, but she really enjoyed the inn. The socialising and the friends she had made there would be things she would miss. Never mind the breakfasts. Then again, many came in for breakfast each morning who were not residents. "I am happy to see what there is. Thank you, both," she said.

"The third thing we wished to discuss is a little more sensitive a matter," Zigferd said.

"Oh. What is it?"

"Alice has been carrying out an investigation for some time now and we believe we have a problem within the council."

"What sort of problem?"

"We believe that one of the members is trying to undermine what we're doing in the town. This is not a recent event and is something that Alice has investigated for the past year. It hasn't been easy for her to gather much information, as the individual concerned is rather secretive at the best of times."

"I see. What can I do to help?"

"I would like you to investigate the matter on our behalf and come to your own conclusions. Our concern is that if they continue to behave in this manner, they will end up damaging the town's reputation with many of the outlying villages."

"And who is it you wished me to look into?" SJ asked, a little concerned at the thought of someone plotting against the town.

"Alice?" Zigferd asked.

"My suspicions point towards Bellakiy," Alice said. "Bellakiy oversees the distribution of trade goods to the outer areas. As part of his role he is required to frequently be away from the town. It is a role he has had for many years, and he's always been thought of as the best for the task because of his merchant skills. The concern is that he is divulging private information about the town and the council members to others. Normal council meetings are held in an enclosed room. You will have seen the guards who are always present, but we also have magical wards which prevent people spying on the meetings."

The fact they had magical wards preventing eavesdropping was something new to SJ, and she was a little surprised.

"Some of the information that has reached our desks from the surrounding villages can only have come from the meetings, and even though it has taken a long time to trace, I now believe that he is the only one who is the common factor."

"Have you not challenged him, or asked him the question?" SJ asked.

"No. We still have no solid evidence. It is circumstantial and nondescript."

"I don't know who he is," SJ said.

"Ah, you probably saw him for the first time today. He is one of the draconian."

"I know who you mean." SJ had seen both the draconian representatives and met with one of them before. Bellakiy had to be the other. The draconian in question was burly looking and had appeared more like a fighter to SJ than anything else when she had seen him in the chamber. "I thought he was something to do with the guard when I saw him."

"He does look that way. He is a very skilled trader, though, but has no skills for diplomacy, as he also has a brashness to him."

"Why would he possibly do anything against the town?" SJ asked.

"I believe it's jealousy," Alice said.

"Jealousy over what exactly?" SJ asked.

"His father was the presiding mayor before Zigferd," Alice said. It was the first time SJ had ever heard her use his first name. "I believe that he thinks the right to being mayor should have passed to him on the death of his father."

"But you have been mayor for over fifty years," SJ stated.

"Yes. I have. Bellakiy had been away for a long time and only two years ago returned to the town and joined the council. His family is regarded very highly amongst the draconian population. Lythonian speaks very highly of them. When he returned from making his fortune trading across Amathera, he joined as one of their representatives."

"I do not know him enough to speak to immediately. It will take time to learn about him, and if he is away from town often, then I will be limited to what I will find out," SJ said.

"That is understandable, but we believe since you are new to the town and are in the process of starting your career, you may be the perfect person to get to know him. He knows he has no direct influence over many on the council, but as you're new, he may try and persuade you otherwise," Zigferd said.

The term *career* struck SJ. She had never even considered the potential of her joining a town council as being called a career. It was strange and rather foreboding alongside everything else she was working towards.

"This looks like it could be very interesting, and perfect for your subterfuge development," Dave said. "Alongside the position of ambassador, I can see there being some rather entertaining times ahead."

"I will see what I can discover," SJ said aloud.

Her display triggered.

Quest: Confirm the Leak
Investigate and confirm who is distributing falsehoods about the town and its council members.
Rewards: 1000xp
Would you like to accept the quest? **Yes/No**

"Woah. That's a lot of experience," Dave said. "You will reach Level 12 easily with the bonus for your reputation."

SJ was a little taken aback by the amount of experience as well, knowing that it really equated to two thousand experience. The benefits her increased reputation had brought to her progression were huge. Anything that triggered a quest related to the town's continuing safety and improvement would allow her to grow exponentially.

Even the less rewarding quests would bring significant bonuses. Accepting the quest, SJ stood. "I need to go and do some training, if there is nothing else?"

"Actually, there is," Zigferd said. From his desk drawer, he removed a small wooden box and handed it to SJ.

"What's this?" SJ asked, frowning. "I wasn't expecting anything."

"Don't worry, this is a formal offering." Zigferd smiled.

SJ took the box and opened the lid. Inside was a tiny silver pin designed in the shape of a great axe, surrounded by laurel leaves. SJ took it from the box and turned it in her hands. "What is this?"

"It is the official emblem of Killic. It proves you are a member of the council. I would ask that you wear it when on official town business, if you would be so kind," Zigferd said.

"Oh. Of course. Do I need to wear it in town?"

"It is entirely up to you whether you do or don't."

SJ looked from Alice to Zigferd and for the first time noticed the small pins that they both wore. "I had never noticed them before," SJ said, smiling, and removed the pin from the box and attached it to her dress.

"It can help you in the town when speaking to townsfolk when they realise you are a council member."

"Before I go, where can I find Bellakiy's residence?"

"He owns one of the large houses opposite the docks," Alice said. "And if you can call back later, I will show you the properties I've identified."

"I will, yes," SJ said. "Thank you both for the confidence you've shown in me."

SJ left the office with her mind racing. She had become a council member, been assigned as an ambassador, and been given a significant quest, the offer of a residence, and the potential to travel in the future, and that was just from today. Then add in everything else she was doing: training, crafting, part-time parenting, and a potential assassination job. SJ had been planning her time ahead with focus on her martial arts training, crafting, and weapon proficiency, and she would need to adjust it.

"So much to do," SJ said as she entered the training ground.

"And all the time in Amathera to do it," Dave replied.

"That is very true, but it never seems like there is enough in one day."

"Well, there isn't, duh! What do you expect, a day to last as long as a year? It would completely mess up the ageing system for the whole of Amathera. Then again . . . I wonder . . ."

"Dave?"

Silence.

"Dave. What are you doing?"

"Nothing," a shy voice replied.

"You realise I was just making a statement, and I really didn't expect there to be more hours in a day."

"I know," he replied uncertainly. "But I just checked anyway, and I can't access the System clock. That would have been so cool if I could have, though."

"Why?"

"I could have time-travelled."

"Sorry?"

"I could have reset the clock back to the beginning of Amathera."

"I am not sure I would class that as time travel."

"What is it, then? If I amend the System clock to its creation date, then the backups would kick in from that period."

"And what do you think that would do to me and you?"

"Erm. Good point, I will scratch that one off my list."

SJ rolled her eyes. "Sometimes you have the strangest ideas."

"I wouldn't call them strange. I would call them abstract."

"Whatever you want to call them, you need to be careful. I am not sure you can be trusted unsupervised."

"You sound like my mother," Dave huffed.

SJ laughed as she walked to the training rings and saw Lorna with a confused look on her face.

"Are you okay?" Lorna asked.

"Yes. Sorry, was just thinking about a joke I was told."

Frowning, Lorna shook her head in dismay. "Are you here to train?"

"Yes. I wanted to get a couple of hours in."

"Excellent. Then you can start with ten laps. That should stop you laughing," Lorna replied with a grin.

"Urgh," SJ said, as she began to run around the ground.

The two hours flew by as she performed her exercises, and Lorna spoke to her about her advancement to Level 6 that she had undergone with Greb. Lorna said she would have to get him involved more in the training of the newer members.

"Wait," Lorna said, staring at SJ open-mouthed.

"What?" SJ said, concerned.

"You're wearing a pin."

SJ looked down at the small pin attached to her dress. "Oh. This, yes. Why?"

"That means you are a member of the town council?"

"I am, yes. I was voted in this morning," SJ said, smiling.

Lorna put her hand up to her face in shock. "I can't believe they allowed you onto the council. How on Amathera did you do it?"

"Do what?"

"You realise that most of the council have previously suffered at the hands of fae. The fact you were voted in is no small achievement."

"There were two votes. The first to add a fae representative and secondly for my membership. The vote to add a fae representative was not as straightforward as I thought it would be."

"Knowing the problems we had four years ago, when our entire crop was destroyed by them, I am amazed that they allowed a fae member to join."

"Four years ago?"

"Yes. When the fae attacked."

"Attacked Killic," SJ said, amazed.

"Not the town, but they decided to destroy the crops. They set the cornfields on fire and destroyed the biannual harvest. The whole town struggled from it, several lost a lot of coin, of which some were councillors."

"I did not know."

"It was a dark time for the town. I don't think we have fully recovered since. The fact you have joined, though, is an amazing feat."

"Thanks," SJ said, smiling.

"No. I mean it. The influence you have since you reached revered status is quite significant."

"My status jumped three levels when it happened. I am not sure how it did."

"I know exactly how," Lorna replied.

"Oh. What happened, then?"

"Cristy, mithril, ogre."

"What?"

"Your selfless act of saving Cristy, a town member, without expecting any reward, is unprecedented amongst all past Legionnaires in the town. The discovery of what is believed to be a mithril mine, which would not have occurred if you had not rescued Cristy. And your subsequent involvement in the battle. Upon striking Bordon, I genuinely believed you were dead, yet you managed to defeat the mage single-handedly."

"I wasn't exactly by myself."

"You were from the town's standpoint. What you have achieved is close to a miracle."

SJ blushed with embarrassment. "I wouldn't call it a miracle."

"I would. To change the minds of some of those on the council is not something to sniff at. The halflings have been trying for years to get on the council."

"I meant to ask the mayor about that, and why they have no representation."

"Halflings are synonymous with 'borrowing.'"

"Ahh," SJ said, understanding the term in relation to the world of Tolkien.

"There have been many issues over items being 'borrowed.' The times I have had to deal with them in the guard is ridiculous," Lorna replied, shaking her head.

"What about the undead?"

"Only Floretta lives in the town, and she has never shown interest in the council."

"Thanks for the training today. I need to see Alice."

"Are you back tomorrow?"

"Hopefully, I will see how I get on. I have already been given a task to do."

"The powers of leadership." Lorna smiled. "I suppose I should now start calling you ma'am."

"You dare and my claws will come out." SJ laughed as she left.

It felt strange having someone she held in such high regard even consider the comment. On getting back to the barracks, she found Alice upstairs in her office.

"Are you free to go now?" SJ asked, after knocking on her door.

Alice looked up, smiling. "Yes. Let's go find you a home."

CHAPTER THIRTY

Angelic Presence

SJ followed Alice as she led her from the barracks. "I've picked three places, and you may choose which you prefer to use for now," Alice said as they walked.

SJ had always stayed in the centre of town because of the inn's positioning and had got used to the hustle and bustle of the vendors and market traders that were there every day and the noise of their daily routine. The inn was after all the hub of the town, and anyone who was someone spent time there. Since SJ had met all the council members during the meeting, she had realised that many of them frequented the inn.

"Is there anything near the centre of town?" SJ asked.

"Unfortunately, not too close to the centre. Those buildings are very rarely free, normally only when a family leaves for Asterfal or one of the other outlying villages," Alice replied.

"That's a shame. I have really enjoyed being at the inn." SJ had got used to the noise every night, the laughing, the singing, and the general camaraderie that was displayed.

Alice was leading SJ into an area of the town she had never been before. It was on the northeastern side, towards the mountain. The first building she stopped at was a two-storey affair. It was in a row of four closely packed homes. The street outside was wide, and opposite was a small open area, with a garden and some seats. It was a pleasant location and SJ stood, looking around.

"Well, this is the first," Alice said, removing a bunch of keys from her pouch. She walked to the door and let SJ inside.

The interior was well maintained, the beams all cleaned and no signs of dust or cobwebs. It reminded SJ of her childhood home. They had lived in a row of terraces and been in one of the middle properties. She had never been a fan because of the noise that used to come through from the neighbours regularly. This house had two rooms on the ground floor, a kitchen and lounge, and up the narrow stairs were two bedrooms and a bathroom.

"It's very nice," SJ said.

"But not for you," Alice replied, smiling.

"Is it that obvious?"

"Ha. You don't seem overly excited, so yes."

"Sorry," SJ said apologetically.

"No, it's fine. This was a last-minute addition."

"How long have you been looking?" SJ frowned.

"The mayor asked me to start investigating a residence three days ago."

"I had only just found out about potentially joining the council then," SJ said, surprised.

"We were both confident you would get accepted. You have done so much for the town already since you have been here. We could not see any objections to you being sustained."

"I wasn't as confident as you were. Not with the concerns over my kind."

"Yes. Many are problematic, but thankfully you and Mistress Francisca are starting to show a different side to the fae."

"I hope it will continue. I don't like being thought of as a nuisance."

"You have been anything but," Alice replied as they walked back outside, and she locked the door. "Okay. Number two."

Alice led SJ down the northern edge of the town, heading down past the church. Lythonian was in the grounds tending the flowers, and he waved as they walked past. SJ knew she would need to speak to Lythonian and get his thoughts on the draconian council member and his family.

The next house was smaller than the first and sat in a small plot by itself, opposite the church hall. SJ liked the look of it from the outside but, as Alice showed her in, realised that the inside was not as well-kept as the first home. "This one does need some work done to it," Alice said, showing her the interior.

After looking around, SJ was quite pleased with it. "I quite like this," she said, smiling.

"Good. Let's show you the third one and then you can confirm which you would like to use."

They now moved to the western edge of town. As soon as SJ saw it, she knew it was the one. Sat by itself in a small plot of land with a garden at the front and rear was a small cottage. It was like Farleck Cottage, although larger. It had a small fence that surrounded the garden, and it looked out directly onto the open cornfields that spread from the edge of town to the forest, where the path to the crags began.

"This is beautiful," SJ said, gawping. She was unaware that there were such idyllic locations in the town.

"It's a nice area. Very quiet and peaceful."

SJ could hear the rhythmic pounding of the smithy in the distance, and looking out from the front garden, she could see the large white sails of the windmill turning. The roof of the mage's academy was not quite visible. On entering the property, it opened into a large lounge area. The main bedroom and lounge were both at the front of the property and looked out over the fields. The kitchen, bathroom, and second smaller bedroom were at the rear, looking into the back garden, which was enclosed with a fence and had two trees, one growing apples, which SJ grimaced at, remembering her initial mistake of tasting one. The other grew a fruit that SJ had not seen before, its skin purple and nobbly.

"What fruit is this?" SJ asked.

"It's called a grapey. They are succulent and very flavoursome," Alice replied.

SJ picked a fruit from the tree and with her knife cut into its flesh. It looked similar to that of a peach, and she lifted the fruit to her mouth to take a bite. The flood of flavour and juice that erupted on her tongue was a sensation to behold.

"These are amazing. Why am I only finding out about these now?" SJ said.

"They are delightful. The owner spent years nurturing the tree as many of them do not bear fruits."

"I think I have a new favourite. I may have to give some to Floretta and see what she can cook up with them."

"I am sure Floretta would be exceedingly happy getting some grapey to cook with. They are not readily available."

As SJ walked around the remainder of the property, she smiled. This would be perfect.

"I am guessing this is the one?" Alice asked.

"Yes. This is lovely," SJ said.

The property was furnished, so she wouldn't need to worry about providing anything apart from bedding and usual household items.

"Excellent. I need to confirm the details with the owner, but I believe she will be very pleased. Once the contract is approved you may move in. It shouldn't take too long to confirm. I will get a message sent to her today via the wagon to Asterfal."

"Oh. The owner lives in Asterfal?"

"Yes. She was a long-standing member of the town council, but when her sister fell ill, she gave up her position and moved to Asterfal to look after her."

"That's unfortunate to hear."

"Yes. She was a breath of fresh air and used to keep many of the grumpy old goats in line," Alice chuckled. "Which I think you will end up doing naturally now."

"I am sure you are more than capable of dealing with any dissent," SJ said.

"You would be surprised. The members can be very stubborn and can take a great deal of persuading."

"I noticed that today about the expansion of the borders."

"Yes. That is going to take time to resolve. As soon as the mine is up and working, we will start considering it more openly, and if we can begin to sell the mithril, it will make a tremendous difference to the town."

"I completely forgot—I got caught up in everything today. My friend has arrived and has said he will be willing to help with that. He's staying at the inn currently."

"Really. You have already got someone here?" Alice asked surprised.

"I messaged him as soon as I found out and asked him to come straight here, and I trust him with my life."

Alice frowned at SJ. "How did you get a message to them so soon?"

SJ removed the gemstone Nexis had given her.

"Nice. They aren't cheap," Alice replied.

"We met in the valley where my cottage is. He gave it to me afterwards. I don't know the cost of them. He said if I needed help to let him know, and he was the first person who came to mind. Knowing that he trades at the auctions, it just made sense."

"How do you know you can trust him?"

"I just know," SJ said, shrugging.

"I am not so sure that letting an outsider know about the mithril so easily was a good idea. It will cause problems if it gets out."

"I promise you that he is trustworthy. He would never do anything against the town or myself," SJ said emphatically.

"How can you be so certain?" Alice was not accepting such a straightforward answer.

"Let me take you to meet him. I'm sure he can put your mind at ease."

"I think it best," Alice replied, a very concerned look on her face.

They left the cottage and began heading straight to the inn.

"How do you communicate with Asterfal normally?" SJ asked as they walked along.

"Through the council mage, William."

SJ realised that the mage who performed all the town announcements was a specialist mage who was aligned to air magic. "I see. I always wondered about the distant communications."

"We only ever communicate distant messages as needed. It's very draining for William to communicate long distance. Most will go via the mail service."

"Mail service?"

"Yes. Every wagon that arrives or leaves to Asterfal contains communications. We also have couriers who travel to the outer towns and villages as necessary."

SJ still had so much to learn about the day-to-day workings of the town and the wider region. On arriving at the inn, the lilt of the bard could be heard, and inside the bar was much busier than usual. SJ frowned as she looked around. The usual clientele seemed to have grown substantially. Many of the patrons were stood up and looking towards the bard, who sang in his usual spot. It all seemed a little strange. SJ couldn't see through the crowd.

Walking to the bar, she caught the attention of Kerys.

"Hi, Kerys. What's going on?" she asked.

"Hi, SJ. Your friend is what's going on," she said, smiling.

"Sorry?" SJ looked down the bar, and from here she had a view of where the bard stood. It wasn't the bard who drew her attention, though, but Nexis, who was sat on a stool next to him playing what looked like a violin. The sound from the instrument was angelic.

"Oh. I'm sorry. I will go speak to him."

"No need to apologise. He's bringing in customers." Kerys smiled. "Hi, Alice."

"Hi, Kerys. Could I have a plum wine please?" Alice asked.

"Of course. Honey wine?" Kerys asked SJ.

"Yes, please," she said.

Moments later Kerys handed the glasses to them, and the music stopped. There was a thunderous round of applause from the watching crowd.

"We will be back after a quick break," the bard called out over the din to some groaned responses.

The patrons refilled their glasses. SJ and Alice took theirs towards where Nexis was sat talking to the bard.

"SJ." Nexis beamed as he spotted her approaching.

"Nexis. This is Alice," SJ said.

"Charmed," Nexis replied, smiling broadly at Alice.

Alice tried to remain stony-faced at his beauty, but SJ could still see slight colouration to her cheeks when she spoke.

"Nice to meet you too, Nexis," Alice replied, calmly.

"Can I speak to you, please?" SJ asked.

"Of course, my dear. What can I do for you?"

"A little more privately, if that is possible?"

"I will be back momentarily, Ptolemy," Nexis said to the bard.

The bard smiled back at Nexis, nodding his head. SJ had never known the bard's name before. Nexis placed his musical instrument on the stool and SJ led them away from the stage area to a quieter area of the bar and took a seat at the table.

"So, what do you wish to discuss?" Nexis asked.

"Alice is the second of the town, and she wished to meet you to discuss a couple of things, prior to meeting with the mayor."

"Of course. What can I do for you?" He gave Alice a dazzling smile.

Alice was handling his Charisma magnificently, not allowing herself to be overthrown by his beauty and charm.

"I wished to understand your reasoning and loyalty to SJ," Alice asked directly.

"I see. You are concerned about the information being divulged outside of the township. I understand fully your concerns, and you can rest assured that I am not one to gossip over my private matters. I have many clients I trade on behalf of whose identities remain secret," Nexis replied.

"You may have, but there is still a trust concern. What if you were offered money in relation to information?" Alice asked.

Nexis laughed, making SJ feel like a spell had struck her. It seemed to cut through her and made her feel giddy. Alice shifted in her seat.

"My dear Alice. Money is no object to me. I make my coin through my trust and worth as a trader. I would never damage my reputation. We all know that reputation matters on Amathera."

"Do you mind if I confirm something?" Alice asked, removing a small item from her pocket.

"Of course, please do check my alignment," Nexis replied.

The item was the same as SJ had seen Lythonian use on the skeletons at the compound. Alice said a few words, and the items turned a bright blue. She raised her eyebrows on seeing the colour. "Lawful good," she stammered, a little taken aback.

"Yes. I am." Nexis smiled.

"Your word is your bond," Alice replied.

"It is indeed. As I say, my reputation matters and I would not sully it through underhand methods or bribery," Nexis replied.

Alice placed the small item away; it still reminded SJ of a magnifying glass, and she would have to discover how they worked.

"You don't need one. When your identification skill levels higher, you will read everyone's alignments," Dave said, taking SJ aback as she had said nothing.

"Would you be free to meet with myself and the mayor in the morning?" Alice asked.

"I can, yes. What time?" Nexis replied.

"Ten thirty?"

"Perfect. It will give me time to have some more of Miss Floretta's amazing breakfast before I come over. I am assuming SJ will accompany me?" Nexis asked.

"Yes, of course. She is our ambassador, after all," Alice replied.

Alice drank the remainder of her plum wine and went to stand. "SJ, I will speak to the owner and see you in the morning."

"Thanks, Alice. That would be great."

Alice turned to face Nexis again. Standing overly stiffly, she nodded her head at him slightly. "Nexis."

"My pleasure," he replied, and Alice turned and left.

"I better get back to it. I can't leave Ptolemy alone up there. This crowd is a little demanding," he said, smiling and standing.

Nexis walked back to the stage, picked up the violin, and struck a few chords. He spoke to Ptolemy briefly before the bar was once again filled with angelic music from the pair.

CHAPTER THIRTY-ONE

What!

Morning, Lythonian," SJ called as she walked up the church pathway the next day. Lythonian was in his usual position when he wasn't running a service: tending to the church grounds.

"Hello, SJ. Is this a social visit or business?" Lythonian grinned with his reptilian smile.

"It's town business. I am seeking some information and would appreciate your input and guidance."

"I see. Well, then, would you like to join me for a coffee, and we can discuss your matter?" Lythonian asked.

"Yes, please. That would be great."

Inside, they headed to the vestry. The church only had a couple of worshippers praying to their respective gods this morning.

Lythonian grabbed a pot of coffee, poured two mugs, and handed one to SJ. "So, what did you wish to discuss?" he asked.

"It's a rather sensitive matter. I am unsure if you know that I am now a town council member."

"I had heard, yes." Lythonian smiled, nodding.

"I don't want to put you in an awkward position. If you do not wish to comment, then I understand," SJ said.

"I see," Lythonian replied, raising his eyebrows in response to her comment. "It must be of a serious nature, then."

"I am not sure yet, but there's a chance it may be," SJ said. "I would like to know more about one of your kin."

"Whom might you be referring to?" Lythonian asked.

"I am after some information regarding Bellakiy."

Lythonian squinted at the comment. "And what did you wish to know about him, exactly?"

"There are concerns that he may have been divulging council details and undermining the good that the town is trying to do. I understand that this may not be easy for you to discuss, as I have been informed that you hold his family in high regard."

"His family, I do, yes. His father was a great draconian, and his sister was an order cleric. I worked with her in Asterfal before I took over the church here."

"I did not know about his sister," SJ said.

"She is a beautiful soul who works at the Asterfal High Church. She is a high cleric who I studied under for several years."

"Oh. I can understand that this may be a little sensitive, then."

Lythonian shuffled a little in his chair. He appeared to be deciding on what he should say. "I can't say too much as I am sworn under the secrecy of information through the order, but I can answer questions that do not directly counter my oath."

"I'm sorry. I did not know that there might be an oath involved, and if I had, I would not have approached you."

"It's fine. If I can answer, I will do it. If I don't, you know why I can't."

"Are you aware of any dealings by Bellakiy that may directly impact the town and its workings?"

Lythonian didn't speak but nodded his head.

"So you know of something that may cause issues to the town?"

Lythonian nodded again.

"Can you expand on the reasoning and issues pertaining to what you may have been privy to?"

"I can indirectly," Lythonian replied. SJ could see a bead of sweat forming on the draconian's' brow. "Bellakiy has been at odds for years since his father's passing. He wasn't present when his father died, as he had been away in the capital, where he made the family fortune trading across the northern territories. He was very astute at business and had been running the family business for almost seventy years. Ever since his father retired and settled in Killic, Bellakiy has argued with his sister."

"I didn't realise he had been running the business for so long."

"Yes. His father, the previous mayor of Killic, was a fabulous draconian. I had the pleasure of knowing him through his daughter. He regularly travelled to Asterfal to visit. I was her apprentice, and I met him many times. This was at the beginning of my journey as a cleric. When he passed, Wystria took it hard. She blamed herself for the loss, for not having taken care of him when he fell ill. She was working towards her advancement to that of a deity representative, which she has successfully achieved, and has held the position of a high cleric ever since."

SJ nodded, listening intently to his tale.

"Wystria had communicated with Bellakiy about their father when he fell ill, but neither was present when he passed. Their mother had passed several years previously from a rare draconian disease. When their father died, it tore the family apart and set the pair at odds with each other. Bellakiy believed he had the rights to the family business as he had been running it before their father's death. Wystria, though, was listed as the incumbent to the business and was given full control under her father's will. This infuriated Bellakiy, and the siblings fought for years over the rights. Eventually, to maintain peace and end the hostilities, Wystria gave up part of her rights to the business and handed it over to Bellakiy.

"Until this time, Wystria had been maintaining the business alongside her duties as a high cleric, completing all the accounting and keeping on top of the business dealings that required her attention. Bellakiy had not fully controlled the business's finances, always having to confirm dealings through Wystria. This had caused many arguments, and their bitter feud was one of the reasons that Wystria ended up giving more control to Bellakiy. She was more reserved and averse to risk, whereas Bellakiy was the opposite.

"In the end, though, handing over control was the worst mistake that Wystria made. Bellakiy got caught up in a scheme at the capital over procuring several mithril mines. He thought he was onto a sure thing and invested all the business capital into the deal. The problem was that the deal was too good to be true. The mines were fake, and only had britlac, a rare ore like mithril but unworkable. It has no viable use outside of basic jewellery. This led the business to eventually collapse after being in the family for over two centuries. He had to close the doors and resign himself to the fact he had fallen to a deal that held no truth.

"This was when he then returned south. He spent several years in Asterfal running several small businesses and doing well for himself, but without the financial capability he had lost, he would never grow the business back to the size it had been before. This was when he returned to Killic to take over his father's legacy."

"But his father hadn't been the mayor of Killic for decades by this point. Why did he think he could come back and take over?"

"Bellakiy is stubborn and very self-centred." Lythonian winced as he finished the line, sweat trickling visibly down his brow. Before continuing, he inhaled sharply.

"He believes in the rite of passage, similar to his stance over the business. Now that he has returned to Killic, he still believes that, as the son of a mayor, he should automatically ascend to the position." Lythonian shook as he finished the sentence.

"Are you okay?" SJ asked, concerned.

"I am walking a very fine line at the moment, and the oath is telling me so," he replied, smiling weakly.

"I'm sorry. I didn't mean for you to break your oath."

"I haven't, don't worry. I know how far I can push the boundaries without undue effect."

"So Bellakiy believes he should automatically become the mayor. Yet, he has no power over the decision to become the mayor, so the only way he can try to take the position is by causing problems that affect the town and make the presiding mayor look bad in the eyes of the populace."

Lythonian did not respond, sitting silently.

"So, there is truth in what has been discovered so far. Yet, you cannot say what exactly that truth pertains to."

Lythonian gave a very slight nod, then visibly winced again as the pain seemed to hit him, making him stiffen in his seat.

"I'm sorry, Lythonian. I never meant for you to suffer in any way," SJ said, looking shocked at the control the oath he was under seemed to have over him. SJ could now understand why the oath that Jabrey had taken was such a valid commitment to not attacking the town in the future. "I need to investigate further, then, and will have to find out what he is doing exactly to undermine the mayor without drawing attention to myself or letting him know."

"I would advise that, yes," Lythonian replied.

"I will have to visit the surrounding villages and find out what is going on," SJ said.

"It may be a good place to start your investigation. Unfortunately, I can't say more than I already have. The dealings are under the oath of my kin, which I am sworn to secrecy over, so I couldn't divulge them without death being the likely outcome."

The power of an oath was startling, and that Lythonian had mentioned the possibility of death made an icy chill run up her spine. She had only just taken an oath to Killic without knowing the potential side effects that it might hold if she ever broke it—not that she intended to, but that was beside the point.

"Thank you for your time, Lythonian, and again, I am sorry for asking you such troublesome questions."

"Do not apologise, my dear. You are a friend and someone I trust. Race oaths hold more sway than most in the realm."

"I am considering moving into a home west of town by the fields. When I do, I would like to invite you for dinner to thank you," SJ said, smiling.

"That would be lovely, and I look forward to it." Lythonian smiled.

SJ bade her farewell and left the vestry as Lythonian dabbed his brow with a handkerchief.

"That was a little intense. Do all oaths carry that much sway?" SJ asked Dave on leaving the church.

"Not all, no. Another oath that replaces or betters it can overwrite the town's oath. Race oaths are something entirely different, though. There are several aspects that, as natural Amathereans, they can't divulge about their races. Not all races hold the same power of direction as the draconian race. It's one of the stronger oaths. Oaths of honour like Jabrey's are also binding and can't be overcome without serious repercussions."

"So Bellakiy could be passing information even if under the oath?"

"He could. It would depend on what he is doing exactly."

"Well, I need to find out. I think I will have to visit the outer villages and see what's going on."

"I think you will. I don't think you'll get any more details from within the town itself."

"Now that I am Level 10, can I use the navigation to find the village locations?"

"Not directly, but if you have access to the regional maps, then you can plot prospective positions. They will only come clear once visited."

"I think I need to see the mayor, then."

"Yes. We also need to go and collect Nexis for his meeting."

SJ looked at the time; it was already 10:10. "I had lost track of time. Thanks for reminding me," SJ said, and hurried back to the inn.

Nexis was sitting at a table with several empty plates in front of him when SJ entered.

"Morning," he said with a smile.

"Morning, Nexis. I see you have been eating breakfast," SJ said, taking in the empty plates and wondering where he had put all the food they must have contained.

"It was delightful. Floretta is an outstanding cook. I had forgotten how pleasurable it is to eat."

The thought of a god not needing to eat had never crossed SJ's mind, but she assumed it was highly probable that they didn't require the usual sustenance that normal beings would.

"We need to get going to see the mayor," SJ said.

"Yes. Absolutely. Let me just pay for my breakfast." Nexis stood and walked to the bar, several pairs of eyes following his movement.

SJ couldn't hear what he was saying, but she could imagine it based on Kerys's giggle and the colour in her cheeks.

"Shall we go, then?" Nexis asked her.

It didn't take them long to walk through the town and reach the barracks. SJ felt very uncertain about all the stares and smiles the pair was getting. She had got quite used to morning pleasantries from many citizens, but today, most were directed to Nexis. The god accommodated all the comments and replied to all those who spoke to him, smiling warmly and disarmingly in response. SJ saw several male and female beings' faces flush at his passing.

"You really need to turn your charm down," SJ hissed under her breath.

"My dear. I am just being me," Nexis replied with a wicked smile.

"Um hmm," SJ sighed, rolling her eyes.

At the barracks, SJ walked straight through the barrier, not disturbing the old orc at the front desk, who was busy dealing with two arguing humans. One had a black eye, from the looks of it, and two members of the guard stood behind them, glowering at them, making sure that nothing else was going to happen.

Upstairs, SJ saw Little Stuart leaving the mayor's main chambers. "Hello, Little Stuart."

"Hi, SJ," he replied cheerily.

"What are you doing?"

"Just starting on the model upstairs. Mr. Cringle has asked me to build the basic structure." He grinned broadly.

"That is fantastic news. Good luck, and I will come and see how you get on at some point," SJ said.

"That would be great," he said, hurrying down the corridor before turning up the stairs.

SJ assumed Mr. Cringle must be the gnome who oversaw the town's model, and she politely nodded at him as she walked by to the mayor's office. The doors were open as usual, and Zigferd stood and walked towards his door on seeing SJ.

"SJ, welcome, and you must be Nexis. I've been hearing so much about you," Zigferd said with a genuine smile.

"I am indeed. Mayor," Nexis replied, taking the mayor's offered hand.

"Please come in and take a seat. Alice?"

"Coming," Alice replied.

SJ watched as Alice came out of her office, and she thought she looked a little different from normal. She frowned as she took in Alice's appearance. Her hair, she thought, was different. She had tied it up in a tight bob, revealing her beautiful dryad features in full. Nexis, had a lot to answer for, she thought as they entered the office and took seats.

"I understand you met with Alice briefly yesterday evening, and she has confirmed your alignment. Therefore, your word is your bond." Zigferd poured four glasses of water and handed them around.

"She did, yes," Nexis said.

"Excellent. That removes that formality from the process, then," Zigferd said. "So we can get straight to business. SJ has informed you of our need and that we wish to remain anonymous in our sales."

"Yes. SJ has informed me of the basic plans."

"So, how do you believe this can be achieved?"

"Quite easily, really."

"Please share," Zigferd offered.

"I plan on opening an auction house here in Killic."

Zigferd, Alice, and SJ all sat open-mouthed at the comment.

"Sorry?" Zigferd stammered.

"Yes. I plan to open a new auction house in Killic."

"But we can't have an auction house here," Alice replied, stunned.

"Why not, my dear? Have the territory boundaries not been realigned, meaning the area is now up to Level 20?"

"Well, yes," Zigferd replied.

"Well, there is no reason an auction house can't be set up here. Trading will still be limited to Level 20 and higher, but it will allow your merchandise to get into the system without anyone asking undue questions. I assume you are aware of how the auctions are interlinked?"

"I am," Zigferd replied, still stunned by the announcement.

"Well, then. The distribution of auction materials is conferred through object transference. The place of origin is irrelevant when moving items, as they are transferred as purchased through the transference stream."

SJ sat wide-eyed, mouth open. She did not know about the workings of the auction houses.

"How would you possibly get permission for an auction house?" Alice said.

"That's my concern to address," Nexis said. "You don't need to worry about the details. I will cover the setup costs and dealings for a licence to be issued."

"You would need to confirm with the auction magistrate in the capital. That could take months."

"Ah. I know Magistrate Hershy very well. We go back a couple of centuries." Nexis smiled.

"You know the magistrate of the auction houses?" Zigferd's eyes could not have got any wider.

"Oh yes. I am his daughter's godfather," Nexis replied.

SJ coughed at the comment. She had been sipping on a glass of water, which now erupted from her mouth.

"Sorry," she spluttered, wiping her mouth and dabbing the spray from the table, knowing her dress would dry.

"Godfather!" Dave laughed hysterically at his comment.

CHAPTER THIRTY-TWO

Magical Transference

Zigferd and Alice turned to look at SJ as she cleaned herself up after spitting water across the table. SJ blushed under their gaze. "I'm sorry. I didn't know that he knew the magistrate of the auction houses."

"It is not normally something I talk about." Nexis smiled broadly, turning and winking at SJ. From the angle he sat, he knew that Alice and Zigferd couldn't see.

"If you know the magistrate at the capital, then we are in the presence of someone with influence," Zigferd stammered, in awe.

Just as SJ began to wonder who the magistrate was, exactly, Dave spoke.

"The magistrate of the auction houses is one of the highest positions in the land. They are responsible for all auction house transactions and have an accuracy rating of 99.99999998 percent for successful transaction completion. It is one of the most efficient services provided across all continents. Only Justilianym has a higher success rate, only by 0.000000001 percent. I still can't believe that Nexis said he was the child's godfather." Dave chuckled.

"We go back a long time, as I say," Nexis said.

"If you have such influence, why would you wish to set up an auction house here in Killic? We are a small town compared to the towns and cities you could establish yourself in," Zigferd asked.

"Why not? The changes happening and the expansion of the boundaries between the territories will eventually happen, anyway. So, it makes perfect business sense to start at the earliest opportunity and confirm the function and standings necessary. There is no point in waiting until some of the rather less reputable auctioneers start clawing at your town for rights to trade. As soon as the territory boundaries expand further, the wyvern will soon circle."

"What fees would you be taking if this is confirmed?"

"The usual auction house fees for all transactions are 3 percent of the value of items. Unless security is required against certain items—security bonds can result in an 8 percent handling fee. You know that anything non-living can be sold through the auction houses; therefore, there are always those who wish to sell more illicit goods."

"Aren't there rules preventing such items from being sold?" SJ asked, curious.

"It comes down to racial considerations. What one race may find abhorrent, another doesn't. All sentient beings from Level 20 can access auction houses. Some items I have seen transferred over my years of dealings are quite concerning, to say the least."

"Can you not decide what you wish to auction or not?" Zigferd asked.

"I could do, but why would I? Unless something is of chaotic evil alignment, then who am I to judge their cultural and race beliefs?"

"You have a limit on what you would agree to auction, then," SJ stated.

"Only related to the alignment of items, yes. Remember that nothing living can be auctioned, so very few items would fall outside of the remit of an auction house. The last item I can remember that wasn't accepted was the cross of Edwardo."

Alice gasped at the statement. "Someone tried to auction his cross?"

"Yes. It was over a century ago now. It is one of the most evil charms I have ever witnessed. You are all aware of the fear and terror that Edwardo brought with his involvement in the scrug wars."

Zigferd and Alice both nodded, but SJ didn't know who he was.

"Edwardo was the most evil of the paladins who terrorised the continent during the Scrug Wars. He had a fanatical following and was known to sacrifice his followers for the God of Death," Dave said.

Considering its chaotic evil alignment, SJ was not sure she wanted to know what the charm could do.

"Who was trying to sell such an item?" Alice inquired.

"Ah, my dear. That would be divulging privileged information, which I am sure you can understand I can't do," Nexis replied.

Alice flushed from his gaze. "Of course," she said.

"Considering that you would be asking for 3 percent of the item fee, how do we know that we will attain the best rates from an auction?" Zigferd asked.

"I am sure you have used auctions before, being your level?" Nexis asked, raising an eyebrow at Zigferd.

Even Zigferd's rustic cheeks coloured slightly. "Unfortunately, no, I have never used an auction house, and how do you know my level? That should be impossible." He frowned, twisting a ring he wore on his finger. SJ noticed the movement and wondered if it was a ward of some kind.

"There is very little that I can't overcome at my level and profession," Nexis replied, smiling.

"As you know my level, may I ask yours?" Zigferd asked.

"You may indeed. I am Level 74."

"What?" Zigferd and Alice said in unison.

Spluttering, Zigferd replied first. "Why are you in this area if you are at such a high level? There is no benefit for you."

"I could ask you the same question. Until this latest update, you would have been getting no benefits either, both of you."

Alice flushed again, knowing that he also knew her level, and she also fiddled with a ring on her finger. Alice and Zigferd looked a little taken aback by the turn in the conversation and completely disarmed by Nexis's comments. "Don't worry. I do not divulge information about others," Nexis said.

"Alice is 21, Zigferd is 24," Dave said, filling in the blanks for SJ, who had never identified either of them.

"Anyway, moving on," Nexis said. "The rules are quite simple if you have never used an auction house. Any item placed for auction starts with a minimum bid, and the mountain top is the limit, as they say. You can also set an item for sale at a buy-out price, for which someone can immediately purchase it outright. Finally, if you wish to cancel an item from the auction, that is fine, as the held funds are immediately released back to the would-be buyer's account. Any bid retains funds from an auction account until such a time as the auction ends, so the funds are always held and kept. Those placing bids really need to make sure what they are purchasing is what they want, as they are not returned while the bidder holds the highest bid position. Only in very extreme circumstances would an auctioneer allow a bidder to withdraw after a set bid. The last time this happened was during the GoblinPox epidemic, when the transference of all items was banned for containment reasons."

"How is everything transferred when an auction ends?" SJ asked.

"Through the transference network. On closure of an auction, the successful bidder is contacted via the System and given a time period to claim the item. Usually, this is seventy-two hours. Once an item is claimed, it will be transferred to the winning bidder's chosen auction house for collection. If items are unclaimed from the System for delivery, the winning bidder will accrue holding charges. Individual auction houses do not control these holding charges; it's set through the magistrate's office. It's a dragon's task to resolve and sort out that side of it."

"So, what does the 3 percent cover?" Alice asked.

"Administration fees, matter transference costs, and storage costs."

Zigferd turned to look at Alice, and without either saying anything, Alice nodded.

"Okay then, Nexis. If you can establish an auction house, we would happily do business with you," Zigferd said.

"Excellent news. I will just have to establish a suitable location. I require little room for the set-up, but storing items requires significant space. I noticed a plot of land on the eastern edge of town heading towards the forest that may be suitable. It may require me to consider expanding into the field there. I would need to find out who owns the land. I can look into starting construction if we can visit the location and confirm its availability and cost."

"Do you not wish to wait for approval before purchasing land?" Alice asked.

"I can guarantee approval. Give me a moment." Nexis placed his hand in his jacket pocket and removed a small, jewelled object. It looked like a small clock face with several coloured gems around the edge.

"Is that what I think it is?" Zigferd asked in amazement.

"If you think it's a messenger dial, then you are right," Nexis replied.

"I have only ever heard of them. I have never seen one before."

"One minute," Nexis said as he touched one of the coloured gems, then several more. Suddenly, a hum was in the air before a sharp ticking sound began. After several moments, the ticking stopped.

"Nexis. It has been too long, my old friend." A disembodied voice emitted from the dial.

"Hershy, you old dog, you. How are Saffy and my little girl doing?"

"They are both well. Only the other day, Lily asked when Uncle Nexis would return to visit. I think she enjoys being spoiled when you're around."

"She deserves to be spoiled. She is my god-daughter."

"When will you next be back in the capital? I know Saffy will be excited to know as well."

"Unfortunately, not for a while yet. I am currently far south."

"That's a shame. What do you need? I assume you need something if you are contacting me from the south."

"I do. I assume the news about the changes taking place has reached the capital?"

"It has, yes. We have sent out parties to several territories to investigate. Do you have news?"

"I do. I am currently in a small starter town called Killic, where the boundaries have just been amended."

"I see. Do you know what triggered them?"

"I have an idea, but that is for another time," Nexis replied, smiling at Zigferd, Alice, and then SJ. "I called to ask a favour."

"Of course, what do you need?" Hershy asked.

"I am going to establish a new auction house here in Killic and was hoping for an expedited licence agreement if possible?"

"Anything for you, my friend. I assume the usual set-up?"

"Yes. Everything as standard would be excellent."

"I can get that written up now. I guess this Killic is an investment opportunity?" Hershy asked wryly.

"You know me too well. I don't set up auction houses without a good reason."

"What is the name of their leader who requires the notary?"

"Zigferd Maxwell is the presiding mayor of Killic."

"Excellent. I will have it sent over very soon. I will let Saffy and Lily know we spoke. They both won't be happy missing you."

"I will call again soon to catch up. Thank you, Hershy."

"Anytime."

The magical hum stopped like a blanket of silence had just swallowed the room. Three faces stared at Nexis in awe.

"Well, then. Shall we visit this plot of land?" Nexis asked.

"Wait a second. Auction houses? How many do you own?" SJ asked.

"This will be my sixth." Nexis smiled.

"Six!" Zigferd exclaimed. "You own and operate five auction houses already?"

"Yes. Only the five. I could have set up many more, but it is more of a sideline than my main profession."

"What is your main profession, then?" Alice asked, intrigued.

"I am a tailor by trade."

"That is a little different."

"Very. I am looking to purchase the tailor shop here in Killic while I am here, as I know the Master wishes to retire."

"He does?" Alice asked, shocked. "I did not know."

"Yes. He's been talking about it for a while. The last time we met, he discussed it, and I said I would come and see what it is like here in Killic. So, I will be trying to complete both transactions while here."

"Are you not staying?" Zigferd asked.

"I will be for the foreseeable future. Yes."

A similar ticking sound began again, and Nexis removed the messenger dial from his pocket. Pressing a few gems, he answered. "Hershy. So soon?"

"I forgot to ask for the transference position for the notary."

"I am sat with the mayor now. Just send it to me, and I will hand it over."

"Excellent. It will be with you momentarily."

The dial dimmed again, and a small ball of orange light appeared in front of Nexis. Nexis reached out into the light, and a cream-coloured envelope appeared as he did. He removed it from the sphere, which instantly disappeared. Nexis handed the envelope over to Zigferd.

The cream envelope was sealed with a bright red wax seal. Zigferd snapped the seal and removed the parchment inside, reading the content. He then handed it to Alice.

"It looks like we have permission to establish an auction house." Zigferd beamed.

"Excellent. Then we have the formalities over. Shall we visit the location?" Nexis asked.

"Alice, would you be willing to go with Nexis? I have Nevik coming to see me soon."

"Of course, Mayor," Alice replied, standing. "Shall we?"

Leaving the barracks, Nexis led them down to the tailor's shop on the eastern end of town, a few buildings from the edge. SJ spotted Fizzlewick inside speaking to a customer while Nexis walked by their side. It was a bizarre experience knowing that they were the same person.

The final building leading out of town before the fields began was a single-storey affair. It had once been a home but looked as though it was no longer lived in. Considering that the hobs' raids used to come across the fields, it made sense that several of the homes on this edge of town were empty. The buildings had previously been used mainly as a barrier.

"This plot here would be perfect, considering its proximity to the tailor shop. I would also be looking to purchase the other one that backs onto it and then expand a warehouse area into the field here." Nexis indicated what he had planned.

"Are you sure you wish to build on the edge of town? We can't guarantee security to the same degree, and we have only recently recovered from a spate of raids. We are not sure what the future may bring yet," Alice asked.

"Security won't be an issue. I will draw up plans for you. I just need to understand the cost for the buildings and land."

Alice took a small notebook, quill, and inkpot from her inventory and made a few notes. "Because of the condition of these buildings, we can let them sell for a reduced price." Alice began pacing out the distances of the width and length of the plots. They were similar buildings, single-storey cottages separated at their rears by small gardens and a wall running along the side facing the field.

"What do you plan to do?" SJ asked Nexis.

"I will have them torn down and replaced with an auction house, then build the adjoining warehouse for storage. I'm guessing from your information that the mine is on this side of town, making the movement of ore or ingots easier," Nexis replied, winking at SJ, knowing full well where everything was.

It didn't take long for Alice to make the notes, and they headed back to the barracks. "I will get the paperwork drawn up for the transfer of the buildings, and then you can proceed with what changes you need to make," Alice said, leaving them to continue back to the inn.

CHAPTER THIRTY-THREE

Fire

SJ was unsure how long she had been asleep when Dave's voice boomed inside her head.

"WAKE UP NOW," he screamed.

When they returned to the inn, SJ had spent the day with Nexis as he drew out his plans for the auction house. It was like watching an architect at work. The details and design were amazing. SJ was sure he could have just conjured the plan up, but had enjoyed watching the god at work as he sketched and adjusted the designs. The main building would be a single storey, housing standard receiving areas for small goods. Several smaller offices were designed for private viewings, and then there was a larger side access for bulkier items, which was linked to a warehouse design.

He had also spent time writing a request for builders, and SJ had promised she would see Terence about coming to do the carpentry work. The auction house would initially require two tellers, four labourers, and a transference controller. SJ had to ask what a transference controller did. Nexis had explained the requirement for a being of lawful good or lawful neutral alignment who could be trusted to establish the necessary transference links to the other auction houses. Surprisingly, they didn't need to be a mage as the transference network was controlled centrally at the capital. Once the building was complete, Nexis could then add the details to the auctioneer's register.

The evening had brought the usual influx of patrons, and it hadn't taken long for Nexis to be called upon to join the merriment, playing his violin. By the time SJ had retired for the evening, it had been getting late, and she wanted to make sure she was up early to attend claw training with Jurgen.

Being disturbed so swiftly from her sleep, she shot up in bed, opening her eyes in panic. Coughing as she sat up, she took in a lungful of the thick, acrid smoke that was filling the room.

"At last. How did you not hear the explosion?" Dave said.

"What explosion? What's happening?" SJ said, confused, coughing, and rolling off the bed to the floor. She could remember back to her time at junior school when the local fire station had brought a large red fire truck and briefed them all on what to do if they were ever in a house fire, and so she stayed close to the floor.

"The whole inn shook from the explosion, and you managed to sleep through it. The thatch has caught fire," Dave replied.

SJ looked up and could see the signs of flames eating at the underside of the thatched roof. Staying low, she crawled through to the other room. Grabbing her boots and dress from a chair where she had put them the previous evening, she wriggled into both. The flames were eating away at the ceiling, and the beams' pitch was beginning to bubble. The weather in Killic, apart from the one deluge of rain she had witnessed, was always dry and warm, which meant the thatch would be bone-dry.

She could hear a cry for help from another room. Coughing, she reached the door and fumbled, grabbing the handle and throwing it open. The corridor was empty, and she heard a scream from the room opposite. "Is anyone there?" she called, crawling over to the door. The smoke was now starting to fill the corridor.

"Help," a male voice cried.

SJ tried the handle, and it was unlocked but wouldn't budge.

"It's blocked," she called.

"A beam is blocking it," the voice called.

"SJ," Fhyliss called, coming from her accommodation and crawling along with Kerys close behind.

"Beam's blocking the door," SJ called.

"We need Bert," Kerys called.

"I can get in," SJ said as she shrank. Squeezing through the gap in the door, she entered the room. Inside, it reminded SJ of pictures of the bombings during the blitz in London. The rear of the room, where a window had once been, was now missing. There was a hole in the floor, looking down into the bar's main area below, and the ceiling that once existed was now open air.

She couldn't see anybody. "Hello?" she called.

"Over here," the male voice replied.

Following the voice, SJ turned and saw an arm sticking out from under a large wardrobe that had toppled over. Thankfully the room was clear of smoke with it billowing upwards into the night sky. The floor looked weakened, not just where the hole had been blown cleanly through it, and she took off flying over, not trusting walking across the fragile remains. Landing next to the overturned wardrobe, she grew and peered over the top to find the face of a young man. His hair looked scorched, and his face blackened.

"My arms are trapped. I can't push this thing off me," he said.

SJ bent, grabbed the wardrobe, and strained to lift it. Her strength was nothing special, and the furniture was made of solid oak or something similar. It wasn't like the DIY flat-pack she used to have back on Earth. The young man managed to move his arm, and he could assist in pushing it upwards until, eventually, it was lifted high enough that he could wriggle out. SJ held the weight until he was clear, then released it, huffing.

Standing, the man took in the damage in the room. Flames still licked at the thatch at the edges where it had caught fire. There was no way SJ or the man could move the thick beam that blocked the room's only doorway. Moving to the edge of the remaining floor, SJ looked out to the street below, where the scattered remains of the glass, stonework, and several furniture items were now strewn. A crowd had started to form at the rear of the inn, and as they stood there, she felt the first signs of a deluge of water beginning to fall, and noticed several people flourishing their hands. One she recognised from the first day she had sought directions to the meadow; she thought his name was Kevin.

SJ watched a cart with hay draw up alongside the building as the water mages continued to make heavy clouds appear and fall onto the burning building, beginning to douse the flames.

"Can you jump down?" SJ asked the man.

He looked down at the cart before composing himself and leaping, and landed with a heavy groan. As he did, SJ shrank and flew down, then landed next to the cart and grew. Kerys, Fhyliss, and Bert stood around the back, looking at the damage wrought on the inn.

The young man began to climb from the back of the cart where he had landed when the furious form of Kerys approached him.

"What on Amathera have you done to my inn?" Kerys shouted at the young, dishevelled, and singed man. His black hair was sticking up, and the streaks of soot on his face reminded SJ of cartoons where the villains' bombs exploded in their faces.

"I did nothing," he spluttered in response.

"Then how do you explain that?" Kerys screamed at him, pointing at the inn. The young man winced from the ferocity in her voice and stepped back. It didn't help that Bert, in his towering, powerful form, stood by her side.

"I was only completing the instructions my master gave me."

"What instructions? What were you asked to do?" Kerys continued to shout.

"I was supposed to mix them and then deliver them to an alchemist, Master Rui. I was following the instructions."

"Are you really that stupid?" Kerys blurted.

"What?" the man replied, looking upset at the comment.

"You were asked to mix alchemical components delivered to a supposed alchemist. Did anything ring in your head that seemed suspicious?"

The man's cheeks went red, even under the soot covering his face. "I didn't consider it, and I am so sorry. I was just after the experience."

"Let me guess. You're a Legionnaire," Kerys huffed in annoyance.

"I am, why? What has that got to do with it?" he said defensively.

"Experience chasers with no consideration, that is why. What the hell did you even mix?"

"The solutions I was given," he replied nervously.

"What solutions?" Kerys screamed, going from angry to furious. Her wrath was palpable, and the man shrank away from her outburst.

"Erm. One was called Plerus, and the other Santine," he stammered.

"Plerus, you had Plerus in my inn. It's one of the most unstable alchemical solutions you can handle. And you thought staying in my inn mixing alchemical solutions would be perfectly fine?"

"I was only completing a quest."

"A quest that has destroyed my business." Kerys brandished her finger as she stepped towards him angrily.

The man took a step backwards. "I'm sorry. I didn't know what would happen. I didn't know what they were capable of."

"Do you bother asking questions or checking before you take on quests?"

"I had a list of instructions I was told to follow."

"Do you still have them?"

The man dug the instructions from his pocket and handed them to Kerys.

"Watch out!" Dave said.

SJ glanced back, hearing the cracking of wood. The remaining floor where the wardrobe had fallen began to give way, and the wardrobe slid forward and came hurtling towards the ground.

"Move," SJ shouted, pushing the young man away as the wardrobe crashed onto the cart, splintering it. The burning wood set the straw in the cart on fire.

One of the mages moved their spell to cover the area, dampening the flames. It was strange watching miniature black storm-clouds move around and empty their contents at will. Turning back, SJ saw the young man lying face-first on the ground where he had landed.

"Sorry," SJ said, looking at his sprawled figure.

The young man rolled over and climbed back to his feet, dusting himself down.

"Even new alchemists are informed of the dangers of certain components. Have you never been trained?"

"I only recently started."

Sighing deeply, Kerys closed her eyes for several seconds before opening them again. "Who is going to pay for the damages to my inn?" She continued berating the young man.

Only the odd patch on the inn remained burning since most of the flames had been extinguished. Apart from the obvious damage caused by the explosion, the inn didn't look too badly wrecked. SJ was no structural engineer, though, so she couldn't be sure.

"I have money," the young man answered. "I can pay."

Kerys's eyes narrowed. "How much?" she asked, hands on her hips, leaning towards him.

"How much will it cost to repair?"

"Bert?" Kerys asked, not taking her eyes off the young man.

"Erm. Structural integrity looks fine," the troll said. "Thatching is normally three copper per square foot. The whole roof needs replacing. The mason work for the walls, new beams, doors, decorating, flooring, any other damages ascertained because of the explosion, and compensation for lost business while repairs are underway . . . The standard work pattern should be able to get most things sorted in three to four days if we get the full team on it. Um . . . I would say three gold and eighteen silver should cover everything, including labour costs."

SJ's mouth opened in complete shock. She had known Bert since she arrived in town, and all she had ever assumed was that he was a bouncer at the bar.

"Are your cousins free at the moment?" Kerys asked.

"Stan and Shirley are just finishing a new build by the docks. The new owners are not moving in for two weeks until they get married, so they have room in the calendar. I'll go and speak to them."

"That would be appreciated," Kerys said.

The young man's face had become ashen when he heard the price.

"So, do you have the coin?" Kerys asked, raising her eyebrow.

He began to fumble with his belt pouch and count out coins. Then, letting out a deep sigh, he withdrew something from his inventory and handed it to Kerys. "Will this do as payment?"

Kerys frowned, taking the object from him. SJ could not see what it was as it changed hands.

"Where did you get this?" Kerys asked, her own face now registering shock.

"I acquired it and have been keeping it for a rainy day."

"A rainy day. Do you know what you even have here?"

"Yes."

"And you know how much they are worth?"

"Yes."

Kerys lifted the round gem up and pointed it towards the moonlight, peering at it. "The cut looks good. Why have you never sold this?"

"I was saving it to place on the auction house when I needed to."

"If you know the auction house process, you must know moonstones sell from three gold anywhere up to seven for the purest cuts."

"I am aware, yes. I have kept an eye on the prices."

"What's a moonstone?" SJ asked, intrigued.

"Specialist druids use them at higher levels. They are how you bond pets to owners," Fhyliss said, speaking for the first time. "Certain creatures are not pleased to be pets, so using a better cut of moonstone can increase the success rate."

The comment about pets made SJ think about the wyvern eggs she had stashed in her room.

"I need to check my room," SJ said, panicking. Sprinting around the side of the inn, she walked in the front entrance. The smell of the burnt thatch hung heavy in the air, and water now dripped from the ceiling as though the inside of the building was raining. The damage downstairs was minimal, apart from where the ceiling had collapsed, leaving a hole looking up and out into the night sky. Thankfully, the room was nearer a corner of the inn, so it was not over the main common room section.

SJ cautiously made her way back up the stairs and to her room. The smoke had cleared and left behind a pungent, sweet, earthy smell from the burning thatch. Apart from the obvious thatch missing, the remainder of the structural beams appeared still in place. In her room, she beelined for the wardrobe. She had collected several items she had been storing in there and began sorting them out, placing the small chest with the miniature wyvern eggs into her inventory as a priority.

She removed a spare blanket from the wardrobe and dropped the items she couldn't fit into her inventory onto it before bundling it up and carrying it back downstairs. The mayor had arrived while she had been inside and now stood out front of the inn with Kerys and the young man, who looked terrified at the huge form of the mayor.

"People make mistakes, Kerys. I am sure he didn't realise what he was doing," the mayor said.

"He should still be locked up. He is a menace to the town if he doesn't understand what he is handling."

"Now, now. Stay calm. I'll deal with this. Please check on the damages inside. I will ensure that Wendil comes to see what is needed once he wakes up. We can't have the inn out of action. It's the hub of the town."

"That would be appreciated, Mayor. Bert will get his cousins to come and start repairs as well."

"Good. There is not much more I can do here until the morning. I'm sorry for the damage, but at least it appears salvageable," the mayor said.

"Bert believes so. Yes."

"Okay. I will send Wendil in the morning. Good night again," the mayor said as he began to walk away.

"What about him?" Kerys said, pointing at the man.

"He isn't going anywhere," he replied, smiling.

SJ hadn't noticed, but two of the town guards had appeared at the side of the man, and SJ recognised Greb.

"Come on," Greb said, ushering the man towards the barracks. "You have some explaining to do so we can write the report."

Dropping his head, the man walked off with Greb and his colleague.

SJ remembered that Shelly and Nexis had been staying in the inn and she had not seen either. "Have you seen Shelly or Nexis?" she asked.

Fhyliss turned to look at her. "Yes. Shelly went to stay with her uncle last night, and Nexis left when the bar closed. I don't know where he went, though."

Thankful that Shelly was safe, SJ walked over to one of the benches. She wasn't worried about Nexis, knowing it was unlikely he could be damaged even if he had been present. She placed her belongings down and sat heavily. Quite a gathering had turned out because of the incident, and as everything began to calm down, folks started to walk off to their homes. Many muttered about being unable to get a drink or meal for the next few days. Kerys was busy talking to Fhyliss when Floretta appeared.

"Kitchen's serviceable," Floretta said.

"Really?" Kerys replied hopefully.

"Yes. No damage. The enchantment held."

"What enchantment?" SJ asked from where she sat, intrigued.

"The kitchen is fireproofed for safety reasons," Floretta replied.

Every snippet of information or detail was another small revelation into the workings of Amathera. "Why only the kitchen?"

"Cost. Enchanters charge a lot of money for fireproofing, which must be renewed regularly because of mana seepage. Thankfully it was only topped up a couple of weeks ago."

"I think it was Malaki who did this," Kerys growled as she sat on the bench next to SJ, looking at the remains of her home and livelihood.

"Who is Malaki?" SJ asked.

"Malaki Fretun. He works in Asterfal for the chancellor. He has been after my rejuvinatus recipe for months, and I have always refused to accept his offers. Mayor Maxwell told me the other week about rumours he was planning something."

SJ could remember the conversation in the bar not long after she had arrived in Killic. She had seen the towering form of the mayor speak to Kerys and had assumed at the time that he had been threatening her or something similar.

"Was that when he visited the bar that night?" SJ asked.

"Yes," Kerys replied, nodding. "He had heard through another councillor that Malaki was talking about getting hold of the recipe by any means as he wished to increase the productivity of Asterfal but reduce the costs of hiring. The last time I was in Asterfal, I had a run-in with him about it. It doesn't matter how often I have told the man, he doesn't take no for an answer. I have recently had several visits from his contacts pertaining to the purchase of the recipe. Each time, I have refused their offers. I am sure he is trying to drive my business under, so I have no option other than to accept his coin," Kerys finished, swearing vehemently.

"Are there no others that know the recipe?" SJ asked.

"It is a gnomish brewer's secret. Only those of gnomish origin know the recipe, and we are all sworn under oath. My family's oath binding is stronger than any to maintain secrecy, never mind the racial and professional oaths that also relate to it. Even if I wished to pass on the recipe and its details, I couldn't without risking death."

"I see. Is he not aware of this?"

"Of course he is, but Malaki doesn't care for others. He has only ever been interested in his own goals. He is an exceptionally skilled alchemist and has tried to replicate rejuvinatus himself, but he will never succeed. Thankfully."

"He couldn't stumble upon it by chance or research?"

"He could get close, but the side effects would be quite devastating if he did. Some processes must be followed that he will never consider in a million lifetimes. If I could tell you, you would understand why."

"What are you going to do about it?"

"I need to wait until the guard questions that idiot who mixed the solutions. I can't believe he was so gullible as to fall for the plot. Unfortunately, over the years, I have met many who fall into the bracket of idiocy. At least in Killic, there are far fewer than when I lived in Asterfal."

"I didn't know you used to live in Asterfal."

"I did for several years before moving to Killic to escape the chaos in the city. I also wanted to be away from the guild's control."

"Guild?"

"Yes. In Asterfal, to operate a bar, you need to be a member of the brewers' guild, and I was sick of paying the cut they took on profits. So I moved to Killic instead. It was the best decision I ever made, going independent."

SJ looked at her display; it was now three. "I need to find somewhere to stay."

"We all do," Fhyliss replied, sadness in her eyes as she looked at the ruined inn.

CHAPTER THIRTY-FOUR

From Above

Alice," SJ called as she saw the dryad hurrying towards the inn from the direction of the docks.

"I'm so sorry it took me so long to get here. The sound didn't travel to the island," Alice said.

"The island?" SJ asked, frowning.

"I live on the fisherman's isle."

SJ didn't know that Alice lived near Setu. There were only a few homes on the island. SJ could now understand Zigferd's anger and frustration when the bridge was damaged, if Alice had been stuck there.

"Kerys, here, take these," Alice said, handing her some keys. "The cottage opposite the church hall is empty, and you can use it for now until the inn is repaired."

"Thanks. I'll grab a few items and head over."

"SJ. I received confirmation this afternoon after we separated. You need to sign the paperwork in the morning."

"That's fantastic news, and the timing couldn't be better. Thank you, Alice," SJ said.

"Bert. Are you going to stay at your cousins'?"

"I am," he replied, nodding.

"Okay. Great, now to sort Floretta out."

"She can stay with me," SJ said.

"Are you sure? I wouldn't wish to impose," Floretta replied.

"Of course, and there are some fruits in the yard you may be interested in," SJ said.

"All those who had rooms will be accommodated at the barracks," Alice said.

SJ had paid no attention, but three others were still standing around the inn. She had noticed Fhyliss speaking to them but was unaware they had been staying there.

"Okay. Floretta, should we go to our new home?" SJ smiled.

Leaving Fhyliss and Kerys to sort out the other patrons with Alice, SJ led Floretta to the small cottage that she could call her new home. Opening the cottage door, she found it furnished but bare of day-to-day items, and she would need to go to the market and get supplies tomorrow.

"This is very nice," Floretta said.

"A previous council member moved back to Asterfal."

"That must be Miss Prewitt," Floretta said.

"Alice didn't tell me her name."

"Miss Prewitt was lovely. She had a caring soul and did everything she could for the town. I was sad to hear she was leaving when her sister fell ill. It's been a while now, though, since she left. I'm surprised that this place has been empty for so long."

"I need to get some sleep. I think I've had enough excitement for one night," SJ said.

"I will just be in the lounge," Floretta said.

"Do you not want to use the bedroom at the back?"

"No. I'm good. I have a book to read so I will sit here," Floretta answered, sitting at the small dining table.

"If you wish." SJ smiled and walked into the bedroom.

The bedroom had a large double bed, and SJ dropped the blanket with her belongings on the floor, tipped them out, and then climbed onto the bed, wrapping herself in it. It took her moments for sleep to take her.

The smell that filled SJ's nostrils was the heavenly scent of fried hogling. Sitting up on the bed, she heard whistling. She made her way through the lounge and down the short hallway to the small kitchen at the rear of the cottage. SJ opened the door to see Floretta cooking a wholesome breakfast.

"Morning," SJ said.

"Morning," Floretta replied, turning and smiling. "I thought you might like some food, and it seemed only fair after you allowed me to stay here."

"You didn't need to, and where did you get the food from?"

"I went back to the inn and took what I needed. It's my pantry, after all. The water is just heating for coffee."

SJ walked over to the stovetop, where a kettle was sat as it began to boil. She allowed it to cool briefly before making the coffee. A barista boyfriend back on Earth had told her never to make coffee with boiling water, and it had stuck ever since.

"Go on in to the lounge. I will bring it through in a few minutes when it's finished," Floretta said.

SJ wasn't going to argue and returned to the lounge area, where she sat at the small dining table. Out the window, the sun was already bright in the sky, and it was nearly ten, which was much later than she usually got up, but considering the disruption from the fire, she felt she needed it.

Floretta walked through from the kitchen, whistling a merry tune, and placed the perfect-looking full breakfast on the table for her. "Enjoy."

SJ's mouth watered at the sight. "Thanks." She took her cutlery from her inventory and began to eat.

"I will go to the inn later and see if we can still get food sales, at least. I moved some tables and chairs out this morning and should still be able to serve from the kitchen into the garden at the rear. At least that way, Kerys and Fhyliss will still have income."

"That sounds great," SJ said, grabbing mouthfuls of delicious fried hogling and mushrooms. After finishing the breakfast, she sat back in her chair and patted her stomach. "I could get used to this."

"Ha. I bet you could. You don't always have a full breakfast. Only normally twice a week; the other mornings you have either toast or cereal, and rarely porridge."

SJ looked at Floretta before replying. "I assume you know what most people eat?"

"I know all the regulars."

"That must make it easier to provide for them."

"I pretty much know what I need daily. Only occasionally do things change. Most have their favourites that they stick to."

"I will have to tell you more of the recipes from Earth and see if there are any more you can create here on Amathera. That reminds me: a grapey tree is in the rear garden."

"I had forgotten about Miss Prewitt's tree. I hope someone has been looking after it."

"Seeing how the cottage was left, someone has maintained it. I don't know who, though I must speak to Alice and find out."

"Probably Kevin. He is the most dab hand at gardening, even better than many druids."

"Is that his profession, then?"

"Yes. I always chuckle because he is a mage who is so negative about other mages. He's always criticising enchanters especially. Despite being a water mage himself, albeit low level, he has a habit of regularly hurling abuse at the academy mages. He only uses it to support his gardening, but it is somewhat contradictory."

"Are you able to make anything special with the grapey?" SJ asked.

"I am, yes." Floretta smiled her skeletal smile. "I can make hogling jerky."

"Jerky? With a fruit?"

"Yes. It goes well with hogling and gives it a sweetness to support the meaty taste of the strips when dried. It also gives nice bonuses."

"Oh. When I arrived, you made that pie with the bellpops, but I never used it as it went off in my inventory. Jerky I am guessing lasts a long time?"

"It does, yes. Once made, it will last for about a year, although it starts to lose its potency over time."

"What bonuses does it grant?"

"It will imbue someone who eats it with +5 Constitution for eight hours."

"That's amazing! That is a huge step in health."

"It is. Grapey is highly sought after if you can get a fruit-growing tree. The fruit growing is the rarity."

"How long does the jerky take to make?" SJ asked, excited at the thought of boosting her Constitution so easily.

"That's the downside. As it is a jerky, it takes over a month to cure and flavour properly."

Considering how long SJ might live in her new life, a month was a mere second in comparison.

"That isn't too long. If we get some from the tree, could you make some?"

"Of course, it would be my pleasure. There are very few ingredients around this territory that can add bonuses to anything when cooked."

The potential of the benefits that food could bring and the buffs they may induce was something SJ knew from games but hadn't even considered since the initial bellpop pie. It was a profession to keep at hand, and having a Master level chef in Floretta was a huge bonus for the town, which SJ believed was not being fully used or appreciated.

"Is the mayor or anyone else aware of the benefits you can get from your cooking?"

"Several are, but the ingredients are often rare or costly."

"Food items are a massive thing in large cities with a population large enough to justify the outlay," Dave interjected. "Here in Killic, though, it is so small a population in comparison that there isn't the same need or uptake, especially as they have no dungeon or anything near here that they can use as justification."

"Floretta, do you know how large the population of Asterfal is?"

"I'm unsure, but I think it's nearly fifty thousand."

"Wow. That is much larger than I expected."

"It's a large city. Not the largest, as the cities farther north are much larger, but in the southern region, it is the largest by far."

"Is the population that sparse here?"

"It is not that the population is sparse; it's more that there are many more tribal or clan-based factions in the south than in the north. The northern region around the capital is diverse and heavily populated."

"You have been to the capital?"

"Yes. I worked there for a while, many, many years ago now. I was the personal cook for a guild until it went under."

"Went under?"

"It collapsed because the guild leader syphoned off too much of the income from the members. There was a revolt and a dispute that caused it to break up."

Guilds were still a way off from SJ's consideration until she reached Level 20, but because the town had now increased its base level and allowed an auction house, she would need to speak to Zigferd about the potential for guilds. There was so much to consider with the continuing expansion plans of the town and what it may entail, and SJ had decided the more they could plan the better. If the next trigger occurred when she reached Level 20 in the town, she would want them to be ready.

"I'm going to head to the inn and see what's happening this morning," SJ said.

"If you see Fhyliss or Kerys, let them know I will be over for lunch to cook as usual. I think we will still get a few patrons coming through."

"I will do," SJ said as she stood to leave.

On her way towards the inn, SJ had a thought.

"Dave?"

"Yep."

"The territory increased in level when I reached Level 10. Does that mean if a Legionnaire who is Level 20 comes here, they will trigger the next border changes?"

"Ooooooo. That is a very interesting question."

"Dave?"

Silence.

Dave didn't reply for several minutes.

"Sorry. I raised an immediate concern, which meant it went straight to the adjudicator panel. I have the answer, and it is no. Only a Legionnaire who originally started in a location can increase the threshold further."

"They could tell you that?"

"Yep. It's the first time I have interacted with them since the border alignment. Apparently, the adjudicators are more well-informed than us administrators!"

"They know what is happening, then?"

"Nope. I asked that question. They are only being given specific details about the changes. I guess that Nexis probably knows more than they do."

It still amazed SJ that one of Amathera's beings, even if a god, could know more than those supposedly overseeing the interfacing.

"I wish he would tell us."

"I bet he couldn't even if he wanted to. If he knows details, he will be under a stricter oath than anything you will probably ever see."

"If a Legionnaire who started in an area is the only method of triggering growth, that means I am the town's only hope for it to continue." The realisation hit SJ like a train. She had personally disposed of the other two Legionnaires in the town who had originally started there and, to her knowledge, was the only one who could trigger the next growth effect. "Do you know if I left the area, would it stop the impact of the growth?"

"I asked that same question already, and no. As long as you are alive and levelling, whichever town you originated in will continue to expand territories as you level, whether you stay here or not."

"That means several towns may not even know what will happen to them."

"I agree. It will bring a little more chaos to Amathera."

"A little! It will be like playing roulette and never knowing when the ball will land on your number."

"Roulette. Now, that is a game I enjoy playing." Dave sighed deeply.

"Sorry. That was a bad reference to make."

"There's no need to apologise; I need to deal with it. I have stayed clean long enough now, and I have you to keep me busy," Dave replied cheerily.

"I am assuming that new Legionnaires are starting in more advanced areas," SJ said.

"Unlikely. There are five continents, remember, and from what I am aware, only this continent is being trialled. That means there are still many starter towns that can be used outside the influence of the sandbox."

A screeching sound filled the air, and SJ winced as her heightened hearing picked up the horrendous sound. "What was that?" SJ said.

"Oh no. I was afraid of this."

"What?"

"It seems we have a cross-border visitor."

"What is it?" As SJ asked, a swift-moving beast flew over the street she walked down. She ducked instinctively from the cast shadow.

"Wyvern," Dave answered.

SJ stared at the sky above but could see nothing as the surrounding buildings blocked her view. A harrowing scream came from up ahead, and she ran towards the sound. Others who had been on the street stood looking skyward.

"Wyverns are vicious predators. I didn't catch its level, but they are normally 30-plus."

Turning the street corner and following the shouting that had erupted, SJ came onto a horrendous scene. An orc lay face down, blood pouring from wounds that had been torn across its back.

A gnoll guard SJ recognised screamed for them to grab him and get him off the street. Looking up, SJ saw what could only be classed as a dragon soaring above the town and turning back towards where the members had gathered. Its wings were large and leathery, and its body sleek with a long prehensile tail. It banked sharply, turning back towards the street, and SJ noticed the mottled green colour of its scales.

SJ ran towards them as another guard member pointed a crossbow at the flying beast. The wyvern let out another screech as it again swooped towards where they stood. The guard released his bolt, and it flew towards the wyvern, who saw it coming and twisted its path, continuing its dive.

"MOVE," SJ screamed.

Those near the fallen orc scattered, some grabbing his bleeding body as the wyvern approached. SJ had no ranged weapons. As those on the immediate street were moving, the guard who had fired stood reloading his crossbow. He wasn't paying attention to the wyvern, cursing as he wound the loading mechanism. It looked like a heavy crossbow with a very slow loading time. SJ had witnessed them being used at the training ground.

As the wyvern swooped, SJ turned and sprinted towards the guard who was the wyvern's target. Hurtling into his side as the wyvern reached him, talons extended,

SJ pushed the guard unceremoniously to the side, and he staggered and groaned from the force of SJ's hit.

It meant SJ was now standing in the guard's position, and the wyvern's talons struck true. The force of the impact and the pain from the flying beast's strike flung SJ backwards, sending her hurtling towards one of the building walls. Her display flashed madly as she crashed into the wall. It could not have been a killing blow as her precognition hadn't triggered. But as she banged her head against the stone surface, she saw stars and slid to the ground.

"STAY AWAKE," Dave screamed at her as she lapsed into unconsciousness.

CHAPTER THIRTY-FIVE

Wyvern

The screech from the wyvern brought chaos to the streets of Killic. Townsfolk ran for cover and got indoors as quickly as they could. It had struck in three places, and the orc who had received its initial strike had unfortunately succumbed to his wounds with no healers nearby. The wyvern stood on the roof of one of the buildings, screeching, its talons digging deeply into the thatch.

"SJ!" Dave screamed.

SJ came to. Two town members had grabbed her and she was now lying on her back in the hall of someone's home. Panic and cries could be heard outside, and as she began to regain her thoughts and lose the dizziness she was feeling, she sat up.

"Thank the gods," Dave said.

She knew none of the beings in front of her well. She had seen them around the town but never spoken to them. A large bugbear knelt at her side.

"You okay? That was a nasty hit you took. Absolute stupidity, I might add," he said, smiling at her.

"I think I will be," she said, wincing at the pain from the talon strike. Her dress was soaked in blood where she had been pierced in her abdomen as the force of the impact had thrown her backwards. She placed her hand on her pounding head and felt the matted hair from the cut she must have received after hitting the wall with such force. Her head felt like cotton wool, and her health was reduced by three-quarters from the one strike. Her dress was repairing itself, and the tears from the talons and the blood were beginning to disappear. The bugbear looked in amazement as it self-repaired.

"Neat trick," he said.

"Did the gnoll survive?"

"He ran into a house on the far side of the street. Thanks to you for saving him. He owes you a drink."

"Ha." SJ winced again, her head throbbing. "I need a health potion. I don't suppose you have any?"

"No, sorry."

Grunting, she got to her feet. She was not in active combat and knew that her dragon blood would boost her healing process, but damn did it hurt. She peered out the open front doorway. Glancing up and down the street, she could not see the wyvern. "Do you know where it went?"

"No. I am not sure where it is now."

"I need to get to the barracks. We need guards to take this thing out."

"I am sure they will already be doing what they can."

"Thank you for dragging me from the street," SJ said, turning to look at the bugbear.

He only nodded in response.

SJ could hear the wyvern screech. Thankfully, it didn't sound too close. Taking a chance, she stepped outside and looked up at the sky. She could not see the beast. She went to shrink to her miniature form and pain flashed across her abdomen where she had been struck. She stopped the process and remained her larger size.

She held her hand across her stomach as she moved, her abdomen tender. She could still feel the dampness of blood caused by her movement as the wounds still hadn't closed fully.

"Any ideas?" she said as soon as she was away.

"It's two streets over on a rooftop. Just sitting there screeching," Dave replied. Having Dave's vision was proving invaluable.

Staying close to the building sides, SJ hurried along the street. The barracks were on the other side of town from where she was now. The streets were empty, and SJ saw several faces peering out of windows or doorways, looking skyward. "Did you get its level?" SJ asked.

"It is 31," Dave replied.

"There is no way we can fight something so strong. I can't do anything against something like that."

"Unlikely. The mages may affect it, but really, you need archers and rangers. Even if they can't kill it, it should eventually leave if they can hit it enough. They are not known for liking to receive damage."

"If anything can even damage it."

It took SJ several minutes to work through the streets, and she heard the wyvern's screech but didn't catch any sight of it.

"What is it doing?" she asked.

"It's just sitting there, doing nothing. It's probably just waiting for someone stupid enough to go outside—a little like yourself." Dave chuckled nervously. "Oh, hang on, it's airborne again."

SJ stopped and moved to the side of the building she had been passing, standing under a small lean-to where an owner kept chopped firewood. Peering into the sky, she spotted the beast circling the town again. It was miniature compared to Bob's humongous form but still large enough to strike fear; its wingspan must have been almost thirty feet, its snake-like body allowing it to turn quickly. It also didn't have forelegs like a dragon. SJ knew that with her identification skills, being able to work twenty levels higher than her own, she should be able to get more details on the creature. Unsure it would work at the distance she was from it, she gave it a go. It didn't work initially, and she watched the timer cool down before trying again as it swooped lower over the town.

Mottled Wyvern	
Level:	31
Hit Points:	415
Mana Points:	0
Armour Class:	42
Attacks:	Talons, Bite
Special:	Acid

SJ let out a low whistle as she read the details. "That thing is untouchable. What does its acid special mean?"

"They have various special attacks depending upon the variant, like dragons and their abilities, but on a much lesser scale. Mottled wyverns are the commonest of their species. They are susceptible to fire damage, which plays havoc with their acidic blood."

"That's good to know. I still need to reach the barracks." Watching the path of the wyvern, SJ continued her movements, darting from one piece of cover to the next. The wyvern screeched again, and SJ saw it disappear down another street to her left. Taking advantage, she sprinted the final distance. Her wounds were healing well, the tenderness in her abdomen easing, and her dress had been repaired and cleaned. At least she no longer felt like the torn piece of meat she had done.

She did not slow as she approached the barracks entrance, ploughing through the door. The guard standing on the other side shouted in shock and surprise.

Captain Broadaxe stood in the main area, shouting orders to guards filing down towards the armoury. Lorna was busy talking to two other guards who were holding very long pikes, which must have been nearly twenty feet.

SJ hurried over to the captain.

He noticed her coming, finished shouting his last instruction, and turned to her. "SJ. What are you doing here?"

"I am here to help if I can. I know it's a Level 31 mottled wyvern and is susceptible to fire damage."

"You know its weakness? I didn't realise your identification skill was so high," Ballentine replied, surprised.

The main area had nearly twenty guards, most equipped now with crossbows or bows. "Get me cloth swabs and oil now," Ballentine shouted to one of the attendants who would normally be sitting at a desk doing his daily work. The kobold jumped at being addressed by Ballentine and sprang to his feet, then ran towards the armoury, pushing through a guard who was just heading back up the corridor with a bow and quiver in hand.

"Have you fought these before?" SJ asked.

"Never," Ballentine replied. "I have fought hatchling red dragons but never a wyvern."

"They also spit acid, so the guards need to be aware."

Ballentine hurried the guard to sort themselves out, and they moved towards the entrance. The double doors were opened, and the captain stood looking outside up to the sky. The screech of the wyvern carried easily over the quiet streets of the town with everyone indoors.

"Okay. We fan out and line up on the street sides. It can't swoop to attack if we are against the walls."

"Here," panted the attendant whom Ballentine had ordered away as he ran forward carrying a bucket of oil and a cloth roll under his arm.

"Before you go out, those with bows must make burners."

Only half a dozen had bows, and one of them moved forward to take the cloth. SJ watched as he removed a knife from his belt and started to cut the cloth into strips that could be soaked in oil.

"Here," SJ said as she equipped her claws. "Hold it taut." The guard and attendant held the cloth stretched between them as SJ pierced the material and cut it into strips much faster than a single knife blade could.

"Thanks," the guard replied.

Taking the cloth strips, the other archers began to remove arrows and wrap the cloth tightly around the ends before soaking them in the oil from the bucket.

"Ready?" Ballentine asked.

"Sir," came the reply from several guards.

"On my order, we move out and line the streets. Ready, move."

The guards streamed from the barracks entrance and split to both sides of the street. The wyvern was not visible now, and as they reached their positions, SJ watched from the barracks doorway as two crossbow wielders took flint and steel and began striking them to support the archers, setting their wrapped arrows alight.

The whole town lay silent apart from the wyvern's screech and the sound of flint and steel being struck.

"You need bait," Dave said. "Wyverns are not the most intelligent of beings, and if you can draw it to attack, that will allow the archers to strike."

SJ groaned, knowing exactly what Dave meant. She shrank to her miniature form, thankfully without the previous pain, and flew out the barracks door. She turned up and headed towards the roof of the three-storey building. As she flew past a window, she saw the wide-eyed face of the gnome who worked on the miniature town staring out at her.

Reaching the roof, she landed and scanned the sky. The wyvern circled above the far side of the town, where SJ thought she remembered there being livestock. It dived out of sight and moments later reappeared, this time with a cow in its talons. SJ could hear the panicked mooing as the beast was taken. The wyvern carried it upwards, beating its wings, before releasing it. The bovine lowed as it plummeted back towards the ground and smashed into and through the roof of a building.

"I need to get its attention somehow," SJ said. She took off again and flew straight towards it, diving low down to the roofs of the buildings. "Of all the stupid things to be doing, flying towards something that could eat me for lunch . . ." she sighed as she continued.

Compared to her six-inch miniature form, it looked like a mountain, its huge leathery wings accentuating its body size dramatically. As close as she was getting now, its skin reminded her of that of a python with its mottled colouring and green-brown tones. It had not noticed her yet, and she was only a few streets away from it.

"Don't get too close. They are fast when they want to be. You need lead time to keep away from it," Dave warned.

"It's not paying attention, though."

"Land, grow, and then get ready to run like your life depends on it. Which it will," Dave added unhelpfully.

Dropping to the nearest rooftop, she checked her footing on the thatch and then grew, not taking her eyes from the direction the wyvern was in. Once again, it had circled away, making its way out of the town area. "It seems to be moving away," SJ said.

"It won't go far, if anywhere. Once they have found an area to hunt, they are quite persistent unless driven off or killed," Dave said.

SJ stood on the roof and began to shout and wave her arms; in her green dress she hoped to draw its attention at least. It flew out over the fields and turned as it neared the windmill. SJ saw a flash of blue streak into the sky, followed by another of red. "It looks like it found the mage academy," SJ said.

The wyvern let out another screech, which even in the distance still made SJ's ears ring as it headed back towards town. That is when it saw her. SJ ran as she saw the creature's gaze fall on her. Throwing herself off the side of the building as she finished shrinking, her brilliant green form flew as fast as it could towards the barracks and where the guards lay in wait.

"Faster. It's gaining on you," Dave shouted.

Glancing over her shoulder, SJ could see the speed at which the beast moved. Its wings were tucked in like that of a diving bird. It had been higher than the rooftops, so it had approached her at a slight decline, increasing its speed as it did. SJ gritted her teeth and flew as fast as she could, zipping over the building tops until she reached the street of the barracks, then dived and skimmed the street's surface.

"Get ready," she screamed as loud as she could in her small form. Ballentine and the other guards saw the bright green missile of SJ fly down the centre of the street, which was followed by the snake-like head of the wyvern, following her path. The guards were a little slow on the uptake, and several didn't even react before the wyvern passed their location. Others farther down the street had time, and missiles got fired towards it. SJ watched the flash of bolts soar by her as at least three burning arrows also did so. She didn't know how many had fired, but the sudden draught she felt behind her as the wyvern adjusted its flight path and rose again into the air told her it was getting out of their way. She reached the main barracks entrance door and flew straight inside before stopping under the shelter of the building.

Panting from the exertion, she turned and looked back outside. At least four of the projectiles had struck the beast, one of them a burning arrow. The wyvern shrieked as it circled upwards out of range of the archers, whose arrows fell short and back down to the ground.

"That didn't work as well as I hoped," SJ said.

"Maybe we should have informed them what the plan was first," Dave said, chuckling nervously.

"Grrr," SJ said, annoyed at her stupidity for not even letting them know. She had been so caught up in getting its attention that she hadn't even informed anyone what she was going to do. That was why so many were not ready for its appearance. "I doubt it will work a second time."

"They are pretty stupid beasts. If you attract its attention again, it will probably attack," Dave said.

SJ flew back outside again and straight over to where Ballentine stood with a heavy crossbow. He had just finished reloading it.

"Sorry. I should have said what I was going to do," SJ said as she approached.

"No problem. I just wish we had more archers and rangers available. As fighters, we are not skilled in archery, and these crossbows do not reload fast enough to allow for successive attacks."

The wyvern screeched again as it now hovered high above the street. She noticed it draw its head back and then throw it forward as though spitting.

"Duck," Dave shouted as the green ball of acid came hurtling downwards towards where she and Ballentine stood. She flew sideways, screaming at Ballentine to move. He dived out of the way at the last second as the ball of acid struck the wooden door that he had been standing in front of. Its acid sizzled against the surface, charring the wood. She turned and looked again as it spat towards another position where guards stood by the wall. One of the guards did not react quickly enough, and the ball of acid struck him in his leg. Screaming in pain, he fell to the ground. Another guard grabbed him and dragged him back towards the wall edge. A door opened from one of the homes they were stood by, and the guard was dragged inside.

"We need more than this," Ballentine said.

That was when a blazing arrow hurtled towards the wyvern. It screeched in response and tried to jink out of the way, but this arrow flew with unnatural precision and speed. It lodged itself in the beast's wing arm. The wyvern wailed in frustration as the flame from the arrow began to spread onto its wing. The wyvern reacted by diving downwards, and the draught caused by its sudden descent made the flames flicker, then extinguish.

That was when SJ saw him. Standing in the doorway to the jail was the half elf who had managed to blow up the inn. He held a glowing short bow in his hands and again took aim at the wyvern. The arrow tip began to glow a blue colour, and he released it as the wyvern neared. The wyvern had no chance to react, and the arrow struck its elongated neck. That was when the effect took hold. The scene reminded SJ of people she had seen Tasered on Earth as a flash of blue lightning erupted across the surface of the wyvern, making it spasm and lose control. It hurtled towards a building and crashed into the roof, disappearing into its interior.

SJ heard screams from the building as the wyvern's head reappeared above the remaining wall. With effort, it hopped and flapped from the debris until it could jump again into the air and fly. Another flaming arrow again sped towards it from the half-elf and successfully struck it. SJ noticed Zigferd stood in the jail entrance behind the half elf. The wyvern cried again as it flapped its wings, cascading dust and debris from the building across the street, and took off, gaining height.

They watched as the beast moved away from the town and towards the mountains to the east.

CHAPTER THIRTY-SIX

Darren

As the wyvern continued to move away from the town, Ballentine began shouting orders to the guards.

"Get the clerics now. I want all those injured across the town treated. I also want you four to check the building that the wyvern landed on. The rest of you need to start cleaning the streets, and I also want the livestock herd checked out. Tell Gregor to ensure that any livestock is moved into the barns immediately. I am sure we all saw the flying cow. Find out where it came down and check for injuries," he called.

SJ grew to her human size and looked at the devastation of the building where the wyvern had crashed. The front wall was at a precarious angle, and she was surprised it hadn't collapsed fully from the impact of the beast landing inside it. Glancing towards the wyvern, she ensured it was still heading away from town.

"It will be back," Dave said.

SJ walked some distance from Ballentine before whispering. "How do you know?"

"It is a predator, after all, and the town is an easy source of food for it, especially with livestock. I am surprised it didn't just take one of the cows and leave."

"These changes and monster levels could get very dangerous very quickly."

SJ saw Zigferd place his hand on the half elf's shoulder, nod at him, and follow as he slung his bow over his shoulder and re-entered the jail area. Watching him head back inside after what he had just done for the town concerned SJ, and she walked straight over. Zigferd stood at the desk with the half elf.

"If you sign here and here . . ." SJ watched Zigferd indicate. "Then you are free to go."

The half elf picked up the quill from the desktop and, dipping into a pot of ink, scrawled his signature as requested.

"Thank you. Make sure that you don't do anything else stupid while in town," Zigferd warned.

The half self looked at the huge form of Zigferd, and his shoulder sagged. "It was an accident. I honestly did not know what may happen."

"I know it's obvious that Master Fretun wasn't expecting you to survive or that you would be able to inform us that he sent you here," Zigferd replied. "SJ. What brings you here?" he asked, smiling.

"I just came to see who saved the town from the wyvern attack," SJ said.

"Well, Darren here is a ranger with experience fighting wyvern," Zigferd replied.

"He has. It's good to know that there is someone in town to help with it. I'm guessing it will be back at some point," SJ said.

"I hope not too soon," Zigferd said.

Darren was still in the same state he had been the previous evening. His face was covered in black streaks from the fire and the explosion in his room. His clothes were unkempt, and he looked dishevelled. "I'm going to see if any of my stuff survived the explosion," Darren said as he headed to the door.

"Level 20 Legionnaire," Dave said.

"Level 20," SJ said in surprise.

Darren stopped, turning to look at her. "You could have asked," he snapped angrily.

"Asked what?" SJ said, shocked by his response.

"To identify me before going ahead and doing it," Darren replied.

"I didn't," SJ spluttered defensively.

"Then how do you know what level I am?" he asked, scrutinising her.

"That is a separate story. Let me accompany you to the inn, and I can explain it."

"Whatever," he replied, shrugging as he walked out of the jail.

"SJ. Please keep an eye on him," Zigferd said as she followed Darren out the door.

Darren was walking off down the street, ignoring the guards and others who had now come out to clean up the mess left by the wyvern. SJ hurried to catch him up.

"Wait," she said as she got to his side.

"Wait for what? To be thrown in jail again and locked up? I don't think so. I'm going to get my things and leave this dump of a town," he snapped.

"*Dump of a town*?" SJ repeated angrily. "This dump of a town, as you call it, is my home, and I don't take kindly to someone from out of town coming here and saying otherwise."

"How would you feel after the way I have been treated?"

"Typical Legionnaire. All he thinks about is himself," Dave said.

"Treated? You blew up the inn, which was my home, and you don't see me having a go at you, do you?" SJ retorted, frowning.

"I paid for the damages and apologised. I'm unsure why I spent the night in the cells."

"Precaution, probably. Would you let someone who had just caused an explosion walk off without questioning them?"

Darren stopped and turned to look at SJ, his eyes narrowed and filled with anger. SJ stood, looking back at him with a blank expression, showing no malice towards him. His face softened slightly. "At least you aren't looking at me as though I'm a piece of dirt," he grumbled.

"I have no reason to look at you any other way. I'm more interested in finding out about you being a Legionnaire."

"So how do you know I'm a Level 20 Legionnaire if you didn't identify me?" he asked, pursing his lips, clearly expecting to hear a lie.

"I know what level you are because I'm also a Legionnaire with an administrator who speaks to me, and he informed me. I guess yours doesn't," SJ said, smiling.

Darren shrugged nonchalantly. "All administrators talk to their Legionnaires, but mine has never given me any details about anything useful."

"Erm. My administrator may not be that normal," SJ said.

"Hey. I can hear you, you know," Dave complained.

"What do you mean not normal?"

"He's a little sarcastic."

"I am. I have a first in sarcasm," Dave replied smugly.

"Sarcastic. My administrator rarely speaks, and when it does, it's in the most annoying metallic voice, like a nail on a blackboard."

"He must have an old model. They are rather boring to talk to. I wonder who he has?" Dave mused.

"Dave wonders who you have and says they must be an old AI model. He even said that they can be rather boring to talk to."

"Dave?"

"My administrator."

"He has a name?"

"It's not his official name, but I couldn't keep calling him blah blah blah or whatever his designation was. I couldn't remember it, for a start."

"How can he speak to you about levels though?" Darren asked, frowning.

"Dave can do much more than that. He is my best friend in Amathera and always helps me out."

"You're kidding me, right?" Surprise registered on Darren's face.

"No. Why would I lie about it?"

"My administrator only tells me about basic upgrade stuff. Its voice is the most frustrating part."

Darren's face was a picture—a mixture of confusion and surprise—as he stood looking at SJ.

"What does he tell you?" Darren asked, intrigued.

"Whatever he can."

"Ooooo. I found his administrator," Dave said. "He *is* an old model—probably one of the first. I can't speak to his administrator for obvious reasons, as we have Legionnaires, but he is the only Darren registered on this continent."

"Dave thinks your AI model may be one of the first ones on Amathera."

"How would he know that?"

"He found your name and traced it."

"I wish my AI was as helpful and interactive as yours sounds," Darren replied in disbelief.

"Dave is great," SJ said, smiling. "You realise that we are the only two Legionnaires in the town."

"Aww, shucks. You'll make me blush," Dave said.

"I'm not surprised. There isn't anything to keep Legionnaires of higher levels here."

"There will be in the future if things continue."

"What do you mean?"

"With the territory and border expansions that are occurring."

"What?" Darren asked, frowning.

"You may not be aware, but the starter areas are starting to get the opportunity to level higher. This town was a 0–10 and now is a 0–20."

"How has that happened?"

SJ spent the next few minutes explaining what had happened with the System since she hit Level 10 as they neared the inn. On arriving in the town square, there were several broken stalls, and it was obvious the wyvern must have struck here. Thankfully, there was no evidence of injuries. Instead, it was filled with the frantic and worried expressions of the town members who were busy cleaning up. Many of them were glancing up into the sky continually. The damage to the inn was visible in daylight, and SJ stopped to survey the scene. The front looked fine, apart from the fact it was missing its thatch. There were several blackened marks on the walls caused by the smoke, and there was a large sign posted by the door: GARDEN ENTRANCE OPEN.

Around the rear of the inn where the garden area was, the damage to the building was more substantial, with the missing wall and clear damage caused by the explosion. SJ watched Darren cringe when he saw what he had caused. SJ spotted Fhyliss and headed over.

"Hi, Fhyliss."

"Hi . . ." Fhyliss stopped in her tracks when she saw Darren. "You are either brave or very stupid," she finished, looking at Darren.

"I just came to see if anything I brought had survived, and then I will be out of here," Darren said.

"You are lucky Mum has gone to help at Lucian's, where that cow landed. She will probably be there for a while. I would advise you to go and look and then make yourself scarce. Her temper is legendary in Killic."

SJ couldn't help but half smile at her comment. She had seen the effect that Kerys could have on some exceedingly large and drunken beings before and the way they had shrunk away from her, and after seeing her tear into Darren the night before, SJ could believe she'd do it a second time.

"Can I get in the back to look?" Darren asked.

"Go through. Bert is inside, clearing the worst away still."

Fhyliss and SJ watched as he walked through into the back of the inn.

"I can't believe a wyvern attacked the town," Fhyliss said.

"I know. It moved off, though, because of Darren."

"Darren?" Fhyliss asked, raising an eyebrow at SJ.

"Yes. He is a Level 20 ranger. You should have seen him with his bow. It was glowing as he fired arrows at the wyvern."

"Hmph. I think Mum would say he would need to do a lot more than that to get in her good books."

"He has paid for the damage. She can't hold a grudge to that degree."

"You know Mum," Fhyliss replied, shrugging.

"While I remember—Floretta thinks she may still serve food today."

"With the wyvern in the area, we will have to see how many of the town venture outside today."

SJ had automatically turned to look in the direction that the wyvern had flown. There wasn't a clear view of the mountains from here, but she couldn't see any signs of it being airborne. The streets were much quieter than she would have expected. Many stood in doorways, talking in hushed tones to each other.

"You need to try to keep him in town," Dave said.

Fhyliss had returned inside the inn, so SJ could respond to Dave. "Why?"

"I have seen all the town's archers, rangers, and fighters. As with the magic users we have seen, very few can damage that wyvern. If it returns and attacks the town, there is virtually nothing they have of an offensive capability to damage it enough. Even multiple runs, as you did with it being shot at, would take forever to take its health down. As we saw with his shock arrow, that ranger has the best chance. Once it's on the ground, you stand a chance, but airborne, you won't."

"I'm not sure how we can make him stay. He sounded pretty determined to leave as soon as he could. He is also Level 20 and won't be able to level further in this territory."

"That is true, but there may be a way around it."

"Really. How?"

"I think I may have found a loophole you can manipulate to your advantage."

At the thought of a loophole, SJ felt a rush of excitement. "Go on, what loophole have you identified?"

"I have been considering how the System will have allowed the growth changes to occur. I have also been considering the quest system and how it is associated with territory levels. With the expanded territories and the variance in levels that are now permitted to enter, I believe that an open quest may provide the answer. An open quest is one which can be completed across boundaries, so you could assign one to Darren to allow him to progress still."

"Me, give a quest?" The revelation startled SJ. Never in a thousand years had she considered being able to assign quests.

"Yes. You are now a member of the town council. You should be able to assign quests on behalf of the town. If the mayor authorises you."

"Can't that be seen as cheating?"

"Potentially, but remember you are not signed up to the terms and conditions. Unless we try, though, we won't know. I can't guarantee that it will work, but maybe if you can assign a cross-border quest, you can assign experience gains. It would be like how guilds operate with their quest system. Many quests are within different territories than where a guild is based, and they accept them on behalf of the guild, allowing members to complete them."

"So to allow for Darren to be issued a quest, since he is Level 20 I would need to be in a territory that allowed quests for his level? I thought assigned quests were within a territory? You mentioned before if I leave a territory the quest is released."

"Most are, but not all. Several quests cross territories at higher levels where they complete certain tasks or are after certain items or information. An example would be a quest relating to information. A being maybe required to go to a territory to attain information, even if they are a higher level than the area. Just because they are at a higher level doesn't necessarily mean they will not gain experience if they complete the quest. It is no different from what I assume Darren was working under."

"What do you mean?"

"He said he was completing a quest. The quest was to deliver the alchemical components to someone in Killic, a lower-level territory. He could still accept the quest."

"So even if it did work, I would need to enter a Level 20–30 territory and assign him a quest that allows him to gain experience."

"Basically; it is hypothetical. The problem is I have never known one that involves killing something or someone because of restrictions. I think that because the beast is above the threshold of the normal territory levels, it may allow it to happen as a kill quest. No one has tried it before, but you won't know unless you try. It wouldn't even be a consideration in normal circumstances as the levels are aligned directly with the territory."

"It still sounds like a way of cheating."

"I wouldn't call it cheating. I would call it playing the System." Dave laughed at his joke.

SJ groaned in response.

"I think the wording of such a quest must also be carefully considered. Because I have never heard of a cross-boundary kill quest, I think it would have to be deemed a protection quest."

After several minutes, Darren returned down the stairs carrying a blackened backpack on his shoulder.

"Did you get your things?" SJ asked.

"What I could. Thankfully, some of my clothes survived, and I will get changed out of these," he replied, indicating his state. "Is there another nearby inn where I can get cleaned up?"

"Unfortunately, no. The only inn in town currently has no roof." SJ smiled.

Darren grimaced.

"I will let you come back to mine to clean up, and while you're there, we need to talk," SJ said.

"About what?"

"About you staying in Killic," SJ said, smiling.

CHAPTER THIRTY-SEVEN

New Allegiances

It was afternoon before Darren finally finished cleaning himself up and changing at SJ's cottage. Floretta had been kind enough to make some lunch before she left for the inn. There had been no further sign of the wyvern since it had left the town, and SJ sat in the front room as Darren walked down the hall from the back room where he had changed.

He was wearing a dark leather suit of armour with metal shoulder plates. He had cut away the scorched parts of his hair with a knife, and his unkempt looks were cleared to show a young, clean-shaven appearance. SJ could see the slight point to his ears poking from behind his hair. Across his body was a bandolier-style leather strap, and on his back, he wore a large quiver of arrows. He carried his short bow at his side. He was much younger-looking than SJ had thought and had an Asian look. His olive skin tone was similar to Nexis's, and now that he was cleaned up, he looked quite attractive.

"Floretta made some lunch," SJ said, smiling at him as he entered the lounge.

Darren had been taken aback when he had first arrived at the cottage to find a skeleton residing inside. He stated that he had previously had some poor experiences with the undead. It had taken a while for him to begin to relax, watching every movement that Floretta made. Now the table was laid with Floretta's usual amazing spread; she always presented the most amazing-looking food, and SJ saw Darren swallow.

Placing his bow on the table, he sat down before taking a plate and beginning to fill it with food.

"Thanks. I haven't eaten since yesterday morning," he said, popping a small ripe tomato into his mouth. As he bit into it, his eyes widened in surprise. "Damn, these taste so good."

"Floretta makes everything taste amazing. She is a Master cook."

"What is a Master cook doing in a starter town area?"

"She has been here a long time. She is an integral part of the inn and one of the reasons it has such a good reputation."

"I need to ask you. What level are you?"

"I'm Level 11," SJ said.

"I must admit, seeing how you're dressed, I didn't think you were a Legionnaire at first," he replied, looking at her dress.

"This dress was a gift and is quite special," she said, not adding any detail. Dave warned her to be careful about what information she gave Darren.

"You know I am a ranger. What class are you?" he asked, biting into a chunk of bread smothered in butter.

SJ could feel her face heat up at the question though she knew it would come at some point.

"I am an assassin."

The mouthful of food Darren was eating at that moment nearly came back out as he forced himself to chew and swallow it, coughing before he could respond. "You're an assassin?" He stared in amazement. "I thought you were a druid or a mage."

"I think many others think so too," she said, smiling again.

"What made you choose to be an assassin?" he asked, surprise etched on his face.

"It may sound strange, but I wanted to help people fight for good against evil. I had always liked the class from games back on Earth, and the skills seemed to align loosely with my previous life."

"What were you, a hitman or something?!" he exclaimed.

SJ blushed as she said, "A forensic accountant."

Darren guffawed at her comment. "How did you think an assassin would align with a forensic accountant?"

"Okay. Maybe it isn't the most direct relationship, but it has done me well so far," SJ huffed. "And what were you?"

"I was trying to make it in the music industry."

"That sounds interesting."

"It may have been until I died while attending an audition."

"Oh."

"Yeah. They had been advertising for the next boy band, and I had made it through the preliminaries for this new group they were putting together to fill the void between the K-pop and UK music scene. I was more of a dancer than a singer. That was until one of the stage lights fell on me."

"At least you weren't squished by a tree." His previous career intrigued SJ. "You could have been the next big act, then."

"I'll never know, unfortunately," Darren replied, shrugging.

"How long have you been on Amathera?"

"Sixteen months now."

"Wow. I have not been here three yet or anywhere outside of the town."

"You are lucky, then. You seem to have people here who you trust and speak to. I had to leave my starter village to continue levelling, and it was not a great journey. Things only recently started to get better when I arrived in Asterfal."

"Why?"

"Legionnaires are seen as a nuisance by many normal Amathereans outside the starter areas. Many are not held in high regard."

"Dave has told me that before. It still seems strange that some shun us."

"I think it relates to jealousy. Amathereans can't level as easily as we can or have the same chance to experience what we do."

"In what way? They can still level."

"Yes, but they can't go into a dungeon and die multiple times as we can."

SJ was excited about the chance to enter a dungeon. "Have you been in one?"

"No, not yet. I wanted to reach a higher level before I did, but I needed to level my alchemy skill first."

"For what reason?"

"Healing potions are very expensive, normally, and my Constitution isn't as high as I would like it to be, which I am sure your AI has told you."

"No. He hasn't told me your stats. He can only tell me your level. He can't give me details of your attributes."

"Oh. I assume that you have the identification skill?"

"I do. It's part of my class."

"Yeah. There are a few classes that have the option to choose it. Unfortunately, it's not available to rangers. Mainly the magic-user classes. It would have been nice to have."

SJ had never considered which other classes would have the option to learn identification. "I couldn't see your stats if I did identify you, anyway. It doesn't give me those details."

"I assumed it would do. I suppose it must have some barriers."

"I am not that high a level in it yet. I am unsure what it may advance to in the long term."

"Anyway, you wanted to talk to me about staying in town?"

SJ had been enjoying their topic but didn't want to push too far in asking questions. "Yes, I do. I would like you to remain and help protect the town."

"Why would I remain in an area where I cannot level or advance?"

"Because in time, you will be able to."

"In time? You just said you are Level 11, and it's going to take you at least twelve months, if not longer, to reach Level 20. I know; I have done the slog. Repetitive, boring quests, just to grind the experience needed."

SJ had not had to repeat any quest to continue levelling and hadn't considered the need to with so many options available within the town, never mind the new quests she was offered. She had not actively sought quests apart from the very first one when she had gone crypt diving for Lythonian; everything else had been offered as she had naturally interacted with others in the town. "I have enough quests to keep me busy without worrying about repeating things currently."

"You haven't had to do grind quests yet?" Darren asked, surprised.

"No. Not once. Every quest I have completed so far has been different."

"There must be a lot of quest issuers in the town, then."

"I am not sure, although I assume I could have got more if I had sought them."

"What? You didn't even go looking for them?"

"No. Only my first. Since then, everything has been offered to me."

"How?"

"I don't know. It just has."

"I'm guessing you have at least a liked or popular reputation with the town, then, if that's the case."

"I have revered status."

Darren gasped. "Revered? How on Earth did you achieve revered status?"

"That's a longer story," SJ said, smiling.

"Do tell," Darren said.

SJ reached for a piece of crusty bread. Then, she began to tell Darren about her time on Amathera since her arrival.

It was mid-afternoon when SJ finished relaying her history in Killic.

"You are a member of the town council?" Darren echoed in amazement. If his eyebrows could have risen any farther, they probably would have fallen off his face.

"Yes. Newly appointed as the ambassador for Killic."

"I can understand why you may want to stay here, then. I have never been so lucky."

She'd never considered it luck but rather a chance of circumstances. SJ shrugged. "I'm not sure I would say I was lucky. I have made some good friends since I have been here and trust many in the town. It has become my home."

Darren shook his head in disbelief at SJ's story, he couldn't comprehend what had occurred. "I can't believe that you have had so much involvement across the town already. In my starting village, all I had available to me were my training quests and profession."

"What profession are you?"

"My main profession is a tanner. What about you?"

"I am a tailor."

"Explains the dress, I suppose," Darren replied. SJ wasn't going to contradict the assumption.

"Yes. It was a gift from my trainer. I may have some items that are of use to you."

"What do you have?"

"I have some leather and a couple of other items that you might use. I have no need for them but have never sold them."

"If you let me see them, I can let you know."

SJ stood and walked through the bedroom, collecting the items she had gathered since arriving in Amathera. Bringing them back through, she placed them on the table in the lounge.

"Umm. I can use the leather and the wolf pelt. The chitinous plates are more of an armourer's thing. What are these other plates you have? I don't recognise them."

"Rock gobbler plates."

"Let me check my recipes." Darren's eyes seemed to blank out as he was obviously looking at his display. She had never witnessed anyone before doing it, and it was as though he had a vacant expression. After several moments, he turned back to her. "They can be used to create bracers and greaves. They are listed as a material that I can use, but I don't have a recipe for them."

SJ was pleased with the information. "Where can you get a recipe?"

"The only place is probably an auction house. It's a rare recipe, so the closest place would be Asterfal."

"Actually . . ." SJ said, pausing.

"What?"

"We are building an auction house here in Killic."

"But you can't use one."

"There are locals above Level 20 who can, and it seemed like a good opportunity to get one set up early."

"I don't know about auction houses apart from the ones in Asterfal, where I checked the prices of items."

"I have a friend who may find out, but with this recent wyvern attack on the town, I am not sure if the build will be delayed or how long it will even take."

"You are thinking of expansion, aren't you?"

"Yes. This town has no choice but to grow with the changes, and I have no plans to leave here for now." With all the details SJ had given Darren, she left out some key points she was unwilling to share, specifically about the mithril mine. She was already aware of the secrecy issues surrounding outsiders finding out.

"Even with what you have said, I still can see no benefits for myself staying here."

"I think you need to give it a chance to grow on you."

"Without being able to quest and level, there is nothing I can do to gain a good reputation."

"That's not true," Dave said. "Reputation gains do not require a quest completion. Take your raise because of saving Christy as an example of a boost that was not quest related."

"Dave states that isn't the case. You can gain a reputation without completing quests by acting on the town's behalf."

"It still doesn't boost me, though."

"Imagine if you reach revered status, though, and the benefits it will bring long-term as the town grows."

Darren sat contemplating the information from SJ. It would be amazing to get 100 percent experience bonuses for quests, but from what she had explained, until SJ reached Level 20 he still couldn't see a benefit.

"I also need to see if something else will work. I don't want to say anything until I try, as I don't want to give you a false sense of hope."

Frowning, Darren looked at her quizzically. "I can't go back to Asterfal straight away, and the quest I had from Master Fretun is showing as failed, so the experience I should have been able to get has been lost."

"I guess that your Master will send someone to Killic to investigate what has happened and whether his plan worked."

"I still don't know what he was hoping to achieve. Or how I was stupid enough to fall for his tricks. I knew he was manipulative but naively accepted his word."

"We all make mistakes," SJ said, not wishing to discuss Kerys's concerns about Malaki Fretun. She had so many questions that she wanted to ask Darren but also needed to be careful about what she divulged. "Hopefully, you will at least stay here a few days while I see if I can sort out what I am hoping to."

The cryptic comments did not give Darren much peace of mind. "I will probably just start travelling north and head towards the capital. Most of the trade routes are well protected across territory boundaries, and once there, I can get lost in the crowd and leave Asterfal and the south behind me."

"Look. Give me a few days at least to see if I can sort things out for you here," SJ said, and then continued. "You can stay here. There is the spare room in the back, which you have already used. I just need to go to the market and get the basics. I only got the cottage last night after the explosion."

Darren closed his eyes, shaking his head again at the reminder. Opening his eyes, he said, "Doesn't your skeleton companion stay in the room?"

"No. Floretta never sleeps. I need to go into town and get what is needed for the cottage. Would you like to join me?" SJ asked, hoping that he would accompany her. If Darren got to meet and know some others in the town, he might feel more inclined to stay, and the town's safety might depend on it.

CHAPTER THIRTY-EIGHT

Setting Quests

D ave? Which is the closest area to see if quests can be created?" SJ asked. When they entered the town again, SJ visited several shops where goods were sold after finding many closed. Many of the usual market traders were not running the stalls in the square through obvious fear of the wyvern returning. This gave the town an eerily quiet feeling compared to normal. She had ordered what she needed and arranged for delivery of most of the items to the cottage, saying she would be back there later that afternoon. The open traders had been more than receptive to her requests and grateful for the business on such a day. Now Darren was standing in the tailor's shop looking for new clothes to replace his ruined ones.

SJ had shown him inside and introduced him to Fizzlewick's quarterling form. She now stood outside, waiting for him to finish. Despite her struggle to adapt, she acknowledged that Fizzlewick was Nexis, no matter where Nexis might currently be. No one had seen him return since last night, and she wanted to speak to him about the rock gobbler recipes without arousing suspicion by talking to his quarterling version.

It was still mind-blowing, considering she knew who he was and that he was a god performing the menial tasks of shopkeeping, but the smile on the quarterling's face showed that he really did enjoy the daily interactions.

"The easiest option would be going to Asterfal. Designated cities do not have level caps. So you can go there and try. It is a four-day journey, so you are looking at an eight-day return trip," Dave said.

"Is there nowhere closer?"

"There is, but it means going into the desert region to the south and crossing it. The region is not very large, but the dangers there are quite real compared to travelling the much safer route to Asterfal. The main route is regularly patrolled, especially as you get nearer the city. It helps keep the bandits away. If you go via the desert region, you could get across and back in four days. With your flying speed, it may work out faster, but the temperatures can be limiting, so I suggest wagon travel. Either that or flying at nighttime, but more hostiles are around at night."

The sound of going to the desert region wasn't very appealing to SJ, but she wanted to see if she could assign a quest, and eight days seemed too long to wait with the wyvern threat and Darren's eagerness to leave Killic. She needed to devise something to keep him here in the meantime. As they walked through the town, the streets had been empty, and the usual hustle and bustle had been subdued. There was also an increased guard presence with pairs walking the streets, one carrying one of the large pikes and the other holding a crossbow or bow.

Darren walked out of the tailor's ten minutes later holding a large bundle of clothes under his arm. He scratched his head with his free hand as he looked at SJ.

"I spent much more than I expected, and the quarterling is strange. He kept asking how I knew you."

"Oh," SJ said. "I am a regular customer and his apprentice tailor. He has helped me out quite a bit."

"It was like being questioned by a relative of yours."

SJ laughed nervously. "Was it? I suppose he is a little protective of me being his apprentice." She could not get the thought out of her head that a god was quizzing Darren.

"He said he is leaving soon, and someone new is taking over. Is that not going to mess up your training?"

"No. The person taking over is a skilled tailor, and I know them already." The conversation was making SJ feel a little uncomfortable talking about herself. "I bet an alchemist in town could help with your training. It would probably be easier to increase your basic levels in a starter town, no?"

Darren tilted his head slightly, considering SJ's comment. "I suppose it could make it easier. Do you know who the best alchemist is?"

"I haven't a clue as I have never investigated it, but I am pretty sure I can find out and confirm easily. I have worked for one of the regular healing balm sellers, Grewlas, who could be a good place to start asking questions. I know you mentioned Master Rui, but I have never heard of that name in the town before. That doesn't mean he's not here, though."

Darren scrunched his face at the reference to the name. "I am not sure either."

SJ watched him visibly slouch as he walked, reflecting on the previous evening's issue. Turning, she headed towards Grewlas's store, Darren's dejected form following her. Not surprisingly, the shop, like many others, was closed after the attack.

"It looks like we are limited today after the attack. At least you have new clothes and can stay at the cottage tonight. Then tomorrow, we can investigate finding you an alchemist," SJ said hopefully.

"When is the next wagon run from town?"

"I don't know. I've never used it. I assume someone at the stables would know." There were so many aspects of the town that SJ was still unaware of herself. "If you head back to the cottage," SJ said, removing a key from her inventory, "I need to call in at the barracks and check on a few things. I will find out the details for you and meet you later."

Leaving Darren to head back to the cottage, SJ headed to the barracks to speak to Zigferd or Alice about her plans.

* * *

Darren let himself into the cottage and dropped his bundle on the table, then sat heavily in an armchair. He couldn't believe how stupid he had been or the problem he had caused with the alchemical solutions he had brought. If only he hadn't been focusing on the experience gains, he might have considered that the whole quest had seemed too good to be true, just as the innkeeper said. The experience alone had been high, but also, being paid the fifteen silver to cover expenses . . . he hadn't even considered the details. He could have kicked himself for his stupidity.

What intrigued him the most was SJ. She appeared so naive in the ways of Amathera yet had successfully achieved revered status with a starter town. He had only achieved a popular status within his village, and he had helped who he could when he could, completing their quests, but had never progressed further. With the restrictions on the level cap when he reached it, he had no choice but to leave and find new areas to continue his growth. Thinking back, he knew that he would have happily stayed in the village if it had offered him further growth.

Killic was much larger than the village he had started in, and it had much more to offer in the long term. Because it could now accommodate growth to Level 20—and from what SJ had told him, potentially even higher—staying here was an interesting possibility. If he could find an alchemist trainer, he could just stay here for a short time, at least to begin his levelling process. With the expense of paying for the damage he had caused to the inn, his funds were even more restricted now.

He owned another moonstone that he could sell, but he needed an auction house to get the best value as he doubted anyone in the town could afford it or needed one. Plus, he didn't want to sell it unless it became essential. Looking at the town and its growth potential, there could be consideration for producing leather goods for sale. He could make scaled leather at the professional level of Journeyman Level 4. He had spent so long grinding that once he had got into a routine, he would work on his profession every evening with little else to do in the starter village. This had accelerated his profession levelling, and the armour he wore he had made himself. It was not the best, but it was good for his level.

Killic was idyllic, with clear blue skies and beautiful weather. It was very different from the village, which had a much cooler climate with regular rainfall. He stood up from the chair, getting a glass of water before picking up the bundle and moving to the bedroom to try on his new clothes. That tailor had been ridiculously persuasive and made him buy more than he normally would have.

He had just finished getting changed when there was a knock on the cottage door. Walking through, he opened it to recognise one of the traders they had visited earlier that afternoon.

"I have brought the goods as requested," the trader said, indicating toward the cart parked at the end of the small footpath.

"I will help you bring them in," Darren said.

Several trips later, the dining room table was covered with all SJ's purchased items. Darren believed she had bought pretty much one of everything that she thought may be useful in time. He had been the same back on Earth when he had moved into his first home. The fact that she was looking to furnish and equip it so well meant that SJ had no plans on leaving Killic anytime soon. It was strange for him to consider making a home in one area, and the thought intrigued him. It cost her a small fortune, and Darren was surprised she could afford it all. When he left his village after finishing his basic training and levelling, he only had a couple of silver coins to his name.

While Darren was still finishing sorting out the first delivery, there was a second knock at the door, and the remaining ordered items arrived. Taking receipt again, he began to make the cottage homely. Darren spent the rest of the afternoon sorting through what had been purchased and turning the empty cottage into a home. He had always taken pride in his flat back on Earth and gone the extra mile, keeping it clean, tidy, and well-presented in case he ever entertained. He could do the same for SJ.

After speaking to Zigferd, SJ was authorised to assign quests on behalf of the town. She had also stated that she would need to travel to a 20–30 territory at least to attempt to create the quest's level. Zigferd was amazed at the consideration of the open protection quest. The only quests he had ever raised were basic town support quests that had nowhere near the expectations of what SJ was suggesting. He also mentioned Asterfal as the easiest as Dave had, but she really didn't want to be away for eight days; she was concerned that Darren might just up and leave in that time. He had not appeared to wish to stay in Killic, and the sooner she could confirm whether a protection quest could be assigned, the better. At least that way, he would have a reason to stay alongside his alchemy training.

Master Rui was indeed the town's Master alchemist, and Zigferd had told her where Darren could find him. Master Rui spent most of his time collecting herbs or similar for his potions, but he also trained apprentices and took them on field trips. SJ would take Darren to see him tomorrow.

They had discussed the wyvern attack and their concerns over the ability to damage the beast. Apart from the town guard changes, all the hunters were being called in to support, and every able-bodied member of the town who knew archery would be issued a bow and quiver of arrows. The fallout from the wyvern visit had seen two of the town killed: the orc SJ had seen when she had saved the gnoll, and a daughter of the family from the home where the wyvern crashed. The young human girl, whose name SJ didn't recognise, had been crushed by an interior wall when it collapsed. SJ's heart sank at the news. The funerals were already planned, and both were going to be private affairs.

As she stepped onto the road to her cottage, SJ heard the wyvern's cry. Panic flooded her, and she looked towards the mountains where the sound had originated. She watched the shape of the wyvern high in the sky, a distance away from the town itself. It appeared to slow and hover before it dived, tucking its wings in and disappearing out of sight behind the buildings.

Hurriedly, she passed through the cottage's fence. The wyvern had not cried again, and she kept looking towards where she had last seen it, but it hadn't risen. Darren stood in the front garden area, scanning the surrounding skies. He had his armour on and stood with his bow in his hand, with an arrow knocked on the string.

"Did you see it?" he asked, noticing SJ's nervous expression.

"It dived into the forest area by the mountains away from the town. I didn't see it rise again."

"It may be hunting. I am guessing there is a decent hogling and deer population around here?"

"I know there are both. I don't know how strong the population is, although there are always hunting parties out there."

"If it has a ready supply of food outside the town and the potential of attacking here, I can't see it moving away anytime soon. Having fought them before, they are tenacious regarding easy food sources."

"I forgot to ask you about your experience with them. When was it?"

"Several months ago. I was completing a quest chain for my class, and the final stage was to kill a wyvern. That quest allowed me to learn the shock arrow skill."

"I did not know about class-specific quest chains."

Darren looked at her, frowning, "Do you not have a class trainer?"

"No. I train my skills myself through both weapon and skill training."

"That will mean that you have never started any class quest chains?"

"No. Never."

"They help with the progression of your class skills and give options to increase them. I would advise you to find a trainer as soon as you can. Do you mind if I ask what your skill levels are?"

SJ contemplated his request for a few moments before replying, "My skills are in martial arts and subterfuge."

"Really?" Darren looked surprised. "They are unusual. I have met a few assassins over the past sixteen months, and none have had that combination. It is a very specific set of choices. Not limited, but at lower levels, I bet it isn't easy to achieve much."

It was SJ's turn to frown now. "I think I am doing okay overall at my level. I have both my initial skill choices open in each branch."

"Well, I don't know the skill trees for assassins, but without you having a trainer, you are stunting your growth. The quests they offer relate directly to skill opportunities."

The screech of the wyvern sounded again, cutting off their conversation as they both looked skyward.

"It sounds distant still," Darren said.

"I hope it remains that way. The impact on the town was bad today, but if it stays, it will get much worse."

CHAPTER THIRTY-NINE

There and Back Again

Now that Darren is training with Master Rui, I think I have time to see if it's possible to raise a quest," SJ said.

It had been four days since the wyvern had visited the town, and although it could be heard towards the mountain peaks, it hadn't yet returned. It still meant the threat existed, and the town was continuing to work out plans for dealing with any future attacks. The guard force was undergoing extensive archery training. Many of them would never be anywhere near the level of proficiency of an archer or ranger class or that of a hunter profession, as none of them had the dexterity level necessary. Still, they would at least be able to fire arrows rather than depending on the slow reload time of the crossbows. They hoped that anything with a hundred arrows fired at it would think twice about trying something again.

The general guard force was also being trained in using pikes and standing in a line, forming a wall of spikes that could be used as a deterrent. They had been performing drills around the town, and the mage who completed the announcements called dummy attacks to help improve the guard's and the town's reaction times. Gradually, life was returning to the streets, and Zigferd had made an announcement via the mage about the plans so that all were aware. Several had not even left their homes since the first attack had happened, being too scared to venture outdoors.

The mages under Fran's guidance who were able were beginning to learn lightning spells. Many could not do so because of their elemental alignment, but at least four could cast the spell now. The same training was underway for the fire mage apprentices who were of a high enough level to learn fireball or fire-bolt.

The town's training and adaptation to this new threat were exemplary, and even Darren commented on their professional approach.

Over the past four days, Darren had begun to settle in, to SJ's relief. When SJ arrived back at the cottage that first day and saw what he had done inside, unpacking and arranging everything, she was grateful. He had apologised for doing it but stated he couldn't just leave everything on the table waiting for her to return. He was still staying in the back room, and Floretta spent her nights sitting in the lounge reading while the repairs at the inn were finished.

The repairs had got underway, and Bert's cousins were commencing work quickly. The walls were already rebuilt after new floor cross-beams had been installed. The two massive trolls, who were his cousins, dwarfed Bert. SJ had never seen trolls so large. They both towered nearly twenty feet tall. They moved stone blocks around as though they were made of polystyrene. It was effortless for them, making the building process much faster. SJ had wondered why they had not previously helped defend the town when the hobs attacked. She had taken the chance to use her identification skills to discover that one was Level 4 and the other Level 6. Their size made them appear much more than they were.

Nexis had also returned and apparently finished the "dealings" at the tailor shop. The quarterling had been seen leaving town with a wagon full of his possessions to move back to his family's village on the far side of Asterfal. The rumour was that he had sped up the process of selling the shop after the wyvern attack. Nexis was becoming a town celebrity. Everywhere he went, beings spoke to him. SJ believed he loved the attention he was getting from his admirers. She had spent some time with him discussing the auction house further and had promised to get Terence up from the cottages to go over the plans and discuss the carpentry works.

That was why Fran was currently standing in the lounge of the cottage. Darren was off with Master Rui today. They were going on a field trip into the forest on the opposite side of the wyvern's known location, searching for herbs and other alchemical components.

"This cottage is lovely. I have never been inside before," Fran said. Darren had done an excellent job sorting the place out, and everything already had a home. It felt to SJ that she had been living there much longer than the five days it had been.

"It is. I am so lucky to get it," SJ said.

"I know you don't own the deed, but as you are the agreed tenant of the property, I should be able to set a soul stone. Remember what I said about how it affects your health. Are you sure this is what you wish to do?"

"Yes. I want to get to Farleck Cottage and visit the skeletons."

"Okay, then. The way it works is that the soul stone will attach itself to the essence of the building. Where do you wish it to be located?"

"I think my bedroom is the best place," SJ said, indicating the front bedroom.

Following SJ, Fran walked into the room. It was large, with a wide double bed, bedside tables, a large wardrobe, and a desk covered in her possessions with a comfy writing chair. The final touch was a large mirror that hung on the rear of the bedroom door. Lighting in the room was provided by a lantern that sat on one of the bedside tables. "You need an open floor space that can be used as the portal spot," Fran said.

"I think in front of the window is the best place." The bay window with nothing in front of it allowed an open view of the cornfields across from the front garden.

"Stand where you wish it to be placed. To return, this area must always be clear, or you will lose the link capability."

Nodding, SJ stood in front of the window. "Here."

"It has been a while since I cast the spell, and it is quite complex. You need to stay perfectly still. When it begins, you will feel the sensation of the spell. Some have told me it is painful. Others haven't, so I can't guarantee what effect it will have on you," Fran said.

SJ took a deep breath. "Okay. Let's do this."

Fran began to whisper, closing her eyes and moving her hands in a slow, rhythmic motion. A beam of light appeared in front of Fran and shot at SJ instantly. She gasped as the light struck her. The sensation of warmth suffused her body, and then it began.

Initially, the warmth was pleasant, and as Fran continued to cast the spell, the sensation of heat increased. It moved from pleasant to bearable to uncomfortable to painful in the space of a minute. The light enveloped her fully now, and she winced. It felt like her whole body was being dipped in a red-hot bath, and she gritted her teeth, resisting the urge to tell Fran to stop. She then noticed the health on her display dropping. Slowly, as the light from the spell increased in intensity, her health reduced by 5 percent as Fran had mentioned. As it did, the light intensity became unbearable, and she closed her eyes and let out a deep groan from the pain.

The pain faded but there was a residual effect from the spell, which still made SJ's skin feel as though it was on fire. She opened her eyes and looked at Fran. Fran's demeanour had changed, and her shoulders were sagged. As she staggered slightly, SJ stepped forward, caught her, and steadied her.

"Are you okay?" SJ asked, worried.

Fran smiled weakly. "I will be. I had forgotten how taxing the spell is to cast. It uses virtually my whole mana pool."

SJ helped Fran to the edge of the bed and sat her down. "I will get you a drink," SJ said, leaving the room to grab her a glass of water.

When she returned, Fran sat leaning on her knees, breathing heavily, her brow glistening with beads of sweat.

"That has taken it out of you. If I had known it was that challenging, I would never have asked you to perform it."

"I wouldn't have agreed if I didn't know what I was getting into," Fran replied.

"I guess that it worked. My health was reduced by 5 percent." SJ's health bar, previously a full red ninety-eight points, was now greyed out down to ninety-three.

"It was successful, yes," Fran said.

"I can now portal and return again," SJ said, feeling trepidation. She hadn't even attempted to use the portal at the cottage yet, and thinking about it was both exciting and nerve-racking. "I told Darren that I would be going to the cottage today, and with the cool-down, I hope to return this evening."

Fran had drunk the glass of water and placed it on the bedside table, then removed a blue potion from her inventory. Popping the cork in it, she drank it before replying.

"No time like the present," Fran said. "It can be a little disorientating until you get used to the feeling of using portals."

SJ bit her lip nervously. "I need to give it a go."

"Open your map. Select the portal, and boom," Dave said.

SJ jumped at Dave's sudden interruption in her mind. He had been very quiet the past couple of days, and she had been getting concerned.

"Are you okay?" Fran asked, frowning.

"Yes. Yes. I am just a little unsettled. The sensation of that spell was not pleasant. It felt as though my skin was on fire." It was still wearing off, and the burning sensation dimmed to that of warmth again.

"The spell seems to affect different beings in different ways. Some complain of heat, others of cold, others nothing. There doesn't seem to be a reason behind the differences."

"Thank you," SJ said, smiling at Fran.

"My pleasure," Fran said.

"I am going to try my portal now."

Fran smiled at SJ, watching intently.

SJ opened her map, zoomed in on the cottage, and selected the portal where she had placed it. *Here goes,* she thought.

It was as though all light had been absorbed from the world; her eyes were open, but she couldn't see. Not knowing what to expect from using the portal, the shock of losing her vision made her gasp. She knew she could see, but the darkness enveloping her was absolute. Her body felt tingly and cold, a welcome sensation after the heat of the soul stone spell. As quickly as the darkness had come, it disappeared, and she was standing in the clearing before Farleck Cottage. She heard shouting, and as her vision came into focus, she saw Charlotte's startled face above an arrow nocked on her bowstring, drawn and ready to fire.

"SJ," she cried in shock. Terence stood behind her with a large mallet in his hand. Brian was nowhere to be seen.

"Hi," SJ said, smiling broadly at them, amazed because she had just travelled so far so quickly. The portal was going to be amazing, and with it in place, she could now visit the cottage whenever she wished.

"We wondered who was opening a portal in the yard," Charlotte said, releasing the tension on the bowstring. Terence dropped his mallet to his side.

"At least we know for the future that if a black pool of light suddenly appears in the yard, it's just you," Terence said.

"Is that what it looks like? I have never seen one."

"Yes. A black pool of light appeared, and then moments later it went, and you were stood there," Charlotte replied.

SJ took in the cottage in front of her. She had appeared nearly fifty feet from it in the corner of the garden where she had set the portal away from any structures. Now what she saw was not what she remembered. The front of the cottage looked similar but different somehow. The gazebo that had been constructed now had a swinging seat hanging from its beams. The side of the cottage had a lean-to that had been extended beyond what SJ remembered. Her mouth dropped open at the transformation. The garden area was a picture of perfection, with neatly aligned rows of plants and brightly coloured flowers lining the pathway of stone slabs that led from the short picket fence surrounding the property to the front door.

"You guys have been busy," SJ said, wide-eyed.

"There is still so much more to do," Terence replied, smiling his skeletal smile. The large-boned orc skeleton now stood with the mallet on his shoulder.

"Has anything happened since I was gone?"

"No. Nothing. It is the most peaceful we have ever been," Charlotte replied.

"Where is Brian?" SJ asked.

"He is down at the second cottage gardening," Charlotte said.

"Thanks for getting the chisels dropped off. They have sped up the process of building things," Terence said.

SJ had completely forgotten about the chisels and the chimney needing to be aligned. "I meant to speak to Husa to confirm that everything had gone okay!"

"It was a simple job. No new stone was needed. It just needed resetting, which he did while here," Terence said.

"So the chimney is all fixed. That's amazing."

"Yes. Let me show you what else we have been doing."

Terence turned and walked around to the rear of the property. What met SJ's gaze was the framework of an extension. It stretched back from the rear of the property, almost doubling its footprint. The previous storage locker that Terence had constructed was now placed at the side of the cottage under the lean-to, and out towards the woods, which began a couple hundred feet from the rear of the property, SJ could see where Terence and the others had been cutting trees down to allow for him to construct the extension.

"Wow. This is amazing. This place will be huge once finished."

"I need to keep myself busy," Terence said.

"You have all been busy already. I need to ask you a favour," SJ said, looking at Terence.

"Of course. What do you need me to do?"

"I need you to come to Killic if you can. A new auction house is being constructed, and the owner needs some carpentry work done."

If Terence's eyes could have shown more emotion, SJ would have sworn he looked excited at the chance to do more work. "That sounds interesting. What do they need to do?"

"There are various items and some internal structures that he has designed, and I thought of you when I was discussing his plans with him."

"When do you need me to start?" Terence said, and SJ could hear his excitement in his usual gruff voice.

"I plan on returning later today. If you can travel to Killic in the next day or so, that would be great. I can give you directions."

"No problem. Whatever you need me to do."

"Hi, SJ," Brian said as he appeared from nowhere only a few feet from her.

"Ahhh," SJ squeaked in shock.

"Sorry," Brian said, looking as embarrassed as a skeleton could.

"It's okay. You are just so quiet I didn't even sense you nearby."

"Class perk," he replied, smiling.

"I was letting Terence know I need him to come to Killic. There is some work that needs completing for a new build there."

"That sounds interesting. Do you need me and Charlotte to come as well?"

SJ had discussed with Dave about the skeletons accompanying her to the desert region as extra support, which she had initially decided would be the route she would take to get to the closest territory level increase. Dave stated that the only route to the desert region was down through the valley and then through the southern tunnel system—unless she wanted to go over the cliff edge where the rock gobbler had met its demise. He had also reminded SJ that the skeletons were low level still in comparison, and even though they may be skilled in various areas, they would be ineffective against many hostiles there.

The mention of hostiles had made SJ reconsider going via the desert and take the extra time to go to Asterfal. She was still only Level 11, and her skills were only useful up close and personal. She had no ranged ability skills and didn't fancy getting into fights with monsters or beings that were a higher level than she was. Going to a Level 20–30 territory could be a significant risk. And now that Darren was working with Master Rui on his alchemy profession, he seemed more likely to stay for at least a short while.

SJ had concluded that she needed to take the safer option and travel to Asterfal even if the journey would be longer. Over the past four days, she had begun to put things in place. Alongside her daily training, she had also been working on her tailoring, and she had been so close to managing to install an enchantment slot that she just wanted to get it done and advance her profession further. Going to Asterfal would also allow her to sell off the extra items she had from looting various victims and to inquire about the miniature wyvern eggs she had.

"No. Just Terence for now. I will be heading to Asterfal soon, but I wanted to introduce Terence before I go."

Charlotte joined them at the rear of the cottage. "How long are you staying?"

"I will be going back later today. It is only a fleeting visit," SJ said. Taking in the cottage and its surroundings, it was so idyllic that she wished she could stay longer, and she would have to bring Cristy here at some point. With the wyvern near town, getting her out of there might be good. She always had something to contemplate or consider, and there was never a day that she wasn't busy doing something. She still had the quest offer from Fran to consider, as well as the quest from Zigferd.

"Did you want anything to eat?" Brian asked.

SJ frowned, confused. "I didn't think you ate?"

"We don't, but I have been fishing at the lake in my spare time and can easily catch one if needed."

"That would be great," SJ said, smiling.

"No problem. I will be back in a while." SJ watched in amazement as Brian turned and walked off, whistling.

SJ found the inside of the cottage immaculate as well. The items she had purchased and brought down previously were all perfectly placed, and not a spot of dust rested on anything. She walked to the stove area and lit the fire, putting some extra wood in the burner. Then, walking outside to the well, she drew a bucket of water before filling one of the pans. She set about making herself a pot of coffee, removing the container of coffee from her inventory that she had got from Floretta that morning.

While the water got up to temperature, SJ stood in the cottage doorway. Charlotte had returned to gardening at the front, humming away as she carefully worked through and between the plants and flowers along the path. She heard an axe being used and then the sound of a saw and knew that Terence had just returned to his task of building the extension. Leaning against the door-frame in this heavenly place, SJ relaxed fully for the first time in a while. She only realised quite how long it had been when the serenity of the place took hold.

Once the coffee was made, she carried the pot and a mug out to the swinging seat, where a small table stood. She placed the mug down and poured a coffee, then sat in the seat, swinging and sipping her drink.

CHAPTER FORTY

Missing

"Y ES!" SJ screamed.

The look of absolute shock on a skeleton with its mouth wide open made SJ chuckle.

"Sorry," she blurted out around her excitement. She had just managed to install her first-ever enchantment slot in the bundle of cloth she had brought with her. After arriving at the cottage, she performed her daily kata routines and then proceeded to work on her tailoring quest. It was her display triggering that had caused her to scream in delight.

Congratulations! Tailoring Apprentice Level 5 completed.

Quest: Tailoring Apprentice—Level 6
Produce ten items of common or higher rarity clothing.
Would you like to accept the quest? **Yes/No**

Charlotte was still staring at her, wondering what had caused her to get so excited that she screamed. SJ had been sitting watching Charlotte work in the garden and had been so relaxed that she had paid no attention to her mana streaming. It appeared that the relaxed state had given her what she had been missing to create the enchantment slots. Brian had returned with a large fish from the lake. She did not know what type it was, but Brian had been quite adept at filleting it and was currently frying it off over the stove for her. His head appeared in the cottage doorway, and Terence came walking around the side of the cottage.

SJ couldn't still her excitement. "I just levelled my profession."

"Ahh." Charlotte nodded in understanding.

"Congratulations," both Terence and Brian said as they returned to what they were doing.

SJ was not going to be deflated by their lack of appreciation for her success, so she performed what she called her happy dance.

Dave perked up. "We spoke about this before."

"You aren't knocking me today," she whispered in response. Even though the skeletons were her followers, she didn't want to be seen talking to herself.

"Dance lessons, perhaps?"

Dave would not wipe the smile from her face now that she had achieved Level 5. *I wonder*, she thought as she looked at her display, and switched to her inventory screen, focusing on her dress.

Haber's Dress of the Tailor Level 5	
Grade:	Astral
Quality:	Perfect
Durability:	Infinite
Enchantment Slots:	1
Armour Class:	5
Attributes:	+2 Charisma
The god Haber himself made this dress. It is unmatched by any other and provides the wearer with unique skills that are available as levels are gained.	
Self-repair	
Transmogrification—the dress's appearance can be changed as your tailoring level increases. Current available choices: colour	

"Wow," SJ said, much louder than she meant.

"What?" Charlotte asked, looking up.

"Oh. Just my next profession quest," SJ said, grinning like a Cheshire cat and not telling the truth about her dress. She noticed how easily she had begun to lie. Lying had never been something she did; maybe she'd told the odd white lie now and again to not hurt someone's feelings, but it seemed she was becoming adept at changing the narrative of her thoughts. *I wonder if it is aligned with my class?* she thought.

"I wish I could still level my profession," Charlotte replied sulkily.

"I thought you could still learn new things. It just doesn't level?"

"I can. It's just you don't get any profession perks."

"What perks do you get as a gardener?"

"Increased nutrition, sturdy stalk, brilliant blossom, and many perks can support the profession. I had those three before I was killed and returned but was close to my fourth."

Not appreciating or understanding the effects of perks that other professions gave, SJ looked quizzically at Charlotte. "What level are you?"

"I was at Journeyman Level 9. At every ten profession-grade steps, you receive a new perk. I would have been due a fourth perk with all the gardening I have been doing. It's annoying, but the benefit is that I can keep doing what I love without ever having to worry about dying of natural causes."

Charlotte's comment shocked SJ. She had never considered how the skeletons felt about being skeletons. She needed to spend time getting to know them better when she could and would have to visit more frequently. They had, after all, given themselves to her as her followers, and she felt as though she had an obligation to them, which for now she had not met.

She was mulling over what she needed to do when Brian appeared at the cottage door.

"Food is ready," he called.

Brian had laid a place on the table inside for her, and a perfectly grilled fish fillet was presented with a small sprig of green herbs and a green sauce. SJ was unsure what they were and picked one of the leafy stalks up and bit it. Even though it didn't look like parsley, it had the same taste. Taking her cutlery from her inventory, she cut into the fish, the flesh flaking under the slightest pressure from her fork. It tasted like cod, and the soft white meat was delicious.

"This is good," SJ said, nodding her appreciation at Brian.

"I may not be good at cooking many things, but I have experience with fish. I used to fish a lot."

"You have cooked this to perfection." Finishing the fillet and wiping her mouth with a napkin that Brian had folded, SJ felt content.

Brian returned outside to help Charlotte in the garden. Charlotte had moved on from working on the flowers by the path and was discussing making a vegetable patch to the side of the cottage. SJ could hear them through the open cottage doorway and smiled at the conversation. Not discussing the threat of a wyvern, the political intrigue surrounding the council, or the threat to Fran was a pleasant change.

"I can't believe the skill my dress has opened up," she whispered.

"That looks like it could be an amazing perk as you increase your tailoring levels further. Hopefully now you are Level 5, you can get through the next few levels quicker than you have been," Dave said.

"With everything else I have been doing, I don't think I have been that bad at levelling my profession," SJ said.

"No, I agree, a snail may have been slower," Dave sarcastically replied.

Huffing at Dave's comment, SJ stood and cleared the table, washed up, and placed the items to drain. Then she headed back to the seat under the gazebo. The sun was beating down as usual, and the gazebo gave respite from its relentless rays. The area around the cottage appeared to have a microclimate, trapping the sun's rays in the confines of the surrounding forest. It was blissfully warm, with a gentle breeze blowing from the lake. It had been a few hours since her arrival, and she still had to wait before returning to Killic.

"When I return, I assume I just focus on travelling back?" SJ had not asked at any point and was now wondering how the soul stone worked. Charlotte, Brian, and Terence stood by the side of the cottage, discussing the vegetable garden. Charlotte was busy instructing Terence on what she needed to create for the borders and planters. SJ smiled at their interactions. The three of them had settled at the cottage so well, creating their new lives.

"You stand on the spot you arrived and basically go in reverse. You can't just travel to a soul stone. Otherwise, people would use them to place a portal. You must be at the original portal location," Dave said.

"That makes sense. I should mark it properly." Rising from the seat, SJ walked to where she had arrived, noticing for the first time that the grass where the portal must have existed was flattened. "I may as well mark it with stones or something similar. Guys?"

The three skeletons turned to look at SJ. "Yes?" Charlotte asked.

"Could you possibly mark the spot where the portal is with stones to prevent anything from being placed there going forward?"

"Of course. It would make sense to prevent Brian from trying to be creative with his newfound love for gardening and planting a tree there."

"Hey!" Brian replied.

"Well, I do keep finding random new plants dotted around."

"They improve the garden."

"Not when you plant weeds just because they have colourful flowers, which would take over the whole garden, I might add."

"That was only once," Brian huffed.

Terence patted Brian on his shoulder sympathetically. "Don't worry, Brian. Charlotte is just as mean to me."

SJ laughed heartily when Charlotte thumped Terence in the shoulder. Their friendly banter felt therapeutic. Even though SJ had friends in Killic, she hadn't yet allowed herself to get as close to anyone as these three were.

"I have a couple of hours yet, so I will go for a walk and see what the other cottages are like. I'll be back in a while," SJ called over to the skeletons.

"I can come with you if you wish?" Brian said.

"No. I'll be fine, and I am sure Charlotte has chores for you." SJ smiled wickedly.

Brian sighed, turning and looking at Charlotte's skeletal smile.

Walking down the path to the lake, SJ couldn't remember the last time she had felt as relaxed as she did now. The sweet scent from the flowers and the tall grasses along the edges of the forest that enclosed the path to the cottage was intoxicating; their heavenly aroma filled her nostrils. Reaching the lake's edge, SJ walked out onto the small wooden jetty where the rowing boat was moored. In the keel of the boat sat two fishing poles and tackle.

She smiled, thinking about Brian rowing out onto the lake to go fishing. Standing for a moment, she took in the peace and the scenery: bubbles breaking on the lake's surface where fish must be, the gentle breeze through the grasses by the lake, and the sounds of the wildlife in the surrounding forest. A flock of brightly coloured birds flew across the lake, heading north.

"I need to bring Cristy here, and I would love to get Patch and his family here as well," SJ said.

"It's a nice place, but do you think it is best for Cristy? She has been doing so well at the orphanage, and Madeline said last time you visited that her literacy and numeracy were coming on brilliantly," Dave said.

"I know. I just think she is missing out on an opportunity."

"You can always bring her for a visit. I wouldn't advise her to move here full time," Dave said, sounding like a concerned parent.

"I know. I just think she would love it here. She is never happier than when she is out with Patch in the forest, and here, they could stay much closer and she could visit them more easily. I could also ask Charlotte to teach her archery. She is still determined to become a hunter."

"She is, but I think you also need to consider her future class."

"I've thought about it, and I thought druid was probably the most aligned for her."

"Maybe, maybe not. The bond she has with Patch and the wolves has already been formed to a strange degree. I have never seen one like it before between wolves and beings. I have witnessed wolves as familiars, but Cristy and Patch's bond is stronger than that. It appears that they class each other as a family."

"Druid will allow her to help heal the wolves if they get injured."

"So would any other healing class."

"I still think druid would be best."

"Considering her age, classes would not normally be something to consider for another few years yet."

"Is there anything stopping her class training early?"

"No. Not that I am aware of. It just isn't usually something done at such a young age, to allow them to experience the world more and decide on their own."

"I may speak to her about it and see if she has ever given any thought to a class. I don't want to force her into a class she doesn't want to do."

"I agree. Next time we visit, we can discuss it."

The way Dave spoke about Cristy made SJ grin.

"What are you grinning at?" Dave said cautiously.

"Oh, nothing," SJ said, smiling even more.

"I don't trust that look on your face. You are up to something."

SJ ignored his comment and did not give him the privilege of a reply. Turning, she walked from the jetty and around the lake's edge towards the other cottages.

A while later, SJ returned to her own cottage. As usual, the skeletons were busy. It still amazed her that they never tired or stopped working. Everything they did had a purpose. Floretta relaxed and spent time reading in the evenings—SJ would need to discuss resting with her followers.

The area where the portal appeared had already been marked out during her absence with a ring of stones. She had looked at her display and knew that the eight-hour window for returning had now elapsed. SJ took out the notebook and pencil she had brought with her and, sitting at the dining table, sketched out a rough map and instructions for Terence.

"Terence?" SJ said as she found him cutting some timber at the rear of the cottage.

"What do you need?" Terence replied.

"I have the directions for the way to Killic and the cottage I stay in there."

Carefully tearing the page from the notebook, SJ handed it to him. Taking the note, he read the directions. "*Hit the main path turning south, head through the crags, and then continue along the path until you reach the cornfields. Don't enter the town but turn left on the far side of the cornfields and look for the small cottage with the picket fence.* Sounds easy enough," he replied.

"Excellent. When do you think you could set off?"

"I can leave now if needed. There is nothing that can't wait here."

"That would be great. I am going to portal back now, so if you can head there, I will see you . . . tomorrow, perhaps?"

"Easily. I don't sleep, remember." Terence smiled.

"I will look forward to seeing you in the morning, then."

Terence began putting his tools away, ensuring he had a hammer tucked into his belt. He wished Charlotte and Brian farewell before heading down to the lakeside, whistling. SJ watched him go before promising Charlotte and Brian that she would be back to visit again soon and thanking them for all the hard work they were doing.

When she'd toured the other buildings, she'd seen they had kept pristine the cottage that belonged to the millworkers, Gladys and Hubert, and the skeletons had even sorted through the derelict cottage. They had dismantled the walls fully and planned on moving the stone to SJ's cottage. They couldn't use it to build, not being stonemasons, but they wanted to make sure it was there if required.

Walking to the portal spot, SJ opened her display and saw a return option that hadn't existed before she used the portal, so she selected it. The world went black again, and the same cold sensation flooded her body. She did not know how long the transportation took, as once the blackness enveloped her, time seemed to have no meaning. The sun had begun to fade in the sky as time passed before her return, and she appeared in the area of her bedroom window with the shadows of the evening sun. Hearing raised voices, she walked from the bedroom into the lounge.

Darren stood leaning back from Zigferd's towering form.

"I am not going to ask again. Where is she?" Zigferd snarled.

"I told you already. I d-don't know," Darren stammered.

Four other guard members stood in the open doorway of the cottage.

"You were seen with her last," Zigferd said.

"We were just talking about the wyvern, that was all. We walked from town to the edge of the forest, and I left her there and returned here," Darren said.

"What's going on?" SJ asked, shocked at the scene unfolding in her lounge.

Zigferd turned, startled by SJ's sudden appearance. "SJ. Where did you come from?" he questioned.

"I just came back."

Zigferd looked confused. "Alice is missing, and this individual was the last person seen with her this morning," he said.

"I have already told you. I have nothing to do with her going missing. Why would I?"

"I don't know. Maybe because you blew up the inn?" Zigferd snapped, his fists clenched, and SJ was sure she could see the hair thicken around his face.

Concerned he was about to transform into his were-bear form, SJ stepped forward and placed her hand on his arm. "Zigferd. Please, calm down." She looked at him with concern. She could feel how tense he was, his fists clenched and his face full of fury. SJ had never seen him so angry before. Even when fighting Bordon, he hadn't shown so much emotion.

Zigferd turned and looked down at SJ; his towering form was almost two feet taller than herself. Taking a deep breath, he relaxed his fists slightly and closed his eyes. They still contained the same hostility when he opened them again, but his voice was calmer. "I want to know exactly what happened and what you spoke about, and I mean exactly word for word."

SJ looked from Darren to Zigferd and noticed that the table had been knocked before her arrival. "Look, sit down, will you?" SJ said. "And let's talk civilly."

Snarling, Zigferd watched Darren as he moved to sit at the dining table. Zigferd did the same, sitting opposite him, his hands braced against the table's edge.

SJ hurried to the kitchen, grabbed some glasses and a jug of water, brought them back through, and placed them on the table, pouring three glasses. Taking a seat between the two men, she looked from one to the other, the hatred visible between them. "Now, let's start from the beginning. Shall we?"

CHAPTER FORTY-ONE

Into the Dark

The argument—it couldn't be described as a conversation—between Darren and Zigferd eventually concluded. Zigferd agreed to leave Darren in the hands of SJ. As a town councillor, she was putting her reputation on the line to support Darren and his version of events. Nothing she had heard or seen from him since he had arrived in Killic, apart from his stupidity with the alchemical components, led her to believe he was to blame for Alice's disappearance.

SJ had suggested that Darren's alignment be confirmed, and Lythonian had been summoned. Alice was the only other in the town with an alignment token. Once Lythonian had arrived, he had confirmed that Darren's alignment was neutral good. Not even that had put Zigferd at ease.

"We need to find Alice," Darren said. Now that Zigferd had left, he wouldn't stop pacing.

"We only know she went into the forest. Did she give you any information as to what she was doing?"

"Nothing, as I told that idiot town mayor on multiple occasions before you returned. What is his problem anyway?" Darren snarled.

"That is obvious, and her importance to the town has already been explained," SJ said with frustration. "Now, will you stop pacing and sit down so I can think?"

Darren stopped and looked at SJ, who was sitting in one of her armchairs. He sat down facing her. "If they would just let me leave and go and search for her . . ." he said.

Two of the town guards remained at the cottage, and Zigferd had given them strict instructions not to let Darren go anywhere alone.

"It's best that, for now, you stay here and let the town do what it needs to."

Floretta had returned, and the evening dragged on, with tension in the air because of Darren. Eventually, he retired to his room. Not long after, there was a knock at the cottage door and Terence arrived. Floretta was shocked initially at seeing another skeleton. Once SJ introduced him, the pair of them began to chatter away as if they had known each other for years. SJ didn't want to leave Darren alone in the cottage, so Floretta said she would go and introduce Terence to Nexis, who had returned to stay in the inn. The inn repairs were well underway, and now the floor had been repaired, the downstairs could open again, even if not all the accommodation was available yet. SJ went to her room once Terence and Floretta left. As she lay back on her bed, Dave talked.

"I believe Darren," Dave said.

"So do I. I am not sure what has happened to Alice; from what Zigferd said it is the first time she has ever missed an appointment and not been seen. I hope she hasn't been injured in the forest."

"With the wyvern's arrival, chances are many of the forest creatures will have moved. That could cause creatures or beasts that wouldn't normally come to certain areas of the forest to move closer to town."

SJ shivered involuntarily at the thought of Alice being attacked by any beasts. "I hope she is okay."

The next morning, SJ woke to Dave speaking. "We may have a problem."

"Morning. And what problem?" SJ asked, yawning and stretching.

"Darren has disappeared."

"What do you mean *disappeared*?"

"He left early hours this morning."

"How? Zigferd left guards."

"He left out the back garden."

"Why didn't you wake me if you saw him go?"

"Erm. I wasn't watching."

SJ frowned at his response. "I better go search for him."

"I would advise that you don't. Let the guard do their job. You have enough to do."

"But it's Alice."

"And it's Fran, and it's Bellakiy, and it's Nexis, and it's Cristy, and your training, and your ..."

SJ cut Dave off. "Okay. I get the message." Huffing, SJ slammed her fist onto the bed.

"I know you want to help with everything, but you can't. You need to leave things to others. Remember the townsfolk use quests too, not just you, and you have two important quests to complete already. I would also still suggest that you create the quest for Darren."

SJ was unhappy with the thought of not helping to find Alice but could understand Dave's point. "Why would I even bother looking into a quest for Darren now that he has run off?"

"He hasn't run off. He left a note."

Frowning, SJ climbed from the bed and walked through to the lounge. Sitting on the table was a folded piece of parchment.

Sorry!

I have to go and look for Alice. Yesterday when the mayor was here,

I didn't tell the whole truth. I know Alice from Asterfal and did not know she lived in Killic until two days ago. We met at the forest to talk so as not to draw attention to ourselves.
I am sorry for lying. I need to find her.

Darren

SJ was shocked at the revelation that Darren knew Alice from Asterfal. She did not know Alice had ever been there, and she wasn't sure how long Darren had been there either.

"I should go and tell Zigferd. Otherwise, I am not sure what the guards will do if they find him," SJ said.

"Considering he is a Level 20 Legionnaire, I doubt many of the guards could do a great deal to him unless they really outnumber him. It isn't as though he is a new Legionnaire, and his level is much higher than the vast majority in the town," Dave replied.

Where the hell has she gone? Darren thought as he moved deeper into the forest. His tracking skill was active and following the faint trail that he believed Alice had left. The skill was at Level 10 and allowed him to focus on and follow a track set. He had used it frequently since his arrival in Amathera, hunting and tracking down injured animals he had failed to shoot cleanly, and it had levelled because of his initially poor archery.

At first, his tracking skills only allowed for track identification, but with his level now and skill improvements, he saw what could only be described as a faded path, as though a mist or haze existed where they had passed. With each track set he analysed, he could assign it a colour, selecting a bright blue to contrast with the greenery of the forest. It wasn't something that could be used well in large towns or cities due to how many beings they contained, but in quieter and more rural areas, the skill came to its own. The forest had come alive with the sounds of creatures as the early morning sun had risen from the near silence during the night. Unfamiliar with the area, he waited until the first light to enter the forest. He didn't fancy walking upon one of the nocturnal beasts that frequented forest areas.

Just after three, he left the cottage by sneaking out of the window and climbing the fence in the back garden. He then skirted around the edge of the town to reach the spot where he had left Alice the day before. Since daybreak, he had spent a few hours travelling into the forest following the trail, winding through the mountain peaks. Looking at his display, it was nearly nine. *I hope SJ forgives me,* he thought.

He had met Alice in Asterfal at the Bugbears, and they had shared a couple of evenings in each other's company. Nothing had happened between them, but they had seemed like kindred spirits. He knew she was a druid after they had spoken about their classes. He had only bumped into her in Killic on an off-chance when he had left Master Rui two days earlier after finishing his training. She had been walking along the street, and they had nearly walked into each other.

The shock on both their faces had transformed to genuine smiles. Darren had felt his heart skip on seeing her again. After a conversation in which Alice learned Darren was the culprit for the inn explosion, as well as the wyvern defence, she made him aware of her role in the town. She didn't want to draw attention to him after his start in town, so they had planned to meet by the forest to talk the following afternoon in secrecy. They had spent several hours catching up properly, and Alice had promised to meet him again. He now had a reason to stay in Killic. Alice was a beautiful creature.

It was as they had been just about to leave the forest edge when a hunting party had come upon them. Alice had passed pleasantries, as she knew them all, and they had continued to the town carrying their successful haul of two hoglings. Alice had then told Darren to leave first so as not to draw attention, and he had headed back to town. That was the last time he had seen her.

The trail led him deep through the forest, curving towards the base of the mountain area to the east, towards where the wyvern had flown. Darren didn't feel happy approaching the wyvern territory, but he had no choice. He needed to find Alice to clear his name.

The trail had grown fainter as he had followed it, and its dispersion made him stop and survey the forest area more closely. The brush was thick around him with tangling vines and thorn bushes. It was obvious from the surroundings that only forest animals would usually be anywhere near this area. There were none of the usual animal trails that covered many forest floors.

As he searched the area, he identified tracks he didn't recognise. There were several pairs of what could only be described as humanoid footprints, but nothing he had witnessed previously. The prints only had four toes. He squatted, looking at the tracks, tracing their outline with his finger. Based on the size and depth of the prints, he guessed the creatures were similar in size to most humans. He triggered his skill. A new coloured trail appeared, and this one was much stronger than the faint trail. It had a red colour to it. Unslinging his bow from his shoulder, he lifted an arrow from the quiver on his back and nocked it on the string.

He could easily walk and hold the arrow on the string without loss of balance or hampering his stealth. His high dexterity increased his balance and ability to track almost silently. It was uncanny how quiet he could be while moving through forests. He followed the new trail while keeping an eye on the remainder of the other. Both trails followed the same path. The trees began to thin out as he progressed, and he believed he was a few kilometres from the wyvern location and had to be at least seven from the town. The undulating land began to rise at an incline as he approached the side of one of the mountains.

He stopped as the tree-line thinned further, observing the mountain ahead. The stark, grey rock face created a drastic contrast with the richness of the forest.

The animal sounds had begun to fade as he moved nearer the edge. Even being on the edge of a forest, he was surprised at how quiet it had become. Looking up the rock face, he could see no movement, although a couple hundred feet up the side, he thought he could see the opening to a cave—and the trail led in that direction.

The bright blue trail was only just visible now, and he had seen no signs of any footprints for a long time, which led him to believe that if it was Alice, she was being carried by whatever or whoever had taken her. His heart was beating hard as he moved towards the cave entrance, nervous tension building as he approached. The wyvern cried in the distance to the north of his location, and he froze, scanning the skies. He couldn't see it airborne. Relief flooded him, and he edged closer, his hands clenched on his bow with unnatural tension.

Calm down, he thought as he edged closer.

When he got within fifty feet of the entrance, the sun reflected off the brilliant white polished skulls of several animals that covered the ground. He wasn't sure what lived in the cave, but this wasn't a good sign. A ranger walking into a cave was never a good idea. He was not skilled at mêlée fighting; he had a sword, but a cave was a mêlée-class territory. Any cave systems he had ever visited previously were only ever as a support member of a party.

At the entrance to the cave, there were red streaks around the sides as though someone had dipped their fingers in blood and drawn them across the rock surface. What or whoever had done so only had four fingers. The trail led inside, and he stopped, listening carefully. The sun was high in the sky, and his display showed it was 10:55. It had taken several hours to reach the cave following the tracks. He could hear no sound, and he checked his inventory. He withdrew a torch and lit it. The cave was dark with no visible light source. His half-elven heritage gave him improved sight, but he couldn't see in the dark.

Once the torch was lit, he held it and his bow, gripping around its length and the bow's grip. The arrow he had nocked did not rest perfectly with the bulk of the torch in its way. It was not the easiest of options, but at least he wouldn't be walking into a cave blind and could use his bow, even if not with the level of accuracy he could normally maintain.

Listening keenly for any sound, Darren edged his way inside. The cave was natural and had no sign of being carved out of the rock face. It also surprised Darren that there could be previously unknown creatures or beings this close to town that may have kidnapped someone. The forest had been thick, but he would have expected that the areas around the town would have been cleared fully of anything hostile, knowing how long the town had been established. It still amazed Darren the vast areas of Amathera that possessed the characteristics of untouched wilderness.

Darren's senses were heightened with his increased apprehension of entering the cave. Leading into the mountain's interior, a tunnel with rough stone walls followed the entranceway, winding upwards at a sharp incline. His thighs burned by the time he reached the top of the tunnel, as the going was tough. As the tunnel's width narrowed significantly, he lowered his bow while approaching the narrowest point. The path ahead was the shape of an inverted V. Even crouching, he could not move through easily. He could crawl, but that would make him unable to respond to an attack. Looking at the dirt-covered floor, he could see what he assumed were drag marks created by someone's heels. He placed his bow on his shoulder, drew his short sword, and proceeded forward.

He had been through a cheese press when caving as a teenager, and the tight feeling of the rock against his chest as he turned sideways, squeezing through, brought back unpleasant memories. The tunnel walls parted again, and as he continued, he returned his short sword to its sheath and took up his bow once more. Darren edged forward approached the entrance to a cavern.

He stood just out from the entrance and listened. The only sound he could hear was the spluttering of the torch as it continued to burn, casting a glow ahead of him. The cavern looked small, and he eased forward. As he entered, he swung his bow around in a wide arc, covering the extent of the chamber. On either side, there were two further tunnels leading off. The trail he had been following headed to the left, and looking down again at the ground, he squatted, seeing the outline of the four-toed creatures in the dirt. There were no longer any signs of anything being dragged.

He had lost the ability to work out where he was in the cave system, and he took a moment to open his display to ensure that his map was updated with his location. He didn't want to continue following a maze of tunnels and not be able to return. Once confirmed, he moved across the small chamber and entered the trail tunnel. The blue trail had ended. Darren knew that all trails faded. He believed that this red trail he followed was still so easy to track only because of the potential number of creatures that had made it.

He could feel the sweat on his palms as he continued, his breath shallow, trying to be as quiet as possible. It felt as though his heart was in his head, and he could feel his blood pumping in his temples. Letting out a deep, controlled exhale, he tried to steady his nerves and relax. He had travelled what he believed may have been another few hundred feet when he heard a noise. Instantly freezing, he listened intently. The sound was distant and low, but he was unsure how far it was; sound travelled differently in tunnels. There appeared to be more than one variation of whatever was making the sound. He couldn't see ahead as the tunnel was winding, and he was unsure of the sound. He cautiously crept forward, now straining to hear.

When he approached a fork in the tunnel, he saw the first sign of a light being cast from ahead. Not wanting to give his position away, he backed down the tunnel and found a crack in the wall where he could wedge the torch. He flexed his fingers where he had been gripping both the torch and bow and then, nocking an arrow again, proceeded forward to the fork.

CHAPTER FORTY-TWO

Pit

The light being cast flickered like that of a torch, and listening intently, Darren could hear several of what he assumed were voices ahead of him. They were guttural and animalistic in sound, with more grunts than any language he had ever heard. He followed the tunnel wall, its rough surface rubbing against his shoulder as he pressed to its side. The tunnel began to widen, and he stilled, looking into the space ahead of him.

The smell of cooked meat wafted down the tunnel, and Darren began to panic, thinking that Alice was the food source. He moved forward faster than he should have, continuing to the edge of the tunnel-mouth. Before him was a large open cavern containing a large deep pit. The light was being created by a fire burning below, the smoke from the fire drawn upwards to an opening in the cavern roof, and torches were stuck into the walls. The pit was over a hundred feet wide and eighty across, with a roughly hewn path cut into its side leading down to the bottom. Moving cautiously to the edge after ensuring nothing was at the top level, he peered down.

The bottom of the pit was fifty feet below. What drew Darren's attention were the beings moving around. They reminded Darren of pictures of aliens from science fiction stories back on Earth, with their long, thin, gangly arms and legs. Their bodies appeared emaciated, with large bulbous heads, no hair, and eyes that reminded him of a fish's. The pit contained sixteen of the creatures. The fire had a spit built over it, containing the remains of a hogling.

At the base of the pit, he could see what could only be described as tepees made from multiple animal furs and skins, stretched skins on tanning frames, and various implements or weapons that reminded Darren of cavemen. At the far end were wooden cages, and lying in one of them, he could just make out, was the still form of Alice. Two others contained animals, one a hogling and another a puma. Darren's anger flared, and adrenaline flooded him as he saw Alice. He didn't know the creatures' levels, but considering he was in what had been a starter area until recently, he didn't think they could be very high level. He wouldn't be able to tell their health until he shot one and it took damage. He only wished he had the identification skill.

He knelt, looking down into the pit, observing the creatures. One walked to the spit on the fire and turned it. The hogling leaked its contents onto the fire with the sound of sizzling fat and a flare of the flames. Another one of the creatures walked to the other, and Darren watched as what he thought was an argument took place. The new arrival tried to adjust the spit and was struck by the other. They hissed at each other in animalistic tones before a larger creature barked an order, and they fell silent, turning to look at it.

Darren couldn't tell if they were male or female; although naked, they didn't seem to have any recognisable signs. Considering the options open to him, he had two choices. One was leaving and returning to the town to get help, and the other was attempting to free Alice alone. Looking at the scattered bones on the pit floor, he didn't dare leave Alice behind now that he had found her, considering she looked as though she would be a meal rather than a prisoner. It would take him too long to return and get help, and he did not know what reception he would get if he did, considering that he had left without permission.

One of the creatures cried out, and Darren watched as two more walked over to the cage containing the other hogling. It squealed as they approached, and the puma growled. Alice still lay motionless. Picking up a rough-looking short spear from by the cage, the larger of the two creatures began to poke at the hogling. The hogling squealed each time the spear struck it. Darren could see well with the light in the chamber from the fire, and his vision was boosted from being half elven. The hogling continued to squeal, and the puma hissed at the creatures. Several of the other creatures were looking towards the cages.

There was a call from the larger creature, and the two who had been bickering began to remove the hogling from the spit and placed the carcass on top of a pile of bones. Several of the others moved towards the food. The scene which unfolded reminded Darren of a savage gnoll tribe he had visited, with less decorum. The creatures tore at the remains of the hogling in a frenzy until the larger one barked and walked forward, shoving the others aside. Their would-be leader would have to be Darren's first target.

The squeals of the hogling lessened because of the protracted damage it was receiving, and Darren watched as it fell onto its side, quietening. A creature moved close to the cage containing the puma, and it snarled hissing towards it as it backed into the corner of its cage. The creature struck out angrily at the bars of the puma's cage, shouting something in a language Darren didn't know. Alice was still motionless, and Darren only hoped she was alive. As the creatures kept their other prey alive, he hoped it was the case.

Darren silently positioned his short bow, selecting his true flight skill. He aimed at the largest of the creatures. His vision improved from his ranger class, and his skill when using his bow seemed to act like he had binoculars on as he zoomed in on the creature's head. The bonus with being underground was that there was no wind to contend with, and he let his arrow fly.

The shriek of shock from the beast as it was struck in one of its bulbous eyes sent a shiver down Darren's spine. The high-pitched wail left its mouth as it fell backwards. Its health bar was now visible and had been reduced to almost zero. It lay on the floor wailing, rolling with its hands covering its face as the others began to react. They turned and looked upwards at the lip of the pit, their eyes falling on Darren. The screaming and snarling that erupted below echoed off the chamber walls as they reacted.

Damn, Darren thought as he drew another arrow and took aim at another, releasing again. His arrow struck true again and sent another creature to the floor, where it remained still. His arrow had pierced its chest. The creatures moved, grabbing their crude weapons and running towards the path leading from the pit. Darren saw the choke point and aimed at the first as it started to ascend. He hit it in its leg, making it stumble and fall. The creature directly behind it tripped on its comrade's fallen body and slipped from the path, only falling a few feet to the pit bottom. Standing again, it growled in anger.

More creatures began up the path, not caring for the fallen, climbing over and standing on the injured one with the arrow in its leg, having no thought of assisting it. Darren triggered his burning arrow, took aim, released it, and hit another in its side. The screams and shouts from the creatures were now deafening within the confines of the chamber. Continuing, he fired arrow after arrow at them. Thankfully, most hit their targets with his skill level. Many of those hit were incapacitated or killed outright because of the damage bonuses they received from archery.

"Come on," Darren cried as he continued to fire. Several were nearing the top of the path. as he realised that he would have to resort to mêlée combat if they reached the top. He triggered his lightning skill, focusing longer to ensure he hit his desired target, before releasing the arrow. The blue streak of light cut a brilliant trail in the chamber's dim surroundings. There were still seven of the creatures ascending the path.

As the arrow struck the lead creature, it froze in place before beginning to convulse as the lightning coursed through and around its body. The others, pushing up behind, still trying to reach the lip, touched the affected one, and the reaction he had hoped for began. The blue light lanced between anything that touched the stricken creature. Four of the remainder were affected, two of which fell from the side of the path and, at a distance above the pit floor, screamed as they plummeted to their deaths below.

The three that hadn't been affected stopped on the path, turning and snarling towards Darren while the lightning continued. Darren took the opportunity to pick off another, who died instantly, toppling forward. The lightning skill ceased, and as it did, the remaining two charged the final distance to the lip of the pit and turned towards him. Pulling two arrows this time, he drew back on his bow as they charged him. He had used dual shot several times, but his skill level was low, and he released the arrows. One arrow flew true as expected, striking his target and sending the beast backwards from the impact. The other arrow missed, passing harmlessly by its side.

The distance between them was only several feet, and Darren didn't have time to draw and fire again. He stumbled backwards, dropping his bow and drawing his short sword as the creature closed in, a club held high in its hand as it charged towards him. Darren lifted the sword, deflecting the club's blow, sending shock waves down his arm. The strike had been more powerful than he expected from such a weak-looking creature. Taking a step backwards again, he slashed at the beast. It withdrew from the strike with an unnatural agility, its body seeming to curve out of the way of his sword before it struck again with the club.

Darren raised his bracer-covered arm to deflect the blow, grunting from the pain as the club struck but holding his ground as he thrust his blade forward and upwards into the creature's gut. Its eyes widened in shock from the attack as the blade dug in. The beast's weight fell towards him as it became a victim to his attack. He staggered backwards, allowing the lifeless creature to fall to the ground.

There were still several of the injured creatures in the pit where they had been hit, screaming what Darren assumed were obscenities at him as he ran forward, scooping his bow and heading to the path, short sword in hand. The path down was treacherous. It was cut so roughly, and he was surprised as he descended how easily the creatures had headed up it. As he reached any of the creature's bodies or those injured, he finished them. His display had been firing the whole fight, and he now knew that the creatures were greylings. He had seen nothing like them before in his time on Amathera.

Darren reached the bottom, having disposed of four on the way down, he noticed that one creature had got back to its feet from where it had fallen off the path. It screeched at him as it stumbled forward on a twisted leg. It was broken, and sheer hatred towards him allowed it to move. It reached down and grabbed one of the short spears. Darren was over thirty feet from it and, sheathing his sword, drew his bow.

He reached back for an arrow and found only thin air. *Have I really used all my arrows?* he thought, panicking and feeling vulnerable. He had his short sword, but his bow was his comfort. As he shouldered his bow, the creature cried as it threw the short spear at him. Darren, distracted and unprepared, hadn't expected the spear to be thrown, considering its length and how he had seen them used by the creatures so far. Quickly trying to move out of its path, he stumbled, only his increased dexterity kept him on his feet. The head of the spear missed him by millimetres, its haft striking his side as he moved.

He turned drawing his sword and, with a cry, ran at the beast. It staggered toward him, and with its elongated arms, which ended in four fingers with large claws, it raked at him. Darren dropped his shoulder as he charged inside its swing and stabbed it in its chest. His sword was buried deeply. The creature instantly became limp as its life left it. Pulling his sword free, he let it fall to the floor before continuing around the pit, ensuring those others that had fallen were dead. He eventually reached the larger creature he had initially shot in the eye and found it had bled out from the wound.

There were no more visible threats, so he sheathed his sword again and hurried towards the cages at the end of the pit. The smell of the area, apart from the cooked meat, had a mustiness to it. It reminded Darren of a damp, cold cellar. As he neared the cage, the puma snarled at him. The dead hogling still lay on the floor of the next cage where its body had been left when the greylings had reacted to his appearance. The cage containing Alice was only held closed by a wooden peg, and he worked it free. It would not have held her captive if Alice had been conscious.

Darren threw the cage open, stooped down and entered, kneeling by her side and reaching out to feel for a pulse in her neck. Alice's heart beat steadily, and he let out a breath he hadn't realised he was holding. Grabbing Alice's shoulders, he rolled her onto her back and then, placing his arms under her knees and shoulders, lifted her gently and removed her from the cage. After laying her on the floor outside, he removed his water canteen and, lifting her head, poured some onto her lips.

There was no reaction, and he noticed the mark on her neck. There was a red circle with an apparent puncture wound in the middle of it. Traced around the puncture wound was a faint tint of green. "Poison," he said. He triggered his display before searching through his inventory. He had a class-specific bag as part of his tanning profession, allowing him to increase his inventory size. He could not sell it, as it was only useable by the maker, but it increased his capacity significantly. He grabbed one of his antidote potions and, uncorking it, carefully placed it against Alice's lips and poured the liquid into her mouth.

She didn't swallow, and Darren was concerned it could choke her, so he tilted her head, allowing the liquid to drain out of her mouth. He lay her on her side and placed her in the recovery position that he had been taught as a child. before carefully pouring some of the antidote onto his finger and then rubbing it on the inside of her mouth, hoping that through absorption, it would take effect. He continued the process until the vial was empty.

Alice's face looked serene and beautiful. She was angelic to his eyes, and he had fallen for her the first time he had met her. "Come on, Alice," he said, stroking her hair. When she didn't respond, he cursed, stood, and kicked at a rock in annoyance. "I wonder if they have anything to offset it," he said as he began searching the area. The stench inside the tepee was horrendous when he opened the flaps to the first. He recoiled from the smell while still holding the flap, but couldn't see inside and went to the wall, grabbing one of the weak torches they used to light the area. With the torch in hand, he checked the tepee again. The floor was covered with the skins of animals the creatures must have hunted and nothing else of value that he could see.

He worked his way from tepee to tepee, finding nothing of use until he reached the final taller tepee where the larger creature had been. The inside was just as filthy and dishevelled, but it also contained a chest, which he hauled out by one end and into the stronger light of the fire. Dropping the torch, he opened it. Inside were rather crude-looking tubes and wrapped leaf parcels. He opened one of the parcels to find a green paste inside. At the bottom of the chest was a selection of what could only be classed as needles made from the thorns of a plant. *It must be a crude blowpipe*, he thought as he began placing the items into his inventory. He didn't recognise the paste, so had no clue about the effects it might have. Cursing under his breath, he turned to head back to Alice, when she coughed.

CHAPTER FORTY-THREE

Following Orders

SJ sat in the inn. Cristy was opposite her eating lunch. The inn was packed now that its downstairs was open again for food and drink. That morning, she had been to see Zigferd after informing the two guards who had been standing watch at the cottage about Darren's disappearance. It was the most furious that SJ had ever witnessed of Zigferd as he turned the air blue and swore that he would have the hides of the guards who were supposed to be watching him, never mind what he would do to Darren if he caught him. It took SJ a long time to calm him down, and even as she tried to explain that they knew each other, he screamed and bellowed his frustrations. He was missing his second and one of his closest and most trusted friends.

Eventually, SJ left him as Ballentine had come to see him to receive a berating from him for his inept guards. To Ballentine's credit, he had not responded and just taken the abuse hurled at him by Zigferd. As SJ had left, she had seen the dwarf walk over to where Zigferd sat in a chair, holding his head in his hands, and placed his hand on the lycanthrope's shoulder, speaking to him quietly.

SJ had promised to see Cristy, so she collected her and brought her back to the inn for lunch. Terence had stayed to help Floretta in the kitchen all night and was planning to meet Nexis the next evening to look through the auction house plans he had drawn up and understand the work that was necessary. SJ and Cristy were going to visit Patch and check on him and the pack. They had not been out there since the wyvern had arrived, and Cristy was worried about them.

An hour later, they arrived in the south of town and crossed the cornfields to the forest. As soon as they reached it, Cristy began to call, and within moments, the form of Patch appeared, bounding through the brush. SJ could have sworn Patch had as much of a worried look on his face as Cristy had on her own. SJ felt relief as Cristy gripped Patch around his huge neck, squeezing.

SJ knew that the wolves were predatory animals but also was aware of how well wolves could track. "Cristy. Do you think Patch could help find Alice?" She had told Cristy about Alice's disappearance, and Cristy had been upset.

"I don't know. I can ask him," Cristy said, looking at Patch. Patch's eyes held clear intelligence to SJ, and she had begun to realise that he could understand the common tongue from their previous interactions. "You know the lady who came and healed Dark Paw?" Cristy said. SJ had never known that the other wolves had names.

Patch lowered his head in response and let out a low growl.

"She's missing. Do you think you could help find her?" Cristy said.

Patch growled again in response and turned his head, looking into the forest.

"I think he can help," Cristy said.

"That would be amazing," SJ said.

Patch let out a howling sound, and a couple of minutes passed before the remainder of the pack arrived. SJ now recognised the grey wolf called Dark Paw. Across the wolf's side, where the rock gobbler had struck it, there was a break in the fur, showing where it had received the damage. Apart from the missing swath of fur, he looked fit and strong. Patch growled at the pack members before they all moved off again into the forest area. Patch turned to look at Cristy and let out a low huffing sound.

"Patch says it may take time," Cristy said.

"What do you mean he said?" SJ said in shock.

"He said," Cristy replied, looking at her.

"You understand him?"

"Yes. I never used to, but recently, I have begun to understand him when he speaks."

SJ stood staring at Cristy and then Patch in amazement, not sure how to respond. Patch tilted his head sideways, looking as though he was smiling.

"He likes you, by the way," Cristy added.

SJ's eyes went even wider at the comment. "I like him too."

Patch walked forward and pushed his head towards SJ's hand. SJ stroked the top of his head.

"There isn't much we can do now but wait," she said. "The guards are also out looking, and the mayor has ordered one of the hunting parties to see if they can help track Alice's whereabouts. We should head back to town now that we know Patch and his family are okay. There's still a wyvern in the area."

Cristy looked at SJ with sad eyes. "We have only just got here."

"I know, but I don't want you to be in any more danger out here."

Cristy's eyes narrowed as she said to SJ, "I am not a baby. I am growing up and can defend myself." A short dagger appeared in her tiny fist.

"Where did you get that from?" SJ asked, surprised.

"Uncle Gary," she said.

"Uncle Gary?" SJ frowned. "You mean Gary the orc guard?"

"Yes. He gave it to me to protect myself."

"When did you see Gary?" Surprise etched SJ's face.

"I see Gary nearly every day when he passes the orphanage on his patrol. He always stops to talk to me."

The thought of Gary stopping to speak to Cristy regularly made SJ break into a smile. "I didn't know," she said.

"He has promised me when I am older that he will teach me to fight. Like he does," Cristy said, stepping forward and thrusting her small dagger out in front of her.

"So you plan on joining the guard?" SJ asked.

"No. I will be a hunter, like Dad."

"I know someone who may be able to help train you in archery. If he ever returns."

"You do?" Cristy replied excitedly.

"Yes. Hopefully, when we have some time, I can bring you to meet him."

"That would be amazing."

"We better head back."

"Okay," Cristy said forlornly. Turning, she spoke to Patch. "If you find anything, can you howl and let us know?"

Patch lowered his head again in response to her comment, and Cristy grabbed him around his large neck again, hugging him. "I'll be back soon," she promised as she turned to leave with SJ.

After SJ had returned Cristy to Madeline's care, she decided that she would focus on trying to find out more about Bellakiy today. Dave had been adamant that she must focus on her quests rather than getting involved in Alice's disappearance. The agreement that she had made with Dave was that she would see if Patch could help.

Kerys had informed SJ about the office Bellakiy had. It was a single-storey building not far from the docks area and close to where she believed he lived. As SJ approached the building, a tall elf who she recognised as one of the councillors was leaving.

"Hello, SJ," the elf said as he saw her approaching.

SJ couldn't remember the councillor's name and felt embarrassed. "Hi," she smiled. "Is Bellakiy in?"

"Yes. He is just finishing up a requisition, and I believe he plans to leave again tomorrow."

SJ did not know what his regular plans were, but the councillor acted as though it was normal behaviour. "That's great. I wanted to catch him before he left. I didn't have the pleasure of speaking to him before I was voted in."

"Ahh. That doesn't surprise me. He is always on the road," the elf responded, and wished SJ a good day as he walked off.

SJ knocked at the office door before trying the handle and walking in. The draconian was sat at a large desk strewn with paper and parchments, holding a quill in his hand and writing in a ledger. Looking up from his paperwork as SJ entered, he smiled at her. The office was decorated ostentatiously. A large stone-carved desk was the main centrepiece, and the legs were intricately detailed, with several of Killic's races portrayed. Tapestries hung around the walls, with various scenes and several paintings showing Bellakiy himself. To SJ, it felt like a pretentious setting. Compared to Zigferd's stark and practical office, it was a league above.

"SJ, isn't it?" Bellakiy said, placing the quill in a silver holder and pushing back from the desk. He stood and walked around his desk with his hand outstretched in a friendly greeting.

"It is, and you are Bellakiy," she said, smiling.

"I am indeed. What may I do for you?"

"I came to introduce myself and was also seeking some advice."

"I am glad to be formally introduced. What advice are you seeking?" he replied as he offered SJ a seat and returned to his on the other side of the desk.

"I am not sure if you are aware of my new position on the council?"

"I am not sure, no. I am not in town very often, and when I am, I am usually too busy to catch up with what is happening apart from meeting several of the merchants before heading back out again."

"Well, I have been assigned as an ambassador for Killic."

The draconian tried to hide his surprise but didn't entirely manage it. "Really? That is amazing," he said, his smile delayed.

SJ could sense that he didn't appear genuinely pleased with her comment. Her ability to read people's behaviour had always been a strong trait she had used in her previous life, and it seemed to be the case now.

"He doesn't look happy and is nervous," Dave said.

"As part of my new role, I am required to make relationships with the outer villages, and from what I am told, you are the one to speak to."

Although SJ was not 100 percent confident in her ability to read draconian expressions, his look seemed to become smug.

"I have been building relationships with all the local villages and towns for years now. I have great relationships with them all. As you correctly state, I have an uncanny ability," Bellakiy replied.

SJ hadn't stated anything of the sort, and his arrogance about his own ability was sickening. "It would be fantastic if you could please introduce me to the various settlements over the coming weeks."

"I would be delighted to. I am due to leave in the morning on a route around four of the closer villages. Would you like to join me?"

"How long will you be gone? I will not be available immediately."

"The route takes me three days to complete, with two overnight stops on the way. There are several villages that I frequent regularly with the trade caravan."

SJ had assumed that pedlars rather than trade caravans would visit most villages. Several pedlars regularly came to Killic and set up stalls in the market square alongside the regular traders. SJ had never considered the use of a specific trade caravan. She had seen wagons and carts coming and going through the streets of Killic but never considered what they were doing or where they were going. It made sense with the regular movement of food and goods to the villages.

"I don't like or trust him," Dave said.

"Unfortunately, with Alice currently missing, I don't want to be too far from Killic," SJ said.

SJ could have sworn that Bellakiy had to hold back a sneer at her name being mentioned. His eyes narrowed slightly. "It is a shame she is missing. I have always held her in such high regard," he said.

"He is such a liar," Dave shouted. Dave was getting more annoyed at Bellakiy than SJ was.

"It is more than a shame. She is a rock for Killic," SJ said, still holding her smile. "I will see you again on your return, if that is okay, and hopefully by then, I may be free to accompany you."

"That would be lovely," Bellakiy said.

Saying farewell and thanking him for the time, SJ left his office.

"What a pompous, self-centred asshat he is," Dave blurted as soon as they were outside.

SJ couldn't hold back a chuckle. "I agree. His office is all about his wealth and showing off. It's completely impractical."

"What were those paintings all about? Why have paintings of yourself plastered around the walls? Do you think it's so he can remind himself who he is?"

SJ could not hide her laughter this time as she returned to the town centre. The next place on her list that afternoon would be the Wandering Ogre. She wanted to talk to Niweq about his thoughts on being absorbed into the town's borders once it expanded. It was now mid-afternoon, and she didn't fancy going there in the evening, knowing that was when it received its main clientele.

"Okay. Time to see Niweq. I want to see if I can get an eye on this kobold that Harrietta has mentioned."

"You are on a mission today," Dave said.

"You scolded me earlier, so I better do as I am told," SJ said sarcastically.

"And have you listened to me before?"

"I always listen to you. I have no choice."

"Hmph. I mean, really listen."

"Yes. My dark overlord," SJ said, chuckling.

"Oooo. I like that. Dave the Dark. Dave the Destroyer, Dave the . . ."

"Douchebag?"

"Oi," Dave said.

SJ laughed heartily, getting some strange looks from others on the street.

Having never visited the Wandering Ogre in daylight, SJ was surprised at how different it looked. The building was plain-looking, and its architecture seemed cold and clean. The front door was open, and no trolls were standing outside, as there had been on her first visit. SJ could also not hear any noise coming from inside.

When she entered, her eyes took a few moments to adjust to the dimly lit interior. There were no acts on the stage, and only a couple of patrons sat at tables drinking. Looking towards the long bar, SJ recognised one of the trolls and walked over to him. He was leaning on the bar with a huge tankard in his hand, talking to the scantily clad human barmaid.

"Hi," SJ said as she neared him.

The pair turned to look at her.

"Can we help you?" the troll asked, frowning deeply.

"Is Niweq around?"

"He should be in his office if he is up yet. It is still a little early for him. The shows don't start for another couple of hours," he replied.

"I assume I need to go around the side?"

"Yeah. Use the stage entrance," the troll replied before turning back to his conversation with the human. The girl giggled at something he said, and SJ guessed it was about her as she turned and left through the main entrance, then walked around the side to the stage door.

The door was closed, and she tried the handle with no joy, then rapped on the door sharply.

Several moments passed before she heard a bolt being withdrawn, and the orc she had met previously stood in the doorway, yawning and rubbing at his eyes with his free hand.

"Hello again," Pethtu said, recognising SJ.

"Hi. I have come to see Niweq."

"Not sure he's up yet. You just woke me from my afternoon nap," Pethtu replied.

"Apologies. I thought you would be preparing for the evening's entertainment."

"There isn't much to prepare for," Pethtu replied, shrugging his broad shoulders. "Why?"

"Since that damn wyvern arrived in the area, the number of patrons has dropped significantly. If it keeps going like this, there won't be much point in being here," Pethtu said, stepping to the side and holding the door open. "You know where his office is. Feel free to see if he is there yet."

SJ walked past Pethtu, thanking him, and headed down the corridor. When she had visited the place for the first time, the interior was lively, with music playing and the dressing room full of acts. As she passed the changing room doors, she glanced in to see that there was only a lone half elf sitting at a large mirror doing her hair. SJ nodded towards her as she caught her eye in the mirror. Continuing down the corridor until she reached Niweq's office door, she knocked loudly on it and waited for a response.

Grey Matter

Enter," Niweq's voice called. SJ opened the door and walked inside. The interior hadn't changed. The posters on the walls of various acts reminded SJ of a theatre office. Niweq was not alone; sitting in a chair in front of his desk was a kobold.

"Hello, Niweq," SJ said.

"Ah, the fae. You have returned. Are you seeking employment this time?" Niweq asked with a smile.

"No, thanks. I am here on town business," SJ said.

"Town business. I see. What business do you have with the town and my establishment?" Niweq asked, raising one eyebrow inquisitively.

"I'm here to talk about a delicate matter." SJ turned to look at the kobold, who had paid her no attention since she entered. Its back was still turned to her.

"Delicate, you say," Niweq replied, looking at the kobold. SJ couldn't see any movement from the kobold.

"It relates to the expansion of the town's borders."

"I see. What does that have to do with you?"

"I am the town's ambassador and here as a representative to discuss this matter on the town's behalf," SJ said, knowing that she hadn't even had an express discussion with Zigferd as yet over whether she should be here.

"The town's ambassador?" Niweq said, surprise registering on his face. "I did not know. Congratulations on your appointment."

"Thank you. As I mentioned, I wished to discuss this delicate matter with you," SJ said again, indicating towards the kobold.

"It's fine. Please continue," Niweq responded, waving his hand towards the kobold, who still hadn't moved.

SJ hadn't been invited to sit and didn't wish to assume she might be, so she remained standing, feeling a little awkward. "The town is considering expanding its borders, and with the proposal, the land around the Wandering Ogre would fall within its new boundaries. As you are the deed holder of this property, I do not wish to force anything on you that you don't want to do. I wished to discuss a proposal for the Wandering Ogre and its land to come under the town protection."

"You wish the Wandering Ogre to become a protectorate of the town?"

"I wouldn't say a true protectorate, as we don't wish to control what you do. We wish to offer you the ability to consider being a more permanent part of the town in the future. You would benefit from the standard elements relating to all those who live in the town."

"What benefits does this bring me? All I can see from your initial proposal is that we would fall under the taxation and remit to the council."

"No, that is not what I am saying. I am saying you would receive the same protection rights as any other member of the town, with guard support." SJ felt completely out of her depth and suddenly wished she hadn't started this path of inquiry with Niweq.

"Do you think I require guard support here at the Ogre? I have some of the most capable fighting staff around these parts."

"You may have once."

"Once? What do you mean *once*?" Niweq's brow furrowed.

"With the territory and boundary expansion, which I assume you are aware of by now, there is the potential for many more to move into the area, and also, many of those here already will grow stronger."

SJ noticed a movement from the kobold for the first time. One of his clawed fingers raised and wagged towards Niweq, the slight gesture not missing her.

"I was unaware of these changes. What are you referring to exactly?"

"The town now accommodates all up to Level 20 for growth." SJ could feel a bead of sweat on her back. She really wasn't content with the conversation's tone or direction.

Niweq's eyes narrowed slightly. "Then why would I require protection, as it will mean that my own people can also level?"

"I really don't like him," Dave said. "The way he is acting. The fact he didn't introduce the kobold. He isn't to be trusted, and I would advise cutting the conversation short and leaving it here. You are outside the town's boundaries currently, and he doesn't seem to be receptive to your offer. You need to be careful."

Niweq had been charismatic and charming when she had first met him, even if he did run a seedy club, but his mannerisms today were completely different. He didn't show any of his charm. *I wonder if that kobold is controlling him*, SJ thought.

"Maybe he has something on him," Dave said.

Did you just read my mind? SJ thought.

"I don't think so?" Dave said.

"What!" Dave said, and SJ thought, at the same time.

SJ had lost all sense of direction at the sudden revelation that Dave could read her thoughts. The interaction had only been seconds in duration, but Niweq now sat staring at SJ, awaiting a response. Trying to control herself and not react, she considered her options.

"Niweq. It is obvious that I have caught you at a bad time. Pethtu has informed me that your clientele has reduced since the wyvern attack, and I only hope your business continues as it has done. I don't wish to try to force or change the way you run your establishment. I only wish to offer you the consideration of integrating into the town as it grows. Consider the thought of future growth. I will leave you to dwell on the proposal," SJ said, and turned to leave.

SJ noticed Niweq's expression change to one of confusion as she cut the conversation short and walked from his office. Hurrying back down the corridor to the side entrance, she let herself out and called a thanks to Pethtu, who raised a hand in response from behind the counter he sat at.

"What just happened?" she said as soon as she was a safe distance to talk to Dave.

"I don't know," he replied, sounding confused.

"You read my mind!"

"I think I did."

"You must know if you did or not."

"Think of something now."

Dave sucks.

"Hey! Oh, damn, I did read your mind, didn't I?"

"It seems that way. Has this ever happened to you before as an administrator?"

"No, never. I am as confused as you are. I know I can see your neural pathways, but I never realised that I could communicate with you without you having to speak to respond."

"At least I can walk around town without looking like I am always talking to myself."

"Yes. I don't know what has allowed me to read them. I'm looking through my code currently and trying to see any changes . . . but I don't see anything."

"It's a little disconcerting knowing you can read my thoughts."

"How do you think I feel?! It's not as if I want to know everything that goes through your mind. *Oooo, isn't that dress pretty? Her hair looks nice like that. He's cute,*" Dave said, sarcastically.

SJ stopped, still considering what Dave had just said, uncertain if she even had thoughts like that. She supposed she may occasionally but hadn't ever considered how they might appear to others.

"You realise I can now understand what you were just thinking about."

Embarrassed, SJ began walking in earnest towards the town again.

"I can't understand why it has happened. I know we have got close, but I never expected this to occur," Dave said.

"You said you can see my neural pathways?"

"Yes. I can see the patterns of your electrical signals as your brain triggers. That is the basis of the integration coding that allows us to communicate directly with your brain and converse with you."

SJ couldn't get her head around the concept that Dave could see the internal workings of her brain at the same time as seeing everything around her. "How does it work?"

"It's hard to explain. I suppose the easiest explanation would be like seeing a holographic projection of your brain."

SJ had seen movies and TV shows back on Earth, whether science fiction or science based, that gave her an impression of what he meant, but she'd never imagined a real version of them. The concept was not alien, just very difficult to comprehend. "What does this even mean?"

"No idea. It is as new to me as to you. I am in as much shock as you are," Dave said.

"If you can read my thoughts, what else can you do?"

"What do you mean?"

"Can you control them?" SJ sounded concerned.

"I don't know. I wouldn't have thought so. That would mean integration and neural transition. I know I previously joked about taking over a dragon or beastkin, but I never thought it would be a serious option. This may mean it is a possibility."

"That's scary."

"But also, exciting."

"For you, maybe."

"For us. Just consider if I could help out during situations. I have a greater visibility of the world around you and could support you during times of need."

"You already have that ability and do."

"I mean reaction times. If I could control . . ."

"Don't even go there!" SJ snapped. "There is no way you will ever be able to control me."

"No. I don't mean control."

"That is exactly what you just said."

"Yes. I didn't mean *control* control. I meant control as in help. Say someone attacked you, and I could see the attack before you could and react before you could react."

SJ shivered at the thought of being controlled. "The fact you can read my mind is frightening enough. If you could ever control me, I'm not sure I could cope."

"I honestly don't know what it means. I will have to speak to the System about it."

"NO," SJ shouted, stopped again.

"Why?" Dave asked.

"I am sure if this is normal, you would know about it. I don't need to draw more attention from them. They already class me as an anomaly."

"Okay. I won't. I will continue to work on my code, though. The recent levels have been challenging to break the algorithmic locks they implemented."

"Has this got anything to do with what you have been working on previously?"

"No. I was just freeing my mind and removing restrictions. I don't believe anything I have done would have caused this."

Over the past couple of weeks, SJ had not considered Dave's coding and the changes he had been investigating. She had been too busy with her new life.

"Ohhhhhh," Dave said.

"What?" SJ said, concerned.

"Erm, you have a new entry on your character sheet."

"What?" SJ said as she called up her display and switched to her sheet. Reading through it, she saw nothing different until the final line.

Synchronisation:	7%

"Synchronisation!" SJ exclaimed.

"It appears that way. Maybe because we have communicated so often. I don't know."

"Why is it only showing now? I have never seen it before."

"The fact I can read your thoughts may have triggered it to show. The System has many hidden features to which I am not privy."

"If we ended up synchronised . . . would that not mean I could also see your code or what you know?"

The comment startled Dave, and he spluttered a response. "I—I don't know. Maybe it would." His voice now contained a nervous inflection.

"Why are you worried suddenly?"

"No reason." Dave coughed.

"You're afraid I would discover all your dirty little secrets, aren't you?" SJ asked.

"No. I have nothing to hide. Well, not that much anyway." Dave chuckled nervously.

Standing on the path back to town, they both stayed silent. SJ was trying not to think of anything, which, under the circumstances, was virtually impossible. She looked around, trying to focus on the trees and the plants, considering the animal sounds that filtered from the nearby forest, anything apart from what she wanted to think about. Giving in, knowing it was pointless, she spoke. "Can we agree? Whatever happens, we will never divulge each other's secrets or use anything we learn about each other against each other."

Dave did not hesitate to agree. "I agree fully that whatever happens, we will always keep each other's thoughts secret."

"This is a little one-sided. I can't read your thoughts."

"It's not exactly comforting for me either. It's a good job we are best friends."

Yes, we are, SJ thought before realising he'd hear her anyway.

"Now, that's the kind of thought I like to see," Dave said cheerily.

"This is going to take some getting used to."

"It is, for both of us. I am now going to have so much more to do."

"Consider this option. Unless I am involved in a conversation with another or in an area with others, I will always speak to you normally. Does that sound fair?"

"It does. It stops me having to continually monitor your thoughts, although that doesn't take much processing power."

"Are you saying my thoughts are not worth the effort?" SJ huffed.

"No. I would have expected the continual load of neural processes to take up much more processing than they do, that's all. It is minuscule in comparison to other things I do, which is strange considering the complexity of the human brain."

"You just said *human brain*."

"Yes. Why?"

"I am a fae. Is my brain not a fae brain now?"

Silence.

"Dave?"

"Sorry. I just had a moment of realisation."

"What?"

"You are absolutely right. You should have a fae brain, but you don't. It's still human."

"Sorry?"

"When any other Legionnaire has selected their race and transformed, their metabolism and physical changes fully morph into those of the race they choose. Your brain hasn't changed, meaning that you are actually a fae with a human brain. I had never even considered it until you mentioned it."

"Is this a bad thing?"

"I don't think so. Let me check something quickly."

Silence.

"I think I understand why you still have a human brain. Reincarnation protocols state that only a human brain can be integrated into the System. With your adaptation of the terms and conditions and waiver status with the potential for future reincarnations, if your brain had been physically altered to that of any other race, they could not reintegrate you again."

"What about those who go in dungeons and die but get reincarnated?"

"It's not really a reincarnation. They are basically in a subsystem of Amathera and then reinstated in Amathera. It's the same with world events. They create subsystems. If you die in the main Amathera system, you are then reincarnated in the primary system. It's again one of those Oxford and MIT moments—too difficult to fully explain or comprehend."

"What about those who decide to be humans? Does that mean they could be reincarnated if the System wished?"

"No. Their brains are Amatherean human brains, not Earth human brains. You still have your full on original grey matter. This is mind-blowing."

"You're telling me?!"

"I will start doing some research. I need to understand the synchronisation process more."

"We both do," SJ said, and once again continued back towards town.

SJ returned to the cottage and settled down to eat until there was a sharp knock on the cottage door. "Who is it?" she called.

"It's the guard," Dave said before they replied.

"Councillor. We have been asked to inform you that the dire wolf has been seen near the town entrance, breaking the rules for it to remain away from Killic."

SJ jumped from her table, knocking the chair over, and ran to the door.

"Is he howling?" she asked excitedly as she swung the door open.

Surprised at her reaction and the look on her face, the guard in front replied, "Yes."

"Amazing. Let's go," SJ said, pushing between the guards and pulling the cottage door closed behind her.

Both the guards looked confused at her reaction, but turned to follow SJ.

"I will meet you there," SJ said as she transformed into her miniature form and took off. Her flying speed was much faster than her walking pace. She sped through the streets to the far side of town. It didn't take her long to arrive and see a group of six guards standing in a line facing out towards Patch, who sat approximately a hundred feet from the street on the path between the cornfields. SJ had heard Patch's howl as she crossed the town.

Ignoring the guard, she flew straight past them towards Patch, landing and growing as soon as she did. "Have you found her?" she said excitedly.

Patch gave a low growl and turned back, leading towards the forest.

"Wait," SJ said, turning back to the guard. "Get me the mayor now."

The guards just stood looking at her with confused looks.

"NOW!" SJ shouted.

One of the guards reacted before the others and ran towards the barracks. Several minutes passed, and SJ stood waiting impatiently. As soon as she saw Zigferd appear, she yelled at him, "The wolves have found Alice. Get some guards to follow."

Zigferd's look of confusion disappeared in an instant, and he shouted orders at the guards who had been standing facing Patch. They moved towards SJ, who again switched to her miniature form, and as Patch bounded across the cornfields, she followed.

SJ heard a roar behind her and turned to see that Zigferd had transformed into his bear form and was pounding across the fields in pursuit. This left the poor guard to try to keep up with them. Zigferd soon caught up as Patch started to lead them into the forest.

CHAPTER FORTY-FIVE

Unknown

As the three of them left the guard behind, they crashed through the under-brush. All around them, there were the squeals of beasts, creatures, and birds. Patch hardly made a sound when passing through the forest. SJ was airborne, zipping above him, but Zigferd was like a mountain. Even saplings didn't hamper his movement as he flattened them with his huge bear form.

Occasionally, SJ would hear the howl of a wolf in the distance, and Patch would respond as his pack directed him to where they were. It took much longer than SJ had expected to reach the wolves' location. As SJ swerved the lower branches of the trees, Patch and Zigferd broke through the brush into a clearing with a small stream running through it. Patch came to an elegant stop as he entered, and Zigferd slammed to a halt, his paws digging deep gouges into the soft ground. SJ slowed to a hover.

In front of them, the four members of Patch's pack stood surrounding Darren, keeping their distance from him. He was backed up against a tree with his short sword drawn. Alice lay on the ground by the stream, appearing motionless.

Zigferd roared, charging across the clearing at Darren, his huge maw salivating and his teeth on full display. Darren's eyes opened in sheer terror at the bear charg-ing him. The wolves moved out of Zigferd's path. Darren reacted, jumping around the rear of the tree as Zigferd's huge paw swung where he had stood a moment earlier, gouging a chunk out of the tree and littering the ground with bark and splinters.

SJ had flown straight to Alice and grew at her side. Feeling a strong pulse in her wrist, she called to Zigferd, "She's alive!"

Zigferd didn't respond, instead swinging another huge paw at the form of Darren, who was now moving from tree to tree, trying to stay out of reach of the bear's sharp claws. The wolves all stood in the clearing, watching as Alice groaned and croaked in a dry, cracked voice.

"Stop," Alice said.

"What?" SJ asked, not hearing her clearly.

"Stop. Darren saved me."

SJ's eyes opened in shock, and she felt guilty. She knew Darren had left a note about Alice but, being so worried about Alice, hadn't even thought about Darren's safety in the face of Zigferd's wrath. She should have come alone.

"ZIGFERD, STOP," SJ shouted.

The huge bear glanced at her briefly, let out another roar, and swiped at the tree Darren was behind, tearing more bark from it. Zigferd stepped back, not taking his eyes off Darren, who was cowering behind it.

"Darren saved Alice," SJ said once Zigferd had stopped his onslaught.

"What do you mean saved her? She wouldn't have been missing if it wasn't for him," he said in the very deep voice of the bear form he was in.

SJ was helping Alice sit up; her eyes were half closed still, but she was conscious at least. "He saved me, Zigferd. If it hadn't been for Darren, I would likely have been a greyling's meal by now."

Zigferd turned to Alice. "Greylings here?"

"There is a cave network a couple of kilometres from here. We had only stopped because I needed to rest. Whatever they poisoned me with still isn't out of my system," Alice said.

Taking another step back, Zigferd turned again and looked at Darren, who was still crouched but now peering from behind the tree. "Am I safe to come out now?" he asked nervously.

"Zigferd. Let him be," Alice said more sternly.

If bears could look scolded, SJ wasn't sure, but to her eyes, it seemed like they could. Zigferd responded by backing farther away. Slowly, Darren stood and moved into the clearing; Zigferd still let out a warning growl.

"Zigferd, I said stop," Alice said.

"What happened?" SJ asked, looking between Darren and Alice.

Darren tried to move towards Alice, but the pack reacted by growling at him, making him stop in his tracks.

"I tracked Alice's trail after I picked it up. It led me through the forest to the mountain, where there was an entrance to a greyling cave. I entered and found Alice in a cage with a puma and a hogling. They were in the middle of getting the hogling ready to be roasted, and I didn't want to chance leaving Alice there, so I attacked them."

"How many?" SJ asked.

"Sixteen."

"You killed sixteen greylings alone?" SJ asked.

"Yes. They were in a pit, and I could pick them off as they tried to reach me, clambering out. I then released Alice, but she had been poisoned, so I gave her some antidote I had, which began to bring her around. Whatever they used, though, is quite toxic, and the antidote hasn't fully combatted it."

Zigferd began to transform back into his human form, his presence no less threatening. He still glared at Darren with a look of mistrust.

"Alice. What happened to you? Why were you in the forest?" Zigferd asked.

"I was heading back to town when Rex informed me of some strange activity in the forest, so I went to investigate. That is when the greylings attacked me. They shot me with a poison dart, making me fall unconscious. I have vague recollections of being carried and also dragged on their way back to their cave. When we got there, I can remember being placed in a wooden cage, and that was all until Darren awoke me. I couldn't tell you where the network is, but I am sure Darren can."

"I could show you, but there was nothing left alive."

"It isn't them being alive that's the issue. There is an unknown network that has an entrance on that side of town. In all the years we have been in Killic, no greylings have ever been reported there," Alice said.

"It's probably because of the wyvern," Dave said.

"Maybe the wyvern caused them to change their usual routine?" SJ asked.

"It is possible, I suppose," Zigferd said.

Darren still held his short sword in his hand. "Put that away, please," SJ said, nodding at Darren.

He looked down at his tight grip on the sword before returning it to its sheath.

"Patch. Leave him be, please," SJ said.

Patch looked at SJ and growled at the wolves, who backed away, allowing Darren to approach.

"We need to get you back to town to see Master Rui," Zigferd said. Walking over, he bent and scooped Alice up into his arms as if picking up no more than a piece of paper. Darren looked a little dejected by his actions but didn't say anything.

"Thank you, Patch, and your pack for their help," SJ said.

Patch tilted his head down in acknowledgement, the gesture not unnoticed by Alice, who smiled weakly at SJ. Alice looked terrible. Her usual glow was dimmed to grey, her eyes sunken, and her lips pale.

The party began to make its way back towards the town. The wolves moved in front through the brush ahead of them as though they were forward scouts. The path that Zigferd's bear form had made crashing through the underbrush easy to follow, and they had been travelling for a distance when one of the wolves howled. Stopping, the group waited, listening, until they heard someone shout.

"Wolves," it cried, panic in its voice.

Not too far ahead, they heard the drawing of swords.

"I bet that's the guard," Zigferd said. "Hello," he called.

"Mayor. Is that you?" a voice replied.

"Yes. It's me. We have Alice. Sheath your weapons."

"Sir. There are wolves?!" the voice replied, alarmed.

"They are with us," Zigferd replied as he continued forward.

Moments later, they reached the group of four guards they had left behind in town.

"Mayor. Is Alice okay?" a gnoll guard asked.

"She will be once we get back to town," Zigferd replied.

As they neared the town again, Patch approached SJ's side and nudged her. SJ turned to look at the huge wolf. Patch looked off back towards the forest.

"It's fine, Patch. You go. Thank you for your help. Please let the rest of the pack know as well," SJ said.

Darren was the one to react this time, frowning at SJ's interaction with Patch. "He understands you?"

"Yes. I am sure he understands common fully," SJ said, watching as Patch turned and led the pack back deeper into the forest.

"How?" Darren asked.

"I don't know. I think it's because of Cristy."

"Who's Cristy?" Darren asked.

"You haven't had the pleasure of meeting her yet. You will love her when you do, and she has a favour to ask of you."

"Me? What would she be asking of me?" Darren said, surprised.

"You'll see when you meet her. Zigferd, can you confirm that Darren won't be facing any problems going forward?"

Zigferd turned to look at SJ, and she watched as his face went through several emotions before he responded. Alice had fallen asleep in his arms as he carried her like a baby. At no point had he slowed or complained about carrying her in his arms. "No. There will be no repercussions."

"Good. Glad to hear it, and Darren, you owe the mayor an apology."

Darren flashed a glare at SJ, obviously not happy with being put on the spot by her, as she smiled sweetly at him.

"Mayor. I apologise for running off," Darren said curtly.

"Accepted," Zigferd replied. The pair were obviously not happy, but neither was in a position to argue.

Alice was taken to see Master Rui, and Darren stayed since he was now his apprentice. Zigferd had to get back to the barracks, as he had disappeared without telling anyone and needed to stop any alarm it may have caused. The news that Alice was back soon spread, and everyone seemed to know by the time SJ reached the cottage.

Entering, she looked at the food she had been sitting down to eat. Not feeling it now, she left again to head to the inn and see what she could get. It was later that evening when she returned to the cottage, having bumped into Terence and Nexis. Darren hadn't returned, and she guessed he was staying with Alice until she was better. Floretta would be back later with Terence once the inn closed.

SJ was making the most of some peace and quiet. She had read through her recipes for cloth items and decided it was time to start tailoring. As she laid her items out on the dining table, she decided she would need to sort out a permanent area to perform her tailoring. The extension at Farleck Cottage that Terence was building would be ideal, and now that she had her portal, she could go there daily when she wasn't needed in the town.

She still had so much to do and keep on top of. She hadn't been working long when her eyes fluttered, not realising how tired she was. Dave had been chatting to her, asking about an old TV series he had been watching recently. The mundane conversation made her feel even more relaxed. As the stresses of the past couple of days had faded, so had she. Placing the scissors down, she walked into her bedroom before collapsing on her bed.

"WAKE UP," Dave screamed in her head.

SJ's eyes fluttered. *No*, she thought.

"NOW. YOU ARE BEING ATTACKED."

That comment brought SJ from her slumber faster than she would ever have wished, flying upright in bed as a shadowy figure lunged towards her. She saw the glint of a blade in the moonlight coming through the window, and in a half-drunken state of sleep, she tried to focus on defending herself. Her claws appeared on her hands as she raised them, attempting to block the blade. Her movements were slow and disorientated, and she only deflected the blade slightly. Rather than the blade striking her in the centre of her chest, it plunged deeply into her upper left shoulder.

"SHROUD," Dave screamed.

Crying in pain, SJ lashed out with her claws and triggered her shroud skill. Whoever her attacker was, they were fast and dodged the attack as she saw the blade coming for her again. Her eyes adjusted to waking up, and the low light in the room gave her the green glow of night vision. Trying to block the strike again while sitting on her bed was difficult, and this time, the attacker adjusted his strike and, rather than going for her chest, spun the blade at the last moment and brought it down into her thigh.

Her display flashed brightly with the dramatic loss of her health. Whatever they were using or whoever they were caused considerable damage. Grunting from the second hit, she tried to push herself backwards away from the attacker. Her attacker wore a cloak and a mask concealing their face. She needed to get to her feet. She was too vulnerable on the bed, rolling sideways to try to get away from the attacks. Throwing herself down off the edge of the bed, dragging her legs behind her, she felt the blade again strike into her calf. Her health was down to 30 percent. Another couple of hits and she could be dead, even with the benefits her shroud skill gave her. If she hadn't activated it, she would have been dead already.

"Level 19," Dave said.

SJ stumbled to her feet as her attacker moved around the bed. She stood weakly on her injured leg, feeling the blood running down her thigh and calf. It was then that the cottage door opened, and she heard footsteps running.

"SJ. Are you alright?" Terence's voice called.

Her attacker had been moving around the end of the bed to reach her but, on hearing the call, turned back towards the open bedroom door. As Terence's figure appeared in the bedroom doorway, hammer in hand, the attacker ran towards it. Taking Terence by surprise, he knocked him flying back into the lounge. SJ heard

Floretta scream. Staggering, SJ collapsed, leaning on the side of the bed for support, lowering herself. Her leg felt like jelly, and she could not support herself.

"Oi," Terence called. As she heard him charge out the front door and down the path, the front gate squeaked on its hinges.

Floretta came bursting into her room. "Are you okay?" she asked, panicking.

"Not sure," SJ hissed through gritted teeth. She hadn't been wearing her dress, and her armour class was nothing without it. *No wonder those hits did so much damage*, she thought.

"Not just that, they were also at a much higher level than you. If they had got a critical strike on you, I doubt you would have survived," Dave replied, concern in his voice.

"Who attacked you?" Floretta asked.

"I don't know. I didn't see their face. From what I could tell, they were wearing a cloak and mask."

"Here, let me help," Floretta said, walking over to her, picking her leg up, and swinging it onto the bed. SJ winced but could feel the blood ceasing as her active combat status dropped and her dragon blood kicked in, boosting her healing.

"Thanks," SJ said, grimacing. Her legs throbbed from the two strikes, never mind her shoulder, which felt as though it was on fire. Flopping back onto her bed, she closed her eyes. She heard the front gate go and footsteps on the path.

"Terence is back," Dave said.

"SJ. Are you okay?" Terence asked on entering the room.

"I will be," she said, smiling at him. "Thank you both. If you hadn't arrived when you did, I'm not sure I would have survived."

"I'm just sorry we were so late back. We got tied up making some pies for tomorrow and lost track of the time," Terence replied.

SJ couldn't help but smile at the thought of the large, burly, skeletal orc making pies in the kitchen with Floretta. "No need to apologise. You shouldn't need to be here when I am sleeping."

"And you shouldn't be getting attacked in your home," Floretta replied.

"No, and I don't know who it was either," SJ said.

"It has to be that kobold," Dave said.

We can't be sure, SJ thought.

"Who else would have it in for you?"

Bellakiy, perhaps.

"Oh, maybe, but why? You haven't said anything to him to make him react like that."

I told him I was the ambassador, and he wasn't happy with me visiting the villages. You saw that as well as I did.

"I think it's time you started to get some more levelling done and experience claimed. You can't keep fighting higher-level beings. You are going to fall foul if you do."

I agree, but can I just rest and heal for now, please? SJ pleaded.

"I will go and inform the guard," Floretta said. "Terence, get SJ some water, and can you switch her blankets, please?"

"Of course," Terence replied, moving around the side of the bed and leaning to pick her up.

"I'm fine," she protested, but Terence scooped her into his arms, carried her through to the lounge, and placed her in an armchair.

"I will be back in a few minutes," Floretta said, walking to the door. "And lock the door behind me."

Terence locked the door, then went and got SJ some water before busying himself in her bedroom changing the blankets that were now covered in blood. Her wounds were healing now, and the blood flow had ceased. She could feel the itchiness of the wounds as they scabbed before they closed and cleared fully. Injuries in Amathera went through such a rapid healing process; it was still strange.

Terence moved around the cottage, checking all the windows and doors to ensure they were secure. SJ couldn't remember locking the front door and assumed the attacker had let himself in. She had never expected to be attacked in the town, and the thought that there was now someone willing to assassinate her sent a shiver down her spine. Not long later, they heard the gate go and the sound of voices coming along the path to the front door.

"Only me," Floretta called as she unlocked the door and let herself in, followed by Gary and Greb.

CHAPTER FORTY-SIX

Progressing Well

W hat the hell has happened?" Gary asked, his face in shock at the blood-stained blankets lying on the floor where Terence had dropped them. "Floretta says you were attacked."

"I don't know who it was. They wore a cloak and a mask," SJ said.

"Do you have anything to describe them by?" Gary asked.

Greb walked over to the blankets and poked them with a spear he held. "Did they drop anything or leave anything behind?" he asked.

"I haven't looked, sorry. Terence was kindly sorting the bedroom out," SJ said.

"Do you mind if I look?" Greb asked.

"No."

"SJ. Do you need a healing potion?" Gary asked, a look of concern on his face.

"No. I will heal soon enough. Whoever attacked me was at a much higher level. They were doing serious damage. I think they were Level 19. If Terence and Floretta had not returned when they did and disturbed them, I doubt I would still be here," SJ said.

"Level 19!" Gary exclaimed. "What would someone that level be doing attacking you?"

"I don't know. I have been trying to think who or what it may have been, and I haven't been able to come up with anything or anyone," SJ lied.

"No ideas at all?" Gary quizzed.

"Nothing, sorry."

"I can't see anything left behind. There doesn't seem to be anything dropped or marks to track," Greb said, walking from her bedroom.

"How did they get in?" Gary asked.

"The front door, I think. It was unlocked as I knew that Floretta and Terence would be back, and I also never expected to be attacked," SJ said, shrugging.

"It's a little strange. I know of no one in the town who has got a bad word to say about you." Gary frowned.

"I wish I knew so that I could help, but I really don't," SJ said.

"I am going to get a guard posted at the cottage while this is investigated," Greb said. "I'll go and let the lieutenant know."

"There really is no need to," SJ said.

"Someone has tried to assassinate one of the town council. I think it is absolutely critical that we have a guard posted," Gary said with authority.

SJ had never witnessed the professional side of either Greb or Gary when on duty and it gave her a sense of pride knowing how they both behaved.

Terence cleared up the bloodied blankets and offered Gary refreshments while waiting for the guard to return.

"Don't you need to get back on patrol?" SJ said after a while.

"You think I'm leaving here before the guard arrives? You have another thing coming."

That made SJ smile. If there was one thing about Gary, it was that he cared for his friends.

It was sometime later when Greb returned, not just with another member of the guard but with two new guards, plus Lorna. SJ then repeated the whole incident from the start. Lorna asked for specifics, even in relation to how they had attacked, whether she could remember anything about the blade, if they were short or tall, their build, and the colour of their clothing. SJ felt overwhelmed by the end of it, feeling like she had been at the end of an interrogation.

Eventually, Lorna, Gary, and Greb left, leaving SJ in the care of Terence and Floretta, who were both fussing around her, and two guards who now stood watch at the front entrance. SJ had been instructed to come to the barracks the next day to submit a full report, which she had agreed to.

Terence was returning from checking the back entrance for the third time.

"Okay. I can't cope with this," SJ eventually said, much more firmly than she meant to.

"With what?" Terence asked, confused.

"The pair of you. Treating me as though I can't look after myself. My wounds are almost healed."

"I know you are a Legionnaire, but someone attacked you, and we just want to make sure you are okay," Floretta said.

"I know. I'm sorry. I didn't mean to sound snappy. I just think I'm overtired now," SJ said.

"Try to get some sleep, then. You know we are both here and the guard, and we don't sleep," Terence replied.

"I think I will go to the cottage. That way, I am away from here, and there will be peace and quiet."

"Are you certain?" Terence said.

"Yes. Charlotte and Brian are there, and I will just grab some food from the kitchen before I go."

"I will go and sort you something," Floretta said, standing and hurrying into the kitchen.

It didn't take Floretta long, and when she walked back through with some food wrapped in a napkin, SJ stood and walked into her bedroom, promising she would be back once the cool-down ran down. Checking her display, it was two, and her eyes felt scratchy, but she knew she couldn't sleep there after what had happened. Standing in the bay window, she selected her portal and transported to the cottage.

When she awoke mid-morning, her nostrils were filled with the smell of fresh coffee. Charlotte stood by the stove in the cottage and, seeing SJ stir, poured her a mug and brought it over.

"Here you go," Charlotte said, smiling.

SJ had explained to Charlotte and Brian what had happened last night, and they had both been shocked, swearing they would hunt the assassin down. SJ eventually calmed them both and, feeling exhausted, excused herself, collapsing on the bed and falling asleep instantly.

"Did you make the coffee deliberately?" SJ said, sitting up and taking the mug from Charlotte.

"Whatever gave you that idea?" Charlotte smiled.

"It worked," SJ said, sipping the steaming mug. The hard bitterness soothed her already overactive mind. The instant she woke up, thoughts of last night flooded her head.

"Yesterday. We need to focus on you levelling. If there is another attempt on your life, you may not survive," Dave said.

I know, SJ thought. Aloud, she said, "I am going to drink this, then do my morning exercises."

"That sounds like a plan," Charlotte said. "Do you need anything from me?"

"Actually, now you mention it . . ." SJ was mulling over an idea. "I think what I will do for the foreseeable future is transport here daily to sleep. I can go back after eight hours, and I should be able to get into a routine of completing my training and, once the extension is finished, working on my profession. I want to make one of the new rooms into a tailor's workspace. I would also like to get some training dummies built if possible?"

"I don't see a problem with any of that. It will be nice to have female company here more often. The boys are great, but sometimes . . ." Charlotte sighed.

SJ chuckled. Climbing from the bed, she placed the mug on the side next to the coffee pot and walked outside into the front yard. She decided that if she was going to train, an area at the rear would be best. Moving around the side of the cottage, she found Brian tending to the newly-dug-out vegetable patch.

"Morning, Brian. Can I ask you a favour?" SJ asked.

"Morning, SJ, and of course. What do you need?"

SJ continued walking around the cottage's rear and started planning a training ring and where she would like training dummies positioned. She even discussed having some archery targets set up, mentioning her plans to bring Cristy here at some point.

"Charlotte will like that idea," Brian said. "I am sure she would enjoy training her."

The remaining time at the cottage passed quickly, and as her display showed it was twelve, she decided she better return to Killic. This would mean that the earliest she could return was twenty that evening, and she wanted to try to get the cool-down timer aligned as soon as she could. SJ considered what she was deciding to do to be no different from commuting to and from work.

Leaving her friends behind, she returned to an empty cottage in Killic. No guards were there, nor were Terence, Floretta, or Darren. She made her way to the barracks and then had to go through the process of being interviewed again, this time with a scribe present taking notes of everything she said. The news of the attack had travelled the town in her short absence, and she had to spend a substantial time calming down Zigferd, who wished to tear the town apart looking for her attacker.

Alice was improving but still very weak from the poisoning. SJ learned that Darren was staying with her at her property on the island while she recuperated. SJ could read the look of disgust on Zigferd's face when he told her. Having explained her plans to Zigferd, she'd taken him aback by having a soul stone at the cottage and a portal to use. Zigferd was happy with her plans, and although the skeletons didn't sleep, neither Floretta nor Terence were high enough to combat a Level 19.

SJ now had one priority.

Level.

"Okay. That's that finished," SJ said, wiping the goo from the spider onto her dress, knowing it would clean.

Quest: A Tangled Web—Complete
You have cleared the spider infestation at the caves northeast of town.
Rewards: 200xp + 100% reputation bonus = 400xp awarded

"What's next?" SJ asked.

"Closest is the Cellar Dwellers. At Mrs. Westerby's," Dave said.

"Okay. Let's get going, then," SJ said, shifting to her miniature form and taking off.

"Two more quests, and you should reach Level 15," Dave said excitedly.

Since the attack at the cottage, things had begun to change. SJ had spent the past month questing full time. Zigferd had given her leave from any council responsibility to allow her to focus on her growth. They had no reason to rush into solving the issue with Bellakiy, as it had existed for months before SJ was offered the quest. SJ had been spending every night at Farleck Cottage and only using the cottage in town during the daytime. Since Terence had returned to Farleck, the extension was almost complete, and SJ had created a tailoring room where she would work for at least an hour a night once she returned there each day before turning in. This had been helping her immeasurably, and she had increased to tailoring Level 6 after completing the initial clothing quest. Her next task had been to create a rare set of trousers, which she had been struggling with.

SJ eventually admitted to Zigferd that she had spoken to Niweq, and he had not been pleased. He had made her swear she wouldn't go anywhere near the place again without speaking to him first.

The auction house's main building was completed. Terence had done an amazing job with the carpentry before returning to Farleck Cottage. He had promised to come back and visit Floretta. They had been getting on so well together. The walls of the adjoining warehouse were currently being finished, with only the final section left to go up and then the roof to be built. Nexis had spoken to the magistrate again and the transference network was to be configured within the week. Nexis could have set it up but, for obvious reasons, didn't, asking the magistrate to send one of his nearest mages to configure it.

Nexis continued to be the town's star, and the tailor shop had never been so busy. He had even mentioned to SJ that he should have run a shop properly before, as Nexis, because he was already aware of several new followers because of his work.

After the repairs were completed, the inn was fully operational. Fhyliss had arranged a grand reopening, which had been the only night SJ had stayed in Killic since the attack. Nothing had happened back at the cottage, and when she moved around the town in the daytime, there were always beings around, and Dave was on permanent over-watch, which always comforted SJ.

The wyvern had revisited once in the past month, attacking the livestock in the field. An unfortunate cow had been seen being carried off back into the forests, mooing loudly. The guards and townsfolk had reacted to the mage's announcement, meaning everyone had cleared the streets apart from the guards and hunters who were present. They had attempted to shoot at the wyvern, but it had not come close enough. It had been enlightening for the town to know their training and hard work had been paying off. Their drills had been so slick. The town was not letting its guard down, though, and everyone had remained vigilant.

The mine was operational, and SJ still hadn't been down to visit it yet. She had meant to go weeks ago, but with everything that had happened, she had left it in the capable hands of others. She spoke to Shelly regularly when she saw her and had been getting updates first hand. They were currently finishing building the smelter on the ridge above, back from the edge itself. Nevik had been overseeing its build, and it would likely be operational in time for the completion of the auction house, meaning they could start making mithril sales as soon as possible.

"Where is Mrs. Westerby's?" SJ asked.

"Fourth street, southern edge, fifth house on the left," Dave replied.

Dave had turned into her chief navigator and quest controller as she moved from one to the next, completing as many daily as she could. The experience needs had increased dramatically with each level, giving SJ an appreciation for why it had taken Darren so long to level.

"I think Darren is back today," SJ said.

"Yeah. He should be."

"I wonder how he got on?"

"I am sure we will find out soon enough."

Darren had travelled with Alice to Asterfal. After her recovery, Zigferd decided that there was no point in SJ going to see if she could set a quest when Alice was due to meet with the Asterfal council soon. Alice was going to discuss the new tax levies that Asterfal was trying to implement and would try to set up the quest at the same time. Zigferd ordered Darren not to leave the wagon, as he didn't need any problems if Master Fretun discovered he had returned. Darren and Alice were due back soon.

"Which quest is this one?" SJ asked as she flew across town. Her green dot had become a frequent expectation by many, and several often waved to her as she flew overhead.

"Cellar Dwellers. The description is a little vague, but I would guess it is a rat infestation to clear," Dave said.

"URGH. Spiders to rats. But they all add up," SJ finished, trying to be cheery. Many of the quests had begun to repeat, if not specifically then the experience of them. She had initially started picking up what she could do, including delivery or search quests, but soon realised that combat was the best option for her. At least they allowed her to practise her skills outside of training. Her kata had been improving with her daily routine and punishing quest schedule, and she had recently reached Level 7. Her identification skill had also been getting its use and was now at Level 8. The biggest bonus since she had begun to focus on quests were her developed combat skills. She was now adept at triggering all her skills whenever she could per their cool-downs. It was what she should have done a long time ago.

"Here we are," Dave said.

SJ flew down to the house and grew before knocking on the front door. The house was one of the larger ones on the street.

A kindly-looking ratkin opened the front door. "Councillor. What may I do for you?" Mrs. Westerby said.

"Mrs. Westerby? Please call me SJ. I am here to complete the quest I accepted."

"Oh. Please call me Silti. I did not know it was you. Please come in," Silti said.

"Thank you. What seems to be the problem?" SJ asked as she entered the hallway.

"There is something in the cellar. I don't know what, but my Hawey won't go near it."

"Hawey?"

"My cat."

The fact SJ was talking to a ratkin who owned a pet cat didn't go amiss, and she smiled.

"I see. Well, hopefully, I can resolve the problem."

"I never go down there personally. It was Goji's workroom before he passed away."

"Oh. I am sorry to hear."

"Oh no, dear. No need to say that. Goji passed twelve seasons ago now. Silly old fool he was. Here, let me show you where it is."

SJ followed Silti into a large kitchen area with a heavily bolted door. "It's secured well?" SJ asked.

"Yes. It always was, and as I say, I never go down there. Hawey was going down weekly as a treat to clear the rats, but he won't go anywhere near it now."

Listening to a ratkin mention a cat being let into a cellar to clear rats was one of the most bizarre experiences SJ had had since arriving in Amathera. SJ watched a large tabby cat walk into the kitchen, weaving around Silti's legs and purring. Silti walked to the door and began pulling back the various bolts. Hawey hissed as soon as she did, and his hackles rose.

SJ frowned at the cat's reaction as Silti turned a key and opened the door. The smell of musty, stale air wafted from the entrance, and SJ stepped forward. "Okay. I will see what the problem is," SJ said as she stepped through the door.

The light from the kitchen only shone so far into the cellar's darkness, so SJ removed a torch from her inventory and lit it, striking the flint and steel. She heard a sound as though someone was scraping nails on a blackboard. The hairs on the back of her neck stood on end. *What was that?* she thought.

"I can't see anything yet," Dave replied.

CHAPTER FORTY-SEVEN

Don't Go Down There

The previous similarly titled quests she had been completing over the past month would be classed as usual. Go here, kill giant rats, go there, kill spiders, et cetera. Nothing she had done had ever sent a shiver down her spine like the noise she heard from this cellar.

As the torch lit, the sound travelled up the stone steps. It sounded even worse this time, and SJ equipped her claws, holding the torch out in front of her as she edged downwards. The steps were enclosed on each side and then turned at ninety degrees halfway down, so she couldn't see the cellar area below.

"How large is the cellar?" SJ called to Silti.

"Same size as the house, I think," came the reply.

"One room or multiple?"

"Three," Silti replied, her voice sounding very distant.

What's making that sound? SJ thought again as she shivered on hearing it.

"Still can't see, sorry. It's too dark in there, and I look down on things, not up, unfortunately," Dave chuckled weakly.

As she reached the bottom step, the flickering torch cast its orange glow into the cellar. The light did not reach the farthest corners, and much of it was still in darkness.

Anything yet?

"Nothing," Dave said.

Once again, the sound came. This time, being down at the bottom of the steps, SJ could tell it was coming from the far corner.

Over there, SJ thought, moving the torch to point in its direction. She crept forward, her senses on overdrive. Even with her improved vision, she could not penetrate the far gloom. Not wanting to make a sound, she checked the floor and placed her feet as silently as possible.

Having only taken about five paces, she froze as a sense of foreboding crept over her. Her whole body felt like it was being dipped in an ice bath, and her teeth chattered. Every hair on her body felt as though it stood on end.

"Still nothing," Dave said, sounding frustrated.

The first thing SJ saw was the flash of something coming towards her.

Instinctively, she moved her head sideways, and whatever it had been passed by within an a couple of centimetres. *What was that?*

"Oh no," Dave said nervously.

WHAT? SJ screamed in her thoughts.

"I think I know what Goji was."

WHAT?

Before Dave could answer, almost instantaneously, a being appeared in front of her, hands outstretched to grab her. SJ screamed, staggering backwards and knocking into a table. She lost her balance and tripped, releasing the torch as she did.

"Are you okay?" Silti called from the kitchen.

SJ didn't respond, busy clambering back to her feet as fast as she could. Spinning, she looked in the direction the thing had been. The torch continued to burn, spluttering against the stone floor. At the edge of the light, SJ saw them. The glowing green eyes of the creature.

"It's a lesser lich. The good thing is they are weak magically. The bad thing is that I think Goji was a necromancer, and that is him."

The being moved farther into the light. It wore dark, tattered robes and stood almost five feet tall. Its once fur-covered ratkin body now looked withered and skeletal, with ragged patches of fur still clinging to its gaunt features. A brilliant green gem hung around its neck, which flashed in the torchlight as its robes fluttered around it.

It didn't make a sound, but SJ saw its husk of a mouth move. A thin needle of white flashed towards her. She was too slow; the missile struck SJ in her left arm. Searing pain shot through her as she looked down. It was a thin, needle-shaped bone. Gripping the end of it with her right hand, she pulled it out, grunting.

"Up close and personal is the only way," Dave said.

Her fear receptors were on overdrive, and it took all her will to begin moving towards it, rather than run away. Its hands ended in thin, needle-like claws, and she believed they were what had been making the sound. As she stepped forward, it again vanished into the darkness.

"Damn," SJ cursed out loud this time.

"Is everything alright?" Silti called again.

"Yes," SJ shouted back, although every inch of her said it wasn't.

"You have to get close enough to hit it. As I say, it's a lesser lich. They are not very strong and have low health. You must destroy that gem around its neck to kill it once you have injured it enough. The gem is its phylactery."

"The quest said nothing about the undead." SJ grimaced, cold seeping into her arm where the needle-like bone had struck her. Her health had not dropped by much, but her left arm was starting to feel heavy. "I think it poisoned me."

"Necrotic poison, probably. You will need to see a cleric once you kill it," Dave said.

"That's if I can even see the damn thing," SJ hissed.

SJ caught a flash of movement in her peripheral vision and threw her claws out defensively. Her claws caught the extended hand of the lich, which was again reaching for her. The blades dug deeply into the soft flesh, and it let out a screech.

If the nails had sounded bad, the screech sounded ten times worse in the confines of the cellar. SJ's enhanced hearing took the brunt of the high-pitched sound. She winced as the lich went to strike at her with its other hand. Using mind over matter, she moved her left arm up, blocking the claws from the lich from reaching her body, but they didn't fail to penetrate the skin of her arm. Thankfully, it was the left again. She felt a colder and sharper pain this time as at least three of its long nails pierced her skin.

Thrusting with her right, she aimed for the lich's head, her claws catching it on the side of its face as it pulled away again. Quickly triggering her identification skill, she took a step back.

Lesser Lich	
Level:	18
Hit Points:	76 of 121
Mana Points:	85 of 115
Armour Class:	20
Attacks:	Claws
Special:	Necrotic Needles

At least I'm doing decent damage when I hit it, SJ thought.

"Just stay away from those claws. You have two doses of necrosis now. They stack over time, and it will spread faster the more times you're struck."

My health is good, though.

"It wants to immobilise you to turn you," Dave said. "They can control undead."

That thought drove the fear of god into SJ. Noticing another movement, she spun just in time as it again appeared from the darkness to strike her. Kicking out, she caught it in its abdomen, her foot seeming to sink into its weakened body before striking a solid bone. The blow made the lich double over, and SJ tore her claws across its shoulder as it did.

Again, the screech it made deafened her as it vanished backwards into the dark. Its health was down to forty-one.

"I wish I had more light," SJ said.

"I have a lantern. I'll get it," Silti replied, hearing SJ.

Before SJ could respond, two more needle-like projectiles flew at her from the dark. She managed to twist from one while the other struck her in her right leg. "Argh," she cried.

"Careful. That's three now," Dave said.

"I can't see the damn thing to attack it," SJ hissed as she pulled out the needle, dropping it to the floor. The torch continued to splutter on the floor, and she moved towards it to stay in its light. Another needle flew at her. This time, she just managed to deflect it with her claws. Her right leg felt weakened and heavy, her left arm almost useless now.

"Here you go," Silti said as she came onto the steps and started heading down, not understanding what she was getting herself into.

"Wait," SJ called in panic.

It was too late as the lantern light bathed the cellar with its much brighter flame. The dark, shadowy figure in the robes screeched again, and Silti stopped dead in her tracks two steps from the bottom. Wide-eyed terror was on her face as she took in the robed figure.

SJ moved as the figure looked at the new target.

"Goji. Is that you?" Silti said in a terror-stricken voice.

The figure didn't respond, instead flicking its hand out and firing a needle-like dart at Silti. SJ was too far away to help, and the needle struck her in her chest. Silti screamed in pain and shock, dropped the lantern, and fell backwards, clutching at her chest.

"Damn," SJ cried, moving towards the figure as fast as she could. She triggered her shroud skill, unsure if it would help her that much, and lunged at the lich. The lich turned at the last moment and tried to move backwards but backed into a cupboard, stalling its escape. Striking out with as much fear as anger, SJ attacked. Her left arm was now useless, and she only had her right to fight with. She couldn't even kick out of fear of losing her balance because of her right leg.

The lich threw one of its skeletal arms up to try to block the blow, and her claws ripped through the robe and flesh, striking against the bone underneath. Another screech left its mouth as it tried to attack back. The one saving grace that SJ had above everything else was her high Dexterity and initiative. Since her levels had increased, her Dexterity now sat at twenty-six, having added two extra points to it on top of the level increases. She had also increased her Constitution and Charisma by a further two each. Swinging her right arm down as though it was one movement, she parried the lich's attack and brought her elbow around and inside, catching the lich across its jaw. Its health dropped to eight.

"Once more," Dave said.

"I'm trying," SJ said through gritted teeth, her movement impaired by the necrosis. She moved her right leg forward and, overreaching, stabbed towards the lich. The green of the lich's eyes met hers as her claws caught their target, and its health finally dropped to zero.

Staggering backwards, gasping for breath from the extra exertion of moving half-paralysed limbs, she watched the light from its eyes fade.

"Good job," Dave said. "Now smash the phylactery."

SJ had already turned away from the lich's form and was heading to Silti. *I will in a minute,* she thought. "Silti. Are you okay?" she said as she approached.

Silti was lying across the steps where she had fallen, the thin needle of bone still protruding from her chest. Her face was pale and ashen-looking. "I can't feel my chest," she gasped as she tried to breathe.

"You will need to get help as soon as you can. The necrosis is working on her chest and affecting her breathing," Dave said.

"This may hurt," SJ said as she pulled the dart from Silti's chest.

Wincing from the pain, Silti struggled to sit upright slowly, taking rasping breaths.

"I need to get help. I will be back as quickly as I can," SJ said.

Silti just nodded as she lay there, looking over at the corpse of her deceased husband.

"The phylactery," Dave said.

It can wait until we are back, SJ thought as she moved up the stairs as quickly as she could in her injured state. The numbness was spreading through her right leg, and she had to get help before her leg became useless. Forcing herself up the steps, leaning heavily against the wall, she made it to the top before stumbling down the hallway to the front door. Managing to open it, she stepped outside into the street. Seeing an elven couple walking down the street, SJ called out.

"Help. Please."

The elves stopped and turned before recognising her and running over. SJ recognised one of them from the inn. "SJ. What's happened?" Jolian said.

"We need a cleric as fast as possible. Necrosis," SJ said.

Jolian and his partner's eyes opened in shock. "I'll go," the female elf said as she turned and ran down the street seeking help. SJ was leaning heavily against the door-frame of the property.

"Here, sit," Jolian said.

"Silti was hit. She's in the cellar," SJ said.

"What caused it?" Jolian asked with concern.

"A lesser lich. It appears Silti's husband may have been keeping secrets from her," SJ said.

Concern changed to fear on Jolian's face.

"I killed it. Don't worry. Please check on Silti," SJ said. Her right leg was now useless and felt like a lead weight. Her left arm flopped at her side, immovable. She could feel the cold spread of the necrosis as it worked its way up her leg and into her hip. It wasn't painful, just ice-cold.

Jolian stepped past SJ and hurried inside. "In the cellar," SJ called.

SJ felt a nudge on her right arm as she sat leaning against the door-frame. Turning, she saw the face of the tabby cat Hawey. It let out a purring sound and rubbed up against her. SJ smiled and, reaching with her good arm, stroked him.

A few minutes passed before SJ heard the calls, and heading down the street came the female elf with a man. The man's name was Gregor, and he was a cleric who served as the town guard at the training grounds. SJ had been healed by him regularly after receiving the odd cut or blow while training.

"You have got yourself in a bit of a state this time," Gregor said, seeing SJ slumped against the door.

"Don't worry about me. Please check on Silti first. She was hit in the chest and was struggling to breathe."

"Will do," Gregor replied as he headed straight inside.

The female elf crouched by SJ as they waited for Gregor to return. The cold had now crept across her lower abdomen, and it felt like her left leg was cut off. The necrosis in her arm had now spread into her shoulder and across her back.

I would have thought the lich being killed would have stopped the damage, SJ thought.

"Nope, not from necrosis. It will basically end up paralysing you and then suffocating you as it stops you from breathing and takes hold fully," Dave explained.

Gregor appeared back at the front door. "Silti will be fine once she rests," he said as he knelt by SJ. "Where were you hit?"

"Left arm, right leg," SJ said. The wounds had healed over, and there was no visible sign of the damage because of her healing ability, just the effect of the necrosis that remained.

Gregor pulled the sleeve of her dress up, placed his hands on her upper and lower arm, and began to chant. A tingling sensation and then heat began to blossom from where he held her, and slowly, she felt the cold of the necrosis beginning to lessen as though it was being pulled back to the source of the injury. Feeling the movement come back to her arm, she flexed her shoulder, smiling gratefully at Gregor. "Thanks."

Gregor then moved to her leg. "Do you mind?" he asked as he moved her dress. Laughing, SJ said, "What do you think?"

Gregor slipped his hands under her dress and she felt the warmth of his hands on her thigh. Again, he began to chant. SJ felt the cold dissipate and bent her knee.

"Thank you, Gregor." SJ smiled.

"No problem. I'm surprised there was a lesser lich in the town."

"No more so than me," SJ said as Gregor helped her back to her feet. "What can I give you as payment?"

"No need. You are a councillor of the town, and I have seen how hard you train and what you do for Killic."

SJ flushed from his comment. "Thank you."

"I better get going. I am supposed to be at the grounds by now," he replied, smiling at her.

Entering the house again, SJ found Jolian, his partner, and Silti seated at the kitchen table. Silti still looked pale from her ordeal.

"Silti. I am so sorry," SJ said, embarrassed that the ratkin had been affected.

"It wasn't your fault," Silti replied.

"I need to go and finish the job," SJ said as she returned to the cellar.

The fallen lantern stood upright at the bottom, and picking it up, she walked over to where the robed figure lay on the floor.

"Don't get scratched by those claws," Dave warned.

SJ flipped the body over. The green jewel glowed brightly, appearing to pulse. Reaching out, she grabbed the jewel and pulled, snapping the chain from around the neck of the creature that was once Goji. The jewel felt cold in her hand.

"How do I destroy it?" SJ asked.

"Smash it," Dave said.

Taking hold of the remaining chain, she looked at the glowing light before swinging it onto the stone floor of the cellar. There was a cracking sound, followed by a howling wail as the shards of the gem flew across the floor, the green light fading from the shattered pieces.

SJ had not been ready for the wailing sound and had thrown herself backwards, banging her head against the wall as she did. "Damn. You could have warned me," SJ huffed, rubbing the back of her head.

"Sorry," Dave said, coughing and feeling embarrassed.

SJ's display triggered.

Congratulations! Level 18 Lesser Lich killed. 180xp awarded.

Quest: Cellar Dweller—Complete
You discovered Mrs. Westerby's husband had been up to no good and disposed of his undead presence.
Rewards:
1 x Silver
400xp + 100% reputation bonus = 800xp awarded

"I don't feel right looting the corpse of Silti's husband, even if it was now a lich," SJ said.

"Understandable. Okay. Next quest," Dave said cheerily.

Rolling her eyes, SJ stood and scanned the room with the lantern, moving and checking the other two smaller rooms the cellar had. Nothing appeared out of the ordinary or any signs of necromancy. It was obvious that Goji must have been a necromancer to have become a lich. Dave had explained that many necromancers would attempt to have a lich fail-safe if they died. The chances of returning as a lich were never guaranteed, and it could also take years for them to develop. Even Dave didn't know precisely how a lich was formed.

Walking back upstairs, she checked on Silti and comforted her. Silti gave her the silver coin, even though SJ tried to refuse because of the turmoil she must be going through. Not long after, she left and thanked Jolian and his partner, who she learned was named Lucial, for their help.

"I think I have had enough excitement for one day," SJ said as she left the house.

"Yes, but you are only one more quest from Level 15," Dave said glumly.

Sighing deeply, SJ checked out her character sheet to see how much experience she required. Her development had been going well. Her hit points calculation now included the 5 percent reduction caused by the soul stone.

Legionnaire 25007077			
Name:	SJ	↻ Level: 14	
Age:	27	**Experience:**	4985 of 5250
Race:	Fae	**Hit Points:**	107 of 107 (112) (55 * 2.04) − 5%
Class:	Assassin	**Mana Points:**	67 of 67 (55 * 1.22)
Alignment:	Neutral Good	**Armour Class:**	26 (10)(16)

Attributes	
Strength:	10
Dexterity:	26
Intelligence:	11
Wisdom:	11
Constitution:	18
Charisma:	15

Skills	
Racial:	
Night Vision—you have improved vision in poor light conditions.	
Flight—when in miniature fae form, you can learn to fly. Flying is not available in humanoid form.	
Shapeshift—you have the ability to switch between fae forms.	
Class:	
Martial Arts:	Kata Level 7, Clawed Avenger Level 3
Subterfuge:	Identification Level 8 (278 of 300 to Level 9), Shroud Level 3
Profession:	Tailor Level 6
Symbiosis:	
Dragon Sense—your senses (touch, hearing, smell, and sight) are heightened.	
Precognition—foreknowledge due to increased perception will allow you to evade a killing blow. (24-hour cool-down)	

Divine Lightning—your blood is combined with that of a blue dragon, increasing healing speed while out of combat.	
Malware:	Waiver (Sandboxed)
Inventory:	10 slots (10 special)
Followers:	3
Synchronisation:	17%

Resigned to the fact she was so close to Level 15, she said, "Okay. Where now?"

CHAPTER FORTY-EIGHT

The Root of All Evil

The easiest and fastest option would be a repeat quest, Spinners in the Dark," Dave said.

"I don't fancy going into the dark again today," SJ said, shivering involuntarily.

"All your current quests probably involve cellars or caves to visit."

"Let's go back to the inn and see what else is on the wall," SJ said, shrinking and taking off.

Flying back to the inn only took a minute, and SJ landed in the rear garden. Human sized again, she entered. After ordering a coffee, SJ walked over to the quest board to see what was available. Most of them were the usual ones; SJ recognised them as starter quests as the experience was so low for each. As her level increased, several more quests had appeared, as though they were being released in response. One in particular drew her attention now as she looked at the description.

Plant Infestation—visit Blossom for the details

The problem with the quests in the inn was that you didn't know any of the experience gains until you spoke to the person who had issued them. "Plant Infestation sounds above ground and more interesting than saving Shelley the cat from up a tree," SJ said.

"It was a one-hundred-and-fifty-foot tree," Dave said.

"It may have been. Reaching her was fine. It was the fact she thought I was a play toy as I was in miniature form."

Dave giggled. "Seeing you run along the branches as she followed you down again was funny."

"For you to watch, maybe," SJ sulked. SJ knew where Blossom lived. She was a florist who lived near the church east of town and ran a stall in the centre most days. Her stall was always full of the brightest and most fragrant blossoms. SJ finished her coffee, placed her mug back at the bar, and headed to see Blossom.

"Hi, Blossom," SJ said as she approached her stall. The sweet scents of her flowers filled the air.

"Hello, Councillor," Blossom replied.

"As I have told you before, call me SJ. I am not on town business. I am here to find out about your quest," SJ said.

"Really? That would be amazing. It has been posted for a couple of days now with no takers. I need the place sorted out. Otherwise, my next season's flowers won't be grown in time."

The weather and seasons of Killic were strange. Due to the constant temperature and the rare deluge of rain, they had two harvests a year. SJ had only witnessed two storms since her arrival, the first being when the hobs attacked the town. The most recent was two weeks ago. Even more rain seemed to have fallen that time. The quest popped up on her display.

Quest: Plant Infestation
Investigate what is causing the problems in the flower garden.
Rewards:
1 x Stem of the Angelus
200xp
Would you like to accept the quest? **Yes/No**

Stem of the angelus, that's something new, SJ thought.
"Unusual reward. It's something that alchemists use, quite rare," Dave said.
Auction house?
"Maybe. Darren may want it, or Master Rui."
"Where is the garden?" SJ asked Blossom as she accepted the quest.
"Between the church and the Wandering Ogre, there is a clearing in the forest that I have been cultivating for years."
"I have never been into the forest in that area."
"It's not a very large area, but enough for me. It is just outside the town boundary, unfortunately. Otherwise, I could have asked the council to help clear it."
"What is it exactly?"
"I'm not sure. Some invasive species. I have never seen it before. It grows quickly and is covered in thorns. It has slowly been taking over the flower-beds."
"I will go and have a look."

It was early afternoon, and SJ was making her way through the town. The usual hustle and bustle of the streets and the sounds of Killic had become a soothing norm for her: traders calling, carts moving, and people walking about doing their daily chores. The town wasn't huge, but everyone was always busy.

Maybe I should have got some tools if I'm going to be weeding, SJ thought.

"Possibly. I am surprised that a dryad or druid didn't accept the quest to help. Many of them are so adept at nature and growth spells."

The quest isn't exactly very telling. I was expecting moles or something to be cleared, not weeding plants. At least it will be easy experience and above ground.

Reaching the far side of town, SJ followed the path towards the Wandering

Ogre and found the path Blossom had mentioned leading off into the forest. The path was narrow, and as soon as she entered the tree-line, the sun's brightness was cut out by the overhanging canopy of the surrounding trees. The path led a couple of hundred feet into the forest before SJ came upon a clearing. It was much larger than she had expected. The ground was flat and had been worked over the years to provide rows of pristine, perfectly aligned flower-beds. Each of the beds contained a different variation of plants or flowers. Small wooden signs with the names of the species were placed at the end of each manicured row. The vibrancy and mixed perfumes from the clearing were intoxicating.

"I can't see anything unusual," SJ said.

"Umm. Strange," Dave said.

"What's strange?"

"Nothing seems wrong with the place."

"That's my point," SJ said, rolling her eyes as she began to walk between the rows.

It wasn't until she reached the far end of the third row that she noticed the thorn-covered vine that was intertwined with the flowers at that end. She knelt to look at it. Where the vine wove between the flower stems, it had grown smaller vines that were attached to the flower stems.

"It looks like it's feeding from the flowers," SJ said as she equipped her claws. Carefully, she positioned the tip of her claw next to the flower stem and cut through the offending thin vine. "This may take some time." SJ began to work between the stems, cutting the thin, rootlike vines. It wasn't until thirty minutes had passed that she noticed the vines were reattached where she had begun.

"Have you seen that? They are attached again."

"Try finding the source of the vine," Dave said.

Rather than cutting the thorned vine from the stems, she traced it back between the flower-beds until she reached the end of the bed, where the vine disappeared into the earth. It was as thick as a tug-of-war rope, with thorns like a rosebush's running its length.

Placing her blades against the vine, she began to cut through it. The vine was much stronger than she had expected, and she had to place a lot of pressure on her blades to cut it. After severing the vine, she picked it up carefully, scraping the thorns from it, and then lifted it, pulling it back the way she had come, breaking the smaller vines as she did. Eventually, she got to where she had started. The removed section of the vine was at least ten feet long. She moved it to the side and dropped it between the flower-beds. She repeated the process on the next row, where another vine grew.

It was as she cut the fourth vine that things went drastically wrong. A shriek pierced the clearing coming from the forest's edge to the rear. Looking up in shock, SJ came face-to-face with a creature she didn't recognise. It looked like a walking root.

"Mandrake," Dave said casually.

"Didn't you know what it was?" SJ said.

"Nope. They are all unique. No two are alike, unfortunately."

As the creature emerged fully from the forest, it appeared like a land octopus. Thick vines propelled it forward into the clearing, each covered in barbed thorns. Its body was shaped like a carrot, and on its head grew loose leaves that cascaded around its face like hair. It was one of SJ's strangest sights since arriving in Amathera.

SJ identified the creature.

Thorned Mandrake	
Level:	15
Hit Points:	98 of 110
Mana Points:	20
Armour Class:	10/30
Attacks:	Thorn Strike
Special:	Entangle

"It has multiple armour classes?" SJ said as it began moving towards her.

"Their roots are usually weaker than the main body. You need to cut its roots off to disable it. Then you can deal with the main root. I don't think it's happy you're cutting its roots off."

"It took long enough to react."

"They are used to losing limbs and regenerating them. It wouldn't notice losing one or two, but as you cut more off, it has obviously become suspicious."

As the creature moved, its vines disappeared into the earth, slithering just under the ground's surface. Each of its roots moved independently, and it had many. Moving into a space away from the flowers, SJ stood facing it, ready to attack.

"Watch for its—" Dave cut off as a vine erupted from the grass beneath SJ's feet and wrapped itself around her ankles. Dragging her feet from under her, the vine tumbled her onto her back.

Crying out at the sudden shock, SJ sat up and reached forward, slashing through the root. Her blades sliced through it with relative ease. Now she wasn't being careful not to damage the flowers. The reaction from the mandrake was for two more vine-like roots to shoot towards her. She jumped to her feet moving back from its attack.

It began lashing out with multiple vines as SJ cut and slashed, parrying many of the blows with her blades until one hit its target. Wrapping around her right wrist, its sharp thorns digging into her flesh, it yanked her arm forward. SJ staggered off balance from the attack, grimacing from the pain of the thorns. Another vine struck at her and caught her across the side of her face. She felt the thorns rip into her cheek. This time, she cried in pain.

Its multiple attacks seemed never-ending as SJ cut the attached vine off with her free hand and backed away again.

"Any ideas?"

"Just keep severing its roots. Eventually, it will not be able to regenerate as quickly as it has been doing," Dave replied.

"I didn't realise it was regenerating." SJ frowned.

"All mandrakes can when they are in contact with the ground."

Looking at its health, SJ noticed it fluctuating. As she cut through one root, it lost health, then slowly, over time, gained a few health back.

"This may take a while." SJ blew hard from the exertion.

"Usually, their regeneration stops at 50 percent health," Dave replied.

"Good to know." It currently had 76 of 110.

Two more vines flicked at her; she parried one while the other wrapped around her waist, pulling her forward. The thorns again dug into her through her dress, scratching and piercing. Another vine lashed out at her as she was dragged towards it, this time catching her right leg in its grip. If SJ wasn't careful, she would get entangled in it. Slashing with her claws, she cut the vine around her leg, freeing her movement, and leaned back against the pull of the vine around her waist.

The mandrake was stronger than it appeared, pulling her forward again by the vine at her waist. Her arms flicked up from the sudden movement, and recovering, she slashed down through the vine at her waist. It fell limply, uncoiling as she moved away again. It had sixty-two health remaining now. It went to attack again as it lumbered closer on its vines, whipping its appendages towards her. She cut, thrust, and slashed as it continued to attack. It eventually reached fifty-four health. SJ's health was, by this point, down to seventy-one. She hadn't noticed the damage she had taken from all the various attacks and thorns that had caught her. All the small attacks had added up.

The creature's wrinkled features shrieked again, making SJ's ears ring with pain. "I wish it wouldn't do that," SJ hissed through gritted teeth.

"Now it's below half health. You need to finish it by attacking its main body," Dave said.

"And how do I do that without getting caught by the vines? If I get any closer, it will just entangle me."

"It won't die from root damage alone. They only die once you sever their heads."

The mandrake's carrot-shaped body was possibly eighteen inches across. "My blades aren't long enough to slice its head off in one go."

"No, unfortunately, you are going to have to reduce it to zero health and then cut its head off."

"Great," SJ said sardonically, continuing to defend herself from the vines' onslaught.

The mandrake was only a level higher than SJ, and she was doing relatively good damage. The issue was the number of attacks it was getting in comparison. SJ was struggling to get in range of its body without being struck back. As she moved closer, her health was getting whittled down as much as the mandrake's.

"I wish I had a ranged attack," SJ growled as another vine struck her across her side, and she gouged more cuts into the mandrake's body. Her health was now down to 43, and the mandrake still had 31 remaining because of the increased armour class of its body.

The mandrake had lost over half its vine-like limbs but still had many remaining. They were strike for strike, SJ tiring more as the battle continued. This was the longest continuous fight she had ever been in. Even in the main valley battle, she had a respite between attacks.

As her health dropped to 28, the mandrake still had 25, and if they continued at this rate, she would be dead before finishing it. "I can't keep this up." SJ hurriedly backed up and shrank as she did. Pain flared across her body from the multiple wounds, but she gritted her teeth and bared it, taking off as soon as she was able. Flying up and away from the creature, she hovered above it to catch her breath.

"You need to hurry up whatever you are thinking of doing. If active combat drops, it will begin to regenerate faster than you will even with dragon blood," Dave said.

Thinking through her options, SJ opened her inventory and checked it. She still had it with her, thankfully. She had meant to visit Nexis at the auction house to discuss the prices of some of her loot later that day since she had picked up various items and begun the quests. Withdrawing the vial, she dropped to the ground again in front of the mandrake, growing as soon as her feet touched. SJ drew her arm back like a baseball pitcher and she hurled the vial at the creature.

"Ooo," Dave said, realising what she had just done.

The vial of rock gobbler intestinal acid exploded against the mandrake, the white translucent liquid spraying over and around its body. The mandrake screeched in agony as SJ watched its body begin to be eaten away. Its health dropped as the acid took hold, eating into its fibrous flesh and turning it black as it did. It began to look like a charred vegetable. Several of its remaining vines fell off as acid ate through them. The mandrake whipped its vines around in a frenzy, shrieking and unable to do anything to stop the acid.

As its health deteriorated, it slowed its movements. It reached zero, its vines stilled, and it fell forward to the ground. Where the acid had splashed on the ground when the vial exploded, small holes were eaten into the surface, turning the earth into muddy pools.

"That was a very good idea. Maybe if you had thought of it sooner, you wouldn't have taken so much damage," Dave said.

"You think?!" SJ said, looking at the now-smouldered mandrake root.

"Okay. Remove its head but be careful of the acid."

SJ walked forward, making sure she didn't step on or touch the acidic splashes. She began to cut through the root with her claws; its texture reminded her of a swede. Eventually, the top of the mandrake head came away, and SJ lifted it by its green-leaved hair and threw it to one side. Taking in the scene, it looked like she had been shredding lettuce, with plant parts scattered around the flower-beds. Several of them had been trashed in the process of the fight and would need work to get back to their pristine state.

SJ looked down at her body—her dress was shredded, ripped all over from the multiple thorn strikes, and her arms looked like a cat had used them as a scratching post. She moved away from the acid covered area before sitting heavily on the ground. As she removed her waterskin to drink, her display triggered.

> Congratulations! Level 15 Thorned Mandrake killed. 150xp awarded.

> **Quest:** Plant Infestation—Complete
> You have disposed of the mysterious mandrake.
> **Rewards:**
> 1 x Stem of the Angelus
> 200xp + 100% reputation bonus = 400xp awarded

> Congratulations on reaching Level 15

"Congratulations!" Dave said.

"Thanks. Maybe rats would have been easier," SJ said, lying back on the grass, exhausted.

After opening her character sheet, she decided to add both her extra points to Constitution. Her health had been her weakest element of the fight as soon as she had needed to get in range of it with its multiple attacks. The recent questing had been helping her no end. Her updates were:

↻ Level: 15	
Experience:	285 of 6000
Hit Points:	41 of 118 (124) (55 * 2.25) − 5%
Armour Class:	27 (10)(17)
Dexterity:	27
Constitution:	20
Subterfuge:	Identification Level 8 (280 of 300 to Level 9), Shroud Level 3

After resting for several minutes, her dress repaired, and her health continued to improve as the scratches and cuts healed. She stood, walked to the mandrake remains, and looted it.

> 2 x Mandrake Roots, 1 x Potion of Regeneration

"I better see Blossom, and then I am going to head home," SJ said.

"You have had another very productive day. Those two latest quests gave much better experience than the usual ones you've been doing," Dave said.

Shrinking, SJ took off and flew back to see Blossom.

CHAPTER FORTY-NINE

Archery

Having returned to Farleck after completing the quest with Blossom, SJ stood in the kitchen area as Terence stood at the stove cooking. He had picked up some great skills by working with Floretta and had been preparing meals for SJ on her return. It was nice to have the skeletons' company when she was at the cottage. The vegetable garden was fully planted, and apart from the odd pesky mole that Brian and Charlotte had dealt with, the plants were beginning to grow well.

"How did you get on today?" SJ asked. It had become a common discussion point between the pair of them. Terence always wanted to show her what he had completed in her absence.

"This is going to take a few minutes to cook, so I can show you now," he turned, smiling.

Where there had been a wall at the rear of the cottage, the stonework had carefully been removed and Terence had constructed an archway which led through to the extension. Walking along the hallway, there were five rooms leading off.

The first room had been turned into a bathroom, and the second was SJ's tailoring suite. The other three rooms were private rooms for each of the skeletons to use as they wished. SJ had been adamant that they had to have one each, even if they never used them. Terence had built bedframes for each, and SJ had mattresses and bedding delivered from Killic by Greta, the dwarf whose stall was like a hardware store. Greta had become her go-to for anything she needed. Between Greta; Jacob, who had gotten SJ most of her initial supplies; and Zej, she got the majority of the items she required.

There was a rear door at the back of the property that opened onto the training area that had been constructed. There was a ring marked out with small stones around its circumference, with sand footing from the lake. SJ had been training against both Terence and Brian some evenings. Then, three archery targets were placed at varying distances, going back towards and into the forest slightly. Charlotte had been over the moon with the targets and used them regularly when not tending the gardens.

"Ta-da," Terence said, showing SJ the newly constructed training dummy. SJ walked over to it. All the training dummies in the town were basic. This one was anything but.

"What are all the contraptions coming off it for?" SJ asked, confused.

"Here, let me show you," Terence said, grinning. He walked behind the dummy, where several pulleys and levers were positioned. As Terence moved the various levers, the dummy moved, and it could strike back. Its arms and legs could be used to simulate attacks while using it.

"Wow," SJ said, amazed at the work he had put into it. Terence had been keeping this latest project secret.

"It's more realistic," Terence said.

"It's amazing," SJ said. "Can I?"

"After dinner." Terence smiled.

They returned inside, where Terence served SJ a bowl of fish stew. Each day SJ returned, Brian would have been fishing, and there was now always a couple of fish hung up on a frame outside the cottage. Brian was trying to construct a smoker so they could also go hunting for hoglings or similar and preserve the meat. There was no point currently, as only SJ needed to eat. Initially, she told them they didn't need to worry about it, but they all were adamant that they did.

"The food was delicious as always," SJ said, finishing the stew.

Charlotte and Brian had joined them in the cottage now, and the four of them sat around the dining table.

"SJ. Can we ask you a favour?" Charlotte said.

"Of course, there is no need to ask. Just let me know what you need."

"Do you mind if Brian and I visit Killic?"

The question took SJ by surprise. "Why would I mind?"

"We didn't know if you wanted us to go there."

"I have told you all before you can go and do what you wish. I don't control you or decide how or where you live. If you wanted to move to Asterfal or anywhere else, that is your choice."

If a skeleton could blush, SJ could have sworn the pair of them just had. "We aren't used to freedom," Brian replied.

SJ shook her head in response. "You are my friends, all three of you," she said, looking around the table. "You aren't my servants."

The skeletons turned and looked at each other.

"I really want to visit the florist you have spoken about," Charlotte said. "I would love to get some new plants for the garden to work with."

"Of course. Blossom is amazing. I just did a quest for her today."

"What quest?" Brian asked. He was always excited to discover what quests SJ had been completing.

"There was a thorned mandrake that needed getting rid of." SJ then had to spend the next fifteen minutes running through a blow-by-blow account of what had happened.

"What did you want to get from Killic?" SJ asked Brian.

"I am after some fishing gear and also wanted to see about some new daggers.

Mine are getting very worn with all the gardening and digging they have been used for," he said, looking at Charlotte.

"Don't blame me," Charlotte replied, looking guilty.

SJ laughed. "Setu is a goblin friend of mine who works down at the docks as a fisher. He may be the best to speak to about gear when you get there. Here," she said as she removed some silver from her inventory and handed it to them.

"We don't need your money," Charlotte said, shocked.

"What's wrong with my money?"

"We can't take it," Brian said.

"How else are you going to pay for anything?" SJ asked.

"We have a few coppers from when we were with the necromancer," Brian said.

"I don't care what you have. Take these as a thank you for all the work you have done for me at the cottage since you arrived," SJ said, placing two silver coins in front of each of the skeletons.

All three sat with their mouths open, staring at her in disbelief. "And if you see anything else while there that you want but can't afford, let me know," SJ said, pushing her chair back and standing up. "Okay. Who is coming to train?" she asked, smiling.

The rest of the evening passed quickly, with all of them taking turns fighting against Terence's new contraption. It was hilarious for those watching, not so for the one of them struck by the solid wooden appendages Terence had given it. It added a sense of realism to the training, and SJ wanted to speak to Lorna about implementing them at the main training ground in Killic. She even discussed patenting, which confused the skeletons. As the sun set, SJ called it a night and thanked Terence for his amazing contraption, promising she would speak to the training ground.

SJ was standing in her bedroom at the cottage in Killic the next morning, where she had just returned. She walked to the wardrobe where she had been leaving her questing gear. After removing the items, she dropped them into her inventory. As she was finishing, there was a knock on the cottage door.

"Darren," Dave said.

SJ unlocked the door and let him in. "How was Asterfal?" she asked as soon as she saw him.

"Boring being confined to the wagon," he replied glumly. "Alice wouldn't even let me visit the Bugbears."

"You are surprised?"

"No," he said.

Over the past month, the relationship between the pair of them had developed to that of a brother and sister. Whenever Darren had questions about females— she couldn't call them women, knowing that Darren was talking about Alice, who wasn't human—he was always broaching the topic with SJ. It was both sweet and annoying all at once.

"What happened this time?" SJ said, looking at the face Darren was pulling.

"I did something stupid."

"What?" SJ asked, frowning.

"I asked her if she would marry me."

"You what? You have only been seeing each other for a month," SJ said, shocked by his revelation.

"I know. It was stupid of me. We were lying on the wagon roof the night before last while travelling back, looking at the stars, and that just slipped out."

"And what was Alice's response?"

"Nothing."

"Nothing?"

"No, she didn't say a thing."

"So, what's your problem?"

"I mean *anything*. Since I asked, she hasn't said a word to me."

SJ stared at him. "Did you say anything else to her?"

"No. I've been too embarrassed since." Darren stood with his shoulders sagged and looked close to tears.

"He is an idiot," Dave said.

Why? SJ thought in reply.

"Dryads have strict codes for betrothals. Alice has to speak to her parents before she can answer anything."

Explain.

"Dryads have a very complex hierarchical structure within their families. Most requests for marriage would have been organised and confirmed through their families. Only once confirmed would the proposition of a request be announced."

Oh. I did not know.

Darren had walked to the dining table and sat in a chair with his head in his hands. "I am such an idiot. Why did I do it?"

"Agreed," Dave said.

"Because you have feelings for her," SJ said. "I think I know why she isn't speaking to you."

"Why?" Darren asked, looking up at SJ hopefully.

"They have strict familial rules. Any marriage request normally goes through the parents before any communication between the parties. Dave just explained it to me," SJ said.

"She has no parents," Darren replied.

"She must have a guardian or similar, then, or relatives," Dave said.

"Does she have a guardian?" SJ asked.

Darren's face scrunched up as he cringed.

"What?" SJ asked.

"Zigferd," Darren replied.

"Zigferd is Alice's guardian?" SJ was now the one in shock.

"Yes. Zigferd took her in as a child and has been her guardian since her parents' death."

There was so much that SJ still didn't know about her friends. This explained Zigferd's behaviour when Alice had gone missing.

"I did not know," SJ said as Dave burst into laughter at the news.

"If there is one person Darren didn't want as her guardian, it would be Zigferd. Hehe," Dave said.

Stop being mean, Dave, SJ thought.

"Sorry, it's just too funny," Dave gasped.

Darren and Zigferd's relationship had not started well, and it didn't seem to matter what Darren had done since. Zigferd always looked at him as though he was trouble. His continual reaction towards Darren now made complete sense, as he was so protective of Alice. The revelation threw SJ off.

She gathered her thoughts and responded, "Maybe this is a good thing. If you show how serious you are, maybe Zigferd will start coming around."

"And maybe he will turn into a were-bear and eat me," Darren replied.

The comment made Dave laugh even harder than before.

"Anyway. How did it go with Alice being able to set up the quest?"

Darren looked up. "It worked. She could configure it while in Asterfal."

"That's great news, at least," SJ said, smiling.

"Not sure there is much point in my staying in Killic now, though," Darren sulked.

"You don't know that for certain," SJ retorted.

"As if."

SJ wasn't going to entertain his melancholic mood any longer. "Get up."

"What?"

"I said get up."

Darren pushed his chair back and stood, turning to SJ. "What?"

SJ had been trying to think of something to say that would snap him out of his mood. Nothing came to mind, so she did the only thing that did: She slapped him across the face.

"Ow," Darren said, rubbing his cheek. "What was that for?"

"Feeling sorry for yourself. Stop being so stupid and pull yourself together. You're acting like an adolescent teenager. Not a grown man," SJ snapped.

The anger in SJ's voice took Darren by surprise. "S-sorry," he stammered.

"Now man up and put your big-boy pants on."

SJ was certain that Dave was rolling around the floor. He seemed to be struggling to even breathe, he was laughing so hard in her head. She could imagine a little robot doing cartwheels. SJ felt terrible after just slapping Darren and turned away. "I have things to do, so if you have finished feeling sorry for yourself, maybe you can give me a hand?"

"What do you need?"

"I need you to come and meet Cristy."

In the month since the attack on her, SJ had been so focused on her level that she had only briefly seen Cristy and had sworn that she would spend the day with her as soon as she reached Level 15. She wanted Darren to start teaching her archery. She knew she could take her to the cottage, but Darren was at a much higher level than Charlotte was.

"I know you have been to the fletcher's, and I need you to help pick a bow for her."

"Sure," Darren replied, looking a little happier with something to think about other than his predicament with Alice.

"Which bow do you suggest?" SJ asked Darren.

They were standing in the fletcher's shop. SJ had never visited before and was amazed at all the different styles and varieties of bows available to purchase. Cristy was keeping the fletcher busy by asking her many questions. Darren and Cristy had got on like a house on fire. Darren had been acting like the silly uncle and spoiling her rotten. SJ's inventory was currently full of toys and clothes Darren had bought for her. She could see that Cristy could get away with murder with Darren.

"This one," Darren said, picking a small bow from a stand. "It's an elven bow used for training."

Cristy had been experiencing a growth spurt for the last few weeks, and SJ was sure the gnoll had grown another six inches. Dave had explained the basics of gnoll growth, and it sounded like it was normal and would likely continue at this rapid pace until Cristy reached full size.

SJ took the bow from Darren. "What makes this so good?"

"You can vary the string tightness so it can be adjusted as she gets more proficient and stronger."

SJ noted the small screw-style thread at the base of the bow. The bow was two feet, about half the size of Darren's short bow that he used.

"Once she has the basics and grows a little taller, one of these would be better for her," he said, indicating an actual short bow approximately three feet, "before deciding if she wished to stay with short bows or move to longbows."

The longbows were massive and stood taller than SJ and Darren.

"Okay. What about arrows?" SJ asked. There was a selection of available arrows to choose from.

"For training, I would get bodkins. They are easier to remove from targets since they don't have barbs," Darren said.

SJ looked at the differing heads the arrows had until she found them. "What length?"

"Cristy needs to try the bow, and we can confirm. They must be a couple of inches longer than she can draw."

"Cristy?" SJ called.

"Yes?" Cristy said, walking over.

"Darren thinks this one is best for you," SJ said, handing her the bow.

Cristy took it, her eyes wide in awe. "Are you certain?" she said to Darren.

"Yes. This is best for you as you learn and also for your size. Titch," he finished, laughing.

Cristy kicked his ankle in response.

They had been bickering like this all day, and SJ just rolled her eyes.

"See how far you can pull the string back," SJ said.

Cristy got hold of the bow by its grip and then pulled the string back. It didn't go back very far.

"Here," Darren said as he adjusted the string tension. "Try again."

This time, Cristy pulled the string back much farther. "Perfect," Darren said as he selected the arrows she needed. "Now all you need is a quiver and to decide how you want to carry it."

"Carry it?" Cristy asked.

"Yes. My quiver is on my back, as you can see. You can get ones that sit on your belt."

"I want a back quiver like yours," Cristy answered excitedly.

"Do you have anything in her size?" Darren turned to ask the fletcher. SJ had never met her before and didn't know her name.

"Yes. Give me a moment," she said, walking through to the back of the shop.

After a few moments, she returned with a small quiver that Cristy put on. It fit her perfectly after a couple of strap adjustments. Darren had selected twenty arrows and dropped them into her quiver. Darren wore his bow across his shoulder most of the time, and SJ couldn't help but smile when she noticed Cristy copying Darren. She now had the look of a fledgling archer.

"How much?" SJ asked.

"I'll get it," Darren said.

"No. You have been conned out of enough today," SJ said, smiling.

Darren frowned.

"You realise you have bought Cristy everything she has asked for today?" SJ said.

SJ turned to the fletcher before he could respond.

"Fifty-eight copper," she said.

SJ had been expecting it to cost much more. "That sounds cheap?" SJ said.

"You are a councillor," the elf smiled.

SJ blushed at the comment. She hadn't been feeling much of a councillor recently. "Thank you," SJ said, feeling embarrassed.

The afternoon was spent at the training ground. SJ had asked Lorna to allow Darren to show Cristy the basics of archery. Cristy hung on his every word the whole time, and by late afternoon, she had begun to complain that her shoulder hurt. Darren had been really impressed with how she was doing and promised to bring her back in another couple of days.

SJ had taken the opportunity to perform some of her own training and, after finishing a punishing routine under Lorna's guidance, had been watching the pair.

"I think we need to get you home," SJ said as Darren fired a few arrows into the centre of the farthest target. His accuracy was uncanny.

"Probably best," Darren said, collecting his arrows.

After dropping Cristy back at the orphanage and unloading her inventory to the dismay of Madeline, who told them both off for spoiling the gnoll, SJ and Darren made their way to the inn to grab some food. They were walking along, talking casually, when Darren came to a standstill as a huge hand grabbed him on his shoulder, halting his movement.

"We need to talk," Zigferd said.

CHAPTER FIFTY

Mistake

SJ turned to look at Zigferd. Darren's eyes were wide with shock, fear, and panic. His casual humour and banter from the day disappeared in an instant. Darren turned to look at the huge man.

As Darren replied, his voice cracked, sounding rather squeaky. "What would you like to talk about?" he asked.

"You know exactly what I want to talk about!" Zigferd said in a very calm but serious tone. His tone was so flat that it even made SJ feel nervous. She had never seen him like this before. "Come with me," he finished, not removing his hand from Darren's shoulder.

Darren gulped as, without question, he allowed Zigferd to direct him. SJ was as shocked by the sudden appearance of Zigferd as Darren was, and as Zigferd began to direct Darren off, she spoke.

"I will join you," SJ said.

Zigferd didn't even turn and acknowledge SJ. "If you wish," he replied.

Zigferd escorted Darren down a couple of streets until they came out near the lake opposite the docks. SJ had been here once before with Setu, when they had travelled over from the docks back to town when it had been quarantined. The houses along this stretch were much larger than the ones in the town centre. Approaching one of the houses, Zigferd eventually took his hand from Darren's shoulder and directed him up the path. Zigferd then followed and, stepping by him, took out a key, opened the front door, and let him in.

The house was a two-storey building with an overgrown front garden.

"Is this yours?" SJ asked, never having been to Zigferd's home.

"Yes," Zigferd replied. "In here," he said, directing them into a lounge area at the front of the property. The room was sparsely furnished. It contained a sofa, a couple of armchairs, a small cluster of tables, and a bookcase.

Darren was looking pale now.

"Sit," Zigferd said.

Darren moved and sat on the sofa. Zigferd took one of the armchairs and dragged it so when he was sat down he was facing Darren.

"SJ, the kitchen is at the back. Would you mind getting some water?" Zigferd asked, not taking his eyes off Darren. Darren could not meet Zigferd's eyes, and he looked down.

Not wanting to leave the pair of them alone for long, SJ hurried down the hall into the kitchen, grabbed some glasses, and filled a pitcher of water before heading back. She hadn't heard anything being said. The tension in the air was palpable.

"Thank you," Zigferd said. He took a deep drink before placing his glass down. SJ poured one for herself and sat in another armchair, turning it slightly. She felt as though she was a referee between two prizefighters.

The silence continued for a few minutes on both sides, and Zigferd didn't drop his gaze.

"Do you mind?" Darren asked, his voice cracking and sounding dry as he grabbed a glass and poured himself some water. He drank deeply himself before nurturing the glass in his hands, still not meeting Zigferd's gaze.

SJ couldn't take it any longer; her nerves frayed. "Are you two going to talk? Or just sit in silence?"

Darren glanced at SJ, a deep-set fear in his eyes. Zigferd's gaze again didn't flinch from Darren. Shifting in his chair slightly, making it squeak under his considerable weight, Zigferd sat back a little and took a slow, deliberate breath. "I believe you have asked Alice to marry you."

Darren flinched. "I did."

"Think very carefully before you answer this next question," Zigferd said, still in a very calm and controlled tone. "Did you mean it?"

Darren sat upright, his eyes meeting Zigferd's for the first time since arriving, and with a single word, he replied, "Yes."

Zigferd took another long, deep, deliberate breath, closing his eyes as he did. Slowly exhaling, he opened his eyes again. "I am guessing you have absolutely no idea about the dryad culture?"

Darren dropped his gaze again. "No," he said meekly.

"You managed to put Alice in a very awkward position by asking her directly. It broke all the dryads' protocols that are expected to be followed," Zigferd replied.

"I'm sorry. I was unaware until SJ informed me this morning," Darren said.

SJ was struggling to read Zigferd, having never seen him in such a flat and controlled manner before.

"Do you realise what marriage means to a dryad?"

"I had assumed it would have the same meaning as marriage for anyone."

"Once a dryad gets married, it is for life. There is no turning back. A broken marriage for a dryad means death."

Darren's eyes shot open in shock. "What do you mean *death*?"

"When a dryad weds, their soul is split. If a marriage fails, then the dryad will lose half their soul, and most succumb to madness and eventually death," Zigferd replied, his face completely neutral.

"I didn't know!" Darren replied.

"So, I will ask you one more time. Did you mean it?"

Darren again did not hesitate. "Yes, I did. I wouldn't have asked her if I hadn't," he said adamantly.

Zigferd closed his eyes again and took another long breath. Pushing himself up from his chair, he stood and turned, leaving the room without saying a word. Darren and SJ glanced at each other. SJ shrugged, having no idea what was happening. Listening, they heard Zigferd climb the stairs. The pair sat in silence for several minutes, listening to Zigferd move about upstairs, opening and closing what sounded like a chest before he came back down the stairs and into the lounge area.

SJ and Darren were staring at Zigferd as he entered carrying a short staff intricately decorated with leaves and a design resembling vines running its length. At the staff's top was a claw-like grip holding a clear orb.

"You will need this," Zigferd said flatly, handing the staff to Darren.

Darren reached out and took hold of the staff, which was only about three feet. Zigferd didn't let go, and Darren's eyes met Zigferd's, which now contained a look that SJ couldn't describe. It wasn't anger, and it wasn't hatred. It was something much deeper and more meaningful than anything SJ had ever witnessed; a promise.

"If you hurt her, I will kill you," Zigferd said, releasing his grip on the staff and walking back out of the room.

With an uncertain look, Darren sat with his arm out, still holding the short staff. "What does this mean?"

"It means that Zigferd has granted him permission to ask Alice to marry officially," Dave said, yawning.

"What?" SJ said.

Darren turned to look at SJ, confused. "Dave just said it means you have been given permission to ask Alice to marry you," SJ said excitedly.

Darren's face instantly went through several changing emotions before he shouted, "YES." He jumped up from the seat.

"Now you just have to find her and ask her, offering her the staff. The staff offer means that her guardian, in this instance, has approved the proposal," Dave said.

"You now need to go and ask Alice officially and present her with the staff," SJ said, standing.

Darren turned and threw his arms around SJ, hugging her excitedly. The grin that had broken out on his face was contagious, and SJ couldn't help but grin back.

"No time like the present," he said, hurrying from the house.

SJ walked from the lounge and saw Zigferd down in the kitchen with his back to her. SJ walked down the hallway towards him. "Zigferd. Are you okay?"

SJ could see Zigferd's shoulders shuddering.

"Zigferd?" SJ asked again.

"Has he gone?" Zigferd asked.

"Yes," SJ said, turning to see the open front door Darren had left through.

Zigferd turned and looked at SJ, tears running down his cheeks.

"What's wrong?" SJ asked, panicking. Seeing the mountain of a lycanthrope crying as he did wasn't something she had ever expected to witness. Through all the hardship and trials she had seen, the mountain stood in front of her had always been stoic, the strength behind the town.

Zigferd wiped his eyes. "I never thought that I would see the day of Alice being asked to marry. It has come as a shock. I have brought Alice up since she was a youngling, and she has always dreamt of getting married. I am just a little emotional, that's all."

"I assume that Alice wants to marry Darren?" SJ asked.

"Yes. She mentioned not long after returning from the caves how she immediately felt about Darren and hoped he would be the one."

"Why did I think you wanted to kill Darren every time you saw him?"

"I didn't realise."

"You have put the fear of god into him."

Zigferd half smiled. "That's not a bad thing, then."

SJ couldn't help but smile in response. "No. I suppose not. It's better to keep him on his toes," she chuckled.

"I need to sort myself out. I have a meeting with Orik, Nevik, and Shelly this evening. We are discussing the first mithril batch."

"I will leave you to it, then, and allow you to compose yourself," SJ said.

"Thank you. Make sure that Darren understands that I meant what I said. If he hurts her, I will kill him," Zigferd again replied in a flat tone.

The sudden switch to his serious persona made SJ's hair stand up on the back of her neck. She knew that he meant it.

Leaving Zigferd, SJ headed to the inn. She wanted to speak to Floretta about the grapey fruits. It had been just over a month since she had first moved into the cottage, and Floretta had taken some of the grapey to begin producing some of the jerky. At this time of day, the inn was starting to receive the early usuals before the main thrum arrived a little later, once many of the stalls and shops had closed. It was always busy in the evenings.

"YOU CAN TELL THAT FOOL IF HE EVER DARKENS MY DOORWAY, I WON'T HOLD BACK FROM THE DAMAGE I WILL DO TO HIM," Kerys screamed. A tall, elegantly dressed man stood at the bar feeling Kerys's full wrath. Bert stood in his usual spot, not concerned about the ongoings. All the patrons were facing the bar, watching the interaction. SJ walked to the bar, standing just off from the berating. The look in Kerys's eyes was that of hatred.

"Kerys. Is everything alright?" SJ asked.

Ignoring the man she had yelled at, Kerys turned and noticed SJ, her face softening as she did. "Hi, SJ. No, everything is not alright. This pompous idiot thinks he can walk into my inn and threaten me."

"Threaten you?" SJ asked, shocked.

The man didn't even react to Kerys's flippant remarks.

"He is here on the guidance of a supposed complaint raised against my inn by the brewers' guild in Asterfal. Apparently, I have been selling illegal ale."

The statement baffled SJ. "How can you be selling illegal ale? Don't you brew your own?"

"Most, yes. I do purchase some ale from the local villages that we support."

"How can it be illegal, then?"

"They are accusing me of stealing trade secrets and saying that my ale is a stolen recipe that replicates the brewers' guild's traditional ale. I sell excess ale in Asterfal and have several bars which purchase it."

"I'm confused. If you are brewing your own ale, what makes them even consider it the brewers' guild recipe?"

"Nothing! It's that backstabbing idiot Fretun. He is playing dirty games, trying to damage my reputation and reduce my income. It's another one of his tactics to try to gain my recipe, after his failure to blow up my inn. If he causes enough damage to the inn's reputation, he believes that I will give up the secrets to stop the damage he is attempting to cause. I will have to go to Asterfal to meet my buyers and smooth things over. This not-so-kind gentleman has just told me that any further shipments to Asterfal will be prevented from entering the city until the accusation is investigated in full."

"Do you not fall under the town's trade arm?" SJ asked.

"I do."

"Isn't this an issue to be addressed through the councillor for trade, then?" SJ asked. She had, with the time around her levelling, been learning about all the various aspects that helped the town tick over. The infrastructure and workings of the town were very similar to what would be expected back on Earth. All the main areas were covered under the guidance and support of one or more councillors. There were departments in the barracks that oversaw each one. Housing, waste, magic, food, trade, professions, et cetera. It was a complex web of work, with many areas that overlapped each other.

SJ soon began to realise that her role as ambassador could cover all areas if an external party inquired.

"Can I ask who brought the charges?" SJ said, turning to the man. He wore perfectly tailored clothing, and his brilliant white shirt looked soft and luxurious.

The man looked SJ up and down. He wore small, circular glasses on the end of a long needle-like nose. His look turned to one of disgust.

"I have no business with you, fae," he said, turning back away from her toward Kerys.

"Oh no," Dave said.

"What did you just say?" SJ's tone was low and menacing. The instant anger from his comment sent her blood beyond boiling.

The man turned back to look at SJ. "Go away before you get hurt. I do not deal with your kind." He stood looking at her in a derogatory manner, sneering.

"My kind? Would you like to elaborate on what you mean?" SJ asked, her tone measured but still menacing.

"You know exactly what I mean by my statement," he said.

"Do you have a name?" SJ asked, speaking now through gritted teeth.

"I won't be telling you anything. I told you to go away."

"Who do you think you are to tell me to go away?"

"I am an official of Asterfal working within the guidance and remit of the binding unity of our region. You do not have the right to question me nor even speak to me unless I deem that I wish to speak to you. And I will not sully myself any further by talking to one of your kind."

Several in the inn gasped at his statement. The man didn't take his eyes off SJ.

SJ balled her fists the instant he finished speaking. Bert noticed SJ's reaction and started toward them. Kerys's eyes widened, and SJ was unsure if it was because she had equipped her claws or because of what the man had said.

"I suggest you think very carefully before you answer the next question I'm going to ask you," SJ said, almost hissing.

The man raised an eyebrow casually. "You realise the trouble you would be in if you attacked an official of Asterfal?" He showed no fear, glancing at her clawed hands.

"And do you realise that you have disgraced the city of Asterfal with your behaviour?"

"Ha. My behaviour. You think anyone in Asterfal cares about your kind?"

SJ had held her temper long enough. "MY KIND," she screamed.

The sudden change in tone made his eye twitch.

Sighing, the man turned back towards Kerys, ignoring SJ.

"HOW DARE YOU TURN AWAY FROM ME? DO YOU KNOW WHO I AM?"

The man glanced sideways at her as he replied shaking his head, "A disgusting excuse for a race."

SJ's emotions were already in turmoil because of her fear and elation for Darren, and to be spoken to in such a way by this man was too much. Her eyes flew, and her arm moved before she even realised what she was doing as she went to grab him, her other arm pulled back into a punching position, with the claws pointing menacingly at the man. As she did, Bert gripped her shoulder, preventing her from reaching him.

"Not inside, please, SJ," Bert said in a calm voice.

Turning, the man again looked at SJ in disgust and waved his hand. "I suggest you throw the trash out, and I would advise you attempt to get better clientele in the future," he said to Kerys.

"What's going on?" Alice said in a commanding voice as she entered the inn.

CHAPTER FIFTY-ONE

Highs and Lows

The man, hearing Alice, turned to face her. "Ahh, Alice, my dear. My intention was to come and see you. I hope you have been well. I missed you on your recent visit to Asterfal," he said, a smile now on his face.

Alice took in the scene before her. "I asked what's going on," she said in a deadpan tone.

"I would like to raise formal charges against this . . . this thing here," he said, waving at SJ dismissively. "She tried to attack me."

"And what reason did you give the ambassador to believe you deserved to be attacked?"

"She has no rights to even . . ." The man trailed off, his mouth opening in shock, as he looked at SJ and then back at Alice. "What did you just say?"

"Tirelle. I asked, why do you think our ambassador believes you deserve to be dealt with?"

"Ambassador?!" he spluttered.

"Yes. Ambassador."

"What?!" The man looked again from Alice to SJ and back again, the colour draining from his cheeks and his eyes wide in alarm.

Bert still had hold of SJ's shoulder firmly but not painfully.

"SJ, could you please be so kind as to allow me to speak to Tirelle?" Alice asked. "And maybe lose the claws," she smiled.

SJ hadn't taken her eyes off the man as she seethed at his comments, but she took a deep breath and relaxed her fists, exhaling deeply, and returning her claws to her inventory. Bert removed his hand from SJ's shoulder as she did.

"Thank you," Alice said. "Tirelle, I think you and I need to have a talk."

Tirelle's face had lost all colour, his previous bravado and contempt having been replaced with one of shock after Alice's comment.

"Let's go and sit," Alice said as she walked to the far end of the bar, away from any other patrons. Tirelle stood frozen for a moment before hurriedly turning and following her.

"Well, that was boring after all," Dave said.

I can't believe how he spoke to me, SJ thought.

"I told you before about how many feel about fae."

I know, but that level of hate is atrocious.

"I can understand how you feel. You have shown none of the behaviours of the fae. The problem is that many fae behave in a manner which damages their reputation. You are an anomaly of a fae, never mind of the System."

SJ looked over at Alice and Tirelle. Alice looked very animated, and the look on her face reminded SJ of when her mother used to scold her.

"Here," Kerys said, placing a glass of honey wine on the bar.

SJ picked up the glass and drank it nearly in one, then wiped her mouth. "Thanks."

Kerys gave SJ a wry smile. "I'm sorry," she apologised.

"You have nothing to be sorry about," SJ said.

"This wouldn't have happened if it wasn't for the situation with Malaki."

"Are you certain it's Malaki's doing?"

"It must be. There is no one else who has ever brought ill will against the inn."

Alice and Tirelle talked for several minutes before they both stood. Tirelle glanced briefly at SJ, then left the inn.

Alice walked over, sighing deeply. "Sorry. Tirelle is a fool. He is a lower officiate of Asterfal. He only holds a position because of his family name, not his ability."

"I don't care who he is. I have done all I can since being in town to build my reputation, and he thinks he can walk in here and speak to me the way he did," SJ said.

"Don't worry. I will ensure that his father is made aware of his behaviour. Belldon, his father, is a leading councillor for the trade emissary. Tirelle normally only deals with minor issues, as his own father doesn't trust him."

"Did he tell you of the accusation against Kerys?" SJ asked.

"Yes. Kerys, I know you won't have done anything wrong, but can I ask that you allow the investigation to take place?" Alice asked.

"Why should I even accommodate the accusation?" Kerys said.

"Tirelle wouldn't say who had raised the complaint, but by following the process, I can request the details of who made it and on what grounds," Alice said.

SJ still had so much to learn about the political landscape of Amathera, especially now she was an ambassador. The proposition seemed more daunting every time she thought about it.

"Have you seen Darren?" SJ asked.

"Not since we arrived back," Alice replied, sadness filling her eyes.

"Oh!" was all SJ could respond. She was bubbling with hidden excitement, knowing what would come.

Kerys poured them both another honey wine, and they walked over to an empty table, where they caught up on what had been happening since Alice had been away and the outcome of the tax levy.

Ptolemy appeared on the small stage not long after, and his music filled the bar as more of the evening patrons arrived. Alice had excused herself to go talk to one of the merchants she had meant to catch up with that afternoon. SJ saw Darren enter the inn. Spotting her, he walked straight over, looking distraught.

"I can't find her anywhere," he said glumly.

"Try looking over there," SJ said, pointing to the far side of the bar where Alice sat with her back to him.

His eyes shot open, and he had a huge grin on his face that disappeared as the colour drained from his cheeks.

"What's wrong?" SJ asked.

"What if she says no?"

"Just tell him to go ask her already," Dave huffed.

"You'll never know unless you ask her," SJ said, smiling at him.

Darren stood nervously, fidgeting as he processed what he should do. "Okay," he replied.

He walked towards the stage rather than where Alice was sitting

What's he doing? SJ thought.

"No idea. Whatever it is, if she doesn't say yes, I think he will die of embarrassment," Dave replied.

Darren stood now talking to Ptolemy, who was playing a tune. SJ saw Ptolemy smile, and as he finished playing, he coughed loudly.

"Friends and strangers alike, could I have your attention for one minute, please?" Ptolemy said, even his normal voice melodic.

Several in the bar turned to look at him.

"What is it, Ptolemy?" one of the regular orcs called.

"Darren here would like to say a few words," Ptolemy said before he stepped aside, and Darren took to the small stage.

Silence began to fall across the bar, and SJ glanced at Alice and saw she had noticed him standing on the stage; her eyes were wide.

"Hello, everyone. I know I don't know many of you well, if at all, and before I start, I would like to apologise for the issues I have caused Kerys and her inn since I arrived in Killic. I am glad to see that everything is back as it was, if not better."

One of the patrons shouted, "We can't all be born idiots," to which several laughed.

Darren's cheeks reddened with embarrassment before he coughed and said, "I have a song I would like to sing." Reaching towards Ptolemy, he took his lute and began to pluck the strings. SJ sat staring at Darren as he transformed from a nervous, embarrassed wreck to someone she could tell had performed on stage. Remembering what Darren had mentioned about how he had died, SJ couldn't take her eyes off him as he began to play.

"This is for you, Alice," he said, and soon SJ recognized "All of Me" by John Legend.

The patrons were silent as Darren sang with confidence and composure. SJ, caught up in the moment, glanced constantly between Darren and Alice, whose cheeks had reddened.

Kerys had not been in the bar when he had made his statement, so when she returned from the cellar, she walked over to where SJ sat and whispered, "What does he think he is doing?"

SJ turned and looked at Kerys's hard-lined face, which was filled with animosity towards Darren. "Proposing," SJ said with a huge grin.

"WHAT?" Kerys said much louder than she meant to, getting a couple of the regulars to turn around and hiss *shhh* at her.

Kerys stood now, watching Darren perform. He wasn't as proficient on the lute as Ptolemy, but the music came across well. As he struck the last chord, Darren ended with "Alice, will you marry me?"

You could have heard a pin drop as silence filled the bar. Everyone turned to look at Alice. They all knew her. She was one of the most popular beings in the town, highly respected and trusted by many. Darren handed the lute to Ptolemy and got down on one knee, called the short staff from his inventory, and held it towards her.

Alice held her exceedingly red cheeks in her hands, cupping her face as she stared open-mouthed at Darren and the staff he now held.

"What's your answer, Alice?" called the same orc from before.

Silence ensued for several more moments, and tears appeared in Alice's eyes. As they began to flow down her cheeks, she said, "Yes."

The bar exploded in hooting and cheers. Alice stood and walked over to where Darren still knelt. Reaching out, she placed her hand on the staff, around Darren's hand.

"Looks like we needn't have worried about the quest for Darren after all," Dave said.

SJ could feel tears on her cheeks as she sat there, grinning from ear to ear.

The next few hours disappeared in a haze. The drink began to flow, and Ptolemy began to play again. It was not long after that Nexis arrived and joined him on the stage. Alice and Darren had come and joined SJ at her table, and well-wishers came and went as the evening wore on. SJ drank much more than she usually would. Darren got up to join Nexis and Ptolemy on the stage. As they sang, SJ checked her display. It was already getting late, and she had stayed in Killic later than she had for weeks, apart from the one evening when the inn reopened fully.

"I need to head home," SJ said to Alice.

"Thank you," Alice said. Leaning over, she gave SJ a hug. Alice had been on the honey wine as well, and the pair of them were a little tipsy.

"Say bye to Darren for me," SJ said, standing.

"Will do." Alice smiled.

SJ left the inn, turned, and headed out of the town centre towards the cottage. The night sky was bright with a cloudless sky and a full moon. SJ swayed as she walked down the street. "That was fun," SJ said, hiccupping.

"It was okay," Dave replied.

"What do you mean *okay?* Two of our friends just got engaged."

"I'm happy for them. I'm just feeling left out, seeing you all have so much fun when I'm stuck watching it all unfold and can't partake."

SJ had never considered how Dave might have wished to be a part of the evening as it unfolded. It was strange, considering they were two of the same person. SJ could experience everything first hand while Dave was stuck watching from above.

"I never gave it a thought. Sorry, Dave." SJ said.

"It's not your fault," Dave replied, sighing.

She turned the last corner, the cottage lay just ahead of her—a welcome sight. As she reached the gate, she stumbled almost toppling over it.

"Careful," Dave said.

SJ giggled, the fresh air having hit her now she was outside, adding to her intoxication.

She stood upright, and reached for the gate latch as a blade penetrated her back. Half collapsing, half falling, she fell over the gate, her momentum and weight carrying her into a forward roll. The blade that had struck her dug in further.

SJ cried in pain as she tried to understand what had just happened.

"Throwing knife," Dave shouted. "Get up and get inside now. It's that Level 19—he's coming!"

Panic filled SJ's foggy mind as she scrambled to her feet, and she staggered forward before losing her balance and falling down face first. She climbed to her feet again as she heard the gate open behind her. She did not look back—just tried to make it to the front door so she could get inside and lock out whoever was attacking her. Fear coursed through her veins as a voice spoke behind her.

"Sorry, SJ."

The next blade caused her body to convulse as it entered her back aligned with her heart.

Precognition triggered—cool-down 24 hours

As the cold steel of the blade penetrated her body, her knees gave way, and SJ fell forward, cracking her head on the stone step of the cottage. The last thing she saw before losing consciousness was her display flashing.

You are suffering from the effects of bleed. Health will be lost over time until healed.

"WAKE UP," Dave was screaming in her mind.

SJ came to. She was lying on the ground, her neck at a painful angle where her forehead had hit the stone step. Pain radiated from the points where the blades had struck her, and she groaned as she moved her arms.

"Thank the gods. At least they left, thinking you were dead," Dave said.

SJ couldn't think straight. She slowly pushed herself to her knees, leaning heavily on her hands. Lifting one hand, she could feel the free-flowing blood from her cut head. Her display flashed precariously. She had two hit points left, ticking down and back up as she lost health and regained it.

"Your precognition and dragon blood kept you alive. You should have died from that attack, if not from the initial blow, then from the bleed effect. Only gods know how it missed your heart," Dave said.

Slowly climbing to her feet, SJ fumbled in her pocket for the cottage key before entering, then locking the door behind her. As soon as she did, she collapsed to the floor again. Her breath was coming in short gasps, and she knew her lung had been punctured. The blade had entered her back at an angle and should have pierced her heart.

SJ opened her inventory, calling the potion of regeneration to her hand. Her hands shook violently as she pulled the stopper from the vial and drank. The effects of the potion began to work almost immediately. Her health increased rapidly, her breathing eased, and she felt the cut on her forehead stitch together, the skin feeling stretched and taut as it did. The healing didn't remove the pain from the wound, and the potion effects wore off as her health reached 50 percent. Looking at her display, her health was still ticking down from the bleed effect and back up from her dragon blood.

Pushing herself back to her feet, moaning loudly, she grimaced. "Did you see who it was? They said my name."

"No. They were fully hidden again in cloaks. I think I recognise the voice, though," Dave said nervously.

"Who?" SJ hissed.

"I am not sure I should say, just in case I am wrong."

"WHO?" SJ said with anger.

"I think it was Greb."

"What?" SJ said, surprised and confused.

"It sounded like Greb. He has a subtle lisp on his *s*'s, and when he said sorry, it sounded like him."

"Why would Greb attack me? I thought we were friends."

"If it was him, I can only imagine one reason," Dave replied.

"What reason?"

"An oath."

CHAPTER FIFTY-TWO

Secrets

Even after the regeneration potion, the bleed effect wouldn't stop. SJ needed to find a healer. There had been several in the inn celebrating Alice and Darren's engagement, but Lythonian was closer.

"I am going to see Lythonian," SJ said.

"I wouldn't go outside yet. Whoever attacked will not have received any experience for a kill, so they may come back. Luckily, you were only unconscious for a few moments, and they probably expected that the bleed effect would take some time to finish you. Whichever skill or weapon they used is potent to continue doing the damage it is doing. There are few who could have survived without your dragon blood."

"I can't stay like this."

"Why? You won't die. Your dragon blood will keep you alive. You can wait as long as you need."

"If I stay here and they do come back to investigate, I will be trapped inside."

"It's better to be inside than out on the street."

There were no visible signs of injury left from the attacks, but the bleeding effect still attempting to finish her was exhausting. Steadying herself on the edge of the table, she took a seat.

"I can't stay here. I need healing. I can't even think straight." SJ's head was spinning with the potential of it being Greb who had attacked her. This was the first time since the initial attack that she had returned to the cottage after dark, having stayed in the inn the last time she was in town. Now that she was sober, even with the pain from the wound in her back, she could make it to the inn in a minute or two easily.

"If you are going to leave, fly," Dave said.

SJ hadn't considered flying and on hearing Dave's comments shrank. The sharpness of the sensation that flooded her back was nearly unbearable, and she cried in pain as the transformation was completed. As they began to beat, her wings sent pulses like electric shocks coursing through her body. It was the safest way, she knew. She flew into the kitchen, knowing that the window was open, and left immediately, rising into the night sky.

Flying over buildings to the rear garden of the inn, she swooped down to land, growing as she touched the ground. Her back flared in protest, her lungs feeling as though they were being squeezed, and she fell forward to her knees, gasping. There were several in the inn garden, and a couple stared at her.

"Are you okay?" A goblin she recognised as a relative of Setu stood from a bench and walked over.

"No. I need a healer," SJ said, grimacing.

He looked at her with raised eyebrows before walking into the rear of the inn. A couple of others had come over to her and helped her to one of the benches, where she now sat doubled over, leaning on her knees. Her breathing was difficult, and she wasn't sure if the regeneration potion had repaired her lung or whether it was from using her wings. A couple of minutes passed before Sven arrived.

He was dressed in casual clothes. SJ didn't recognise him at first.

"SJ," he said.

"Bleed effect," SJ hissed.

"Okay." Placing his hand on her shoulder, he began to cast. A brilliant white light emitted from his hand. The light made the surrounding area look as bright as day. SJ watched as her health increased again, and it felt as if her lung was being reinflated, it was obvious from the sensation that the potion hadn't healed it fully. After several moments, the rush of power reached her mind, and she felt like she had been injected with adrenaline.

"Thank you, Sven. I owe you again," SJ said.

"No need for thanks," he said, looking concerned. "What happened?"

"I was attacked when I returned to the cottage. It's the first time I have been out at night in Killic since."

SJ could see the anger on Sven's face. "We need to find the culprit."

"I need to speak to Darren. Sven, are you able to sober him?" SJ said, standing and rolling her shoulders, her back no longer throbbing.

"I can," Sven said.

"Good. Do you mind waiting here for a moment?" Walking into the inn, she found Darren sitting with Alice at the same table they had shared earlier. Alice noticed SJ and frowned.

"I thought you had gone home," Alice said, slurring slightly.

Darren turned to look at her, a huge grin on his face. His eyes looked glazed, and he was drunk.

"I'm sorry to disturb you but must speak to you both. Is that okay?"

Darren smiled. "Sure. Come and sit. We can talk."

"No. Not here. Outside, please," SJ said, indicating to the inn garden.

They looked at each other, shrugged, and stood to follow SJ as she wove back through the throng to the garden. Sven was still outside.

"Sven, do you mind?" SJ asked.

As Sven approached Darren, who frowned at him, he reached out and placed his hand on his arm. The brilliant white erupted in moments, and Darren's eyes began to clear.

"Wow," Darren said as his head cleared. "I can start again now," he said, laughing.

"No. I need your help," SJ said.

Alice looked unsteady on her feet, and Sven repeated the exercise with Alice, removing the alcohol from her system with his magic. Once the pair of them were sober, SJ told them what had happened.

"I'm sorry for ruining your evening," SJ finished.

Darren was first to respond. "I'm going to go to the cottage and see if there is a trail."

"Don't go alone," SJ said.

"I will be fine," Darren said, calling his bow from his inventory and hurrying from the garden.

"Are you okay?" Alice asked, concerned.

"I wish I knew why I've become someone's target." SJ had not told them who she believed may be the suspect, only asked Darren to see if there were any tracks. She didn't want to start passing any information without confirming the details.

"I didn't see Greb inside," Dave said.

Alice and SJ sat on one of the benches. Sven had returned inside to leave them to their conversation.

"It must be to do with Asterfal," Alice said.

"Why? I have never been there. I know no one from Asterfal."

It was well after midnight when Darren returned.

"There was a trail. It leads to a building south of town," Darren said.

"Did you see anyone?"

"No. It enters the building and stops. It wasn't easy to track. Whoever it was had trails all over town. It took me a while to find the correct one."

"Okay. Thanks, Darren."

"Not at all." He smiled. "I thought you might know who it is, Alice, if you want to come with me?"

Alice stood immediately. "We need to make sure SJ is safe first. I am going to speak to Kerys."

Alice disappeared inside again and eventually returned, and SJ was made to stay in Kerys and Fhyliss's private quarters. Fhyliss had finished as the bar had quietened, and many patrons were now beginning to leave the inn. Once SJ was secured upstairs in the relative safety provided by the number of patrons and people who stayed at the inn, Alice accompanied Darren.

SJ was lying on the sofa in the quarters. Fhyliss had provided her with a blanket.

I wish I wasn't stuck here, SJ thought.

"Better being safe than vulnerable on the street," Dave said.

I don't like others putting themselves in danger.

"Darren is at Level 20, and Alice is even higher. They are more than capable of looking out for themselves."

It still doesn't feel right.

SJ couldn't sleep and lay on the sofa trying to work out what she had done to end up as someone's target. As the morning sun's first light began to shine through the room's windows, SJ heard footsteps and a knock on the door. Kerys had returned upstairs a couple of hours before and had excused herself to sleep after chatting to SJ.

SJ stood and walked to the door. "Who is it?"

"It's me, SJ," Alice's voice replied.

SJ let her in and asked nervously, "Did you find anything?"

"Yes. We have the culprit in custody. He has confessed to the attempted assassinations."

"Who is it?" SJ asked.

"I am not sure how to tell you this, but it was . . ."

"Greb," SJ finished her sentence.

Alice's eyes opened in shock. "Yes. How did you know?"

"When he attacked me, he said, *Sorry, SJ*. I wasn't sure then, but I thought I recognised it as Greb's voice. Did you find out why?"

"Yes. Ballentine and Lorna have been questioning him, and he broke under their pressure. It is safe to say he will not be causing you any further problems."

SJ frowned. "What happened?"

"I won't go into details as it wasn't pleasant. His oath was very strict, and as he broke it, he suffered the consequences."

SJ gasped. "Is he dead?" She dreaded to think what they had done to Greb to make him confess. Witnessing Lythonian's reaction while talking about Bellakiy's family was frightening enough to make her understand an oath's power.

"No. He isn't dead. His mind has been left broken, though. He will be lucky to speak again. Master Rui has been called to treat him with his alchemical solutions, and I believe Lythonian will be spoken to today as well. Master Rui didn't sound hopeful."

"Did you find out the reason?"

"Yes. Unfortunately, that is where it affects you."

"What have I done that has caused someone to attack me?"

Alice looked weary, and it was obvious she hadn't slept since learning about SJ's attack. By the sounds of it, none of them had. SJ ushered Alice over to the sofa to sit down.

"It's not your fault, but unfortunately, because of the System changes, you have ended up as the target."

"I don't understand. Why?"

"It stems from politics, and this attack appears to be based on fear."

"Fear?!" SJ said. "Why would someone from Asterfal fear me?"

"They don't fear you. They fear what you stand for. Asterfal is the strongest city in the south of the continent. It has built its reputation around its strength and control of what occurs within the south. Killic has always been a small but well-respected town, and over the years, our relationship has allowed us to bring sway to several decisions. We have gained the trust and support of varicus councillors in Asterfal. This relationship recently supported the tax levy negotiations, which I briefly alluded to last night.

"The problem is because of the influence we have as a town already. Someone within the council is fearful that as the town grows, the balance of power could shift from Asterfal to Killic. The easiest way for them to limit the town's growth is to dispose of you."

SJ sat, mouth open at Alice's words. At no point had she ever considered that her position as a Legionnaire and the System's adaptation of allowing Killic to grow as she did would bring such danger to her doorstep. Never mind a potential direct threat against Killic. She had seen it as an opportunity for all to grow and develop. Never to challenge Asterfal.

"I thought Asterfal was huge in comparison?"

"It is. The fear of what will happen over time has driven someone to begin this course of action."

"But it would take Killic years to grow its population, and potentially that long for me to reach a level that allows Killic to even be considered a rival of Asterfal."

"Perhaps. They are also aware of the mithril mine. We had thought that the knowledge of it had been controlled well enough. Unfortunately, with Greb being one of the affected parties, whoever he has been working for in Asterfal is now aware. That now brings a direct threat against the town if the knowledge spreads farther afield. As you say, we are still a small town; our population is less than four thousand."

SJ did not know that it was even that large. "Do you know who he was working for?"

"No. He broke as he tried to reveal a name." Alice's head dropped forward, a look of shame on her face.

"What's wrong?"

"What Greb went through is one of the hardest things I have ever witnessed."

SJ shuddered thinking of what may have been done to him; she did not like the possibilities.

"What do you need me to do?" SJ felt the need to help in any way that she could. Whether Alice or others blamed her or not, she had triggered the potential future impact on Killic. She loved the town and the beings who lived here. Dread filled SJ at the thought of her friends being targeted because of her.

"Nothing currently. The most important thing is that you remain safe. How many know of Farleck Cottage?"

SJ had never publicised where she lived, but several knew about it: Gladys, Hubert, Lythonian, Zej, Husa, Kerys, Fhyliss, Floretta, Zigferd, Alice, Darren, Fran, Gary, Setu. SJ reeled off the names of those she could think of. "There may be more. Possibly Jacob and Greta. I'm not sure." SJ frowned.

"Well, that is a start, at least," Alice replied.

"A start for what?" SJ was concerned by the statement.

"Secrecy. If we are going to keep you safe in the future, we will have to keep your cottage as quiet as possible. Greb was questioned and was not aware. There had been no other attack before last night because you had always been back at Farleck Cottage. Greb had observed the cottage in town regularly and not worked out where you were going. A new oath is going to be created, and all those who know about Farleck will be asked to take it. If they don't, I am unsure what we will do with them yet, but Zigferd's response wasn't very positive."

"Zigferd is aware already?"

"He was involved last night, yes."

The thought of the damage and challenges she might bring to the town was huge, and SJ put her head in her hands, staring at the ground. "I am so sorry," SJ eventually replied.

"None of this is your doing. It is the System and those who are fearful of change."

"If we don't know who is responsible in Asterfal, what does that mean?"

"I'm not sure yet. We have a lot to discuss and work through. Zigferd has yet to decide whether he should inform the council."

"He has to, doesn't he?"

"Not unless a direct threat to Killic is known of. We have confirmation of why you were attacked. It still doesn't mean Killic is currently directly within their sights."

"I can't remain an ambassador for Killic if I am a threat to the town," SJ said.

"You most definitely can," Alice replied firmly. "If anything, it strengthens your position as the ambassador and shows your meaning and true town position. It is not known widely that you are Killic's ambassador, but with your position known, an attack on an official would be the same as an attack on the town. I doubt that whoever ordered Greb knew that you were. Otherwise, they are likely to have tried a more subtle approach rather than direct assassination."

"Subtle?"

Alice coughed nervously. "Poison, et cetera, could have been passed off as an illness rather than a death because of an attack."

"Can you think of anyone in Asterfal who would be that fearful of Killic growing in strength?"

"Several, unfortunately."

"Can anything be done to confirm who it may be?"

"I have contacts who can do some digging and pay more attention to certain information. Our best option is you. You are an assassin, after all."

"WHAT?!" SJ said in surprise.

"If it comes down to it, and we have to, we will remove the threat. We had no thought of ever challenging Asterfal, but only time will tell what the future brings," Alice said, looking ahead thoughtfully.

SJ groaned, having gone from the elation of the previous evening to the sudden realisation that she was a catalyst in a wider scheme. She felt like a very small fish in a very big pond that was potentially full of sharks.

"If Asterfal is aware of the mithril mine, what will they do?" SJ asked.

"I am not sure the chancellor is aware of the mine yet. If he was, I am sure he would have contacted Zigferd by now. Asterfal only has two mines from which it gets revenue. To my knowledge, one is nearly empty. The priority for Killic now is defence. We require walls to be constructed and the crag entrance controlled. They must be our focus."

"Won't the council challenge them? They have resisted expansion already."

"Once we begin to see the mithril revenue, I can guarantee that most, if not all, the council will want to protect the revenue stream."

"I need to get as strong as I can as fast as possible," SJ said with conviction.

"Actually, you don't," Alice replied, facing SJ and smiling weakly

"Why not?"

"If you reach Level 20 and the borders expand again before we have other elements in place, we will end up being even more vulnerable."

Shock registered on SJ's face. She hadn't considered the implication of her continued levelling, even after what they had spoken about. All she could think of was growing in strength to support and defend the town and herself if need be.

Alice registered the look on SJ's face and smiled at her. "It doesn't stop you levelling. It just means that we must consider your growth alongside the town's capabilities directly in the future. None of us were aware of this until you levelled. It is something everyone must consider."

CHAPTER FIFTY-THREE

A Binding Oath

I am not sure where to start," Dave said once Alice had left.

You're telling me, SJ thought. Fhyliss was up, busy getting ready for work.

"I hadn't considered that somewhere like Asterfal would take an issue with one of its towns growing. Most cities would have jumped at the chance of recognition through town growth, never mind the increased income from taxes. These circumstances are strange."

I am not sure what I should do. I want to level, but as Alice said, if I reach Level 20 and they aren't ready for it, I could cause significant harm to the town. We already have a Level 31 wyvern in the mountains to the northeast. If I reach Level 20, what is going to come next?

"It's not so much what will come next after levelling. It is more about what is going to happen next. These System changes are still an unknown." Dave sighed.

You still have not managed to do anything with your code yet?

"No. I have a further 217.3 sextillion combinations to run through on the algorithm lock. So it could be now or in a while." Dave laughed.

The thought of one sextillion alone freaked SJ out. She did not know how fast Dave could perform computations or how long each check took.

That's a lot.

"I did say before it's a doozy."

Do you have any ideas on what I can do? Alice mentioned remaining as ambassador, but all I see is that it makes me a larger target.

"Politically, from what Alice said, it makes sense to remain as the ambassador. She was right in her interpretation that if everyone knew, then it is very unlikely a direct attack or attempt on your life would happen. It is not unheard of, just unlikely."

That doesn't make me feel any better. I'm not even sure who I can trust. I classed Greb as a friend. Not close like others but still a friend, and he was under orders to assassinate me.

"It does raise concern. Hopefully, the creation of a specific oath that beings swear to can remove any concerns."

Can it, though? Racial oaths can outstrip another oath. The town oath is only as strong as someone staying in the territory. I am unsure if anything can be done to guarantee my safety. It fills me with dread.

Dave cleared his throat before he answered. "Trying to look at it from a neutral perspective, there are never guarantees. The world is an unsafe place—all worlds are. Look back at what happened to you on Earth, being squished by a tree. You never know what is around the next corner, but it can't stop you from living the life you wish to lead. You have to make the most of what is available to you, and you have so much. Your relationships with many in Killic are beyond any I have ever witnessed in my millennia as an administrator. You are special, SJ, and you can't let this incident stop you. You must have resilience and fortitude to overcome adversity."

SJ sat silently, contemplating Dave's words. He was right, after all. A tear formed in the corner of her eye. The single drop rolled down her cheek, hanging from her chin with determination before it dripped onto the knee of her dress. SJ watched as the damp spot disappeared as the dress repaired it.

Thank you, Dave. Whatever happens in the future, I know that I have the best friend anyone could ask for.

Dave sniffed. "I will always be here for you. Always. Remember that."

SJ's display triggered.

Synchronisation:	25%

That's gone up a lot, SJ thought.

"It has steadily increased since we first noticed it," Dave replied. "I don't know what it signifies. I asked the adjudicators, and they didn't know, so I asked the System, and they didn't respond."

Why would the System not answer?

"The only conclusion I can come up with is that they don't know themselves."

"SJ. You look terrible," Fhyliss said, walking from her room dressed for the morning shift in the bar.

"Thanks," SJ said, laughing.

"You didn't sleep, did you?"

"No. And knowing what I do now, I am not sure I even could."

"We need to remedy that, then," Fhyliss said as she returned to her bedroom. A minute later, she returned carrying a small bottle. "Here. Drink this."

"What is it?" SJ asked.

"Poison," Dave said, laughing sarcastically.

Not funny! SJ thought.

"It's a sleeping remedy. I use it for nights when the inn stays open, and I have an early shift, so I need sleep."

SJ uncorked the bottle. It smelt of marzipan, sickly sweet. SJ couldn't help but feel nervous, especially after Dave and his sarcasm.

"I promise it won't harm you," Fhyliss said, smiling.

SJ couldn't sense any danger, so she took a drink from the bottle.

"It takes a few minutes to work, but soon you will sleep like a gnomling. I will come and check on you later," Fhyliss said. "I better go." Fhyliss left to go downstairs.

The liquid tasted sweet, and SJ felt like her head was much lighter. Her whole body relaxed. The nervous tension she had been holding on to dissipated, and as it did, she lay back on the sofa. Her eyes began to feel heavy, and she allowed them to close.

Wake me in a few hours, please, Dave, she thought moments before sleep took her.

When Dave awoke SJ several hours later, she panicked, equipping her claws and sitting bolt upright.

"There is no one here. Don't worry," Dave said, sounding concerned.

"Sorry. I had horrible dreams," SJ said. She had been dreaming about being attacked again, and whenever she thought she was safe, another of her friends came at her. Her dress stuck to her skin, its self-cleaning function not even keeping the sweat away while she slept.

"You didn't sleep well. You tossed and turned the whole time."

"Could you see my dreams?"

"No. I can only read your thoughts while you're awake."

Standing, SJ could feel her dress beginning to dry as it was cleaned of her sweat. That was at least one positive from everything that had been happening.

"Darren came to see you while you slept, but Kerys sent him away again before she went to work."

"Did he say where he would be?"

"No. Sorry."

SJ headed down to the bar. Looking at the room below her as she walked down the broad stairs, it was the same as always: laughter, drinking, singing, and eating. Nothing appeared different, but SJ knew that for her, nothing would ever feel the same again. As her eyes moved around the patrons there, she knew many of them by name and recognised all of them. The problem was whether one of them would be her next "visitor." She shuddered at the thought.

"You need to try to not let it affect you," Dave said.

Easier said than done, SJ thought.

Kerys saw SJ coming down the stairs, smiled broadly at her, and began to pour her a mug of coffee. Sitting on a bar stool, SJ took the mug and, inhaling the bitterness, drank.

"How are you today?" Kerys asked. "When I got up, you didn't look very settled."

"I am not sure," SJ said honestly.

"Understandable, under the circumstances," Kerys replied, nodding. "Darren stopped by and asked you to see the mayor once you were awake."

"Thanks. I will go over once I have drunk this."

"Do you not want any food?"

"I am not sure I could stomach any at the moment."

Kerys smiled. "Let me know if you change your mind."

SJ finished her drink and left the inn. Walking outside into the afternoon sun was like any other typical day in Killic. The town square was busy with the usual traders. Customers moved around, talking and bartering. Nothing looked or felt different from what SJ had got used to since she had arrived. Beings she knew called greetings to her as she passed. She responded with fake smiles and nods of appreciation.

The problem was that everywhere she looked, she began to question, *What if? Could they?*

"You need to stop," Dave said, concern in his voice. "Until last night, you loved walking around town. Always wittering away in your head about some of the inanest things. Today, you are so paranoid it's frightening."

Sorry. I just can't help it, SJ thought.

"You need to remember that apart from one person, everyone here is the same as before. You can't allow yourself to be overrun like this. Get control of your own thoughts."

Says the AI reading mine!

"Okay. Get control of our thoughts, because you are concerning me," Dave said sternly. "If you carry on with this paranoia, you will send yourself crazy."

On arriving at the barracks, SJ went straight to Zigferd's office. Zigferd stood from behind his desk and came to meet her.

"I am so sorry," Zigferd said, concern etched on his face.

"For what?" SJ frowned.

"For what has happened."

"You can't control the actions of others."

"Please. Come and sit." Zigferd offered SJ one of the chairs as they entered his office. "How are you?"

"Honestly, I don't know. Everywhere I look, I am now questioning the truth," SJ said.

Zigferd's brow furrowed at her comment, a clear sign of the worry he held. "Alice informed me of those who you believe know about Farleck Cottage. All have been asked to come to the barracks shortly. We have a written oath that we'll request all agree to and sign."

"Do you think an oath will be enough to keep the cottage secret? I said to Alice that I may have told others."

"It's a starting point. You are the most important being in the town. We must keep you safe at all costs. You will allow Killic to flourish and become a better town."

A rush of emotions hit SJ— above all else, the dread that settled in her stomach that the town relied on her growth.

"Am I not just painting a target on Killic?" SJ said, clasping her hands nervously.

"If you mean will your existence and the progression of Killic be down to you? The simple answer is yes and no in equal measure. You may have triggered the territory and border amendments but didn't trigger the mithril mine. The mithril mine, above all else, will draw unwanted attention. Now that others outside of Killic could know about it, we need to begin our plans to expand and control our borders."

SJ sat in silence, contemplating Zigferd's comments. She had made so many friends since arriving, and even now, sitting with Zigferd in his office, she held on to a nervous tension. He had been like a father figure since her arrival. His strength and resolve always provided a sense of security for the town.

It was sometime later that those SJ had named arrived at the barracks; they were shown upstairs to the council chambers, which, for many, was the first time they had ever been there. Zigferd sat at the top of the table, and as they arrived, they were asked to sit and drinks were served. The last to arrive was Alice, accompanied by Nexis. SJ had never mentioned Nexis to Alice as a being who knew about the cottage, which surprised her. Knowing that he was a god, she hadn't even considered him a threat.

With Nexis joining them, the council table was almost full. Several around the table sat nervously, wondering why they had been called here. Most, upon seeing SJ, smiled fondly at her.

"I believe that is the last of our planned arrivals," Zigferd said as Alice closed the council chamber doors and sat at the far end of the table opposite Zigferd and SJ. "Some of you will already know why you are here, and others will not, so first, I need to explain why I have requested you all to attend."

Zigferd spent the next few minutes explaining the occurrences of the previous evening. Several around the table stared in shock at what had happened to SJ. Those who already knew sat with hard expressions of anger on their faces as Zigferd relayed the events. Even though SJ hadn't spoken to Zigferd directly about the attack, he was aware of everything SJ had explained to Alice and was also present at Greb's interrogation. He expanded on the findings from Greb and the reasons behind the attack.

The details caused several to react angrily, but the deepest-set look was that of fear. Even Hubert sat with a concerned expression, and Gladys looked downright terrified.

Only Nexis sat calmly through the proceedings, at no point changing his neutral yet pleasant expression.

"In conclusion, we have to maintain SJ's safety, and to do so, those who are aware of where she lives are being asked to take an oath that will ensure that Farleck Cottage remains a secret."

"Wouldn't she be safer staying in the town?" Kerys asked.

"The two times she was attacked were in town, and without providing her with a permanent escort or guard, we couldn't guarantee her protection. At least with her cottage, she has a place away from town, and with her followers who do not sleep, she has a guard always on watch at Farleck," Zigferd said.

SJ hadn't even considered Charlotte, Brian, and Terence, and now feared they could become future targets. It was true that they never slept and would always be on guard while she was there, but she didn't like relying on others for her safety. SJ could feel the mounting pressure that rested on her shoulders. All those who now sat in the chamber were either very close or very good friends.

"To alleviate any future threat and to maintain the secrecy of where SJ lives, we have written a new oath that I would ask that you all agree to today," Zigferd said as he unrolled a parchment that lay on the table.

"Does anyone object to agreeing to a new oath of secrecy?" Alice asked.

SJ glanced around the table nervously. No one spoke in objection.

"I have one question." Nexis spoke. He had maintained silence since the commencement of the proceedings, and everyone was now turning to look at him.

"Please," Alice said.

"May I?" Nexis asked as he reached for the parchment that Zigferd had unrolled.

"Of course," Zigferd said as Nexis picked it up.

Holding the parchment in his hand, Nexis read the oath and raised an eyebrow.

"Why do you believe this oath will prevent people from speaking of SJ or divulging her secrets? Have you not proven that a being may be forced to comply?"

Zigferd's cheeks reddened at the comment, the colouration not going unnoticed by SJ, meaning that he may have been directly involved in whatever had happened to Greb to make him break his oath. "What else can we do?" Zigferd replied.

"There is one way that we could confirm secrecy. It is not something that can be taken lightly, though, and may be seen by some as interference."

"Interference?" Zigferd asked, confused.

"Yes. Interference. It is unlikely, but some may consider it stretching the rules," Nexis said.

Most around the table now looked at Nexis with confusion, his cryptic comments not making sense of what he was alluding to. Nexis pushed his chair back and began to pace around the table. He muttered as he did, holding his chin with one hand and appearing deep in thought. This continued for a few minutes, the confusion in the room replaced by a nervous tension.

"Nexis. Is something wrong?" Alice asked.

Stopping, Nexis turned to face her and gave her a brilliant smile. "No, nothing is wrong. I am just conferring."

Frowning deeply, Alice looked at Nexis as if he had lost his mind. "Conferring?"

"Yes. With my brethren," Nexis replied.

That statement brought even more confusion to the table.

"Sorry?" Zigferd asked. "What brethren, and how are you possibly communicating with anyone?"

SJ could feel panic building in her chest.

"I think I know what he is going to do," Dave said, sounding in awe and amazement.

What? SJ thought. As she did, Nexis moved to the top of the table where Alice sat.

"There is one way that I can guarantee absolute secrecy from those who know," Nexis said.

"How?" Zigferd asked, a tone of anger in his voice. The scene that had been unfolding had caused everyone to feel uneasy.

"There is one oath that can outweigh any other, even racial. Do any of you know which oath that is?" Nexis asked, looking around the table.

Lythonian nodded his head at the comment. "I am aware of one," he said.

"Please, Lythonian, do tell." Nexis smiled.

"When I worked in Asterfal with the high cleric, I was informed about the oaths and their binding levels. It is a very complex structure, but there is one oath that would indeed replace any others."

"What?" Zigferd asked with apprehension.

"The binding oath of a god," Lythonian replied.

Several around the table scoffed at the comment. "And where will we find a god to perform a binding oath?" Zigferd asked incredulously.

As Nexis replied, SJ could feel the hairs on the back of her neck rise.

"Here, of course," he replied, smiling.

Author's Note

A quick plug! I hope you've enjoyed the journey so far. If you did, I'd greatly appreciate it if you could leave a rating and review—it really helps! Please follow on Amazon to be informed of the latest releases.

Want to stay up to date with the world of Amathera before Book 3 arrives? You can follow along on Royal Road or World Anvil.

For those who'd like early access to new chapters, I post them on Patreon with different tier options here: www.patreon.com/Bosloe.

You can also find me on social media through Tiktok (@bosloe), Instagram/ Threads (@boseloemcanu), Twitter (@boseloemcanu), and Facebook (Bosloe McAnu Author).

If you're looking to dive deeper into the LitRPG community, meet authors (myself included!), and have a great time, check out The LitRPG Group by Aleron Kong on Facebook. Other fantastic places full of recommendations and discussions are LitRPG Books, LitRPG/ Progression Addicts, GameLitRPG Society, and LitRPG Legion.

Acknowledgements

So many amazing authors in the genre have inspired me on my journey.

To name a few ...
Jez Cajiao
Dr. Aleron Kong
S.L. Rowland
Harmon Cooper
Brian J. Nordon
Eric Ugland

I must also pass on a very special thank you to Ryan Maxwell, the charging rhino himself. While mentioned briefly in Book 1, the truth is, I wouldn't have gotten here without his unwavering support and downright *essential* weirdness pushing me forward. Thank you, Ryan!

I can't finish without passing a most important and heartfelt thanks to all those who have read and supported my creativity since I began writing *One Flew Over the Dragon's Nest*.

THANK YOU.
Amathera still has many tales to tell.

About the Author

Bosloe is a math teacher with a military and business background. His passion for teaching comes from a desire to give something back. Born in Northwest England, he discovered a passion for storytelling early on but only recently began writing himself. Inspired by the fantasy and LitRPG genres, he wrote the Amatherean Tales as his debut series. Bosloe lives in Oxfordshire with his wife and fur babies.